I0657923

Savaged Vows

SAVAGED ILLUSIONS TRILOGY • BOOK TWO

JENNIFER LYON

Savaged Vows
Copyright © 2017 Jennifer Apodaca
All rights reserved.

Cover and Savaged Illusions Logo Designs:
Jaycee DeLorenzo of Sweet 'N Spicy Designs
Editor: Sashaknighteditor.com
Copy Editor: www.kimberlycannoneditor.com/
Formatted by: Author E.M.S.

Published by JenniferLyonBooks
www.jenniferlyonbooks.com

This book is a work of fiction. The names, characters, places, and incidents are products of the author's imagination or have been used fictitiously and are not to be construed as real. Any resemblance to persons, living or dead, actual events, locals or organizations is entirely coincidental.

All rights reserved. With the exception of quotes used in reviews, this book may not be reproduced or used in whole or in part by any means existing without written permission from the author.

ISBN: 978-0-9984595-3-0

*Savaged Vows is book 2 in
the Savaged Illusions Trilogy.*

*It is recommended that book 1,
Savaged Dreams, be read first.*

Chapter 1

LIZA GLASNER GAVE IN ON the wheelchair and allowed herself to be rolled out into the bright sunshine. God, she detested hospitals. But she loathed the reason she'd landed there for three nights even more.

Someone had tried to kill her. A man she didn't know had hated her that much. Nothing like an attempted murder by a stranger to make a girl feel special. Okay, not special so much as seriously pissed off. She hadn't been bothering anyone, she'd just been walking to her car when she was tackled and stabbed.

Chill bumps splattered her arms despite the warm day in San Diego. She rubbed her palms over her biceps as her stomach knotted, and pinged her gaze around, careful not to move her head. The orderly had stopped a few feet back from the curb of the horseshoe-shaped pickup zone. Beyond that lay a road and huge parking areas. People milled around, coming and going at a brisk pace.

Did any of them want to kill her too?

Jeez, paranoid much? Liza squeezed her eyes shut, determined to get control. No one was trying to murder her here. She was fine.

"Beth." A warm, comforting hand settled over her fingers digging into her arms.

When she opened her eyes, her world filled with the man crouched in front of her. Justice Cade's blond-streaked brown hair refused to be tamed, and his irises sizzled an angry blue flecked with moody gray and warm concern.

"That was fast," Liza said. He'd gone ahead of her to get the car out of the parking facility, and now the Jeep idled at the curb a couple yards away.

"I figured you'd be in a hurry to get home to your stash of candy." He flipped up the footrests of her wheelchair.

That coaxed a smile from her. "You better not have eaten any, rock star. I don't care if we're living together, some things are off-limits." She stood carefully, trying not to jostle the healing slash that ran from the center point of the back of her neck down to her right shoulder blade. Or the bruises and split lip from getting slammed to the asphalt. The pain pills helped, so she managed.

Justice wrapped an arm around her, avoiding any tender spots. At the car, he opened the passenger door, helped her in then tugged her seat belt across her.

"I can—"

He lifted his head, his eyes hard and his jaw unyielding. "I'll do it. You'll sit there and be a good girl, or all your candy will vanish."

She could almost feel the rage, frustration and worry snapping out from his pores, yet he was gentle and caring with her. "Are you threatening me? I'll have you know I survived a stabbing, and that makes me a bona fide badass."

His face softened. "Definite badass and a tough-as-hell survivor." After locking in her seat belt, he cupped her jaw. "But anyone tries to hurt you again, I'm going badass on them, and when I'm done, they'll be bleeding on the ground. Breathing is optional."

He hovered over her like a shield, and yet he'd called her tough. He didn't see her as weak and reckless, but as a survivor who wouldn't let some maniac with a knife kill her. "Lot of badass in this car." She sank back against the seat, surprised at how tired she was just from dressing, arguing over the wheelchair and getting into the car.

Justice leaned in, kissing her on the side of her mouth to avoid her sore lip. "You're my tough girl." After closing her door, he slid in the driver's side and got them on the road. "We'll get your stuff moved Saturday from your apartment to my house. I'm borrowing a truck and rounding up Sloane and a few friends. We'll get Emily's stuff moved to her boyfriend's for her too."

"But I haven't finished packing." Before the attack, she'd been so busy with her internship and finals, there hadn't been time. Now reality dropped on her like a ton of bricks. She had to be out of her apartment by the end of the weekend, and since she was injured, it fell to her best friend and boyfriend to do everything.

"Emily said she'll handle that." He shot her a look. "You're not going to the apartment. Reporters might be there. And you—"

"I'm not hiding." Not anymore. She'd had enough of that before she met Justice, when she lived with her aunt. "I didn't do anything wrong."

"Damn right you didn't."

"Tell that to my aunt."

Justice clenched his jaw, his head snapping around. "What the hell did your aunt say to you?"

3

She fisted her hands at the memory of the phone call. Despite having been on morphine, she could recite it verbatim. "She said I told you something awful would happen if you kept dating that rock star. You put yourself in danger with bad choices. You have to leave Justice and stop behaving like a drunk groupie."

He slapped his hand on the wheel. "That cold bitch. How the fuck is this your fault? Blaming the victim is bullshit." He narrowed his eyes. "I didn't see your oh-so-fucking-perfect aunt getting her ass in the car and coming to the hospital. You almost died, goddammit."

His arm bulged, making the beautifully inked guitar on his upper arm swell. His shirt sleeve cut off the old-school microphone above it. The whole design was wrapped in a crown of thorns with drips of blood—the only spots of color in the intricately shaded gray-and-black tat. She loved the ink, loved the man who wore it, and she loved the way he defended and cared about her. He'd slept at the hospital to be there with her if she had night terrors.

Stroking his arm, she could feel his fury in his rigid muscles. And it wasn't just her he was worried about. When he wasn't at the hospital, he'd been out searching for his dad. "You haven't found any sign of Noah?"

His jaw tightened. "No. Both he and the man who attacked you vanished."

The worry for his dad poured off him. Had Noah been injured fighting the assailant? "He'll turn up when he's ready. If something happened to your dad and he was hurt, or worse, the cops would have found him." She had to believe that.

He stroked his thumb over the back of her hand. "You're right. And he saved you. I'm grateful to him for that."

The sweet warmth of his words washed over her,

more comforting than any of the drugs they'd given her in the hospital. This man loved her, stood by her, no matter how bad things were. "So am I."

Justice squeezed her hand then released it to steer the Jeep around a slower car. "Let's not worry about my dad right now. The important thing is that you're out of hospital. We'll be home soon, and you can rest. I had a security system put in too. You'll be safe."

"Home," she repeated. "I can't believe I'm actually doing this, not only dating a rock star, but living with him." If she thought too much about it, her head would spin. She'd met Justice Cade and the world as she knew it shifted into a new, exciting place.

And more dangerous.

"I'm the man who's going to keep you safe, Beth. Trust me."

Beth. The name she'd been called for the first fourteen years of her life, until her aunt changed it, trying to erase a huge part of who Liza was. But Justice latched on to that name, making her feel whole and accepted.

"I do. And I appreciate everything you're doing for me." That was what her aunt and grandmother didn't get. Justice made her feel like she mattered and supported her dreams, while they cut her out of their lives when they didn't agree with her choices.

"I won't lose you," he added. "From now on, your security is my first priority. Especially with that fucker who stabbed you still on the loose." Anger vibrated in every syllable.

Concern for Justice welled in her chest. He'd suffered this week too. "Are you and your band okay?" The four other guys in Savaged Illusions were like brothers to him.

His jaw flexed. "Yeah, the guys are in L.A., meeting with Christine and handling things. We're not giving up."

The cold-hearted business manager wasn't Liza's favorite person, but she was more troubled by the tension riding Justice. "That's good, right?"

He glanced over at her. "*Court of Rock* offered us a spot on their summer tour in July. Christine's negotiating that contract now. We need the money and exposure, but will you be okay when I'm gone?"

Was that what had him anxious? They were only a week into June now. But more importantly, this was the life she'd signed on for by loving Justice. He was a rock star—well, right now his star had taken a beating and gotten shoved into the shadows. But he and his band would fight their way to the top. He'd never once lied to her about his goal.

Fame.

Darkness weighed down on her lungs, trying to suffocate her in fear-soaked memories. But Justice wasn't her father, or the bastard her dad traded her to for a shot at stardom. She wasn't letting her past dictate her choices, not anymore.

Lifting her chin, she said, "You have to go on this tour. I'll be fine. I'm going to be working anyway. I wonder if Wylie will let me go back to my waitressing job?" Or would her notoriety be a problem?

"Not until the doctor clears you."

"I can't just sit around."

"You can write your books. Then you can send me chapters when I'm gone. Maybe I won't miss you so much if I can be a part of your secret world."

She hadn't told anyone about her writing until she'd shared it with Justice. It had been her way of escaping her fears and feeling in control. He'd embraced it and encouraged her to write, believing she could one day publish.

Now it was *their* secret world.

"I had this idea about my heroine," she blurted out. "What if she's a groupie who falls in love with the lead singer and—"

Her cell phone rang. It took her a second to remember she'd tucked the device into the plastic bag of all her stuff that Justice had put in the car. She tried to twist to find— "Ouch." Pain streaked out from the cut and her sore muscles.

"Don't move." Justice steered with one hand and reached back to grab the bag and set it on her lap.

Liza fished out her phone and eyed the screen. Her heart jumped. "The police station." Quickly she hit the speaker button so Justice could hear, and answered, "Hello, this is Liza."

"Miss Glasner, this is Detective Jenkins."

Her stomach tightened. "What can I do for you?"

"I'm calling to inform you we may have a break in your case."

Finally. The knot of anxiety in her stomach eased. "Do you have my attacker in custody?" She desperately wanted to feel safe and to know who hated her enough to try to kill her.

"Not for your attack specifically. We've arrested our suspect on another charge, and that led us to evidence that suggests he's involved in your stabbing."

She couldn't stand it. "Who?"

"Noah Cade."

Her fingers went numb. Oh my God, they'd arrested Justice's father.

Justice swerved into a gas station parking lot and shoved the car into park. He couldn't believe this. His dad arrested?

Glaring at the cell phone in Beth's hand, he shouted, "What the blazing hell, Jenkins? My dad didn't stab Liza, he saved her."

Beth winced, which pissed him off more. She was in enough pain without him losing his shit.

"Detective, as you can hear," Beth said, her gaze wide in stark contrast to her pale, bruised face, "Justice is with me. You said Noah is under arrest, but not for my attack?"

"Correct. He was picked up early this morning for an outstanding warrant. He's failed to pay several citations for encroachment."

Justice gripped the steering wheel to keep from punching it.

"What's encroachment?" Beth asked.

"A way to hassle homeless people for setting their stuff on public property," Justice snarled. "I'll pay his damned tickets."

"It's more complicated than that. Mr. Cade was in possession of a jacket covered in dried blood that matches Miss Glasner's blood type. And there's more evidence we're following up on."

"Of course he has her blood on him, he tackled the assailant right off her." He forced calm into his voice and settled his hand on Beth's thigh. "I had her blood on me, and so did half a dozen other people."

"It wasn't Noah," Beth jumped in. "I would have recognized his voice. It's a rusty version of Justice's." She lifted the phone closer to her face. "Why are you doing this?"

"Because I don't have a choice here," Detective Jenkins said. "This story has exploded. People are scared that someone is going around stabbing college girls in our town."

Fuck. Justice didn't require a flashing sign to tell

him that Detective Jenkins and the police department were under pressure and needed an arrest. And a homeless man with a coat soaked in Beth's blood?

Too easy to pin the blame on him.

His head throbbed. After yanking out his phone, he checked for missed calls. "My dad hasn't called. He gets a phone call. Are you allowing him his rights?"

"Yes, he refused to call anyone or talk at all. He stares at a wall and says nothing."

"Don't do this, Detective," Beth pleaded. "Noah's not well. He has PTSD, and you can see he's suffered from his scars." Her eyes filled with tears. "Don't do this."

"I need Mr. Cade to talk to me." Jenkins's frustration vibrated through the speaker. "All we have is a vague description from eyewitnesses—medium height, average build, wearing dark clothes and a beanie. I need more than that to rule out Mr. Cade, and he's not communicating."

Beth squeezed her eyes shut. "I didn't see my attacker, I just heard his voice and saw the knife." She shifted her gaze to him. "I'm sorry."

She was sorry? For what? She'd been fucking stabbed, while Justice had been inside trying to save his career instead of making sure his girlfriend was safe. He'd failed, not her. He took the phone from her ice-cold fingers.

"I'm getting him a lawyer, and I'll be there as soon as I can. You try to pin this on him, we'll go to the media and let them know the guy with a knife is still on the loose while you hassle a former Marine who was seriously injured in the line of duty." He cut the call, ready to kill someone.

Pull yourself together. Beth doesn't need you losing it right now. Get to the police station and sort this out.

"Do you know a lawyer?" she asked.

After handing the phone back to Beth, he put the car in gear and drove while mentally ticking off what he needed to do. "No. I'll call Sloane once we get to the house. He manages MMA fighters now, and a few of them have gotten into trouble, so he knows a reputable law firm." But he couldn't leave Beth alone to work on getting his father out of jail. "Can you call Emily? See if she'll come stay with you?"

While Beth made the call, he eased around a corner. He lasted five seconds before he asked, "Is Emily answering?"

"Not calling Em, I'm— Sloane, hi, it's Liza."

Justice jerked. "What are you doing?"

She held up a hand. "The detective on my case called..." She summed up the conversation, then asked, "Do you know any good criminal lawyers who can get over to the jail right away and try to get him released today?"

Justice gripped the wheel as he heard Sloane's deep voice answering, but he couldn't make out the words.

She sank back against the seat and closed her eyes. "Thank you." She held the phone out to him.

He stared at her for one heartbeat. This was why he loved her so damned much. She was in pain and miserable, yet here she was helping his dad. He took the phone but said to her, "You're amazing."

"We have to get Noah out of there. I saw him after being in the auditorium for less than five minutes, and he looked bad. I don't know how he's handling being dragged to a police station, interrogated and arrested."

Her very real concern for his dad eased his own anguish, outrage and frustration. He didn't have to handle this alone, he had Beth. Putting the phone to his ear, he said, "Sloane."

"I'll contact the firm I use and have a lawyer call you in the next hour."

Justice headed into the decades-old track of homes. "I don't know if my dad will talk to the lawyer. Sounds like he's not talking to the cops." Had his dad shut down entirely? Or was he having panic attacks? He rubbed his chest to ease the crushing anxiety and regret.

"He'll talk to me," Liza said softly. "I'll go with you to the police station."

Oh hell no. She was too weak and sore, and the doctors had been clear—total rest for a few days, and no lifting. The police station surrounded by chaos, desperation and germs wasn't the place for Beth right now. "You're going straight to bed." This was one thing he'd do right—take care of Beth.

Justice turned on his street and hit the brakes when he spotted at least a dozen media vehicles in front of his house. "Goddamn it." Tossing the phone, he threw the Jeep in reverse, shot back up the road and spun around. Flooring it, he glared at the mirror.

Had any of the reporters spotted them? No one seemed to notice.

"Oh crap," Beth blurted out. "Why are they at your house? No one knew I was being released."

Frustrated fury pounded in his head. He couldn't leave Beth there with the media vultures circling. "I don't know." He sucked in air to calm down and took in her pale face, bruised eyes and scabbed lip. "Hang on, I'll figure something out." Seeing her phone where it'd landed in the cup holder after he'd pitched it, he remembered Sloane. Picking up the device, he switched it to speaker. "Sorry, Sloane, reporters are swarming my house."

"The news that they arrested your father is breaking

all over social media and TV. They're calling him a suspect in Liza's attack. They're saying a cop found a bloodstained jacket."

"But we just found out," Beth said. "How did they...?" She dropped her head back. "It doesn't matter, they know."

Exactly. He needed to get her somewhere safe where she could rest. "I'm going to take Liza to her friend's house. I'll call you back."

"Can't," Liza cut in. "Emily's at work."

His neck muscles bunched as he tried to think of an alternative.

"Go to my penthouse suite at the Opulence Hotel," Sloane said. "It's secure, quiet and big enough that Liza can rest in one of the rooms and you can meet with the lawyer in the living space after he finds out the situation with your dad."

It was a good solution, and if he had to leave, she'd be safe and comfortable. He glanced over at her. "You okay with that?"

"Yeah."

The utter fatigue in her voice stabbed him with guilt. She'd hit her limit. "Thanks, Sloane."

Liza said goodbye and cut the call. "What a mess."

He'd done this to her—coaxed his way into her life, and despite her warnings, exposed her past. Her aunt wasn't wrong. If Liza wasn't with him, no one would have paid any attention to her. Beth would have blended in as just another college girl in a college town. He really was a fuckup.

Beth's warm touch settled on his arm. "It's going to be okay. We'll get your dad out."

He took Beth's hand in his, keeping his hold gentle around her scabbed fingers. She looked like hell.

And never more beautiful to him.

It was the love and trust in her green eyes that pierced his heart. She'd chosen him over her family, and even after he'd lost *Court of Rock* and she'd been stabbed, she hadn't left him.

As bad as this week had been, she was the one person who made it bearable, made it feel like together they could handle anything.

Chapter 2

LIZA SAT ON THE PLUSH white couch of the hotel suite, scrolling through the news sites on her laptop. The media was salivating over the arrest of Justice's father with lurid headlines.

Father of Savaged Illusions' lead singer suspected of attempted murder!

Did Justice Cade's father stab the singer's girlfriend Liza Glasner?

She rubbed her temple, unable to believe how badly things were spiraling out of control. It'd been hours since the drive home from the hospital, getting the call, seeing the media covering Justice's house and finally landing in the penthouse. Since then, Justice had gone back over to the house to grab a few things, met with the lawyer and tried to see his dad.

Noah had refused.

Apprehension gnawed at her like a ravenous hellhound.

"No."

Justice's snarl jerked her gaze up from her computer. His face was carved into harsh lines that made him look closer to thirty than twenty-four. He was wearing faded jeans and a T-shirt, his tatted arms bulging with wiry strength as he spun and strode away from her. The lines of his back strained the soft cotton of his shirt. Clearly the conversation with his business manager wasn't going well. The arrest was having a serious ripple effect.

"Back off, Christine. I don't need a damned publicist right now, I need to figure out how the fuck to get my dad out of this mess. He didn't stab Liza." He whirled, glaring at the elevator doors. "I should be doing something," he muttered.

Guilt and worry tightened a steel band around her chest. And beneath all that, a little pang of loss. Another publicist? Liza had been the band's publicist.

And you're part of the reason they lost too.

That pang grew into hurt. Damn it, she'd been good at her job, and she'd loved being a part of his world and having an important role to help him achieve his dream. Now she was being pushed aside.

"Fine. Have the publicist send me the statement." He hung up and dropped his arm. With the late-afternoon light flooding in from the huge terrace behind him, Justice appeared to have the weight of the world on his shoulders.

Setting the computer aside, she got up and went to him, slid her arms around his waist and laid her head against his warm chest. Maybe she wasn't on the inside of his career anymore, but she could give him this—her love and comfort.

His arms folded around her. "Christine's worried *Court of Rock* might pull the summer tour offer she's negotiating. With my dad arrested, the media is spreading crazy rumors. And Jagged Fucking Sin suggested my dad stabbed you because he knew you were setting me up like you did Gene Hayes." He glided his hand beneath her shirt to spread over her back.

Her chest tightened at the mention of Hayes and the knowledge of how much her past caused problems for Justice and the band. "He wasn't arrested for that. It's just a warrant for unpaid tickets." But the truth didn't matter; the media made the link, and now it was out there like a virus, infecting the public.

"The publicity chick is going to craft a statement clarifying that to blast over social media and put out to the news and entertainment sites. My dad's lawyer said he'll probably be arraigned tomorrow on that, and with luck, we can pay the outstanding tickets and fines and they'll let him go. The guys will be here for that as a show of support and unity." His jaw bulged. "Maybe."

Maybe? Another frisson of concern rippled through her. That fight in the greenroom the night Liza had been stabbed...had the damage gone deeper than Justice let on? "You said you and the band were okay."

"We are."

"What are you not telling me?"

He sighed. "We lost, Beth. What do you think is going on? I let the whole goddamned band down. Lynx is drinking himself stupid, River's fucking out his anger with any willing female. Gray's vanishing and reappearing like a magician and Simon..." he shook his head, "...he's gone so cold, he's a machine. I think the only time he feels anything is with a guitar in his hands."

In the last weeks, she'd come to genuinely care about all the band members, and now they were falling apart.

"And when my band needs me the most, here I am, trapped in San Diego taking care of my injured girlfriend with my estranged father in jail on trumped-up charges because they suspect him of trying to kill you."

She flinched. "Trapped?" Was that how she made him feel? A weight and obligation?

Justice lowered his gaze, his eyes losing that icy sheen. "Shit, I didn't mean that the way it sounded. I'm torn, that's all. My friends need me, you need me, my dad's in trouble and he still won't see me." He touched her face. "You're not trapping me. I just can't be everywhere."

It was more than that, Liza could feel it. The squeeze on her chest tightened. "Christine told you to distance yourself from me, didn't she? That it looks bad—like your own dad was trying to protect you from me." If Justice wasn't a musician dependent on fans for his and the band's success, it wouldn't matter so much.

But they needed every fan they could get to rebuild their career. And that was why Justice was so torn; he was getting real pressure.

"Christine doesn't decide who I love. I do, and I chose you."

Sincerity rang in his words, but was it really that easy? The whole reason they hired Christine was to help them achieve the fame they passionately craved. The band planned to record their own album, go on a tour...the pressure was going to multiply. She wanted that for him and yet feared it at the same time. If she was in the way with her past and so many rock fans hating her, would Justice one day realize he'd be better off without her?

Adding to his strain wouldn't help, so she didn't tell him that. Instead, she smiled. "Yes you did, and now you're mine. Christine can kiss my ass." The manager had already made it clear to Liza that she disapproved of her and Justice's relationship.

"There's my fiery Beth." Amusement flickered in his eyes, then he sobered. "What the hell is taking the lawyer so long? She's supposed to call after talking to my dad and meeting with the detective."

He'd barely gotten the words out when her phone rang. Justice released her, grabbed it off the couch and brought it back. "Police department."

She eyed the screen. Was this the break they desperately needed? Her heart thumped as she answered. "This is Liza."

"Miss Glasner, this is Detective Jenkins. I'm here in the lobby with Mr. Cade's lawyer. We'd like to see you. I have some pictures to show you."

Surprised, she asked, "Here in the hotel?"

"Yes. Mr. Cade's lawyer said you're staying here. Since you just got out of the hospital, I thought it'd be easier for me to come to you, rather than asking you to come down to the station."

She looked up at Justice. "The detective and your dad's lawyer are here."

"Give them the code for the penthouse elevator."

Liza relayed the information and hung up. "He wants us to look at some pictures."

Justice led her toward the couch. "How's your pain?"

"It's okay. But I need to run to the bathroom before they get here."

"Call out if you need anything."

She made her way into the bathroom, took one look in the mirror and winced. Yeah, well, she was alive, and the cuts and bruises would heal.

A few minutes later, she shuffled over to the couch. Justice helped her settle in then handed her a glass. "Peach iced tea."

One of her favorites. "Thanks." She took a sip, then

asked, "Did the lawyer say anything to you about pictures?"

"No, but she hadn't seen my dad yet."

Before she could answer, the elevators doors opened. Liza recognized Detective Jenkins from when he came to talk to her in the hospital. The woman with him was fiftyish, wearing tailored black pants, a silk shirt and gray-streaked brown hair and red glasses. She said hello to Justice, then focused on her. "I'm Myra Bolton. You must be Liza?"

After the obligatory handshake, she asked, "Is Noah okay?"

The woman's hard gaze softened. "Mr. Cade is very stressed and withdrawn, but I believe he's coping."

Detective Jenkins slid his gaze around the penthouse as if he expected a bad guy to suddenly pop out from behind a couch or door, then landed on her. "Miss Glasner, you look a little better than the last time I saw you. How are you feeling?"

"Worried. Noah didn't stab me."

The man flattened his mouth. "So Myra has said. Repeatedly." The detective sat on one of the gray chairs facing the couch. "This would be easier if Mr. Cade cooperated."

"You tried to play hardball. That's a mistake with Mr. Cade," Myra interjected. She turned to Justice. "I spoke to your father and read his statement. Mr. Cade told the police he didn't do it. He said he was there, saw the attack on Liza and reacted by tackling the man off her, then the two of them wrestled on the ground. The attacker broke free, got up and ran off. Mr. Cade chased, but lost him because of his bad hip. But he insisted that he recognized Liza's attacker."

Shock punched her. "Who is it?" Who hated her that much?

Justice surged to his feet. "Then why is my dad under suspicion?"

"This is where it gets confusing," Myra answered. "Mr. Cade doesn't have a name, but he swears he has pictures of the man on his cell phone. He said that the guy had been around Justice's house and the auditorium for a day or two."

Liza blurted out, "Wait, you're saying Noah was watching the house? I talked to him the day of the attack. He walked up behind me as I was unlocking the front door."

Myra nodded. "He said he was, well, he claims he was sort of watching out for you."

"Me? Like..." Her eyes burned, and a hot lump knotted her throat as she realized what that meant. "That's why he stayed in the parking lot instead of leaving after Justice's performance." She swung her gaze to Justice. "Your father was there to protect me, and now he's in jail."

Justice eyes narrowed, and his jaw twitched. He stood next to where she sat on the couch, nearly vibrating with fury. He swung his gaze to the cop. "You have pictures of the man who attacked Beth, uh, Liza, and did nothing? Instead you hassled my father? Why? Because he's a scarred, broken man who sleeps on the streets? An easy target to pin this on?"

A chill went down her back at the sharp confrontation riding Justice's tone. How long could he hold it together?

Jenkins glared back at Justice. "Your father has Miss Glasner's blood on his jacket. And he has pictures of her on his phone, along with that video Gene Hayes released. In addition, his phone had been used to go into a private online group of Hayes's fans that brag about how much they hate Miss Glasner and believe she ruined Hayes. They want her to pay, and there are a lot of threats against her. It's possible Mr. Cade believed Miss Glasner was harming your career too and decided to remove her permanently."

"No!" Liza couldn't believe this. "Noah was a Marine. He told me he had friends who laid down their lives so people like Hayes could have a right to a trial. He called Hayes a coward for running. He didn't believe Hayes." She started to shake her head to emphasize her point, but a shaft of pain from her stitches made her clench her jaw.

"I'm trying to get to the truth." Frustration bled through the detective's words. "I want to know who stabbed Miss Glasner, and if it's your dad, he's going down for it. But if it was someone else? Then I'm going to find him and put him in a cage where he belongs."

Liza believed he meant it. She settled her hand in Justice's, trying to calm them both. "How can we help?"

"Mr. Cade was following you for a couple days. It's clear from the pictures." The detective opened his briefcase, pulled out a clipped set of grainy eight by tens and handed them across the coffee table.

Liza took the pages. A seed of pain lodged in her stomach as she flipped through. There was one of her locking up Justice's house, another of her getting in her car in the driveway. More of her walking in the parking lot of the auditorium. And still another outside her apartment building. What was happening? Her hands trembled. "Noah took these? Why?"

"It's not what it looks like, Beth." Justice shoved his hand through his hair, making it stand on end. "Dad wouldn't...there has to be a reason. He's never hurt anyone off the battlefield. Even in his worst rages, he never lashed out at me or my mom." He spun to the detective. "What about the other pictures? Or did you just come here to scare Liza?"

Myra jumped in. "Mr. Cade is insistent the man who attacked Liza is on his cell. He was able to tell me exactly which shots they were and we've printed copies for you to look at."

"The pictures of Miss Glasner showed a pattern of possible stalking. Or Mr. Cade was doing exactly as Jenkins said and watching over Miss Glasner." He reached into his briefcase and pulled out a second set of photos. Returning his attention to Liza, he asked, "Do you recognize anyone in the group shots or the close-up of the man?"

Justice took them and sank down next to Liza.

She leaned in to get a closer look. The first one was definitely a man on a sidewalk, but it was too blurry to identify him. "Is that the sidewalk in front of your house?"

"Yes." Justice flipped to the next one. It was of several people, including some reporters in front of the house.

Liza studied the faces. "I don't... Wait."

Justice turned, his eyes honing in on hers. "What?"

"That one." She pointed to a guy standing behind the reporters. She could only see part of his head. Blond hair, young...but half his face was blocked by a video camera. "Something about him." She glanced up. "I didn't get a look at my attacker that night. But this guy...it's like I've seen him somewhere before." She tapped Justice's thigh. "Keep going."

He went to the next photo.

It was a close-up of the same man. Liza stared, taking in the square face and light blue eyes, struggling to recall why he looked familiar. "I know him, but from where?" The answer was right there, just out of reach.

"Wylie's," Justice snarled.

It snapped into place. "Oh my God. You're right." But why? It didn't make sense. She shifted to the lawyer. "Noah said this is him?"

"Yes."

"Who is he?" the detective demanded.

"All I know is his name is Hans. He was with a friend one night at Wylie's Cantina. Justice and I were there, fans surrounded Justice, and I was taking pictures when I tripped and fell into his friend, who accidentally spilled beer on me. The friend was very apologetic, but this guy..." Liza held up the picture, "...he was a jerk. He tried to take pictures of my wet shirt. I told him no. He grabbed my arm, and I kicked him. He was furious, but Justice came up, and the guy didn't touch me after that. Wylie threw him out." Frustration stewed in her belly. "His voice—that sneer in his voice, it was the same one who told me, 'Message from Hayes...'" She left off the last part, *you cunt*. "It's him. But how did he know who I am?" As soon as she asked it, she flushed with her own stupidity.

It had been less than a week after that scene at Wylie's that the Gene Hayes video came out and Liza's name and image saturated the media. "But why?"

"That bastard. You humiliated him, got him thrown out and then you're all over the news. He had a grudge." Justice flipped through the rest of the pictures. One showed Hans lurking by her apartment building. The last picture was him in the crowd of protesters that had been outside the auditorium the day of the *Court of Rock* finale.

Justice pulled out his phone and snapped some shots of the pictures.

"Hey, I—" Jenkins reached toward the photos.

He jerked his head up. "I believe you want the

23

truth, Detective, but that's my dad trapped in jail and my girlfriend this prick stabbed. I'm not sitting on my ass doing nothing."

Jenkins leaned forward. "Don't do anything stupid that lands you in a cell alongside your father." He turned to her. "Miss Glasner, this Wylie's is where you work part-time, correct?"

"Yes, but I was on leave while doing the intern competition on *Court of Rock*."

"Okay, I'll need the date of this incident and the contact information for the manager of Wylie's Cantina. I'll see if they have a way of tracking his name. We'll find and talk to him."

Liza gave him the information, but her mind tumbled and whirled over everything they'd discovered. "Did you get Ben's statement? He and my friend Emily Manchester were with me when I was attacked. Ben saw Noah tackle the man stabbing me."

Jenkins finished writing down the contact info. "Eyewitness testimony is often unreliable. Dr. Chambers only got a quick look. And you never saw your attacker's face. Additionally, we had conflicting stories from other bystanders. You were out of sight of the parking lot cameras." He took the pictures back from Justice, rose, then fixed a stare on her. "Miss Glasner, I don't know if Mr. Cade will be able to get bail tomorrow. Right now, with the fact that he had pictures of you on his phone, he admitted being in that parking lot waiting for you, and your blood is on his clothes, I'd seriously think about your safety."

Justice jackknifed to his feet. "She's safe with me. I'm not going to let anyone hurt her."

"She's already been hurt and is damn lucky to be alive," Jenkins said. "Next time, you might not be so fortunate." The detective strode to the elevator and hit the call button.

Liza grabbed Justice's hand. "Don't." Anger bled from his stiff fingers and his coiled, ready-to-spring posture.

Myra stood. "We're making progress. If you have any questions or concerns, call me. I'm going to fight hard for your father, Justice. The warrant for outstanding tickets we can handle, but if they arrest him for Liza's attack, he's in trouble."

"What can we do?" Liza asked.

"Hope the cops find this guy Hans. Otherwise, Mr. Cade is the only viable suspect, and the police are under extreme pressure. I'll be in touch in the morning." She joined the detective waiting in the elevator.

Once they were gone, Liza scooped up her computer. "Send me the pictures of Hans."

"What are you doing?"

She opened her search engine, ignoring her throbbing head and the pain in her wound. "Finding Hans. I'm not letting your dad go down for this or Hans get away with trying to stab me."

Justice crouched in front of her, his hands covering her thighs. "I'll make you a deal."

"What?"

"Eat something, take your pain pills and let me get you comfortable in bed. Then I'll send you the pictures, and we'll both search."

"But—"

"Beth, I can see you're in pain. Please. Everything else in my life is fucked up right now, so let me do this right."

"Do what?" Her throat tightened. Worry and stress were carved into his face, yet here he was, noticing her discomfort and fatigue.

"Take care of you. Love you."

"Okay." Her heart swelled. This was what love was, and Liza basked in it, soaking it up. She desperately wanted to give the same back to him "We're going to find him and clear your dad."

Every day she fell deeper in love with Justice. Moments like this reassured her that their love could survive the pressures of her past and his career.

Justice's neck and jaw ached like a bitch. He'd spent the last several hours dealing with the publicist, then the fact that Lynx and River weren't answering their phones, which had held up the approval of the press release. Finally Simon and Justice made an executive decision to approve the damn thing. But where the hell were Lynx and River?

Better not be in jail. Swear to God, he'd beat the shit out of them.

He checked his phone again. Nothing. Fuck.

He shifted his attention back to the laptop, trying to figure out how to locate Hans with only a first name and cell phone picture. He'd searched for the private forums of Hayes's fans that wanted Liza to pay, but all he'd found so far was some public rock music sites where a few people went off on a tangent about Liza ruining a mega star. It was ugly and made his head throb with the need to find and kick their asses.

"Have you found anything?"

Beth's voice startled him. He set the computer down and stood. She had on her glasses, a T-shirt and panties. She'd crashed about thirty minutes after he'd gotten her in bed, and slept several hours.

"No." Frustration and sitting on his ass was driving him out of his mind. "Do you need another pain pill?"

He checked his watch. Yep, it'd been four hours.

"Not yet. I'm getting some water. I..." She scratched at her wrist.

After crossing to her, he caught her chin and studied her haunted eyes. "Bad dreams?" She had night terrors sometimes.

"Gene Hayes and Hans. They were both in the room, and I couldn't wake up. I tried, and I couldn't even scream. I don't want to go back to sleep. I'd rather sit out here." She wrapped her fingers around his arm. "I hate being scared. Hate that we're trapped like animals in this hotel and your dad's in jail, while Hans is out there free. I hate this."

He gently tugged her against him. The back of her shirt was slightly damp. She must have woken up in a sweat. He stroked her hair. "We'll get him, Beth." He led her to the couch and settled her in with pillows and a blanket. After he got her some water, he sat next to her and picked up the laptop. "I can't find the bastard Hans or the site the detective said my dad had been on." He studied her face, looking past the cuts and bruises to the amazingly strong girl who'd survived so much. He wouldn't bring up the other sites that spewed vile things about her, especially after she'd just had a nightmare. They both needed a break.

He wrapped his arm around her, easing her against him. The night was quiet, a silky solitude that settled around the two of them. He stroked her lip, careful of the scab. "I miss kissing you. A real kiss, the kind that gets me hard and you wet, and we both forget about everything else but us." His heart thudded, and heat spread.

"I look like hell."

"You're gorgeous, Beth. I'm going to show you how much I want you once you're healed." All the furious frustration riding him gathered into hot desire. Need. Sex had always been a release for him, but with Beth? It was something more. Bigger. Every time he thrust into her, he felt like he'd found his home. And when she cried out, it fed his desperate need to be loved.

Her mouth parted, and color warmed her cheeks. "How do you do that?"

"Make you want me?" It wasn't cockiness. Okay, it was. But Beth didn't hide how she felt from him. She let him see the desire flowing in her eyes, chasing out the earlier fear. She wasn't up to sex, and she trusted him to know that. But this was something else—intimacy. Knowing they could bask in the want.

"It's a sweet ache," she said softly. "The first time I've felt alive since..."

"Your attack?"

Bringing her knees up, she curled into him and found a comfortable place to rest her head against his shoulder. "Since your band lost and that fight in the greenroom. Simon said I was your Yoko and that you had to choose between me and the band. When I was walking out that night—before the attack—I didn't know which you'd choose."

Regret tugged at him for not reassuring her more at the time, but he was glad she'd told him. Beth didn't have to hide her feelings or fears. "It's not a choice. You're the woman I love, but music is my dream, the one thing that kept me going." Screwing up and getting his ass tossed in juvie, and his mom leaving him there—part of Justice had gone dark that day, turning him hopeless and angry. Then he'd met Lynx, and they'd come up with this dream—a rock band—a chance to prove their worth.

She laid her hand on his chest. "I know. I'm so sorry you didn't win *Court of Rock*. You should have. I hate that I might have been a part of the reason why."

"Beth—"

"No. Let me say this. I'm not your Yoko. I'm here for you, supporting you a hundred percent. When I fell in love with you—it was all of you, and that includes the rock star. A setback like losing *Court of Rock* isn't going to stop you. You guys are coming back, you're going to record your album and fight your way to the top. And I'll help however I can. Once we find Hans and get your dad out of jail, you're going back to work on your dream, Justice. Hear me?"

"Every fucking word." She believed in him even when he'd fallen short. Despite being in pain, exhausted and worried, she'd come out here and soothed him. "I love you so damned much."

"You'd better. And this isn't a free pass, buddy. You're going to be playing gigs and traveling with hot groupies coming on to you. You keep your hands off them."

He wrapped her hair around his hand but resisted the urge to tug her head back. "Only groupie I'm fucking is you."

She snorted into his shirt. "I'm not your groupie, ego freak. I'm not any man's groupie. I don't care how amazing a singer you are or how much I love you."

He couldn't help but grin at her new name for him and the fact she loved him. The groupie tag was a sensitive subject for her. Beth's mom had been a hardcore groupie and dragged Beth around with her following bands, getting drunk and stoned, and young Beth had seen way too much.

"I'm your very possessive girlfriend. I find out you've screwed another woman, I'll go on a chicken-killing spree—every chicken in your house will die. Then I'll leave."

He blinked at the sudden shift in her, the hot

passion riding every word. The chicken threat made him laugh. She seemed to love the chicken decorations living in his kitchen—all courtesy of his grandmother, from whom he'd inherited the house. "My chickens are safe from my jealous, bloodthirsty girlfriend. I'm not going to screw around on you, but I would love to have you travel with me. You can work on your book, and if you get bored, kick some groupie ass. And every night, I'll have you hot and naked in my bed."

Her fingers stilled on his chest. "I don't know. I need to figure out a job, an internship, and I'm finishing my degree this fall."

He stifled the stab of disappointment. What did he want, for her to drop her entire life to follow him around? Besides, he knew how important her goals were to her. She needed to live her own life, not in the shadows of fame like her mom had. "I know. I was thinking for the summer tour—it's two weeks in July and the first week of August. You won't be in school then. I'm not sure you should go back to your waitressing job." She'd be too easy of a target now that her identity had been exposed. "Or you can fly out and meet me for a few days. We can play rock star and groupie."

She laughed. "Only if I'm the rock star. Told you, dude, I'm not a groupie."

No she wasn't, and the sound of her laughter, the feel of her against him, calmed the anxiety that'd been riding him for days. "What you are is mine. But I can work with being your groupie. You can play famous author. Keep your glasses on. I have a thing for chicks in glasses who write." He had a thing for her. So did his rapidly engorging cock. Just the feel of her against him, her husky laugh, the fact that only a T-shirt and panties covered her. He could slide his hand beneath the blanket and up her bare thigh... Nope. Not going there. She was exhausted and too sore. His cock could wait until—

His phone vibrated.

For a second he was tempted to reject the call. He didn't want to lose this moment with Beth.

"You'd better check that. Something could have happened with your dad."

She was right. Snatching it up, he eyed the screen and frowned. "That's weird."

Beth looked over. "Screech? The nightclub owner?"

"Yeah." He switched to speaker. "Hey, man, what's up?" It was nearly 11:00 p.m.

"Got a problem here. Two of them. Lynx and River are stupid drunk."

"In your club?" It took a second for him to catch on. "They're supposed to be in L.A. not San Diego."

"Got a ride with some chicks. The girls left. The guys are fighting and causing trouble. If you don't want them to get arrested, get your ass over here."

Un-freaking-believable. "I can't leave Liza." But he couldn't let his two friends get arrested either. Savaged Illusions couldn't afford any more bad news.

"Go," Liza cut in. "I'm safe here. But if they get arrested, *Court of Rock's* going to pull that summer tour offer."

He didn't have a choice. "I'll be right there." Hanging up, he said, "Are you sure?" She was safe, but would she feel secure?

"Yes. The elevator locks. I can't sleep anyway. I'll watch TV until you get back."

Every time he thought this day couldn't get worse, it did.

Chapter 3

JUSTICE STRODE INTO THE BAR. Music pounded from the speakers, and people got out of his way. He must have worn his pissed-off face. Damn it, he'd had one moment to relax and be with Beth out of the entire shit-fucked week, and this happened—he got his ass dragged away to ride to the rescue of his drunk friends. Leaving Beth alone worried him. Yeah, he'd left her alone earlier in the suite, but it'd been daylight, and she'd already made friends with the concierge in that compelling way of hers. She'd been okay.

Now it was late night edging into early morning, and she was afraid of the dark. He wanted to round up the two idiots and get back to her.

But first he had to find them. Resisting the urge to start shoving the people blocking his path, he scanned the packed club. Where were River and Lynx? He pushed through the crowd, searching every face for his two asshole friends.

He made it two more strides when Screech Rizzo stepped in front of him. "They're in my office. While I was on the phone to you, one of my servers—a newbie who didn't know any better—called the cops. You'll want to get Lynx and River out of here before the cops get here."

And his night just kept getting worse, but he was grateful to Screech. "You're doing us a solid. Thanks." Justice followed him through the crowd. "How much damage?"

"Minimal. Mostly broken glass and a chair." He headed down a hallway. "They got into a fight with a few other drunks. Lynx got on stage and started ranting about losing *Court of Rock*, and a couple guys ran up and shoved him off the platform. I damn near had a riot on my hands, but we got it calmed down." He opened the door to his office.

River was sprawled on the floor, snoring, while a thin line of blood oozed from a cut over one eye. Lynx was prone on the couch, one arm and leg hanging off.

Crouching, Justice smacked River's shoulder. "Get up."

River batted his hand away. "Mrmph."

A couple bouncers came in, and one said, "We'll get the one on the couch." The two beefy men hauled up a protesting Lynx.

He nodded, grateful for the help.

Screech crouched on the other side of River. "Let's go."

"You sure?" Justice asked. The other man had to be in his fifties.

"Yep." Screech got a hold of River's arm.

They hauled the bassist to his feet and headed out, working their way through the throngs of bodies squished around the bar. The two bouncers towed Lynx behind them. Lynx mumbled, but it was slurred nonsense.

Pushing through a gaggle of chattering college-aged

girls, Justice glanced at Screech. "You have free drinks or something?" Seemed busy for a Thursday night.

"End of quarter blowout. Half-priced drinks if they have a student ID." Screech groaned. "How much does River weigh?"

"More than he looks. Lot of muscle." River could have been an MMA fighter, he was that good. But he always said he was a lover not a fighter. Justice stopped for a second and wrapped an arm around River's waist to take more of the unconscious man's bulk. Situated, he glanced around and caught sight of the darkened stage on his right. Pain sliced into his chest. Their band had gotten their start in this club. The last time he'd been up on that stage had been when Screech had thrown a private party celebrating Savaged Illusions' success on *Court of Rock*—they'd made it to the final two shows. It'd been a great night. They'd all been high with their triumph. He'd been so sure they'd win.

"We stopping for a drink?" one of the bouncers snapped behind him.

Justice dragged his attention away from the stage and took a few more steps. A group of guys trash-talking, leering at girls and being assholes stood between him and the door. "Coming through."

One turned, a bottle of beer hanging from his fingers and a sneer on his face. "Go around—" The man froze.

A slap of recognition jerked Justice up short. His pulse jacked. "Hans." The man who attacked Liza was here? Now?

Hans lifted his chin, his gaze sliding to River slumped between him and Screech, then back to Justice. "Taking out the garbage, Cade?" The shock melted off his face, replaced by a smirk. "You hang out with a lot of trash. Even your father knew that when he stabbed your girlfriend."

An image of Liza lying on the asphalt, blood everywhere, her eyes filled with tears of pain and terror flashed in his head. Something cracked in his brain, and hot rage exploded, coating his mind in a red mist. "You stabbed her." Dropping River, he lunged and slammed his fist into the bastard's face.

Hans flew back into a table. Girls screamed, glass shattered, and blood sprayed from his nose. Grabbing a broken glass, Hans rolled to his feet. "You're crazy. Cops arrested your dad. Not me."

Justice eyed the glass. "Think it'll be as easy to cut me as it was Liza?" He wanted the man to come at him. Any excuse to kill the fucker. "What was it like, Hans? Did you feel like a big man sneaking up behind a woman and stabbing her?" All his anger poured out. "Did it feel good? Or were you scared, like the night Liza stood up to you in the bar and made you slink out with your balls all shriveled up?"

Hans roared and lashed out with his makeshift weapon.

Justice snapped a kick, hitting Hans's arm and knocking the glass out of his hold. He kept going, shoving Hans's back to the wall. "That all you got? No wonder you had to come up behind Liza in a dark parking lot. You're too scared to face her like a man."

Hans turned crimson, and his gaze darted around. "She's a whore! Hayes told me how she begged him to fuck her, then cried rape. Bitches like her ruin it for men. I'd have killed her if that bum hadn't gotten in my way." He threw a punch.

Justice blocked with one arm and grabbed the bastard's throat with his free hand. Icy hate ripped through him. He tightened his fingers, slowly cutting off Hans's air. "Liza almost died," he growled. "That bum is my dad." That was how the whole world saw his father now, the scarred bum. That enraged Justice more.

Hans clawed at his hand, panic exploding in his eyes.

"Justice." Screech gripped his shoulder. "Let him go."

His hand stayed locked around the bastard's throat, but he looked at Screech. "He stabbed Liza."

"I heard it, so did everyone else." He held up his phone. "I have it on video. Cops are pulling up out front. Get your hand off him. He's done."

Relief flooded through Justice. They had evidence. Beth was safe, and his dad would be cleared of suspicion. He forced his fingers to unclench.

Hans slid to the floor, his legs folding while he coughed and sucked air. Tears poured down his face, mixing with the blood from his nose.

Justice stared down at the man with zero pity. "Enjoy prison, asshole."

The next night Justice's neck muscles ached with frustration as he circled his Jeep around the jail a couple times. "Do you see him?" It was almost ten forty, damn it. He scanned the road, noting light traffic and no obvious signs of media. But in the dark it was a strain to see the door on the south side of the main entrance where inmates were released.

"Not yet," Beth answered from the passenger seat.

"His lawyer said ten thirty." It'd taken all day to get through the formalities to release his dad. Would he come home? Talk to Justice? Maybe even go into one of the PTSD treatment programs that Justice had found?

Would he finally fulfill his promise to his grandmother to take care of his dad?

Driving past the high-rise county jail that looked like any other office building, he wanted to punch the steering wheel. How many times had he futilely looked for his dad exactly like this?

"Go around again."

"He's not here, Beth. He's gone." Justice shouldn't have let Beth come with him, but what was he going to do? She'd been adamant, and he hadn't wanted to leave her alone again.

"Please, Justice."

He needed to get her back to the hotel and to bed. But the urge to track his father raged inside him, a constant pressure on his muscles. "It's pointless." But he swung around the corner and looped—

"There!" Beth pointed to the lone man on the sidewalk. He wore a dark shirt, backpack slung over one shoulder, and had a rambling, uneven gait that favored his left hip.

Justice slowed and eased the Jeep up to the curb. "Stay inside and lock the doors." He opened his door at the same time he heard Beth open hers too. Damn it. He swung around in the seat, but she was already climbing out of the car.

"Noah, it's me, Liza. Wait, please?"

His dad slowed.

Justice raced around the car to help Beth out. "Easy." He visually searched the sidewalks. A truck and SUV drove by, more vehicles were parked along the street, and a few people strolled on the sidewalks. He didn't spot any reporters or people that triggered an internal alarm.

Holding her arm, he guided her to his dad. As they approached, Justice winced. His father's hair was shoulder length and ragged, his beard more gray than brown. But it was the web of burn and shrapnel scars pulling at his gaunt cheek and temple that gut punched him.

Liza raised her hand as if to touch his dad's arm, then pulled back. "Noah, thank you for helping me Monday night. If you hadn't been there, I don't know what would have happened. Thank you."

He nodded without looking at them.

"Dad, come home," Justice said. "We can talk. I've found two treatment programs that—"

His shoulders notched up. "Can't."

Fuck. Anger choked him. "I'm trying to help you. You're going to end up dead out here on the streets. You're not homeless." Just saying the word *homeless* hurt. "You don't have to live this way." He stabbed his hand through his hair. *I'd have killed her if that bum hadn't gotten in my way.* Even that bastard Hans thought he was better than Justice's dad. They didn't see him as he'd once been—a proud, confident Marine who commanded respect and admiration. Who'd laid his life on the line to protect the country he loved. This man here? This wasn't his father.

Remorse for even thinking that rammed straight through his heart. It hurt, damn it. His own father wouldn't look at him, couldn't bear to be around him. Would it ever change, or would he always have to live with the truth that he'd driven his dad to the streets? He tried again by saying, "You have a home."

His dad flinched and started walking.

Goddammit.

"Noah," Beth said softly. "Justice and I are staying in a hotel tonight. If you'd like, we can drop you off at the house, and you can stay there. If there's any media, I'll divert them, and you can slip inside. You'll be alone, can sleep and eat something. There are clothes there for you too. Take anything you need. All you have to do is let us drive you there." She moved in front of his dad. "I'd feel better if you'd let us do this much for you. I owe you my life. I don't know you well, but you matter to me. Will you consider it? You can always leave."

Justice held his breath. How did Beth do it? She talked to his dad in such an easy, respectful way. As if she didn't see the degradation and desperation clinging to every cell of his ravaged body.

His dad lifted his head, his gaze going to Beth. "Yes."

The air whooshed out of Justice's lungs. This was something. Not a big family reunion, but one step.

"Good. Let's get you in the car. We'll take you to the house, watch you get inside, and drive away." She walked with his dad to the car, talking to him as he slid into the backseat.

Justice held the door for Beth, then pulled the seat belt across her to keep her from twisting and irritating the healing wound.

Halfway home, Liza said, "Noah, is it okay if we drive through and grab some food? I slept through dinner, and I have to eat to take my pain pills. Or do you want us to do that after we drop you off?"

"It's okay."

"Thanks."

Justice closed his eyes for a second, his chest rattling in recognition of his dad's voice. It was rough and creaky, like a rusty door in an old house, but comfortingly familiar. How long since he'd heard it? A year? Hearing it now was all because of Liza, his Beth, a gentle but powerful force of nature. He could almost feel her patience flowing in the car, pouring a calmness over the acid strain bubbling between him and his father.

After heading into the McDonald's drive-through, he gave Beth's order, chose something for himself, and added, "In a separate bag, put another couple quarter pounders, a large French fry and a..." what did his dad like to drink? "...root beer." Grandma had always kept it in the house for his dad.

Once Justice paid, he handed the bags to Beth. Ten minutes later, Justice stopped the car in the driveway of the house. His muscles cramped with the effort of resisting the urge to go inside.

After his dad got out, Liza rolled down her window and held out the McDonald's bag and her house key. "You have my cell number if you need anything."

His dad stood there in the moonlight, hesitating.

"Justice moved the hide-a-key when reporters started following us. Use this one. We'll get another made for me." She told him the new alarm code too.

Noah took the items. "Did you really miss dinner tonight?"

"I did, actually. I watched a movie and fell asleep and slept through dinner."

She didn't mention the late lunch they'd had, but Justice kept his mouth shut.

"Now," Beth went on, "I'm hungry and craving French fries. Everyone knows you need French fries and chocolate when you get out of the hospital."

Noah's eyes crinkled at the edges, as if his face wanted to smile but didn't know how. Then his gaze flicked to Justice and the almost smile fell back into grim lines. He turned and walked up to the door.

He watched his father go, wondering if he'd ever see

the day his father walked toward him, not away. "He'll be gone by morning." No matter how much Justice wanted to help him.

"Time and trust."

Justice looked over at her. "What?"

"We're building trust with your dad, and that takes time. He needs to believe what we say. We told him we'd drop him off and leave, and that's what we're doing. Just like when he came to see you sing, I assured him he only had to talk to me, and I didn't stop him when he left. Or..." she trailed off for a second, "...I thought he'd left. The point is, he can trust that we're not trying to force him into more than he can handle."

"Like when you said you slept through dinner, it was true." Justice had talked her into watching a movie with him on the bed in the hotel room. She'd conked out hard.

"Exactly." She took a breath. "How many times have you looked for him?"

"Hundreds." It wasn't an exaggeration.

"He knows that. He told me to ask you to stop looking, to accept that me and your band are your future, and he's your past."

"He's my dad." He'd never leave him behind.

"I told him I wouldn't do that, and you wouldn't listen anyway. Justice..." she touched his arm, "...he loves you. He was a dry sponge sucking up every tidbit of information about you when I first saw him. But he can't talk to you. After the show, before he left, he told me something else."

"What?" He'd wanted to ask her what his dad had said to her, word for word, but Beth had been stabbed. Now in the cab of his Jeep, he leaned toward her, desperate to glean some insight that could help him reach the father he'd once known and bring him back.

"He told me, 'I hear the screams every time I close my eyes. I failed them, and they died. Not easy deaths, but horrible and agonizing. Because I made a mistake. I can't face my son. I can't.' It was heartbreaking. I could almost feel his agony."

Christ. He dropped his arm on the center console, the weight on his chest unbearable. If only he'd kept his mouth shut all those years ago when he'd screamed at his dad, *I wish you'd never come home.* He'd only added to the anguish his father carried.

"He got some of those soldiers out. Doesn't he get that?"

She leaned her forehead against his. "It's not that simple. If it was, don't you think your dad would have figured it out? We have to remember that what he's struggling with isn't because he's weak or misguided, it's because he's human. Just like us." She touched his cheek. "You told me once life won't break you. But it can. It can break any of us. We're all one moment away from shattering."

He gazed into her bottomless green eyes. "You didn't break." But she almost had. She still struggled sometimes with the urge to cut. That was one of the reasons he hated leaving her alone at night.

"I'm young. Give me time."

A chill went down his spine. "Not funny." It came out harsher than he meant. "Don't break, Beth. Don't let me break you." Then she'd leave him and hate him. "We can be stronger together. We won't break."

Her mouth curved. "All in."

He eased a hand into her hair, careful not to jerk her neck, and kissed her. Soft and slow, marking her the only way he could right now. Once she healed, he'd have her the way he craved, but this was enough for the time being. Tasting Beth, this woman who owned far too much of his heart.

Finally he pulled back. "All in."

With her by his side, he drove away, trusting that they were building something stronger and better. They'd never be like his parents—breaking each other.

The next morning, when Justice returned to the house before going to load up Beth's apartment and get her moved, his dad was gone. Again.

For a second, he squeezed his eyes shut, the pain running deep.

Beth slid her hand in his. Opening his eyes, he gazed at the woman he loved. "He's gone."

"Yeah. And it sucks."

"I don't understand it. He chooses to live on the streets rather than with me. I'd take care of him, you know? I'd..." He shut up. He'd said it all before, would do anything, but what did all that matter if his dad didn't want to be around him?

Beth leaned into his side. "It might not help, but I'm choosing to live with you and to love you. I'm here, Justice. And we're going to keep trying with your dad."

Releasing her hand, he wrapped his arm around his girl. "It helps." Beth's love was everything. The one thing he could count on when everything else in his life went to hell.

God he loved her. And he'd come too damned close to losing her. Even his dad recognized how special Beth was.

He was going to get her all moved in, take care of her while she healed, then Justice was going to prove to her—and to his dad—that he was a winner worth loving and staying for.

Chapter 4

Five Weeks Later

JUSTICE WALKED INTO THE STUDIO in Fairfax, California, *Court of Rock* shared with a few other shows. This afternoon, the set was theirs for the first rehearsal and some promo clips.

"Hey, stranger," Colin said. "Good to see you."

A real grin lit Justice's face. "Colin." He handed the security guard a coffee he'd brought for the man. It'd become something of a tradition when Justice had been on the reality show. Colin always took point guarding the main access door.

"How's Liza?" Colin winced. "I'm so damned sorry that bastard got to her. She was with her two friends when she left the building that night and said she didn't need an escort."

"She's doing well. That guy got by the cops, not you." Colin had been posted at the door, while the police worked crowd control from the street.

"That one's gonna haunt me, you know?"

Yeah, he did. Colin had been at the hospital a few times checking on her, bringing Justice coffee and

44

sandwiches. "I should have walked her to the car. It haunts me too."

"We won't let it happen again. She going on the reunion tour with us? I'll make damn sure she's safe."

"Don't know. I want her to come, but she's hell-bent on getting a job and figuring out an internship she needs for school." Or she was scared. Hiding. Maybe didn't trust him to protect her.

Can you blame her? No, he couldn't. She had every right to doubt him, both in his career and his ability to protect her. So right now, he had to prove himself. The first step was to get his ass into the rehearsal.

He heard a group come up behind him. Turning, he raised an eyebrow. "How the hell did I beat you guys here?" Simon, Lynx, Gray and River headed toward him. They were staying in L.A. while Justice commuted from San Diego.

Lynx held up his energy drink. "Needed fuel and Advil. Got a banger of a headache."

Simon nodded to Colin then glared at their drummer. "Lay off the tequila, and you won't have headaches."

"Blow me." Lynx yanked open the door and vanished inside.

River coughed. "Why don't they just kill each other and get it over with?"

Justice craned his head toward the bassist. "You look like shit. Thought you were getting that cold taken care of."

"River thinks playing doctor with a different hookup every night is the cure. Dumbass." Gray yanked open the door. "You have a sinus infection. Take the damned pills."

"Do they have pills for paranoid assholes?" River trudged into the studio, and Gray followed.

"Morons," Simon said. "Gray's being weirder than

usual, River's sick as a dog and humping like a hound in heat, and Lynx is doing shots with death. Fucking awesome."

Justice took in Simon's tight jaw and the whitening around the scar on his cheek. The tension festering in the band had been growing for weeks. "They'll snap out of it, it's just stress."

"And a glaring lack of self-control." Simon stalked into the room.

"And you have too damned much of it," Justice muttered as he followed. Inside, the stage dominated the center of the room, surrounded on three sides by seating. Crew members moved around setting up equipment, checking lighting and camera angles. They'd film the practice to get clips to run as promos for the tour.

"Savages!" Wendy yelled. All the Fury Run girls rushed over, engulfing them in hugs and back slaps.

Justice hated that they'd won the *Court of Rock* title, but he liked the all-chick band. "So how's it going with Tangent? You guys cutting a record?"

Wendy's face lit up almost as bright as the tiger-yellow streaks in her hair. "Working on it. The Tangent people are pushy as hell, trying to get us to use songs written by their people on our record. Not happening. We write our own songs."

"All right, listen up!" Frank, the producer, shouted. "We've had a change in the lineup. The band Wrexis had to cancel. The replacement band is—"

"Jagged Sin, motherfuckers! We're back." Ace Hollis sauntered into the studio, flinging around his shaggy hair, and reeking attitude. His crew straggled behind.

Next to Justice, Simon jerked then went still. "We've been played. Again."

A throb started behind Justice's eyes. Before signing, they'd specifically asked if Jagged Sin would be on the tour. Traditionally it was the top-three bands from the current year, with guest appearances of previous winners throughout the tour. However, they'd been told Jagged Sin had been passed over for the fourth-place band. So what changed?

Justice strode up to Frank. "What happened to Wrexis?"

"I don't know, Cade."

"Damn it, this isn't what we agreed to."

"You know what? I don't care. Either grow a pair and deal, or walk. But if you do, you pay back the signing bonus."

Fuck. They were screwed. That signing bonus had gone right into their new record label, S.I. Records. Justice had been looking forward to these three weeks of getting out on stage again, only this time without the pressure of eliminations and bullshit.

His muscles twitched with fury and frustration. While Jagged Sin strutted around, trash-talking and bragging about working on an album, he huddled in a corner with his guys.

For weeks, all five of them had been licking their wounds and trying to salvage their pride. It was time to pull their shit together.

He eyed each of them. Lynx, the man he'd met in Juvie when they'd both been kids. Then River, who'd been in the Fighters to Mentors program for troubled boys with Justice and Lynx. The three of them bonded. Later they found Simon and Gray.

This was his band, his life. "Time to step up and do this. No one gets between us. No one. We're going on this tour and showing the entire world who's the best damned rock band. Jagged Sin can go fuck themselves.

We're not playing their game." He held out his fist. "Savages first."

Simon, Gray, Lynx and River all bumped knuckles with him. "Savages first."

They broke up to take their places, when a hand settled on his shoulder. He met the lead guitarist's intense gaze. "What?"

"Nothing comes between us. That includes girlfriends." Simon strode to the stage.

Beth.

The night she'd been stabbed, Simon had been right beside Justice, running alongside him to help Liza. Simon didn't want Liza hurt, but he still thought Justice would have to choose between Liza and the band.

Simon was wrong.

Liza rolled her head, stretching her neck, and tried to calm her nerves as she walked into SLAM Inc. Why did Sloane Michaels want to meet with her? Justice was in L.A. for a rehearsal for the *Court of Rock* Summer Tour that was only one week away now. He came home almost every night, but once he was on tour, she'd be alone.

You could go with him. The temptation tugged at her belly. She wanted to be with Justice. *Like a groupie?*

Now wasn't the time to debate this. Liza pulled her hair down over her right shoulder. The five-week-old wound had healed to a fresh and angry four-inch scar from the center of the back of her neck to her shoulder. She had some lingering pain, most of which was her muscles healing and should go away. She'd been lucky to escape more serious nerve damage.

But she didn't want to advertise her scar. Whatever Sloane wanted to talk to her about, Liza was going to face it as a strong woman, not a pathetic victim with an ugly past.

Steeling herself, she headed into the office and blinked. Wow. Sleek and clean, gray walls and gleaming floors.

"Good afternoon, Miss Glasner. Sloane is ready for you," said a young woman behind a high, curved desk. "You may take the executive elevator up."

Did the girl recognize her from all the media coverage, or was she expecting her? "Thank you."

"Of course. I've let Sloane know you're here. His office is the top floor."

Inside the elevator, Liza smoothed her sleeveless ruffle-front blouse the color of pale sea glass over her pressed flower A-line skirt. Paired with her flat sandals, the outfit gave her confidence.

"You can handle this." Whatever this was. Her stomach pitched. Sloane and Justice had been friends for years, and she feared he was going to tell Liza she needed to get out of Justice's life.

The doors slid open, revealing a reception area. Hanging on one pale-gray wall were tall portraits of a brawny fighter she recognized as Sloane. A leather couch and chairs were gathered on a plush rug, and behind that was a hallway dotted with a few doors. A hallway opened up on her left too.

"Hi, I'm Tess."

Liza focused on the short, heavy woman with deep-brown eyes and an olive complexion rising from a desk and walking toward her. It was hard to judge her age. Maybe forties?

"Liza." Sloane strode through a door. At over six

feet, with dark hair and eyes and a powerful build, he dominated the room. "Come into my office."

She smiled at the woman and followed Sloane into a massive corner office that had a bank of windows overlooking San Diego.

The sound of a door closing rippled up her back, and she spun around.

Sloane lifted an eyebrow. "Would you like it open?"

"No. I'm still a little jumpy." She'd woken a few nights in sweat-drenched terror, and on one occasion, screaming. Lifting her chin, she added, "But I'm fine."

"Sit." He gestured to the sofa and two chairs. "I'll get right to the point."

She perched on the couch and squeezed her fingers together. "I'm curious why you asked me to come." Surprised and confused was probably a better description. Her first instinct had been to call Justice and talk to him, but she'd reined in the impulse. If Sloane was going to tell her she was bad for Justice, she didn't want her boyfriend stuck in the middle.

Again.

He had enough of that with the band, and more specifically Simon. Liza would handle this situation herself.

"I'd like to offer you a paid internship."

"Here?" It was so unexpected, she couldn't think of an intelligent response.

"My current assistant left this morning after an epic meltdown." He leaned forward. "I don't have time for dramatics at work."

Liza's brain caught up. "Your assistant? So Tess is—"

"My receptionist. I need her here in the office handling the phones, some scheduling and my calendar."

Still trying to get her head around the prospect of a

position at SLAM Inc, she sought clarification. "I see. So you're offering me a paid internship as your assistant?"

"Yes. You'd be working with me, and with Tess, doing whatever I ask you to. I'm opening MMA gyms around the country, as well as representing fighters and diversifying my brand, and things are moving fast. I need someone who can learn quickly and think on their feet. As part of the requirements for your internship, you'd be working with my marketing and publicity departments, sitting in on all levels of meetings, and see how we construct and control images of our fighters. You'd log the necessary hours required for your degree."

"You know the requirements?" How'd he get that information?

"I've already cleared it with the school. Or rather, I had Tess do it."

"Well that's...efficient." And slightly unsettling to realize he'd been researching her. But at least he wasn't trying to get her out of Justice's life.

"In return," Sloane went on, "I want a guarantee you'll stay through December. At that point, you'll graduate, and then we can reevaluate if you're a good fit here at SLAM Inc."

All this was a lot to take in, but one question surged to the top. "Why me?"

"I've seen the work you did with the band as their publicist—"

"Student publicist, and I need to point out the band lost." Oh yeah, excellent way to sell herself. She really rocked this whole publicity thing. Liza fought a sigh.

He nodded. "I'm aware. Your work was good, you handled the pressure while juggling the personalities of the band and external pressures of the media storm landing directly on you. That's the kind of calm I need. And you organized getting Cassie and her mom here to see the band, going the extra mile without being asked. I need that initiative. I'm not a hand-holder type of boss. I need someone who can figure out the job and do it, and if you do it well, there's room here to grow."

The opportunity and challenge rushed in, tripping her pulse with excitement. For five weeks, she'd been sitting around feeling like a burden and worrying about her future. Justice never made her feel like a duty, but he was busy building his career. Liza was just...there. Her confidence had wilted. This was a fresh chance to prove herself. "You said this is paid?"

Sloane rose, strode to the desk and returned with a folder. "Here's a list of your duties, a schedule and pay. Look it over, and let me know your decision tomorrow. If you want this, I'd like you to start next week, a few hours a day until you're completely recovered. Once your fall quarter in school starts, we'll adjust your hours. Any questions?"

Probably a million. Standing, she took the folder. "I'll let you know after I look over the offer."

After walking to the door, he held it open. "Tess, please show Liza around, including the office she'd use if she accepts the job."

Liza paused in the doorway. "Thank you, Sloane. This meeting turned out very differently than I imagined."

"Why's that?"

"I wondered if you were going to tell me to get out of Justice's life. He's-a-star-and-I'll-be-in-his-way kind of thing."

His eyebrows went up. "I rarely have time or inclination to get involved in my friends' personal relationships." The amusement hardened. "Your personal relationships are your business as long as they don't interfere with your work. That means you'll be here on workdays no matter where Justice and his band are."

Her mouth dried, but she nodded. "Of course."

By the time she left the SLAM Inc. building, she was almost giddy. The challenge of working as Sloane's assistant in his growing business thrilled her. This was her chance to prove and redeem herself. To show people, like her aunt, that she was making good decisions and didn't have to hide in shame.

Once she was in her car, she scanned the job offer, and her determination to accept increased. Excited to tell her boyfriend, she pulled out her phone and texted Justice. *I have some news. When will you be home?* She started to set the phone in her console. Justice usually answered when he had time.

Her phone buzzed a message from Rock Rooster. *Rehearsal is finishing up. I'm leaving soon. What's your news?*

A pang zapped her right in her vulnerable spot. This was why she needed a job, a challenge. Justice was out there practicing to go on a tour, surrounded by other stars and hot girls. And Liza? Even if she traveled with him, she'd be on the outside. She wasn't even their publicist anymore. She'd end up spending a lot of her time sitting in the hotel room, waiting. So yeah, Liza needed her own life. Focusing on the phone screen, she typed, *I'll tell you about my secret meeting when you get home.*

Rock Rooster: *What meeting? Where are you, Glasner?*

She grinned, unable to keep her good mood at bay. *A girl needs a little mystery. Out.*

Rock Rooster: *OUT WHERE?*

She laughed and pushed a little harder. Time for

Justice to realize she was healed and healthy. *Maybe I'm at the sex store. Or Brazilian wax salon. Or maybe I'm getting a piercing... A girl has needs, you know.*

Rock Rooster: *Are you saying I'm not fulfilling your needs?*

She could almost hear his low, throaty voice, feel the heat burning in his gaze when he said that. An ache settled deep in her belly, and her bra was too confining. She glanced around, feeling a little naughty. She was in the public parking lot of her future employment sending dirty texts to her boyfriend. *It's been almost five weeks of no sex, Cade. Not good for your rock-star image.* They kissed and cuddled, but no sex. *But if you aren't interested...*

Her phone rang.

"Interested?" Justice growled in her ear. "Do you know how many times I've had to jack off while you slept? Holding you close, smelling your skin, feeling you wiggle your ass against my dick, making me so horny I had to slip away into the bathroom?"

"I could have helped. Do you do it in the shower? I like soaping up your dick. Up and down..."

"Beth..." His groan was hot.

"Or maybe you use my lotion? The tropical-peach-scented one? I bet that—"

"You're torturing me. You know that." He pulled in a deep breath. "I was waiting until you get the okay from your doctor. You see him next week."

The edge in his voice told her he was at the end of his patience. "He already cleared me for most activities except heavy lifting, so I can't pick you up in a fireman's carry to throw you on the bed and have my way with you." The thought of her tossing Justice around was laughable. "But I might be able to corner you in the shower, get some of that soap—"

"I'm leaving now. It'll take me a couple hours if I don't hit traffic." He paused and added, "Beth?"

Her smile damn near exploded on her face. She'd told him what she needed, and he was doing his best to get his sexy butt home. "What?"

"You're going to find out just how bad I want you. No, make that *need* you. No backing out now, Glasner, When I get home, you're mine."

Liza walked in from the backyard where she'd uncovered the barbeque and made sure they had propane. She'd start it just as soon as Justice got home and— "Justice!" Slapping a hand over her chest, she laughed at her surprise. "Way to make an entrance, Cade."

"Speaking of making an entrance." His gaze drifted a slow path over her shirt and skirt to her bare feet, then back up. Approval and something dark and needy flared in his eyes. He took a step, then another, crowding her against the back door. "You look beautiful. Very fuckable."

Her heart shot up her throat. Not in fear, but excitement. "Thanks, that's...descriptive." And she loved it. He always told her exactly what he felt, never holding back and making her feel unsure.

His eyes danced. "Can't handle it, baby? You challenged my rock-star ego, now it's time to pay up." He caught her chin. "When I'm done with you, you'll never doubt how badly I want you again."

She opened her mouth.

Justice kissed her, his lips covering hers firmly, tongue demanding she surrender. He didn't let up until she was breathless.

Raising his head, he stroked her jaw and throat. "Take off your shirt. I want to see you."

Shivers went through her at the throaty demand. "Now?" She glanced around the roomy kitchen with the cracked tile counters and chicken-themed decorations.

"In our kitchen that you love so much. This is your home now too. And we're going to christen it with your cries of desire."

His touch ignited her skin, but it was Justice's words that tugged deep in her chest. Home. A place to be really safe. Free. Able to be a little wild without judgment. Her belly turned to liquid heat and made her brave. She tugged off the shirt and bra, freeing her breasts. She wasn't going to think about her slight muffin top riding the waistband of her skirt or her new scar on her neck and shoulder.

He groaned. "So sexy."

Taking her hand, he turned her around, facing the window in the top of the back door. The heat of Justice spread along her bare back. His fingers stroked her belly. Pushing her hair aside, he kissed the curve of her neck.

Hot chills pebbled her skin. Liza tilted her head, giving him more access.

Justice cupped her breasts, brushing her nipples as he kissed and sucked her neck. Yearning streaked down her belly, making her moan and clench her thighs.

Against her lower back, she could feel the hard length of his cock trapped in his jeans.

Justice trailed his mouth to her ear. "Are your panties wet?"

"Maybe."

"Show me. Take them off."

She twisted her waist to meet his gaze without hurting her neck. Looking for...she didn't know exactly.

"Problem? You told me to get home to share your news. And that you need this—not just sex, but to be wanted. You told me, Beth. Now let me give you what you need. I'm going to make you come, then fuck you until you come again—slowly and with care because I love you and I'm not going to hurt you. Now take those panties off and show me that you're ready to take what my brave girl asked for. Then we'll finish whatever dinner you're cooking and you'll tell me your news."

She loved him so damned much. She had told him she needed him, and here he was. All she had to do was be the brave girl he thought she was. Liza kept his gaze while she slid her hands beneath the flare of her skirt. She pushed her panties down her thighs.

Justice shifted to hold her waist but never broke their stare.

She stepped out of her underwear and held the garment up. The late-afternoon sunlight caught the light-blue fabric with the dark center of wetness.

"Fuck." His voice dropped low, almost feral. His cock surged against her back, fighting its confinement in his jeans. With one hand he yanked her skirt up. His fingers slid along her seam and circled her clit. Wrapping his other arm around her waist, he held her firmly. "Rest your head against my shoulder. Don't strain your neck."

She leaned back, sinking into the feel of him. He circled the bundle of nerves, his touch growing faster and more frantic. He angled his mouth over hers, thrusting his tongue in as he pressed one finger inside her.

Her vaginal walls contracted hard, and Liza

writhed. The sounds of their kissing and him fingering her filled the kitchen. Her body burned as need shot up. She gripped his arm, holding on. He curled his finger, rubbing the spot deep inside while his palm pressed her clit.

The orgasm exploded over her, while tremors spasmed. She didn't know how much time passed as she leaned against him, soaking in the pleasure until her muscles were sated.

Blood roared in Justice's veins, his body rigid with excitement. Desperate need pounded along his spine, fed by the scent of Beth—warm peaches and the wet, spicy smell of her orgasm.

"I have to get inside you." He heard the growl in his voice, but he didn't care. Turning her, he lifted her up, and Beth wrapped around him like a blanket. She kissed along his jaw and down his neck.

Christ, her desperation fed his. Long strides took him to their room. Sunlight spilled between the blinds, illuminating his bed that Beth had added a half-dozen decorative pillows to when she moved in. After laying her down, he kicked off his shoes and stripped in record time.

Beth's eyes were glazed behind her glasses, and her skirt was rucked up, baring her pussy to him. He gripped her knees and spread her open. No Brazilian, thank God. This was his Beth with dark curls wet with her desire for him.

"I could take the skirt off."

He lifted his gaze to her face surrounded by the heavy cloud of her riotous hair. "You look like wicked-hot sin with that skirt bunched around your waist, baring yourself to me. Show me your panties that you took off to get fucked."

Warm color stained her face and flushed her chest as she held up her fist. The scrap of blue fabric spilled from her fingers and over the head of his cock.

The cool silk sensation gliding over his throbbing dick had him clamping his teeth. Christ.

Beth dragged the panties down his shaft and back up in a satiny torture. Hot pleasure arced into his balls and gripped his belly. He squeezed his fingers into her thighs. One look to the center of Beth—all the creamy pink flesh, wet and swollen for him—and he was done. Unable to think, to even breathe, he grabbed the panties from her hand and pressed his cockhead to her opening. "Are you going to be good? Let me take this slow? Careful?"

Her eyes fired to a wild green. "No."

"Yes." He growled it as he slid in an inch. Then another. Her hot, slick grasp ripped a groan from him. Without permission, his hips surged forward, buying his cock balls-deep in her pussy. Riding the edge of insanity, he skimmed the lingerie over her tits, teasing her nipples with the cool silk.

Her mouth parted, and her walls contracted hard.

Oh hell yeah. He thrust in and out and guided the scrap of silk down the center line of her belly.

"Justice." Her fingers convulsed in the comforter.

"Stay still, baby. Try not to tense your neck and shoulders." God she felt good. He moved in and out, just hard enough to drive them both mad. Lust squeezed his balls, the need to come building. Now. Holding the panties, he rubbed the material over her clit.

Beth cried out, eyes squeezing shut, belly going tight. Right there. Justice rode her while pressing hard on her clit, and she exploded.

One more thrust and his orgasm shot down his spine, fiery pleasure detonated. His mind hazed beneath the fierce bliss racking his body.

Once he could think again, he pulled out, lay next to her and pulled her against him. He rubbed the shoulder area where she'd been stabbed, but her muscles were so lax, any lingering worry drained out of him. Contentment spread, chasing out all the pressures and worries. "I need this, Beth."

She tilted her head back. "Sex?"

He fixed her glasses on her nose. "Us. This. The way you make me feel." He couldn't help adding, "Everything is so damned tense right now with the band, setting up our record label, money's tight..." He stopped himself from listing all the problems. The thought of leaving her for three weeks made him feel...unsettled. "Come on tour with us." Beth was his sane place. She calmed the frantic energy in him. The only other place he ever felt this way was onstage.

She pulled back and sat up. "I don't think I can."

Irritation climbed his spine. "Why? You gave up your job at Wylie's, and we'll be back before classes start."

She took a deep breath. "Sloane offered me a job today. A paid internship as his assistant. I'll get to work with his publicity and marketing departments, see how they create and control images."

Disappointment weighed heavily on him, but when he saw the excitement brightening her eyes and warming her face, he shoved it aside. He leaned against the headboard and pulled her onto his lap. "You really want this?"

"The money's better than fair. And I'll learn so much." She traced the blue jay tattoo on his chest. "I need this. You're going off on this tour, then you guys are going into the studio to record, plus doing gigs to make money and keep your profile up."

"What does that have to do with accepting the job?"

She sucked in her bottom lip, and her lax muscles firmed.

Worry dug into his gut. Taking hold of her chin, he studied her face. "What?" It hadn't been easy for her these last weeks, recovering both physically and emotionally from the knife attack. She'd had some night terrors brought on by dreams of Hayes. Justice had been there, able to coax her awake and get her to verbalize her fears and anger.

But he was leaving soon... Could Beth handle this when he was gone? Would she cut if he wasn't here? "Talk, Beth." It came out gruffer than he intended.

"It hurts a little, okay? Being pushed out, being replaced as your publicist, the fact that Christine told you to distance yourself from me. Even if I went, I wouldn't be a part of it, I'd be on the outside. Like a groupie."

Shit. He hadn't realized how this bothered her. But what could he do? Christine and the band made it clear—they didn't want Beth connected to their band in any way. She wasn't mentioned on their website, social media, anywhere. He hated this, damn it. "It's for your safety too."

She rolled her eyes. "Don't patronize me. I have a scar that tells me how dangerous it is."

Hell, now he felt like more of an ass. Beth was the one who'd warned him that exposing her identity would bring out the crazies who believed she'd ruined Hayes's career in some scheme with her parents. Then she was stabbed—so yeah, he didn't get to say stupid shit to her about protecting her. At least Hans had been charged with attempted murder, his bail set high enough to keep his ass in jail awaiting trial. "Sorry, you're right. And I'm sorry it hurts that you can't work with us. I wish it were different."

"But it's not. This is the reality we have to live with. But this job, it's mine. Plus it will give me enough credits to finish my B.A. in December, and I have a chance to make a mark here. I won't be chasing after your band like a groupie, or sitting here doing nothing. And the money I make will help both of us too."

She really did need this. "Then you'll take it. And maybe it's better this way. We got blindsided today."

"With what?"

He tugged on her hair. "Jagged Sin, they're on the tour."

"How? They were charged with Simon's attack and—"

"I know. I talked to Christine on the way home. From what she found out, they cut a deal with the court, did a stint in rehab, and the charges were dropped."

"Didn't Simon know this?"

"Yes, but he didn't think they'd do the rehab."

"Oh, Justice, can Simon endure three weeks with those assholes? What about you?"

"We have to, Beth. We need the money and the exposure. As long as they don't go after you, I'm okay. So in that sense, it'll be better if you're not there every day." This wasn't going to be as easy as he'd thought. "But I'll miss you like hell." Another thought occurred to him. "Shit, I'll be gone on your birthday."

She raised her eyebrows. "You could fly home."

The hopefulness in her tone pierced him. "I can't. We're locked in for the three weeks."

Disappointment flickered in her gaze before she shook it off. "Not a big deal. All part of dating a rock star, right?"

Her twenty-first birthday, and the first one they were celebrating together, was a big deal. He needed to figure out a way to— "I have an idea. The tour is in Vegas that weekend of your birthday. Fly out and meet me." Bracing his head on his hand, he looked down at his girl. "We're going to do your twenty-first birthday right. You ever been to Vegas?"

"No. I mean we drove through it, but we didn't stop."

Justice could see both curiosity and worry in her gaze. He smoothed the frown line between her eyebrows. "Do you want to go? I'll keep you safe, but you're turning twenty-one. It's time to live a little, sweetheart."

"Are you corrupting me, Rooster?"

He hugged her against him. "Hell yeah. If you're living with a rock star, it's time you learn to party like one."

And he was just the man to teach her.

Chapter 5

Las Vegas, Nevada

THE JOINT AT THE HARD Rock Hotel was packed. Excitement ruffled the air. *Court of Rock* Summer Tour had sold out the four-thousand-seat venue. Liza loved it. Well, not Jagged Sin. They'd been onstage first, and she'd kept her butt planted in her seat.

"Next up, Savaged Illusions!"

The crowd roared, and Liza surged to her feet, clapping wildly as the band jogged onto the stage.

"What are they singing tonight?" Emily asked.

"'Reaper's Child' by the Hell Blades." Screech's song. Liza hadn't ever seen Justice perform it. Anticipation tightened her belly. It was the song they'd listened to Screech play in the club on what had been their first time out together. It hadn't exactly been a date, but it had been the start of something special between them.

He'd chosen this song for her.

"I don't think I know that one," Nikki said from her other side.

"Just listen." Justice had gotten her two friends

64

tickets, and Liza, Em and Nikki had all driven to Vegas together. Once, Liza'd been isolated and alone. Now she had a live-in boyfriend, girlfriends, and she was celebrating her twenty-first birthday in Vegas. So yeah...she might have lost her family, but she'd gained so much more. Her worst fear had happened—being exposed and then attacked—and yet she wasn't cowering and hiding. Nope, she was out living her life.

Best birthday ever.

Once the band took their places, Justice spread his arms wide. "Hey there, Las Vegas! Who wants to party?" He waited a beat for the clapping to die off. "Let's do this!"

The stage lights went dark, and silence fell. Dramatic chills broke out on her skin. For a few seconds, it felt as though no one in the venue even breathed.

One light snapped on illuminating Gray, his blond head tilted back, eyes closed as he played the haunting opening notes to "Reaper's Child." Gray shined in that moment, his confidence as brilliant as the notes flowing from the piano.

"Wow," Emily said. "He's beautiful."

She didn't have a chance to respond as Justice began to sing, his voice low, as if each word was torn from the deepest reaches of his heart. A second spotlight snapped on Justice, just as his voice climbed the notes, ringing with power as he railed against the Reaper for stealing the soul of his child.

Liza shivered. Reaper meant drugs in this song, and there was a time when she'd felt that the Reaper of drugs, alcohol and partying sometimes stole her mother from her. Everyone had a Reaper they fought for someone they loved.

"My God, Liza." Nikki took her hand. "Justice is amazing."

As she swayed to the song, her dark memories vanished. Instead she recalled the way Justice had wrapped his arms around her in Screech's club as they watched and listened to him.

Once the song hit the first chorus, the entire stage lit up as the band played, Lynx pounding home the anger, River laying down the emotional throb with his bass and Simon ripping up the guitar...and when Justice sang the last note...

All the spotlights went off except Gray's as he closed with the agony of defeat on his piano. The Reaper had won...

The audience sat stunned for a single beat of her heart. Then the entire auditorium exploded into thundering applause.

Liza was right there with them, losing herself in the emotional reaction, even as a part of her desperately wished she was backstage so she could throw herself in Justice's arms and tell him how much she loved him. But she wasn't part of the show or working for the band anymore.

It didn't matter, she was here and having fun.

Two hours later, Liza found herself at the poolside bar surrounded by a crowd. It was after ten, the night warm with the dry desert air of Vegas. Palm trees swayed gently next to groupings of lounge chairs and cabanas. People clustered around tables on the bar patio and swarmed to get the bartenders' and servers' attention.

"All right, birthday girl, what do you want? This one's on me," Gray said, his smile ridiculously sweet.

She glanced at the busy bartenders, the rows of bottles stacked on shelves, the blenders... She repressed a shudder. "Nothing out of a blender." The memory of a hand pushing that frothy pink drink on her rode too close to the surface. Yet surrounded by the crowd of friends and her lover, it was easier to stay in the moment.

"Kahlua Mudslide is made in a shaker. It's sort of like a milkshake," Nikki suggested. "Well, with a punch."

"Same with a Cosmopolitan," Emily said. "You'd like that. Or a Mango mojito. It has mint and lime in it."

"Bellini is made with sparkling wine," Nikki added. "Like champagne. Remember you tried champagne?"

She shifted her gaze to Justice standing at her left shoulder. "We researched drinks on our way here."

He grinned. "Of course you did. I bet you have a list on your phone too."

Making a list made her feel like she was in control of the decision instead of recklessly jumping into a bad choice that could drag her down a life of destruction. She had too many memories of her mom stumbling in drunk and puking, or the screaming fights with men or other women over men. She didn't want to be her. But she didn't want to be her dour aunt either. She just wanted to be a normal college girl celebrating her twenty-first birthday with friends at a bar. "Yeah I still don't know what to order. What do I do?"

His amusement dimmed. "What do you want to do? Any drink you order I'm going to watch them make, then I'll taste it. It's your call. But if you'd rather have a Coke, you tell everyone else to back the fuck off. Got it? No one makes you drink something you don't want."

His calm assurance helped, but the one thing she feared was losing control and being vulnerable. And yet, she wanted to be able to be a normal girl and live, not sit on the sidelines, always afraid to take a risk. "What if I get drunk?"

"I have a two-beer limit on tour. I got you, Beth. You can let go, party, and not worry." He leaned closer. "I'm here. Nothing bad is going to happen to you."

Her eyes stung. He'd protect her, keep her safe while she relaxed years of vigilance and had some fun. Finally she turned and flagged a bartender. "I'll take a mango mojito."

Justice's hand settled on her back, warm and safe. She turned to meet his gaze. But nope, his stare was riveted on the bartender, watching every move the girl made. When the drink was finished and Gray put it on his tab, Justice picked up the glass and took a drink. He made a face and handed it to her. "That's some girlie shit right there. But perfectly safe."

To anyone around them, it probably sounded ridiculous. He couldn't tell the drink was safe with a two-second sip. Most date-rape drugs were odorless and tasteless. But it was symbolic for her. A gesture that he was there, standing between her and danger. It didn't have to be logical, sometimes it was all about the gesture. Holding the cold glass in her hand, gratefulness filled her heart, and she said, "Thank you."

He lifted his beer and clinked it with hers. "Happy Birthday, Beth."

She took a sip as everyone stared. Sweet mango, tart lime with the bite of mint and whoa...that must be the rum kick. She tried another sip.

"Well?" Emily clinked her cranberry and vodka drink against the mojito. "What do you think?"

"Good." She shot Justice a look. "Not girlie at all."

Gray clicked his glass with hers. "*Bon Anniversarie*, Liza."

Startled, she hesitated with her drink halfway to her

mouth. "You speak French?" She'd taken a couple semesters in high school and barely remembered any of it.

The other man grinned. "When I feel like it."

Lynx shoulder bumped him. "Which is usually when he's trying to get into some girl's pants."

"Huh." Liza eyed Gray, curious. "Does it work?"

Gray smiled and said nothing.

"Liza!" a female voice yelled from behind her.

She spun around to see Wendy, lead singer of Fury Run.

Liza hugged her. "You guys were great tonight." Letting go, she took in Wendy's blinding yellow hair with red tips. The singer changed her hair color as often as Liza changed her nail polish. "You remember Nikki and my friend Emily?"

"Sure." After some hellos, Wendy shouted out, "Savages, get me a beer. Come on, let's go sit. Those boots I wear on stage are a bitch. Getting those babies off are almost like an orgasm, but my feet still hurt."

Liza took in Wendy's flip-flops and hid her grin.

"Damn, woman, it's good to see you," Wendy said. "You getting stabbed right outside *Court of Rock* filming was scary shit. You're good now?"

"Yep."

"There's a spot over there." Em pointed to the far end of the pool where a big group was leaving.

"I'll catch up in a minute," Nikki said, and headed off the other way.

Once they locked down the spot, Wendy chatted for a minute, entertaining them with stories about Tangent, their schedule, and then said, "They want me to do this makeover. Like...go blonde and lose twenty pounds."

"What did you tell them?" Liza asked.

She grinned. "Nothing. It was a lunch, and I ordered cake and ice cream for dessert."

Liza high-fived her.

The guys joined them, along with some girls Liza hadn't seen before.

Once Justice sat next to her, she asked, "Where'd the girls come from?"

"River chatted them up at the bar and invited them."

Why was she even surprised?

Emily surveyed their group. "Where'd Nikki get off to?"

"I don't know. Bathroom maybe?" Liza checked her phone, but there was no message.

Gray cut in with, "She's over at the bar now. I saw her by the bathrooms earlier talking to Ace, and it looked animated. I called out her name, she said something to Ace I didn't catch, and came over to me. She said she was fine when I asked, so I dropped it."

Liza started to get up and go check, but caught sight of Nikki striding over to them carrying a drink.

"What did Ace want?" Liza blurted out. "Did he touch you?"

"Nah." She sank into the chair by Em, across from Liza. "Believe it or not, he was trying to get me to go to some stripper bar with him."

"Shut up." Liza couldn't contain her shock. "After the way he treated you when you were his student publicist? Does he not remember that he attacked Simon when you were with him?" Plus Ace'd manhandled Nikki a few times.

"Right? He acted like none of that was a big deal. And why would he think I'd want to go see girls stripping?" She shook her head. "He wasn't bad onstage tonight, but he's still an asshole."

Wendy studied Nikki. "You didn't sleep with him back then, did you?"

Nikki choked, her face turning red. "God no. He used me like a pimp service. If he saw a hot girl, he'd tell me to get her to come to his table or greenroom or whatever. Just thinking about those two weeks gives me a grimy feeling I need to kill off with alcohol and a change of subject." She lifted her glass. "To Liza. Happy Birthday!"

Liza scooped up hers and took another sip, surprised to find it was down to ice. Wow.

Justice leaned closer. "Want another?"

"Sure."

While he walked off, Nikki gestured to the other band members and their entourage. "When did that happen?"

Liza eyed the dark-haired girl on the lounge chair sucking face with Lynx. River had another girl on his lap. Gray was chatting up still another. Simon sipped his drink and watched. She answered Nikki with, "Between the bar and here." More girls were trying to get Simon's attention.

"Jeez. I can't even get a decent first date."

"Oh come on," Wendy said. "It can't be that bad."

"It totally is," Liza teased. "Nikki collects bad first dates. They're priceless. Tell her about the one last weekend, you know, the guy you met at work, which should have been your first clue."

"Where do you work?" Wendy asked.

Nikki wrinkled her nose. "A division of Polly Care." She paused a beat then added, "I'm in marketing for their adult diaper line."

Wendy snorted. "That's where you scrounged up a date?"

Nikki sighed. "Better than Ace, right?"

"Amen," Wendy agreed. "Okay, so what happened on this date that was so bad?"

"This guy is in accounting, so I don't know him very well, but he seemed okay. He picked me up, and we went to Chili's. The first odd thing was he refused to sit in the bar, but I figured maybe he doesn't drink." Nikki paused.

Liza smiled at the sparkle in Nikki's eyes. She loved telling her date stories, or Liza wouldn't have brought it up. Nikki thrived on the attention.

"So what happened next?" Wendy prompted.

Nikki took another sip of her drink. "We got a table, and he spent an entire forty minutes staring at this family—a mom, dad and little boy who was maybe three? I don't know."

River looked around the girl on his lap, and asked, "Was she an ex or something?"

"Tell them." Emily practically bounced in her chair.

Nikki went on, "That's what I wondered too, so I asked him. He swore he'd never met her. But then he added, 'That kid's really cute though, don't you think?'"

"Ew," Wendy said. "Creeper alert."

"Right?" Nikki agreed. "I mean, what twenty-something guy stares at a kid in a restaurant and says that? But then I thought, okay, maybe he's just one of those guy who wants a family. I told myself not to overreact, and asked, 'Do you want kids?'" She paused again.

"What did he say?" River blurted out.

"He leaned across the table and whispered, 'I already have kids. Dozens of them, probably even hundreds. I'm a sperm donor. And I think that one might be one of mine.'"

They all cracked up.

"Wait, it gets better. He then told me he was pretty

sure the movie about the guy who finds out he has all the kids, *Delivery Man*, is based on him."

Liza jumped in with, "Nikki called me from the bathroom, and I went and picked her up."

Wendy laughed so hard she spilled some of her beer. "That's...wow, that's just sad. But you've had good dates, right?"

"Sadly, nope. I've had runners, mommy's boys..." Nikki rolled her eyes. "My dates just suck."

Justice returned, sat and handed Liza her mojito. "You might want to drink that slowly."

"Nah, she should knock it back," Nikki said. "She's gonna need some courage."

Liza swung around, facing her. "What did you do? You didn't hire a stripper, did you?" She'd threatened that on the car ride.

"Nope."

She should be relieved, right? "Then what?"

"I put you, me and Emily on the list for karaoke." She pointed past all the lounge chairs and tables to a stage set up under a big canopy.

Liza looked in horror as even now some guy was attempting a Justin Bieber song. "Shut up! You didn't."

"She did," Emily assured her. "And it gets better. Tell her the song you chose."

Liza glanced around at the entire group. Her mouth dried, and she took another sip of her drink. She didn't sing in public. She never drew attention to herself that way. Finally, she couldn't bear the suspense. "What song?" How bad could it be?

"Britney Spears's 'Oops!...I Did It Again'."

Oh God. She turned to Justice. "Help."

He laughed in her face. "I'll make sure your drinks are safe and you're safe, but this? Nope. If you're too chicken to get on that stage and sing

Britney..." he shrugged, "...you're on your own."

She narrowed her eyes. "Did you just call me chicken?" Oh yeah, she heard the part about him protecting her, and they were safe out here at the pool bar. Security and bouncers damn near outnumbered the guests. But she was feeling...loose. Happy.

Brave.

"Do you cluck like a chicken? Is that why you're afraid to get up there and sing?"

She took another healthy sip of her drink. "You think I won't do it?"

He raised an eyebrow. "You refused to sing at Screech's. Remember? Bock, bock..."

She faced her friends. "I'm in. When do we go on?"

"Liza can sing," Wendy said. "Even if it's a Brit song."

Justice stood at the edge of the stage. He'd walked the girls up here, wanting to be close in case Beth got cold feet or some guy bothered her. Wendy had come along with him, giving the girls last-minute advice. But his concentration was riveted on Liza. After two drinks, she was buzzing. Her hair was a wild mass of curls, her face flooded with color, and she wore a flowing tank top over black skinny jeans and heels.

Not an ugly sweater in sight. When he first met her, she'd covered up in those ugly cardigan things, but now his Beth was shedding her reserve and coming out of hiding.

"Yep, she can sing. But I don't think this group will be getting a record deal anytime soon." The three girls held their mics and strutted around on the stage, half the time bumping into each other and laughing.

She snorted. "They're getting a lot of notice."

The majority of the poolside partiers had stopped their chatting to fix their attention on the stage. Justice looked around. His band, the Fury Run girls, and some of the *Court of Rock* crew had commandeered a spot by the pool. They were partying, laughing, dancing, but they'd all stopped to watch Liza, Em and Nikki.

The girls launched into the final chorus of "Oops!...I Did It Again." Liza belted it out with more enthusiasm than skill, but her voice wasn't bad at all. When they were done, people clapped, and Beth raced down the steps. "I did it!" Her face glowed. "I'm not a chicken."

He chuckled at her excitement. "Nope."

"I want my prize."

He yanked her against him and kissed her hard. Uncaring of who watched, he thrust his tongue in her mouth, tasting her, this girl who shed her fears—rum, mint, lime and that sweetness that was pure Beth. Lifting his head, he stared down at her.

More color flooded her face, and her eyes sparkled. "What was that for?"

"Because I can. Because I wanted to. Because you were so damn hot up there. That's your prize. Me."

"Damn, I wanted another mojito."

Laughter shot up his throat. "Fine. Let's go to the bar." Once there he handed each girl a water while the drinks were being made. He concentrated on watching the bartender make Beth's mojito.

"That's it for karaoke," the DJ said. "Thanks to everyone who took their shot. Let's get back to dancing. Any requests?"

"How about 'Wicked Garden' by Gene Hayes?"

Justice spun around at the too-familiar voice, the same one he'd had to listen to for the last two weeks on the tour. Ace, lead singer of Jagged Sin and pain in his ass.

They stood by the pool, dripping chains, piercings and bullshit attitude. For two weeks they'd kept to themselves and out of trouble. Justice assumed so they didn't get thrown off the tour and lose their bonus for finishing. Nikki said Ace was going to some strip club, but obviously, they'd hung around. Why?

Because Beth is here. She's the draw.

He glanced over at his guys. Simon and Lynx had shot to their feet. Ace knew damn well "Wicked Garden" was the title of Hayes's second album—the one that had dropped and shot to the top of the charts right before he drugged and raped Liza. Bastard was looking for a fight.

A few of the partiers murmured and glanced uneasily at Liza, obviously having figured out that she was the infamous Elizabeth Ranger.

Beth stood frozen between Nikki and Emily, her face draining of color.

Finally the DJ spun a rap beat and people relaxed, going back to partying. Taking the drinks, Justice walked up to Beth. "Let's get out of here. We'll go to another bar." He wasn't going to let Ace the asshat ruin her birthday.

"No." She took the drink and knocked back a quarter of it. When she turned her gaze on him, fire gleamed in her green eyes. "I'm not running and hiding." She swung around and walked—no, make that *strutted*—toward the rest of their crew.

"Hell yeah," Wendy said. "Now that's spunk." She flanked Liza, along with Nikki and Emily.

Justice strode after them, his pride in Beth's grit and screw-you attitude warring with a rush of fury priming his muscles. He caught up to the girls as they passed Ace and his group at the edge of the pool.

"Oh look, it's oops, I did it again," Mick mimicked.

"More like, oops, fuck me again, Hayes. Oh, baby, fuck me again," Ace said.

Rage pounded in Justice's head. Energy snapped at his spine, and his fingers curled with the need to slam his fist into that bastard's face. *Don't do it. Keep walking.* Not only could they be thrown off the tour and forfeit their signing bonus, but Beth and the girls could get hurt.

"Leave her alone!" Nikki yelled.

Justice stopped. Everything happened at once.

Nikki stood in front of Ace with her hands on her hips and her head thrown back. "Gene Hayes is a rapist, and you're a butt-sniffing, coke-snorting loser."

"Shut up, you traitorous slut." Ace shoved the girl's shoulder, knocking her off balance.

Justice leapt forward, grabbing Nikki beneath her arms before she fell. He swung her behind him and set her on her feet, then whipped around in time to see Beth slap her drink on a nearby table and stomp up to Ace.

Oh fuck.

"Don't you ever touch her again!" Beth yelled.

"What you gonna do, suck my dick and cry rape?"

Justice lunged, reaching a hand out to move Beth so he could kill the bastard.

"This!" Beth yelled and rammed both hands against Ace's chest.

His drink flew out of his hands, and his arms windmilled as he tilted back, lost his balance and fell into the pool.

All hell broke loose.

A throb in her head forced her to wake up. Light shafted through the partially opened drapes.

Wait, this wasn't her room.

A bolt of panic clamped her chest, and she jackknifed up to a sitting position, heart pounding, fear drenching her. A buzzing competed with the throb in her head. Where was she? What—?

"Beth, hey." The bed dipped, and Justice rubbed her bare arm.

Damn, it hurt to move her eyes, but once her gaze connected with the familiar stare of her boyfriend, her panic receded. Right, they were in Vegas. It was her birthday trip. But why was there an acute thudding in her sinuses and forehead, as if some monster had slithered in and *pulsed*? What had she done?

The answer flashed painfully in her head. *Mango mojitos*. The memory flooded back. "Oh God, I got thrown out of the bar."

"Yep."

She squinted, then reached over to get her glasses. After slipping them on, she peered closer at her boyfriend. "Why are you smirking? It isn't funny."

"It was hilarious. You pushed Ace into the pool. My favorite part was how he sputtered and fought the poser chains hanging off his belt. He flailed like a beached whale trying to get to the side of the pool." Justice snorted then busted up.

Liza's lips twitched. "He squished when he walked, and those stupid chains clanked." It had been pretty funny, although at the time she'd been too drunk and mad to appreciate it. But then... "I got us thrown out."

Justice sobered and cradled her face in his hands. "Congratulations, baby, now you've partied like a rock star. Happy birthday." He kissed her forehead, then grabbed a bottle of water and a couple pills. "Take this and take a shower. You'll feel better."

After downing the pills, she slowly climbed out of

bed and stood. *Thump, thump, thump.* "Hangovers suck. How did my mom do this night after night?"

"At least you're not puking."

Thank God for that. It was just her headache causing her misery. He'd obviously showered, his jaw was beard-shadowed, hair sex messy, and he was wearing a T-shirt, shorts and flip-flops. "You have no right to look so...delicious."

"Delicious?"

"And bad for me. Really bad. God, what if this gets out? What if people—?" Oh wait, forget about her reputation. "What about you? Are you guys in trouble with *Court of Rock*?"

"Nah. The cops weren't called. No one was arrested or hurt. Simon's already talked to the show execs. We got a warning, which doesn't mean shit."

Her eyes widened. "Can you work with Jagged Sin for the remainder of the tour? I'm sorry, I got drunk and obviously out of control." Her stomach twisted. "I'm turning into my mom."

Justice wrapped his hands around her shoulders. "What did you do that was so bad? Tell me. Get tipsy? Sing a karaoke song? Defend your friend?"

She pressed her forehead to the soft cotton T-shirt stretched over his hard chest. Justice's body heat spread over her skin, and his scent filled her lungs. What had she done that was so bad? Nothing. It was her birthday, she was with her friends, and it was Ace who opened his big mouth.

Don't talk about it, Liza. You're making it worse. People are judging you. Us. Just keep your head down and stay quiet. Her aunt had told her that over and over. She'd wanted Liza to become invisible and stop being an embarrassment. But Justice wasn't upset at all.

She lifted her gaze. "I didn't stay quiet."

His mouth curved. "How'd it feel?"

A little scary. Her anger had shot right past her control and shoved her into an impulsive reaction. She'd been pissed that Ace had pushed Nikki again. He'd done it before when Nikki worked as his student publicist. When he'd said to Liza, *What you gonna do, suck my dick and cry rape?* something had snapped inside her. All those years she'd had to listen to ugly things being said about her while being told she couldn't fight back, couldn't defend herself, to just stay quiet.

"I lost my temper." Something she'd never done before Justice. She'd resorted to cutting alone in a bathroom rather than letting her feelings out, or jamming broken glass into her wrist to escape the emotional barrage and pain.

"And?"

She shifted her attention back to him. A slow smile tugged at her mouth despite her headache. "It felt pretty damned good." There it was, her truth. Losing control like that, defending her friend and herself, had felt awesome.

"That's my girl." His eyes darkened. "But when I'm not there, you don't go near Ace or any threat. I can't take you getting hurt again." His jaw bunched. "I'd have gotten to him first if I hadn't caught Nikki before she fell."

She didn't doubt it for a second. "I know. I think that's why I lost my temper. You were there, you had my back, so I wasn't scared." And that was an amazing feeling.

"Always," Justice said.

Happiness chased out the remainder of her headache. Just under two months ago, everything was a disaster. Justice losing *Court of Rock*, Liza stabbed, no internship.

Now she had Justice, friends, her internship. And soon she'd start her last quarter of college.

The only cloud on the horizon?

Gene Hayes.

Chapter 6

Two Months Later, October

SIX YEARS.

The text from Beth throbbed in his head as he fought the freaking traffic to get home to her. He'd called when his plane landed, but she hadn't answered. Right after that, his phone showed him an update on an entertainment site:

Justice Cade absent from the sentencing of his girlfriend's attacker.

Fucking perfect. It made him look like an asshole, or worse, like he didn't care enough to be there. He'd tried, damn it. Fury and frustration made him want to ram the cars in front of him. Oh wait, let's not forget guilt too. He'd missed his flight from San Francisco this morning, which meant he didn't get back in time.

He really was an asshole. Beth had been under tremendous stress for the last month with school, work and the plea bargain that happened suddenly with

Hans. The media got wind of it, and they'd started harassing her. Some claimed that the D.A. didn't want to put Liza on the stand because she was too tainted by her past with Gene Hayes and all the things said about her in the media.

Others claimed she was afraid of Hayes. They weren't wrong. Her nightmares had escalated in the last month. But she'd have done it—gotten on the stand and testified against Hans. It amazed him that she'd been so willing, even knowing the defense attorneys would bring up Gene Hayes, since he was connected to Hans's motive, and drag her through the mud.

Beth wasn't the problem. Nope, it was his dad.

More guilt dumped in his gut. His father wasn't a reliable witness. And how could the court summon a man who didn't want to be found? Justice hadn't seen or heard a word from him since the night his father had gotten out of jail. It was his dad's pictures that proved Hans had been following Beth. But to get those introduced into evidence, they'd have to bring his dad in. So the D.A. pled it down from attempted murder to attempted voluntary manslaughter.

Six years. That bastard who stabbed and damn near killed Beth would be out in a measly three years with good behavior.

After finally pulling into his driveway, he barely turned the car off before rushing into the house, only pausing to key in the code on the security system.

No Beth. Where was she? Was she so pissed at him for missing the flight she hadn't come home?

Wait, he heard the shower running. Justice hustled down the hall, into their bedroom. A cold pit opened in his stomach. How upset was she? Oh Christ, she wouldn't... Could she be cutting?

Justice stared at the closed bathroom door, hating the barrier between them. But if he barged in now, he'd scare the hell out of her. *Think, man.*

"Beth." He knocked on the door. "I'm home."

"Okay."

That was it. Flat, emotionless. Cold fear pushed at him. Shoving open the door, he strode in. "Beth, tell me you're not—"

She snapped the shower curtain back, her eyebrows raised. "Not what?"

His brain stuttered. Beth stood there wet and naked, her long hair slicked back, eyes huge, and rivers of water streaming over her breasts, her soft belly to that sweet spot between her legs. The steamy bathroom closed in on him.

"Uh..." Four months he'd lived with her, but his desire had grown bigger. Hotter.

"Cutting?"

That word iced a fraction of his lust. She might be pissed at him, but Justice didn't lie to her. He looked her dead in the eye. "Yes, cutting. You've been under too much pressure." Her occasional struggle with cutting wasn't something he'd let fester as a shameful secret between them. He kept it in the sunlight, where he could help her. What he didn't tell her was the fear that one day he wouldn't be here if she needed him, that he'd fail her and lose her.

Her defiance softened. "Cutting crossed my mind a time or seventeen in the last few weeks. But not enough to do it. I'm okay, especially now that it's over. Hans is sentenced, and I just want to move on to concentrate on work and school. I got behind in one of my classes."

As long as she was telling him her struggles, she was okay. It was when she couldn't talk, couldn't find a way to verbalize her terrors, that drove her to cut for relief.

After stripping off his clothes, he got in the warm shower, taking her face in his hands. "I'm so damn sorry I missed my flight." He'd been there with her when she talked to the D.A. and for the interview with the presentencing probation officer. But this time...he'd screwed up.

"When you missed your flight home this morning, I was upset."

Guilt squeezed his chest. "I know. We had a chance to meet with a music streaming service. It's a vital contact. We need them to play our music when we release our album. But I thought I'd make it to the airport in time to catch my flight." *Shut up.* That sounded defensive instead of contrite.

Beth tilted her head back, her naked gaze on him. "It's already starting, isn't it?"

Justice laid his hands on her cheeks, staring down at her. "What?"

"You being forced to choose between something important for your career or me."

The water streamed around them, and he had Beth here wearing only her skin sluiced with water and soap. "I don't give a fuck about my career right now." It came out a growl of possession.

"But you do care about me. You sent Drake to be with me."

"Yes." Drake Vaughn had helped Justice when he was released from juvie, stepping into a mentor-who-will-kick-his-ass role. Beth knew Drake, and liked him. And Drake, as a former MMA fighter, was strong, fast and deadly enough to keep Beth safe.

"Do you know what that felt like? I was in my office, scared to leave and go to the sentencing. I didn't have to be there, and I was half talking myself out of going."

"But you wanted to be there."

"I wanted Hans to see me there, and if he's watching from whatever rathole he's in, Gene Hayes too. I wanted to face Hans and send a message to Hayes. I'm not letting him win."

"There's my badass." The one who survived and persevered.

"Drake walked into my office and announced that you sent him to go with me to court and that he was bringing me home too." She smiled. "It was like having my very own hero."

That sliced him, and Justice brushed her hair back from her face. "I want to be your hero."

"I know. But if you couldn't be there, Drake was the perfect choice. He made me feel safe...and that gave me an idea, one that Drake and I talked about."

Excitement glittered in her eyes. She clearly wanted to tell him. "Spill it, Glasner. What are you plotting now?"

"We can give victims who are afraid of testifying their very own hero to be there for them in court."

Oh he got it. "Like Drake was for you today." And no one really had been when she'd faced Gene Hayes as a young teenager. Her aunt spent too much time blaming Liza to be supportive.

"Exactly like that." She bounced, her wet hair swinging and luscious boobs jiggling.

Justice swallowed, trying to keep his mind on Beth's words. This was important to her, and if it mattered to her, it mattered to him.

"The fighters who work for SLAM are perfect. They're all big and tough, and if the person testifying knows that the fighter is there specifically for them, to make them feel safe, it'll make testifying a little bit easier for them. I even have a name for the program, SLAM Heroes. Drake said he'd help me develop a pitch, but it'll take a few months."

"It's a great idea," Justice said. "And exactly the kind of thing you wanted to do with your degree—help other victims feel safe and heard."

"You think I can do it?"

Easy answer. "I know you can." He leaned closer. "And you will."

Joy filled her face. She rose on her toes and kissed him.

Justice locked an arm around her, taking her mouth. Thank fuck he'd had the foresight to send Drake to go with her to court. Not only had she felt safe, but she'd come with an idea she was passionate about. But right now, all he cared about was the sensual feel of wet, naked Beth in his arms.

She wrapped her legs around him, finding his hard cock and rubbing her pussy along his shaft.

He snapped his head back at the feel of her. Gripping her hip, he pressed her against the fiberglass shower wall and eased his cock inside. "I planned to take you to dinner or pick something up, then fuck you."

Her smile widened. "Plot twist." She tightened her vaginal walls, ripping a groan of pleasure from him. "I'm going to ravish you, then you can take me to dinner."

He grinned. Beth looked a little tired, but he could almost feel the pressure of the last few weeks falling off her shoulders, freeing this wild streak he loved so damned much. "I fucking love your plot twists. And you."

Chapter 7

Six Weeks Later, December

THE FINAL NOTES OF THE deep cut for "Expired Hero" died away. The extra-long bonus version of the song would go to rock media sites like Indie Rock Broadcast, or be given away in contests on their social media sites.

Justice slid off his earphones and looked around the L.A. recording studio they'd rented time in through Christine's connections. She'd kept up her part of the deal, making things happen for them. The last months had been grueling, but their album was in the can, CDs were being manufactured, the music video was in editing, and they had a three-month tour booked. Their release show was at Club Nosh on January 15th, the night their single would drop. Presales on iTunes had just been released, and people were buying. Finally things were on track.

Doug, their sound engineer, stood up from his board. "That's all the tweaks for today. The final deep-cut track will be ready to upload soon."

The lights caught the multiple piercings in his

eyebrow and lip, and his hair was short and spiky. On the small side in stature, the guy made up for it with incredible talent. He knew his stuff. They'd all come to trust him.

"What do you think?" Justice asked.

"Almost there. It'll be in the can a week ahead of schedule."

Lynx leaned a shoulder against the soundproof glass surrounding the recording booth. "You think 'Expired Hero' is a breakout song? Not this version, but the shorter, more commercial radio cut. Can it break out?"

Doug shrugged into his jacket. "With the tweaks River did on the bass, it's your best bet out of the lineup."

But was *best bet* good enough? A familiar burn of worry washed over Justice. They'd invested everything in this album and the record label they'd formed. They'd had meetings with all the players like iTunes, Spotify, radio producers and others to get exposure. Justice had taken a loan on his house, and the other guys had pitched in to get the funding. Sloane had invested heavily in their record company too. That weighed on all of them. It wasn't just their money they were risking.

"Stop second-guessing," River said. "It's a done deal."

The man was right. There wasn't time for changes.

"I still can't believe Jagged Sin is beating us to release," River added. "They waited until we announced our schedule then announced theirs to get a jump on us."

"It gets worse." Simon voice was cold and pissed. "They released it for presale at midnight last night."

Shit, Justice had missed that. "Are they climbing?"

"Oh we're still ahead."

"Then what's the problem?" Lynx asked.

Simon stared at his phone. "You know how we wondered where they were getting the money to make their album and go on tour?"

A frisson of unease went down Justice's back. "Yeah?"

"The album is produced by G. Hayes."

"Fuck." He couldn't believe this. "They really are in bed with Gene Hayes." Pacing back and forth, he thought of Beth. Hell. He didn't want to tell her.

"What difference does it really make?" Gray asked. "It just shows the world what scum Jagged Sin is, right? Hayes is a felon. He can't step foot in the U.S. or any country we have extradition with."

He had a point, but still. "It's the principle." Like that mattered when it came to money?

"Don't be naïve. There's always a way to get around laws and ethics," Simon said. "We aren't letting them defeat us. Hear me? We're going to come out strong and stomp their asses on our way to the top of the charts. Success is the best revenge for all of us."

Justice nodded, one hundred fucking percent in agreement. "We beat them once, we'll beat them again." He glanced at the digital clock on the wall and grimaced. "Gotta bounce." The trek between L.A. and San Diego ate hours of his day. But tonight was special. Beth had finished her last class and was officially done with college. He was damn proud of her and started for the door.

"Hey, Justice."

He spun around, tensing for another of Simon's unsubtle reminders about being committed to the band, yada, yada, yada.

"Tell Liza congratulations."

Oh. Right. "Thanks, man, I'll tell her." He strode out and got on the road.

Anxiety hitched a ride with him.

Jagged Sin and Gene Hayes—that was a match made in hell.

Liza should be thrilled. She'd taken her last final and was officially done with her B.A. She'd worked for three and a half years, going through the accelerated program to get to this point. She had a right to be happy and proud.

But she was worried as hell. She was two days late for her period. Her breasts hurt, she was bloated and feeling a tad off.

This couldn't be happening. She was on birth control.

You were five weeks late for your last shot.

Dang it, she'd gotten the reminder-to-schedule-an-appointment text smack in the middle of the meeting with the D.A. about Hans's plea deal and totally forgot. It hadn't been until she'd gotten a phone message indicating the doctor's office records showed she was overdue for her shot that she'd remembered.

But she should still have been safe. The whole reason she and Justice chose this method was that it usually took months after stopping the shot to get pregnant. Even her doctor had thought she was protected. They'd run a pregnancy test as a precaution, and it came back negative.

"Liza?"

Tess's voice snapped Liza out of her fog. Sheesh, she was standing in the lobby of the executive floor, staring off into space. She'd walked into work on autopilot, barely aware of getting into the elevator.

"Hey, Tess, sorry, I was thinking about something."

"How'd your final go?"

"Great. All done. Pretty sure I passed."

Tess tilted her head. "Have you ever failed a class?"

"Yep," she admitted. "But that was a long time ago." She and her mom had moved around, followed bands, and Liza hadn't always stayed on track in school. It wasn't until she went to live with her aunt and uncle that she'd taken school seriously.

But her aunt Mari no longer cared. Liza hadn't spoken to her since last June when she'd been in the hospital.

"I'm sure you passed and probably got an A," Tess said.

"Thanks. I'd better get to my office." She was only working a couple hours today. Justice was coming home tonight and taking her to dinner to celebrate finishing her classes.

"Actually, Sloane wants to see you."

She considered dropping her purse in her office first, but it was best to see what Sloane needed. "All right then, thanks." She strode to the office, knocked once and went in.

Sloane looked up while holding a phone to his ear. He waved her in and finished his call.

Liza passed the sitting area and beverage bar to the chairs facing his desk. The bright sun lit up the San Diego skyline, but the treatment on the windows cut the glare and kept it from making the office too hot in the summer.

"Congratulations. You're a college graduate."

She forgot her worries for a second and grinned. Setting her purse down, she settled in a chair. "Thanks.

It feels a little surreal." No more thinking about classes and homework.

He nodded. "You've done well here, Liza. If you're interested in staying at SLAM, I can offer you a full-time position as my administrative assistant."

Shock then pleasure warmed her. She'd thought they'd have this conversation after the holidays. But then this was Sloane—he was decisive, and some considered him a cold hard-ass. Which he was, but he was a fair hard-ass, and Liza liked working for him. "Like I'm doing now?"

"With additional duties, including stepping into a more public role as the communications liaison. In other words, if I'm not doing it myself, then you'll be the one to issue public statements. In some cases, you'll be doing it in conjunction with my department heads, but you will be representing SLAM Inc."

Communications liaison? Excitement and fear tangled in her belly, making her almost queasy. Could she do this? She'd be stepping back into the public light and could become a target again. Hayes had backed down after the stabbing and arrest of Hans. Or at least he'd been quieter. Would she bring unwanted attention on herself?

Better question—was she going to let Gene Hayes stop her from taking this amazing opportunity?

Hell no.

"I'm definitely interested." But what if she was pregnant?

Then she'd need the job even more.

Sloane handed her a sheet of paper. "Here's the official offer with salary and benefits. There will be some travel included with the job."

"With you?" That wasn't a problem for her. Sloane had clear-cut boundaries, and Liza was firmly in the employee category. She just wanted clarification.

"As my assistant, yes. Once you gain some experience, and if you do well, there may be times I send you in my stead."

Excitement made it hard to sit still. A job like this would give Liza the tools and chance to become powerful in her own right. People would see what the girl accused of ruining a rock star had become—a successful businesswoman.

She took the paper, hoping her hand wasn't shaking. This was a dream job, but overwhelming at the same time.

You might be pregnant.

She'd think about that later. Right now she focused on the paper, saw the salary and blinked. "That's..." She cut off the words *a very good offer*.

"Competitive. Let me know your decision next week. Now go home. You've graduated, Justice is coming home, and you deserve a break."

The salary wouldn't make her rich, but it was a solid start, and more than she'd hoped for. Then again, she'd kind of assumed he'd move her over to an entry-level job in marketing. This was even better. She liked working as his assistant where she got daily, hands-on knowledge on every aspect of the business, and now she'd get more experience as the communications liaison.

Rising, she met her boss's gaze. "Thank you, Sloane. I appreciate that you took a chance on me and in the last five months gave me the room to prove myself. I'm very interested in your offer."

He gave her a rare smile. "It was up to you to prove yourself. You did that."

She walked out, closing Sloane's door behind her.

"So?"

She was so caught up in her whirling thoughts, she'd almost walked right by Tess. Liza spun around to apologize.

The whole room tilted, and Tess blurred like she was out of focus. *Whoa.* Slapping her hand down on the desk, she dragged in a breath and squeezed her eyes shut. Her entire body broke out in a hot, sweaty flush.

"Liza?"

Opening her eyes, she was surprised that Tess had gotten up and rounded the desk.

The older woman touched her arm. "You okay? You went sheet white and your skin's clammy."

The room settled back into place. "I turned around too fast, I guess. Kind of lightheaded for a second."

Tess's dark eyes narrowed with concern. "Did you eat today?"

"Yes. It's not that." Crap. Another symptom that had cropped up in the last couple days—dizziness if she stood too fast or turned suddenly.

"Then what? Are you sick?"

Liza glanced at Sloane's closed door then back to the woman. *Don't. You haven't talked to Justice yet.* Clamping down the temptation to blurt out her worries, she said, "It's nothing. I'm just overwhelmed." She held up the file. "Sloane offered me a full-time position."

Tess's face lit up. "I know, I typed up the offer letter."

The other woman's genuine happiness made Liza realize just how lucky she was. And how much she wanted this job.

"If you're truly feeling okay, get out of here." Tess flicked her wrist, shooing her like a fly. "I also know Sloane gave you the rest of the afternoon off, and that you and Justice have plans tonight. Go do something nice for yourself, you've earned it."

Impulsively, she hugged Tess. "Thank you." Once the receptionist had warmed up to Liza, she'd taken her under her wing, showing her the ropes at SLAM, and before Liza knew it, they were friends. Liza had been to barbeques at her house and met her kids.

Kids.

Pregnant.

Justice.

On the ride down, another wave of dizziness assaulted her. Justice was one hundred percent focused on his career. What would happen if she was pregnant? How would he react?

How did she feel?

After leaving the elevator, Liza headed to her car and got in. Fretting about the possibility of a pregnancy wasn't getting her answers. She'd been ignoring the symptoms for a couple days to get through her finals.

Now it was time to face this.

And then what?

She pulled her mouth tight. It was one thing to take a morning-after pill to prevent a pregnancy. To her that was being responsible. But if she was pregnant... She already lived with the guilt of shattering her family from her bad choices. She couldn't live with the loss of a child, especially through her own choice.

Or from the fear that a pregnancy would scare her boyfriend into choosing his career over her.

Okay, enough. She didn't know yet, so why go down this torturous path? There was a simple and fast way to find out. She'd take the test, get the negative result, then she could relax and have fun tonight. Enjoy her achievements without worrying.

Decided, Liza drove to Walgreens and headed inside. Focused now, she headed to the back and located the pregnancy tests. Which one? She grabbed the cheapest and wove through the aisles toward the front while scanning the directions on the box.

"Liza?"

Startled, she fumbled the box and dropped it. She looked up, right into her ex-boyfriend's face.

"Dillion?" Seriously? She hadn't seen him in months. The last time had been at a coffee shop when she had been a student publicist for Justice's band on *Court of Rock*. He'd asked her for tickets to the show, and she'd told him to get lost. "Uh..." The pregnancy test lay on the floor between them.

Dillion stooped down, picked it up and lifted his gaze to hers. "For you?"

Heat burned into her face. For so many years, she'd tried to hide from the exact type of judgment that coated his tone and darkened his gaze. She didn't care about Dillion, except that he'd dumped her because she wasn't good enough.

"No." Nothing like a little shame to turn her into a liar. "It's for a friend." Oh, gosh, how original of her. Snatching the test from his hand, she asked, "What are you doing here?"

He held up a box of condoms.

Wild laughter bubbled in her throat. Okay, how perfect was this? Exes meeting up in a drugstore, her with a pregnancy test, him with condoms. Embarrassing much? "Let me guess, for a friend?"

He smiled tenuously. "Right."

Uncomfortable silence hung between them. Where had her anger at Dillion gone? Now she mostly felt...nothing except maybe a little regret that she'd dated a man she didn't really connect with.

"Well, I'd get better get going." She started to turn.

"Wait." He glanced down then back up. "I'm glad you're all right. I heard about that attack last June and that you were in the hospital. I thought about texting, or calling, even coming to see you but..." He shifted uncomfortably. "Well, I didn't think you'd want to hear from me. I wanted to say I'm sorry you were hurt."

She smiled. "Thanks."

"You're okay now, right?"

"I'm good." She rolled her right shoulder automatically. "All healed. I finished my last final today, and once my degree is mailed, I'll be an official college graduate. I have a good job and a great boyfriend." *So you know, other than holding a box that could rock my entire life, I'm doing fabulous.* "And you?"

"I'll finish law school in June, and I'm already working for a firm. Getting married in August."

"Congratulations." So why the condoms? Was he screwing around on his fiancée? He'd tried to get Liza to keep sleeping with him even after he broke up with her and was supposed to propose to the girl Daddy had picked out.

"Thanks. You too." He glanced at the box in her hand and back to her face. "If you ever need anything, you have my cell number. It hasn't changed."

She had no idea what to make of that. This whole conversation was very different than their past encounters. "Well, uh, nice to see you." Before he could say anything, she rushed to the front, paid and escaped.

She had bigger things to worry about than an ex-boyfriend.

Chapter 8

"YOU WERE REALLY SURPRISED?" NIKKI asked.

Liza glanced around the outdoor patio at Wylie's Cantina, which was decorated with streamers and *Congratulations Graduate* banners. Amazing smells emanated from the steaming taco bar manned by her ex-boss Wylie himself. A gorgeous cupcake-laden stand sat in the middle of a table surrounded by cards and presents.

Justice had done all this for her—arranging a surprise party with their friends, including the ones she'd made at work—Sloane, Tess, Sophie from the reception desk and others.

"Stunned," she answered Nikki. "I've never had a surprise party. It's perfect." Although she wished her stomach wasn't so tight with nerves so she could enjoy it more.

"You're lucky, Liza." Nikki hesitated and added, "Let's go back in time to our competition on *Court of Rock* and swap places. I get to work with Savaged Illusions, while you get stuck with the loser band Jagged Sin."

Liza frowned. "Ugh. I don't know how you endured

99

two weeks with them. But you did the best you could." Nikki had tried, but Jagged Sin had been out of control.

"What's going on?" Em strode up to them.

Nikki shook it off. "Just me whining because Liza's got a hot rock-star lover. The truth is I got my ass handed to me today over a project at work. It should have been mine, and I'd have gotten a bonus, but one of my coworkers, who was probably sleeping with the boss, got it instead. I need that bonus to get out of my butt-sweat apartment. Now I'm stuck there until I think of something else."

Liza exchanged looks with Em. Nothing ever seemed to go right for Nikki, and she routinely blamed it on someone else. But she'd worked hard on her pitch to win that project, so Liza could understand her bitterness. "I'm sorry, Nik."

"Yeah. But I have some leads on other jobs. I feel better already." After glancing at her plastic cup of soda, she said, "I'm going to head to the bar to get a real drink. Want anything, Liza?"

Alcohol was off-limits now, but Liza tried to keep her mind off that pregnancy test. "No thanks. I'll go mingle."

"Come on, I'll be your wingwoman," Emily volunteered. "We'll see if we can find you a hot date on the trip to the bar."

"Let's do it."

"No serial killers," Liza teased as they walked off. Turning, she made her way toward Justice, Sloane and a few others, but her mind was on Nikki. Did Liza have any connections to help her get a better job? SLAM wasn't looking for anyone in publicity and marketing right now, but who else—

A hand caught her arm. "So now that you're all educated, you're too good to talk to us?"

She took in the two men gazing at her—one with long dark silky hair that any woman would envy, the other in a leather vest and tats. "River, Lynx." Her throat tightened with grateful joy. "You came." She hadn't known Justice invited them.

"Damn right we did. It's official now, you really are too good for Justice. Think I'd miss a chance to rub that in his face? The dude got his GED in juvie, and you're a college graduate."

River laughed. "What are you talking about? You didn't even do that much. It was Justice's grandma who made you get your GED after you got out of juvie."

"I'm street smart."

River rolled his eyes, hugged Liza, and said, "Any of those cupcakes red velvet?"

She looked up at the bassist. "Ask Tess. She ordered them."

His eyes lit up. "Tess? She likes me. Bet she ordered red velvet just for me. Probably has a whole box of them stashed somewhere."

"Huh, she barely tolerates you," Lynx said. "Bet she has vanilla for me."

The two men walked off, fighting over cupcakes and cornering Tess. Liza guessed they knew her from the Fighters to Mentors program since her son was in it. Justice, River and Lynx had all been in the program too and often worked with kids now.

Emily caught her arm. "Oh my God, you won't believe who we saw on our way to the bar."

"Who?" She was standing close to the fire pit in the middle of the patio, and tried to peer through the large, arched doorway to the main restaurant, but Justice, Sloane, River and Lynx stood there talking and blocked her view.

"Let's go sit down," Emily said. They headed to one of the tables.

Once seated, Liza glared at her best friend. "Spill it. Who'd you see?" A flicker of hope surged—could it be her aunt and uncle? Maybe her grandmother? Had Justice invited them? Maybe now that she'd finished college they would see she wasn't going down the same path as her mom.

"Dillion."

"Oh." Disappointment trampled all over that little glimmer of hope, and she shrugged. "So?" Although it was odd that she hadn't seen him in seven months then ran across him twice in one day. But she wasn't going to bring that up. Emily could read her too well. If Emily happened to ask why she was at Walgreens, she'd end up saying too much. Liza wanted to tell Justice first.

"With his fiancée."

Okay, now Em had her attention. "How do you know?" Liza hadn't met her, so how would Emily know?

Her friend sighed. "Facebook. Jeez, Liza, don't you know how to stalk your ex?"

"It looks just like her," Nikki added, holding up her phone. "See? Look at her ring. Must be the engagement photo the way she's flashing that rock. Her name is Stacy Jo."

Liza leaned in. Ignoring Dillion, she studied the girl. Shoulder-length brown hair with a straight side part. Sleek and shiny—so unlike Liza's own. It took quality time with a battery of hair products and a straight iron to get even close to that look. The girl had classic features, maybe a bit boring, but that ring— wow! A square-shaped diamond cut to create a halo effect.

Em eyed the screen. "It's too square for her man hands."

A bubble of laughter shot up her throat, but Liza swallowed it. She hadn't met Stacy Jo and had no reason to hate her. Liza had enough of ugly judgment from people who'd didn't know her. "I doubt Stacy Jo even knew he was dating me before he proposed to her. Let's just leave her alone, okay?"

"It doesn't bother you that they're here?" Em asked.

Liza shrugged. "Nope." Although she really didn't want to see Dillion again. Not after he'd been buying condoms at Walgreens. She didn't need to think about him and Stacy Jo using them.

You were buying a pregnancy kit.

Right. So better not to see him at all. Plus Justice and Dillion didn't get along. Dillion's very existence had a way of pushing her boyfriend's buttons. "Don't tell Justice."

"Tell me what?" He dropped into the seat next to her and set a plate with two soft tacos and steaming rice in front of her. "You haven't eaten. When I saw you finally sitting, I grabbed you a plate."

Lynx sat down next to Nikki, his plate piled high. "All the women here are after me. You gonna protect me?"

"Depends."

"On?"

Nikki eyed his plate. "I want one of your tacos."

"That's a steep price, but seeing as how I'm driving women mad with lust..." Lynx gave her one of his tacos.

Justice touched Liza's bare thigh beneath the table. "So what aren't you telling me?"

Liza had to think fast. "How many times a week Emily and Ben have sex."

Lynx choked on a bite of food.

"Twelve." Ben sat down next to Emily and handed her a plate of food.

"Ha," Emily said. "More like half that lately."

"Twelve for you, sweetheart," Ben shot back. "I know exactly how many times I get you off."

Emily flashed her boyfriend an evil smile. "I might be faking."

"Nope. It takes a dozen good orgasms a week to satisfy you."

Oh my God, what had she started? Liza swung her head around. "Stop!" Once Ben and Emily got going, they were outrageous. "My boss is here."

Sloane sat next to River. He tapped his glass to Ben's. "A real man always knows, right?"

Justice opened his mouth.

"Don't!" Liza had no idea what he was going to say, but this conversation was causing her to flush like she had a sunburn.

He raised an eyebrow, his mouth tilted with amusement. "Don't tell you to eat? Your food's getting cold." He forked up some rice. "Here."

She narrowed her eyes. "That's not what you were—"

He slid the fork in.

Dang, that rice was good. Of course she knew that, but she'd been so nervous and worried she hadn't felt like eating. One taste and suddenly she was starved. Liza dug in, eating a few bites while Sloane and Ben talked about UFC fighting, and River groused that Tess wouldn't let him eat even one cupcake until dinner was over.

When Liza picked up her second taco, Justice leaned closer. "Eat up. There's champagne with the cupcakes."

Liza's stomach seized instantly. She couldn't drink champagne. Not now. All her worries rushed back. Abruptly claustrophobic and sweaty, she tried to calm herself. "I'm going to the restroom. I'll be right back."

Looking concerned, Justice said, "I'll go with you."

"That's okay." Was her voice too breathy? "I'll be back in a minute." She hurried off, weaving around friends and heading into the restaurant. She passed a group of girls whispering, "He's out on the patio. It's Justice Cade."

Rushing by them, she passed the bar and turned down the small hallway. She already felt better. It had just been a moment of panic. She was tired, scared and on emotional overload. The second she'd seen that positive sign on the pregnancy test, the thought of a baby shifted her on a fundamental level she still couldn't grasp. A child.

Their baby.

That thought sent a surprising wave of longing through her. But the first thing she had to do was tell Justice. No panicking, and no running. They'd talk and figure this out—

"Liza?"

In the hallway, outside the women's restroom, she looked up into the eyes of her ex-boyfriend. Again. At least this time she wasn't holding a pregnancy test. "Dillion." She'd been so preoccupied she'd completely forgotten that Emily and Nikki had warned her he and his fiancée were here. "This is weird running into you twice in one day."

"Not exactly a coincidence."

"What do you mean? You followed me?" That didn't make any sense.

"No. But someone spotted Justice here, tweeted it out, and Stacy Jo is a huge fan of his, so here we are."

"Your fiancée." With the too-square rock riding her not really mannish hands.

"Yeah, she still hasn't forgiven me for not getting the tickets to *Court of Rock*. When she saw that Justice was here, she insisted on coming. She's waiting till he leaves and plans to ask him for a picture."

Unbelievable. "You think I'll get him to do it?"

He shook his head. "No, I'm not asking you for anything. I was just telling you why we're here. But it looks like you guys are having a party out there on the patio. I'll get Stacy Jo out of here without bothering you."

The Dillion she'd talked to twice today was a lot less whiny and petulant than the one who'd broken up with her nearly a year ago. But then, she hadn't seen him in months. Maybe he finally grew up. "Thanks."

He nodded, took a step and stopped when he was even with her. "The truth is I wanted to come here tonight too. I figured if Justice was here, you'd likely be with him, and I wanted to see for myself if you're okay."

Confused, she asked, "What do you mean?"

Dillion touched her bare arm. "The pregnancy test you bought today. Are you pregnant?"

Justice stopped as he rounded the hallway corner. Beth had bought a pregnancy test? And why was she huddled by the bathrooms talking to her ex? That bastard was touching her. What was going on?

He strode forward. "Get your hand off her." Just seeing the guy pissed Justice off. He'd never forget the way the jerk had treated her.

Beth spun around, her eyes wide behind her glasses. "Justice, what—? Uh, we were talking."

"What the hell, Beth? And why are you talking to your ex-boyfriend about a pregnancy test?" His fingers curled into fists. The only pregnancy test Justice knew of was the one she'd taken before her last birth control shot.

Dillion backed away. "I, uh, should go..."

Justice swiveled his head to see Dillion's gaze darting toward the restaurant and back to Liza, his face pale and fear in his eyes. "Get lost," Justice snarled.

Liza settled ice-cold fingers on Justice's arm. "Dillion, go back to your fiancée."

The guy spun around and almost ran. Coward. Shifting his attention to his girlfriend, Justice took in her strained face. *Calm down*, he ordered himself. It wasn't Beth's fault that Dillion pissed him off with the mere act of breathing. "What was that about?"

"I was going to talk to you about this in the morning. Not tonight."

His guts clenched. "About what? How is Dillion involved?"

"He's not. I ran into him in Walgreens today. First time since he asked me for tickets to *Court of Rock*. But—"

Two girls rushed into the hall, chattering. "I ate so much, I don't know if I can go dancing now."

"Oh stop," the second one said. "You barely touched your..." Their words trailed off as they vanished into the women's restroom.

Liza's fingers dug into his arm. "Come to Wylie's office." They walked through the bar, passed a small break room, and into a tiny office.

Justice closed the door and crossed his arms. "What's going on?"

"I'm pregnant."

Pregnant. The pregnancy test. His ears rang. The whole room heated, and he couldn't get his breath. Pregnant. A kid. *His kid.* Wait, it was his, right? No, fuck, don't even go there. Liza wasn't screwing around with Dillion. It'd shocked him to hear them discussing a pregnancy test. But he believed her explanation that she saw him in the drugstore. Justice had no reason to doubt her there.

But a kid. Pregnant.

"You said you took a pregnancy test when you got the last shot." She'd told him about being late to get her shot, but the test results had been negative. How could this happen?

She jerked her head up. "I did, but I probably wasn't far enough along to get a positive reading."

He shook his head, still trying to believe this. "Okay, we'll go get the morning-after pill. First thing tomorrow morning, just like we did when we forgot a condom." Relief washed over him.

It's too late. If I got pregnant when I was overdue for the shot, that was October, so I'm around six weeks along."

Too late? Pressure banded around him, shoving in from all sides. He couldn't be a father. The album dropped in a month, and they were going on a three-month tour. Oh shit, his band would flip the fuck out over this.

Frustrated anger shot up and out his mouth. "What is this, Beth? We talked about this—no mistakes. I can't afford any more screw-ups." Tearing his fingers through his hair, he added, "I trusted you to handle this one thing."

Tears welled in her eyes, and anger blazed across her cheeks. "And I trusted you not to be an asshole. Guess we're both disappointed." She stomped past him.

The sight of her reaching for the doorknob snapped the stupid from his brain. "Don't go, I'm sorry." Damn it, why did he do this? Say boneheaded crap? He caught her arm. "Please. I just... Give me a minute."

She stopped, her head angled down.

Justice could hear her breathing in and out, trying to control her emotions. She'd told him the second she'd realized she'd missed the shot. So why was he acting like the wounded party here?

"I didn't mean it. It's the pressure. Everything is on the line now. This...once you took that pregnancy test at the office, I thought we were in the clear." He hadn't been worried anyway. Her doctor had told them it could take months or a year to get pregnant after stopping the shots.

Beth pulled off her glasses, wiping her eyes. "I never meant this to happen."

He tugged her around to face him. She wore a pretty dress with ankle boots, her hair a cloud of soft waves around her face. This was supposed to be her party—her big night. The one time the attention was on Beth, not him, and he'd made her cry. Even worse, she'd trusted him not to be a jerk.

He pulled her against him. "I'm sorry for yelling." Shit, her whole body was trembling. She'd been carrying this burden all night long. Trying to calm them both, he stroked her hair.

She pulled back, and her green eyes swam with sadness. "This is why I didn't want to tell you here. You did all this for me, this party, and now..." She looked away. "I know how important your career is to you."

"So are you." He needed her, but he needed to prove himself to the world too. He'd already had one painful failure where he'd let his band down. He tugged her chin up. "Do you feel all right?"

"Yeah. I get a little dizzy if I move too fast, and my breasts hurt, but otherwise I'm fine."

He wiped a smudge of her mascara. "There's nothing we can do about it tonight, and obviously we need time. So let's go back to the party. You've worked hard for your degree, and you deserve to celebrate." He'd really wanted to give her this party, to show her how much he loved her before everything changed once the album released.

It was going to be hard enough for them with him being on the road for three months, only seeing her when he could get home or she got a weekend away.

A pregnancy was going to complicate everything. Today was supposed be fun, but instead, it felt like he was getting locked into a pressure cooker with no release valve.

Liza took another bite of the cupcake. Chocolate slid over her tongue, warm and sensual with a dark edge. She sat at the Formica table, the quiet old house settling around her.

A baby.

Her baby. And Justice's. She scooped up another bite of the cake. Her thoughts had boinged around relentlessly, robbing her of sleep. She'd finally slipped out of bed, the lure of cupcakes a much-needed distraction.

Anxiety rushed along her nerve endings, making her too aware of her skin. Her heart thumped uneasily. She ran her finger through the rich frosting, trying to soothe that frantic edge with chocolate.

She caught sight of the small chicken-shaped pitcher sitting on the table by the salt and pepper shaker. "What are you staring at? There's nothing wrong with cupcakes at 1:00 a.m."

The brown chicken with the big yellow tail feather handle didn't look convinced.

"Keep glaring at me, and I'll be eating fried chicken."

"Are you threatening my chickens again?"

Liza pivoted on the chair to find Justice leaning a hip against the sink. His hair was sleep mussed, with just a hint of a rogue wave. His powerful shoulders and arms covered in tats gleamed in the kitchen light. He'd pulled on a pair of shorts, revealing his muscular calves down to bare feet. Despite everything, her body tightened at the sight of him. It didn't matter that they'd had sex on the couch ten seconds after they got home.

She still wanted him. Not with the frantic edge of lust, but a deeper need that felt like it came from her soul. After tearing her gaze away from him to get a full breath, she glanced at her half-eaten cupcake. Guilt pressed down on her. "I didn't do this on purpose."

His eyebrows shot up. "Do what? Threaten innocent birds?"

"Innocent, my ass. He's judging me, and I call fowl."

Justice snorted. "That's really bad, honey. You sure you're a writer?"

She shook her head. "If I wrote this scenario, my heroine would know what to do. What I meant was I didn't get pregnant on purpose."

His half smile dropped away as he strode over and sat on the chair adjacent to hers. "I shouldn't have said that back at the restaurant. This isn't your fault, and we both knew there was a lapse in your shots." He paused a second and added, "But it's a huge wrench in our plans." He selected a cupcake out of the box and took a bite.

"You been thinking about it?"

"Every second." Setting the treat down, he fisted a hand on the table. "How do I do this, Beth? The band is relying on me, we have the album releasing next month, and we're going on the big tour. We've all invested significant money in this. How can I do that and be a father? Be there when you and this kid need me?" He shoved his fingers through his hair. "It's really shitty timing."

Anxiety dug into her chest. She didn't have to write this scene to know how it played out. She'd be accused of repeating her mother's mistakes. Of being a groupie and trying to trap Justice. His band would blame her if he was distracted. No matter what she did, there would always be suspicion following her. She was the girl who destroyed one rock star and now could be trying to ruin another.

And Gene Hayes. He was there, crouched in the shadows. Liza could almost feel him watching her, waiting. What was he going to do once Savaged Illusions' album came out?

What if he found out Liza was pregnant?

Her blood chilled, and she pushed the remainder of her cupcake away.

Justice didn't want this baby, and Hayes was always going to be a threat. Rubbing the pain in her chest, she said softly, "What am I supposed to do, get rid of it because it's a mistake? An inconvenience?" She'd been a mistake and inconvenience. Yet flawed as her mom was, she'd still fought for Liza. "We were both mistakes, you and me."

He took her hand. "You want this baby?"

She wanted a family. "I had to give up the only

family I had left to love you. And before that, I had to give up my mom. But now I feel like I'm getting this second chance. We could have this baby, and I'd love him or her right." Fierce emotion swelled until it was hard to breathe. "I'll love them for who they are, protect and defend them. Not turn my back on them." Like her family had done to her. Liza would fight for her baby. Tears filled her eyes, but she blinked them back and told Justice the truth. "I don't want to have to choose again. Between you and our baby. My aunt and grandmother forced me to choose between them and you. And now it feels like I might have to choose again."

He was quiet, his stare riveted on her face. "I'm afraid I'm not going to have a choice."

Surprise numbed her roiling emotions. "About having this baby?"

"If we have it, do I need to give up my career? We're not pulling salaries out of S.I. Records right now. We're living off my savings and your income. If we have this kid, what am I supposed to do? Give up my dream? Drop out of the band and get a job somewhere? But I have to go on tour, we've signed contracts and..." He grimaced. "Or do I go on the tour, then quit? Leave the band worse off? Where are we going to get the money for this?"

He'd obviously been thinking as much as she had. They were both feeling the pressure. "I'm not asking you to give up your dream. From my calculations, the baby won't be born until summer. And I'm going to make more money with the new job Sloane offered me, plus benefits." She told him the details.

He stroked his thumb over her wrist. "You sound excited."

"I am. I want this job. And now I'll be able to pitch

my SLAM Heroes project too." But she also wanted this baby.

Justice leaned across the table. "What about your writing? You still haven't finished a book. The changes you're making on your rock star-groupie book are good."

Her stomach clenched. "I'm working on it, but it's a hobby, not a career. Not right now anyway. I can't risk publishing my sexy romances. Not with Hayes out there. If he does file to overturn the verdict, he'll use it against me." So many people in the rock world still hated her. And what would her family think? No, she didn't want to put her work out there to be torn apart. Right now she was happy keeping it hers and Justice's secret world. There was something really special about that.

"I hate that that fucker Hayes gets to dictate your choices." He shoved back his chair, and using their joined hands, tugged her up and into his lap. Wrapping his arm around her, he pressed his lips to her hair. "But your safety comes first. Hayes is getting bolder if he's got his name listed as producer on Jagged Sin's album. We don't know what he'll do next. You're right, publishing racy books would make you a target all over again, or even embolden him to file to overturn his conviction."

He understood. She loved that, and that they could talk like this. She didn't have to hold in her feelings until her pain was so great, so brutal, the only thing she could do for relief was cut herself. With her head on his shoulder, she traced the outline of the blue jay tat over his heart. "I want this job. As for the baby, we're not even a hundred percent sure yet. I'll see a doctor to confirm it."

Justice's chest expanded with a deep breath. "We're

working all this week, then the band is taking time off until after Christmas. Make your appointment then, and we'll go together."

Relief and hope tangled in her heart. "Thank you."

His eyes flickered with something. Doubt? Worry? "I'm not making you choose, Beth."

"I know." And she loved him all the more for it.

"Don't make me choose between you and the baby or my dream. I've worked my ass off for years. I'm risking everything. I need to know you understand."

Raw ambition hardened his eyes and sparked a flicker of dread. Yeah, she understood it, but another part of her feared she and her baby would end up as collateral damage.

Chapter 9

TEN DAYS LATER, JUSTICE SHIFTED uneasily. It'd been a long week, anxiety constantly scratching at him. *A baby. A kid.* He didn't know how he could be a father.

The exam room of the obstetrician's office didn't help. He sat in a chair shoved in the corner, facing posters showing the progression of pregnancy from conception to fully developed in the womb. He also had a magnified view of a woman's cervix dilating... Sweat prickled his armpits. Jesus, TMI.

"You okay?" Liza sat on the table, her legs bare beneath that hideous gown.

Was he? How the fuck could he handle this? But what choice did they have? The doctor had confirmed she was pregnant. So what now? Before he could think of an answer, the door opened.

The doctor wheeled in a monitor attached to a machine. "Let's take a look and see if we can determine how far along you are."

Her cheerful voice rubbed him the wrong way. The woman wasn't much more than thirty and had a reassuring manner. But she wasn't the one who had to provide for and raise the child.

Liza reclined on the exam table. An assistant draped a blanket over her hips and legs and pulled up the gown.

After squirting some gel on her, the doctor moved a wand over her belly. Grainy images flickered on the monitor. A moment passed, then the doctor announced, "There's your baby. Dad..." she looked over at him, "...would you like to see?"

Not really, but he rolled up and walked to Liza's side. On the monitor was a gray-toned blob, and in the center was a black hole that almost looked like a gaping mouth.

"Right here is your child." The doctor pointed to the whitish-gray kernel floating in the black mouth. "You're roughly eight weeks along. This is the head, the body..."

Beth's hand grabbed his. Justice leaned over her to focus on the image.

"See this movement?"

A tiny dot pulsed on the screen.

"It's the baby's heartbeat."

His breath whooshed out of him as that fragile little speck pulsed again and again. So small and delicate, but alive. He looked down at Beth, seeing her belly smeared with the clear gel, soft and vulnerable. They had a baby growing in there. He shifted to Beth's face, her skin glowing and eyes shimmering. Even on a table with that ugly gown, she was so damned beautiful it made his chest ache. "Our baby."

Her smile spread like a rainbow, lighting up the dark and lonely place in him.

He didn't care where they were, he leaned down and kissed her. "So we're doing this."

"All in, rock star."

"All in." When he looked at the screen again and

saw that micro-being who would rely on them for everything, the pressure dropped on his chest like a boulder. He couldn't fuck up again.

Once Beth was dressed, they bundled into the Jeep. He drummed his fingers on the steering wheel. "I guess we're going to need a crib and stuff."

She touched his arm. "We have time. I'm not due until late July."

"I know, I just..." He scrubbed at his face, then forced a smile. "Nothing." Beth'd had a huge victory at work today. She'd pitched her SLAM Heroes idea to Sloane and marketing. Not only had she gotten approval, but she was the one who would direct it. She'd been wildly excited about it, throwing herself into his arms once she got home.

He knew damn well how much it meant to her. Liza hadn't had anyone to protect her when she'd testified in court. She wanted to provide people with heroes in their scariest moments. He was proud of her.

"We don't do that."

Her words jerked him from his thoughts. "What?"

"Hold back our feelings. You're the one who made the rule, so talk to me."

He turned in the seat to face her. "I have to go back to L.A. tomorrow. We had the road crew all hired, but one of them bailed. Christine has a bus for us to look at. If we agree, that'll be our tour bus, and it'll meet us in Las Vegas. We'll have to sign the contract for that too and make a massive payment, draining our S.I. Records funds even more. And she wants something changed on the music video. That fucker was done, and now we may have to reshoot some part of it." A throb started in his temple. "I took a loan on the house, Beth. I can't fail. I can't lose that house—I swore to my grandmother I'd take care of my dad, and it's his only home. And now..." His gaze slid down her bronze shirt to her belly.

"You're not going to lose the house. First off, I've heard every track on that album, and they're good. But you're the magic that's going to take Savaged Illusions to superstardom. You know that, you've always known it. You're my Rooster who struts around and shows off because you know you're that good. You're the magic, you and that insanely compelling voice."

Her words and absolute faith washed over him, calming some of the frantic stress eating his guts. Oh, he still believed he was that good, but the *Court of Rock* loss had left its mark.

"And second." She squeezed his arm. "You're not doing this alone. I'm working, making enough money to cover my bills and the loan you took on your house. I'll find us a cheap, safe crib when the times comes. It's going to be okay."

He leaned into her and pulled her mouth to his. Justice didn't care that they were in a parking lot, he kissed her exactly as he wanted to. Long and slow, savoring the taste of the woman who believed in him. Finally, he broke away. "All right, we'll hold off on the crib. We need to celebrate your news today."

"Which? My SLAM Heroes project or the baby?"

"Both." He couldn't get the image of that tiny heart beating in her stomach out of his mind. A baby, a child. One he made with the woman he loved.

"Good answer."

"I'm getting used to the idea, especially now that I've seen the heartbeat," he admitted, although he was still worried. "And I'm really proud of you for going in there and pitching SLAM Heroes. We have the rest of the day together, what do you want to do?"

"There is one thing I'd like."

"What's that?" He'd give her anything he could.

"A Christmas tree. A real one. I'd buy it myself, but I couldn't figure out how to get it home." She sighed. "I never had a real one."

"That I can do. Buckle up, baby. Let's go get you a tree."

He'd do this one way or another. He wouldn't let his band, fans, dad, Beth or his kid down.

Two hours later, Liza beamed at the tree in the corner of the living room. They'd dug through the boxes in the garage to find decorations. Justice had strung the lights, and now she was riffling through a box for ornaments. She pulled out a clay circle with a fading picture on it. Peering at it, she recognized those blue eyes and that smile. "It's you! How old were you?"

Justice glared at her. "Don't you dare put that up."

She snorted and found the perfect branch dead center on the tree. The handmade decoration tugged at her heart. She used to make her mom ornaments in school, but they were all gone now. What happened to them? Liza didn't know. Her aunt and grandmother had gotten rid of everything, except the few pictures and keepsakes Liza had managed to save. Shaking off the memories, she said, "So, what? First grade?"

"Second. We're not keeping that on the tree. It's stupid."

"I love it." She really did. "Did you make it for your grandmother?"

He mashed his lips together and rubbed the back of his neck, then sighed. "My mom."

Her heart wrenched. He seldom talked about her.

"Oh. I'll take it off if you want. But you were really cute." Thin and lanky with a slight smirk riding his little-boy smile. She fingered the picture. "If we have a boy, I hope he looks just like you."

He wrapped his arm around her waist, tugging her against him. "I was pretty damn adorable. Might be hard for a boy of mine to live up to that."

She rolled her eyes. "You're ridiculous. What if we have a girl?"

His gaze slid to hers. "If she looks like you, I'm toast. Burnt toast. I'll crumble the first time she smiles at me."

Her chest flooded with warmth.

He swatted her butt. "Now quit goofing off. Let's get this tree decorated so I can get you naked in the glow of Christmas lights."

"What makes you think I'll let you get me naked?"

"Pay attention, woman. I'm not that cute little boy anymore. I'm a grown man who knows exactly how to make you come. And I'm getting hard just thinking about you naked. Do you want this tree decorated?"

She turned out of his hold. "If you want me naked, this tree had better be dazzling."

"Go find more pictures of me. That'll make you drop your panties."

"Cocky rooster," she muttered as she dug through the box, pulling out typical red and green decorations, when a white 6X9 envelope caught her attention. After tugging it out, she lifted the flap, and a stack of pictures fell out. Liza sifted through them, her surprise growing.

"What'd you find?"

"Old pictures. Looks like Christmas." There was one of Justice on a bike with his dad running alongside him. Liza stared at a younger Noah, his skin free of scars, his eyes shining with pride over his boy. What had Noah been like then?

She studied the woman with the light-brown hair and pretty hazel eyes clapping as Justice rode by. Next was a picture of the three of them—Noah, Justice and the woman in front of a tree. "This is your mom?" Who else would it be? But Justice said she wasn't interested in him, yet here she beamed.

He glanced over—"Yes"—and went back to arranging ornaments.

"She's different than I expected. She looks nicer, like the girl next door."

"You can look through pictures later." He scooped up another ornament and hung it.

Liza frowned. "You never really talk about her."

"Why would I?" His voice hardened. "She walked, Beth. After she made sure I knew I'd fucked up and I wasn't worth staying for."

True. And that pain still lingered in Justice. She put the pictures away and chose a silver bell to hang. "Does she ever contact you? Do you know where she is?"

He stiffened. "Birthday cards started coming a couple years ago. Before that...nothing. Not a goddamned word."

Regret touched down in her belly at the sharpness in his voice. This was their first Christmas together, and she was digging around in his old pain. She laid her hand on his rigid back. "I'll stop asking. I saw the pictures, and my curiosity got the better of me."

His gaze slid to hers. "Her name is Robin. She started a small flower shop here in San Diego after I was born. That required a lot of long days, nights and weekends. It grew, and she sold it for a pretty nice profit. After that, she set out her shingle as a life coach for women with small businesses. That's what she was doing last I knew." He stared down into her face. "I don't care where she is."

His mother had been that successful? Liza hadn't realized that—and yet it made sense. Justice's drive to succeed stemmed from his mom's abandonment, and if she'd been prosperous, then he'd be determined to top her achievement. It wasn't so unlike Liza's need to prove she wasn't making the same mistakes her mom did.

"She didn't deserve you, Justice. And you're right, she doesn't matter." That wasn't entirely true—for Justice his mom was a wound, but he'd formed scar tissue to protect himself. Liza didn't need to pick at that. "You matter, and your dad matters."

"And your mom."

And their child.

"So what do you think of our tree?" he asked.

Liza took in the lush Douglas fir draped in white lights and colorful ornaments. "It's missing something. Wait." She opened the coat closet and took out a box while repressing her grin. Carrying it back, she announced, "We need a top for the tree." With great flourish, she pulled it out, proudly holding it up.

Justice's expression contorted somewhere between laughter and horror. "What the hell is that?"

"It's a Christmas Chicken. Obviously."

"Baby, there is nothing obvious about that." He swiped it from her hand, holding it up. "Where did you get this?"

Liza had to admit, it was...different. It was formed from metal into the shape of a chicken and stood about five inches high. It had a jaunty red Santa hat on, and once it was plugged in, all the feathers lit up in green and red lights. "Online shopping."

"No way are we putting this on the tree. This thing is an insult to Christmas."

Liza stared at him in mock outrage, not willing to admit it had been one of her rare impulse buys. Chickens always made her think of Justice and his closeness with his grandmother. The woman had died before Liza met her, and yet, through Justice and this house, she felt a real connection to her. Or maybe it was just that she wished she had the kind of relationship with her grandmother that Justice had had with his. Of course she could tell him that, but it was more fun to tease him. "You haven't heard the story of the Christmas Chicken?"

"No such thing." Justice pinned her with his stare. "You're making that up."

"I am not." Busying herself with repacking the unused decorations, she tried to think fast. "Come on, you have to have heard this. The one about..." *Think!* "...a chicken named Henrietta who heard the boys talking. She was going to be Christmas dinner. The chicken runs away and goes on a series of adventures." Wow she was ripping off almost every children's Christmas tale she'd ever read.

"Is that right? A chicken all by herself?"

She didn't dare look at him or she'd bust up laughing. "Well, not by herself. She finds friends. You know, um...she rescues a deer after discovering him with his hoof caught in a fence."

"Is that right?" Silky derision flowed in his tone. "Let me guess, a reindeer?"

"Sure." Getting into her story now, Beth carefully closed the box lid. "Only the chicken hasn't seen deer before, so he doesn't know that this is a very special deer—"

"I call bullshit."

She spun around, feigning outrage. "Are you doubting my Christmas Chicken?"

"I think you're lying through your pretty teeth." He advanced on her.

Liza backed up. "Nope. Totally the truth. I can't believe you'd accuse me of lying."

"I'm accusing, sweetheart. And I'm going to prove it with a little truth test."

She spun, running around the couch. "No! You can't!" Liza'd had no idea she was ticklish until Justice discovered that when they were playing around. If he caught her, he'd use tickling to make her confess her lie.

"Oh I can."

"I'm pregnant!" Beth glanced back at the hallway. She'd never make it to the bathroom where she could lock the door. It was all about winning their little game.

"I was at that appointment. Your doctor said normal activity is fine. And sex. Lots of sex."

"Tickling is not normal." He never held her down, nothing vicious. Justice never held her down at all. Even if she had a nightmare, he stroked her arm and talked to her, letting her wake up. Once she was fully aware, she always scooted into his arms and he'd hold her. She never feared him; this was just fun. And she liked to win.

He grinned. "Not the way I do it." Justice took two steps and leapt over the couch, landing next to her.

Hell. Liza tried to run, but he snapped an arm around her waist, pulling her back to his chest. "Caught you." He slid his hand beneath her shirt, spreading it on her belly. "Want to confess anything?"

God. His voice rumbling in her ear slid down her nerve endings. Her nipples tightened, and tremors of desire spread beneath his fingers. He held her gently, his hand circling her stomach. He'd been home two days. Christmas was in a week. It was all going too fast... Once the holidays were over, Justice had a packed schedule of prepublicity for his album release and tour.

Dread flickered in her heart. He'd be gone, out there performing, growing more famous and starring in women's fantasies while she'd be here getting fat with their baby.

And what about Gene Hayes? What was he doing?

No. Liza leaned back into Justice, trying to grab on to this moment when things were good. Craning her head around, she looked up at him. "I'll confess that I love you."

"Nice try, but I believe you've lied to me. There's no such thing as a Christmas Chicken story. You made that up. Admit it, or I will tickle you." He licked her ear.

Shards of pleasure raced through her, making her shiver.

He went on, "In deference to your condition, I'll use my tongue to do it. As long as it takes to get a full and complete confession."

She closed her eyes, savoring the feel of Justice surrounding her. How had she gotten to this place of such happiness? But she wasn't going to play the game his way. "What if I confess? Will there be a punishment?"

He dragged his hand up, skimming beneath her bra to tweak her nipple. "Hmm. What would you consider suitable?"

"Well, if I used my mouth to lie, maybe I should put it to better use." She turned in his arms and undid his belt, along with the button and zipper on his jeans. His engorged cock spilled out into her hands, hot, smooth skin stretched over steel. Running her fingers along the length and around the swollen head wrung a shudder from him.

"You make me so fucking hard." He leaned down, kissing her, driving his tongue into her mouth.

She loved the way he showed her exactly how excited she made him. It was so real and sexy, she squirmed. Breaking the kiss, she slid to her knees, fisting the base of his cock. The head strained toward her, and Liza leaned forward, dragging her tongue over the sensitive slit.

Wild heat slammed into him, searing Justice's balls. He couldn't resist taking the big clip out of Beth's hair and burying his fingers in it. The heavy strands filled his hands, as sensual and sweet as the woman licking his dick.

He gazed down at her, and his chest caught. Beth. His girl. He'd never had this with anyone, this ability to play and laugh, and in the next second, unleash a passion that stripped him raw. It was so much more than sex.

She swirled her tongue around his head, then closed her lips over his length and sucked him. Watching his cock slide deep into her mouth nearly undid him. He hissed, his entire body bowing at the sensation. He wasn't going to last. She did this to him, drove him to the edge of the cliff.

Pressure swelled. "You're going to make me come," he warned her, giving her a chance back off. But she cupped his balls, her thumb brushing over the sensitive strip of skin.

His orgasm raced down his spine. "Fuck," he growled. His control snapped. Planting his feet, he pumped into her mouth and exploded, totally surrendering to the bliss crashing through him in wrenching waves. Finally, his cock slowed its pulsing and slipped from Beth's mouth.

Pulling her up, he buried his face in her hair, inhaling the warm peach scent. "What you do to me." He didn't even have words. Tilting her head back, he eyed her flushed face and wet lips. He wanted more, wanted to drive her to the wicked edge of pleasure until she came with wild abandon. "That's only half your punishment. The other half is going to require you to get naked and—"

Her cell phone dinged a text message. Justice reached into her back pocket, tugging it out. "No distractions." He glanced at the screen and froze. "Noah." Shock blasted through him. Shifting his gaze to her, he said, "My dad?" Beth texted Noah occasional little things and sent pictures of Justice on stage. But Noah rarely answered her.

The heat of passion cleared from her eyes. "Open it. See what he says."

Dual sensations of jealousy and relief clashed inside him. His dad was talking to Beth, reaching out to her but not him. He knew logically his dad couldn't talk to him for reasons of his own.

But that old pain kicked logic's ass, and it just hurt.

Beth smoothed her fingers over his face.

Getting out of his head, he focused on her. She'd told him to look at the message. He wanted to, but his dad was building a trust with Beth, something Noah hadn't been able to do with his own wife, his mom or his son. Was Justice going to stomp on that? Hell no.

He forced himself to hand her the phone. "You read it. He's reaching out to you, I don't want to screw that up." He stepped back to give her space and yanked up his pants. The sharp edges of his old pain blunted. If he was going to trust anyone to connect with his dad, it was Beth.

She opened the message and scanned it. "Oh no. Noah says, *Hit by a car last night. Arm broken. Can you help me?*"

Adrenaline powered into his veins. "Where is he?"

"He didn't say that."

His worst fears materialized—his dad was injured and Justice didn't know where he was to help him. "Shit. Will he answer if you call him?" Was his dad even in San Diego? For a few years, he'd traveled around the state, sometimes farther.

"Maybe." She thumbed her screen, then put the phone to her ear. "Ringing."

Justice held his breath, his head pounding with helplessness. They had to get to his dad. And what would happen when Justice was gone on tour? Would Beth try to go to his dad alone? That sent a chill down his spine. His dad wouldn't hurt her, but someone else could. Beth was pregnant and too damned softhearted.

"Noah, I got your text." She motioned Justice closer so he could hear.

He leaned in.

Beth added, "Where are you? Can I come get you?"

"Don't want a hospital. Hate them." His dad's voice was thin and stressed.

Memories of his dad in that bed in the VA hospital, burned and broken, washed over Justice. Noah had gone through months of pure hell. And the whole time, he'd rarely talked. Except at night when he screamed.

Justice shuddered and stepped away. "Tell him we won't leave him in a hospital. Swear it. We'll just get him treated."

"Noah, I promise, I won't leave you in a hospital.

But if you're hurt and I can't treat you, I have to get you help. Trust me, I won't let them admit you unless you agree."

Relieved, Justice leaned in to continue listening.

"He's there, isn't he?"

Justice's heart jammed into his throat.

"Yes. Justice is right here with me. He wanted me to reassure you that we won't let them keep you in a hospital. Noah, please let me help you. I'll come alone if you want." Her eyes turned to him. *Sorry,* she mouthed.

In that moment, he loved her so goddamned much. But no way would he let her go alone. Most homeless people were safe, but a few were on the run from more than their internal demons. He slipped his hand beneath her hair to cup her nape and listened.

"Maybe need him. Dizzy."

Beth trembled beneath his hand, but her voice was calm. "All right. We'll be there. Just tell me where you are."

"By Petco Park."

Justice nodded. "The baseball stadium, I know it." He'd found his dad near there in the past where some homeless people gathered.

She nodded. "Noah, can you stay on the phone with me?"

"No. Call me when you're here." He hung up.

In the car, Justice drove while Liza frantically tried to think of the best way to get Noah treatment. "Ben!" She scrolled through her contacts, found Ben's number and typed out a quick message.

"What are you doing?"

"Telling Ben what's happening. I don't know if he's on shift at the hospital or home. But he might be able to help us if he knows Noah's situation. Does your dad have VA insurance?"

"He's eligible. No idea if he keeps it up. I'll pay for him, we just have to—"

She put her hand on Justice's bulging arm. "I know. I'm trying to give Ben information." She finished up and sent the message.

He turned to meet her gaze. "Thank you."

"I haven't done anything yet."

"Yes, you have. He texted you for help. He hasn't done that. Not to me and not to Grandma, who was his mom."

"I don't know why he talks to me. My only guess is it's a connection to you. Did you see his face the night he watched you sing? It was heart wrenching. Like a starving person staring at food they can't reach. He loves you, Justice."

He took a breath in what seemed like an effort to believe her. "Will you feel safe with him staying at our house?"

Startled, she said, "It's his house too. Always. He can come home anytime he wants to." Stroking his arm, she added, "Your dad isn't going to hurt me." But he might hurt himself. She'd learned from her research that was more typical behavior of people suffering severe forms of PTSD rather than hurting others.

He tapped his index finger on the steering wheel. "He has nightmares, well night terrors really. He doesn't sleep much. He's skittish and jumpy. The tension of living with him can be tough."

In that second it all came flooding back to her. Her own night terrors, the absolute fear that if she slept, bad things would happen to her while she was helpless. Hot tears filled her eyes, shocking her.

"Hey, Beth. Sh, it's okay. I'll figure something out."

She shook her head and wiped away her tears. "You know that moment when you're almost asleep and you sometimes jerk?"

"Yeah?" His voice softened as he checked the road then looked at her in concern.

"I'd jerk awake in full-bore panic. Sweating, screaming, guts churning. I'd throw up from the terror. Then lay on the bathroom floor, the only place I felt safe—in the small locked space with blazing lights."

Justice grabbed her hand. "What did your aunt and uncle do?"

"They tried to help, but they were so stressed, tired and worried about their own kids." The memory calmed her stupid tears. "But this isn't about me. I meant that I'm not going to judge your dad. It'll be rough, but I'll understand. I won't make things worse for him."

"Have you slept on the bathroom floor when I'm gone?"

She hesitated.

He jerked his head around, gaze intense. "Beth? The truth."

"Not all night. I've sat in there once or twice, calming down. Then I sit in our bed and write, like we often do when you're home. Sometimes I play your music on my phone. That calms me."

"Shit. I'm going on tour, I won't be here." He glanced at her, his mouth flattening. "You can handle this, right? My being gone, being pregnant, dealing with my dad if he's there. You won't cut."

"Stop worrying about me, I can handle almost

anything." A face loomed up in her mind. "Except Gene Hayes. As long as he leaves me alone—" She shook her head, stopping herself. How had they gotten off track? This wasn't about her right now. "Let's get your dad. It makes me sick to think of him hurting and alone. And I know it's a million times worse for you." Her phone rang. Glancing at the screen, she said, "It's Ben."

While Justice drove, she talked to Ben, quickly running down the situation.

"Bring him to the emergency entrance, ask for me. Two doctors here are former military, and I believe some nurses are too. They might be able to connect with Mr. Cade. We'll get him treated. And, Liza, don't worry. Just stay calm. The last thing Mr. Cade needs is anyone else getting upset as he tries to cope."

"What do I do for his arm?"

"Immobilize it the best you can. Call me if you need to. I'll do my best to help over the phone. Otherwise, get him warm and assure him we're not going to do anything without his agreement."

"Thank you, Ben." Gratefulness overwhelmed her.

It took them another twenty minutes to find Noah in the park area across from the stadium. He sat against a tree, shivering in the late-afternoon sunshine. She wasn't close enough to see his face clearly, but the way he cradled his right arm across his body telegraphed pain.

Noah saw them and hunched his shoulders.

Stopping, she laid a hand on Justice's arm. His muscles were rock hard, almost humming with his worry and frustration. He shoved his sunglasses up, his eyes dark and troubled.

"Let me talk to him first," Liza said.

He glanced at his dad then back to her. "Go."

Crossing to Noah, she knelt close enough to see fresh, raw scrapes on his face over the scars. One cut near his temple had dried blood around it, but still oozed. Concussion? His jacket and pants had streaks of dirt and some rips. "Hi, Noah. You're looking rough."

He shifted his stare to her. "It's my good arm. Can't fight without it. Other arm isn't good for much except eating and pissing."

She snorted in surprise. "Ah. Now I see where Justice gets his bluntness."

The man's gaze went to his son. "Hate him seeing me like this."

"He's not liking it either." She didn't see any reason to lie, Noah wasn't an idiot. "It made him crazed to think of you in pain. He wants to help you, Noah."

He nodded once. "My forearm is broken, hit my head pretty good. Confused most of the night, not sure how I got here."

God. "All right. The plan is to take you to the hospital where my friend Ben is a physician. He's arranging your care. He promised me they won't do anything to you without your permission. I'll stay with you where I can if you want me to."

"You going to buy me French fries and chocolate too?"

It took her a second to remember the night she'd told him everyone needs French fries and chocolate after they get out of the hospital. He had to be in agony and was still able to tease her. She frowned at him. "Only if you agree to come home to heal."

Noah closed his eyes, pain wrenching his features. His scars whitened. A few seconds passed, then he seemed to regain control and opened his eyes, his gaze flicking to Justice and back to her. "Don't have a choice. I want my fries supersized, and a chocolate milkshake."

Justice waited as Beth knelt by his father, her voice pitched too low for him to hear. But he could see his dad relaxing. She turned and motioned him over.

It had been six months since he'd last seen his dad for those brief moments when they'd picked him up at the jail and drove him to the house.

And now, there he was, looking so damned old and fragile. Not the big, strapping man who fought wars and laughed loudly enough to wake the dead.

Go. Take care of your dad.

Up close, his dad looked worse. Ragged beard streaked with gray, cuts and abrasions on his face. Weary lines digging into the tender skin around his eyes. And the scars on the side of his temple, cheek and neck from the bomb that exploded, marking his father forever. Those scars made people's eyes slide away in horror.

"Dad, the car isn't too far. Can you walk?"

Weariness radiated from him. "Yeah."

"He says his right forearm is broken. I'm thinking he might have a concussion too." Beth looked up at him. "Can you get your arm around him and help him up?"

Justice moved slowly, positioning himself at his dad's left. He ignored the smell of old sweat and sickness. "I'm going to help you to your feet, then keep hold of you to get you to the car."

His dad stared straight ahead. "Sorry."

That one word dug in so deep it nearly undid him. What had it cost this man to ask for help? "I'm not. I'll come any time you need me." He didn't give his dad time to respond, just said, "Now let's get you up."

Once Noah stood, it didn't take them long to get him in the car. Beth fussed around him, cushioning his arm on a pillow and covering him in a blanket.

His dad didn't protest, just sat in that distant, quiet way that Justice had found strange as a teenager. Almost frightening.

Now? It broke his fucking heart.

Chapter 10

ALMOST A WEEK LATER AND Justice was on his last damned nerve. He'd run nearly twice his normal three miles this morning. He was increasing his cardio and weight training to prepare for their tour.

But those bastards Jagged Sin had beat their band to the punch—they'd scheduled the release of their album one week before Justice's band. God he hated those pissant wannabes. But what worried him more—what was Gene Hayes doing?

I can handle almost anything...except Gene Hayes.

Beth's words nagged at him. What if Hayes made a move when Justice wasn't here? Could Beth handle it? Hans's plea bargain, meeting the probation officer to give her version of the story, and going to the sentencing hearing had stirred up her nightmares. Add to that the pressure of Justice on the road, her pregnancy and taking care of his dad, and Justice worried she'd crack.

She'd need him, he wouldn't be here, and Beth would pick up a razor blade or maybe break a glass and cut. He swiped an arm over his sweaty face as he headed up his driveway. Once he went inside, he had to deal with more frustration—his dad.

Noah had been there five days and barely spoke to his own son.

The hell of it was, part of Justice wanted to leave, to go on tour and get on that stage where he could make audiences fucking adore him. He wanted it all, damn it—Beth, his father back, and to be a star so big no one walked away from him.

Steeling himself, he walked through the door, but the sounds in the kitchen made him grit his teeth. Pausing in the living room, he swept his gaze over the eight-foot tree in the corner topped by that ridiculous Christmas Chicken. Christmas had exploded in the house—Santa, elf and reindeer figurines had landed on every flat surface, and the dining room table proudly boasted a festive tablecloth and red candles. It turned out Beth loved Christmas. And she missed her family, especially now that she was pregnant.

He was getting more and more worried about her. He looked up to the ceiling as he heard her chatting to Noah. Typically his dad didn't say anything, but that didn't stop Beth.

"The whole band locked me up in the ship's brig, then took pictures of it. All because I'd merely suggested that we stage one of them falling off the side of the ship and the others jumping in to save him. Like Savage Heroes."

A deep sound filtered out, a half cough, half laugh.

Justice closed his eyes. Oh yeah, his dad listened, and laughed, the sound so rusty it raised the hairs on Justice's arms. Old memories of his dad laughing rippled and teased him. He'd all but forgotten the sound.

"Right, stupid idea. But not jail-worthy."

Nothing then except the sounds of utensils on the counter, pans on the stove. Did Beth hope Noah would say more?

Of course she did. This was the girl who'd believed her dad at fourteen and let him lead her into hell. Beth was smart, but Noah tugged at her profound need for family. It was more than that too. Beth simply connected to Noah, maybe because they'd both had traumas.

But Beth had found a way to keep living, and Noah had shut down. He'd leave, and it would hurt her. It was bad enough his father did it to him, but to Beth? He couldn't bear his father rejecting her the way her aunt, uncle and grandmother had.

Crossing into the kitchen, he swept his gaze over the room. Ignoring the chicken-shaped wall hangings that all now had their very own Santa hats—Beth was on a mission to convince him there really was a Christmas Chicken—he focused on his girlfriend. Dressed in her black and pink pajamas, her hair piled on her head and glasses perched on her nose, she was beating eggs in a bowl.

His dad sat at the table, thumbing through Beth's laptop. He read news sites obsessively.

"Hey, how was your run?"

He yanked his gaze from his dad and went to her. "You should be sleeping." She'd worked five long days this last week, plus catering to his dad and getting ready for Christmas. "You need rest." The doctor had emphasized that, along with a good diet and prenatal vitamins.

"I'm fine. I heard Noah up and thought I'd make breakfast." Beth poured the eggs into the pan, then looked down and stilled. A second later she swallowed. The color drained from her cheeks. "Uh—"

Oh crap, he recognized that pale, sweaty sheen on her face. "You're sick." Another thing the doctor mentioned to expect—morning sickness.

"Just queasy. Not—" She clamped her mouth shut.

"Go lay down. Now." His words came out harsher than he meant. Gently prying the spatula from her hand, he said, "I'll do this, then bring you some 7 Up. Touching her face, he noted the clammy feel to her skin. "Please, go back to bed for an hour or two."

She nodded and headed out.

Brittle silence filled the kitchen, broken only by the hiss of eggs cooking and the pop of the toaster.

After plating the eggs, he buttered two slices of toast and set them in front of his dad.

Noah closed the laptop and stared at his food. "What's wrong with her?"

It was one of the few times his dad had addressed him. So far, they had only told Sloane, since he was Beth's boss, and Emily and Ben about Beth's pregnancy.

Justice didn't want to think about telling the band. Dread crapped a few bricks in his gut. He might not want to do it, but he'd man up. He owed the guys the truth and to make sure he told them before they heard it somewhere else.

But his dad wouldn't tell anyone, and he seemed worried about Beth. Justice needed to clear things up now before they got out of hand. Much as he wanted to take care of his dad, he now had a woman he loved to protect too. "Beth is pregnant. We're having a baby in late July."

Noah froze mid-bite. Carefully setting the fork down with his left arm, he kept his gaze on his plate. "A baby." He glanced up, then away from Justice. "She seen a doctor?"

"Yes. She's in good health." And this was where it got tricky. "I love Beth, Dad."

"I know."

It was surreal. This was the first real conversation that wasn't about food and what Noah needed. He eyed his dad's right arm in the dark-blue cast, his left arm covered in scars and weak. That, along with the pain in his hips and general weakness from the life he'd been living, kept him here at the house with them.

But for how long? Justice didn't let himself hope too much. The man would leave again.

"Dad, Beth doesn't have a father. Do you see what's happening here?" Could Noah get outside of his head long enough to grasp it? She was stopping on her way home from work each night to bring Noah a supersized fries and a chocolate milkshake. As if the treats would entice his dad to stay. Justice had kept his mouth shut, but now he had to make his father understand. "Her own family won't have anything to do with her because of me."

"She told me."

He blinked. Shit. How much was Beth confiding in his father? Apprehension knotted his guts. "Don't break her heart, Dad." It was out before he could stop the words, a primitive need to protect his woman, the mother of his kid.

Noah stared down at his plate. "I'll leave."

Justice grabbed his dad's scarred hand. "I don't want you to leave, damn it. I want you to—"

"What? Stay like this? Up at night and walking circles in your backyard so I don't scream? You don't want me, son. You want the father you once had, and I'm not him." He shoved up to his feet, jerking his hand back. "You don't want me."

Fury ripped into him. "What are you doing to do? Walk in front of another car?" Shit. Goddamn it to hell. "Beth thinks you were hit by accident. But you were trying to end it, weren't you?" It pounded viciously in his brain. The one thing he hadn't wanted to face. But he'd known it.

Noah stopped, his thin shoulders bowed. He wore the pajama bottoms and shirt Beth had bought for him. "Yes. Couldn't even do that right."

"So why did you text Beth?" Why not just fucking end it if that was what he wanted? Why keep torturing them all?

The second he thought it, Justice hated himself as much as he had when he was sixteen and told his dad he'd wished he'd never come home. He didn't want his dad to die, he wanted him to *want* to live.

His dad turned his gaze to him. "Because she doesn't remember what I was. She's never known me as anything but broken and useless." He walked out.

Justice clenched his fists, struggling to rein in the kaleidoscope of whirling emotions. Anger, hurt, fear, frustration, love, and maybe hate. But his dad had a point. For the first time, Justice began to see how unfair that was. Noah had come home a different man, and no one wanted to accept that.

Most of all, his son.

Beth slathered peanut butter on a piece of toast, and said, "Stop staring at me. I'm fine."

Justice leaned back against the counter. "You look better. Want some tea?"

"I have water, thanks." Sitting at the table, she added, "No more eggs for a while." It'd been so sudden. She hadn't felt great when she got up this morning, but she hadn't expected to look at the eggs and get so nauseated. At least she hadn't actually thrown up. Fortunately, she'd fallen asleep, and once she woke, she felt better. "Emily and I are going out shopping."

Justice crossed to her and slid his hand beneath her hair. "You said you're done with Christmas shopping."

"But Emily's not, so I'm helping her. I'm going."

"I'm not trying to stop you if you feel up to it." Backing up, he dropped into a chair. "How are you going to work with morning sickness?"

Was that what had him hovering over her? "Women do it all the time." She could tough it out. "I'm off next week for Christmas anyway."

He didn't look convinced. "What happens when I go on tour? You'll be here alone."

"Not alone. Your dad is here. And—"

He took her hand. "He's not going to stay, Beth. He never stays."

"But—"

The doorbell rang.

"You finish your toast, I'll get the door." Justice got up and walked out.

Beth assumed it was Emily and followed, or Justice would make a big thing of her bout of queasiness, and the two of them would gang up on her. When they opened the door, it was Ben.

"Where's Emily?" Beth said, surprised.

Ben's gaze swept over them. "She'll be here soon. I've come to talk to Mr. Cade."

Surprise trembled through her. "You mean Noah?" He wouldn't call Justice Mr. Cade. What was up? "Come in, I'll get him."

"I'm right here."

The three of them turned to Noah. He stood by the couch, a thrashed backpack in his hand. Worry and confusion clashed in her stomach. "Noah, what are you doing?"

He locked his attention on her. "Justice told me you're pregnant."

"You're leaving because I'm pregnant?" Liza didn't understand.

Misery swirled in his eyes. "I want to be in your baby's life. But not like this."

Did he think she would object? "You can be. I won't ever stop you. You can see the baby and—"

"Not like this." He set his jaw beneath his beard exactly as Justice did when he was being stubborn. "That car didn't hit me on accident. I walked in front of it."

Liza stumbled at the impact of his words. "Oh, Noah." The man's pain radiated off him, raising goose bumps on her skin.

"Ben knows it and so does Justice. But you...you just see me. Broken and crazy, yet you seem to believe I'm worth the effort."

"You are." How didn't he get this? "You're Justice's dad. My child's grandfather. Did you know that Justice has changed the oil in my car? You taught him that." She didn't know what she was saying, it was all emotion tumbling out. "You didn't just teach him how to change the oil, but how to take care of someone he loves. Okay, he didn't love me then, but—"

"Beth, easy." Justice put his arm around her, tugging her into his side.

His warmth flooded through her muscles, and she realized how selfish she was being. "Sorry. He's your father, not mine. I just—" She cut off the words, looking up at Justice's harsh face. "He's our family."

Her word's punched him right in the throat. She really did accept Noah in ways Justice hadn't been able to. Every time he looked at his dad, he searched for the hero of his childhood.

Beth just wanted a family.

He faced his dad. "What are you planning to do?"

Noah stared at the floor. "I'm going into a program, one that Dr. Gunderson in the emergency room mentioned to me. Ben emailed me more information days ago. I've been considering it."

Ben stepped up. "Dr. Gunderson is a veteran who does some work for the program. The Transitioning Warrior Recovery Center is a live-in treatment facility, run by veterans. They treat some of the most difficult cases of traumatic brain injury and PTSD. With Noah's permission, I was able to get his records and have them sent over. They've reviewed his case and are willing to take him on."

Of course, Noah hadn't said a word to him. He eyed Beth. "Did you know?"

"No." She touched Noah's arm. "If this is what you want, we'll support you any way we can."

Relief settled into his dad's eyes.

"Dad," Justice began. "I'll take you. Wherever this place is, I'll take you there. Check it out."

Noah shook his head and strode for the door. Once there, he stopped, his back to the room. "The last thing I thought of before that car hit me was you, Justice. As much as I'd like to see your son or daughter, my real reason for trying again is you." He opened the door and walked out.

Justice's lungs locked, and the room closed in on him. Had his dad really said that? Did he mean it? But when had his dad lied?

Never.

Noah said nothing rather than lie.

Throat clearing got his attention, and he focused on Ben. "What happens now?"

The other man handed Justice a dark-green folder. "Here's the information, including the address. Your father will have his cell phone. The only requirement is that it's turned off during any therapy. There are emergency numbers in there for you to reach him if he's not answering. Otherwise they'll admit him and do an evaluation, not only of his mental and emotional condition, but his physical. The first goal will be pain control. Then they'll focus on therapies and strategies to work through his specific issues and to help him cope." Ben laid a hand on Justice's shoulder. "I honestly think it's his best chance. I'd leave my own father there without a second's hesitation. I didn't recommend this to your dad lightly."

Justice held out his hand to Ben. "Thank you, man. Thank you."

After shaking his hand, Ben said, "I'll text you once he's there. If he sticks it out, it's going to take time. Mr. Cade has been dealing with this for a decade now. I've seen his medical files, and the fact he survived his injuries from the explosion is a testament to his strength. If he wants this badly enough, I believe he can achieve a substantially improved quality of life."

"How do you know so much?" Beth asked.

"I have a friend." He grimaced. "*Had* a friend who was in the military. We all missed the signs when he came back from a tour in Afghanistan. He didn't have to die. And neither does Noah."

She hugged Ben. "I had no idea, I'm so sorry."

He squeezed her once and let go. "Thanks, Liza. Now look, guys, this isn't an easy fix. But it's hope. Let him settle in, send a text or email, but any more personal interaction is harder for him. Especially with you, Justice. He thinks he failed you." Ben moved to the door.

Regret kicked him in the gut. Justice could hear himself screaming at his father that he wished he'd never come home. "He didn't." It was Justice who had failed to be the son he'd needed.

Stopping, Ben turned. "Don't lie to him. Your dad is a highly intelligent man forced to live in a state of constant hyperawareness of a soldier in danger even though he's been home for a decade. He did fail you, Justice, and lying makes it worse. But the system also failed him. Get that shit out in the open and let it breathe, and you'll all have a better chance to move forward." Ben lifted a hand and added, "Noah's waiting, I need to go."

Justice shut the door and tried to get his balance back. Before he could do or say anything, Beth walked straight into his arms. For long minutes they just stood in the Christmas-cheer-filled living room.

Beth. Would this have happened without her? No. She came into his life with her sweet yet damaged spirit and somehow reached Noah in a way no one else could. Beth was the bridge between him and his father.

As long as he had Beth, Justice could deal with everything else. He'd go on tour, make Savaged Illusions' album a success and give her the life she deserved. But he was going to be gone for months, and he wanted to know for sure she was his before he left.

The idea grew in urgency. His dad had just walked out the door again. His mom had walked out. He needed to know Beth wasn't going to leave.

Christmas morning, Liza plopped down on the floor in front of the tree and handed Justice her gift. She was so excited, even morning sickness couldn't compete. She hoped he'd like it. "Open yours first."

He stared at the box. "We were supposed to get gifts for each other? I don't remember that in the story of the Christmas Chicken."

Liza jerked the box back. "Fine, I'll give this to someone who believes in Santa and the Christmas Chicken."

Justice grabbed the end of the present and tugged. "Mine."

She laughed, seeing a flash of the little boy in the picture on the ornament. "Say 'I believe in the Christmas Chicken.'"

He narrowed his eyes. "That's blackmail."

"Say it."

"Maybe I won't give you your present."

"Ha! I knew you got me one." Of course he had. "Now say it."

"I believe in the Christmas Chicken."

The wiseass smirk totally ruined his serious voice, but she released the box anyway. She was too excited to torture him properly.

"Who." he added as soon as he had possession of the gift, "shows up in the middle of the night, can sniff out all secret stashes of chocolate and carries them off to sell them on the ChickenDeals4U website."

Of course he thought he could get in the last word.

"Well sure, for bad kids. But I'm good, so he'll leave me extra chocolate. Now open your present."

Justice tore into the wrapping, his long fingers ripping off the box lid.

Liza grinned at his eagerness.

After shoving back the tissue paper, he pulled out the garment. His eyes lit up. "Is this a Lazaro? For real?" He turned it, studying the distressed leather blazer.

Worry edged into her chest. Would he care? "It's preowned. I couldn't swing a new one, but it's in good shape." Her neck muscles bunched. She couldn't return it, and yeah, the price had been steep. But she'd haggled shamelessly, using her position as Sloane's assistant and throwing in a pair of tickets to a UFC fight. "I could picture you strutting out on stage in it."

He ran his fingers over the black handcrafted jacket, then popped up to his feet and swung it on. Holding out his arms, he focused on her. "Tell me how hot I look."

She ran her gaze over his naked chest and flat stomach, down to the plaid PJ bottoms he'd pulled on when she'd bounced on the bed and insisted he get up. Despite her usual morning queasiness, she'd been too excited to sleep. "Like a rock star. Perfect."

He hunkered down, taking her face in his hands and kissing her. "Thank you. I love it."

"You don't mind that it's preowned?"

"No. I'll wear it for the tour opening at the Nosh."

She was so pleased he liked it and didn't mind it was secondhand. "Are you going to make me beg for my present?"

He grinned. "Not this time." He rose and strode down the hall. A minute later he returned, still wearing the leather blazer. He sat in front of her, crossing his legs, the coat long enough to brush the floor around him. He had a bag in his hands and silently handed it over.

Beth took the pretty red bag and pulled out the tissue. Nestled deep inside was a blue velvet jeweler's box, small and square. Her heart tripped and pounded.

Wait, don't jump to conclusions. It could be a necklace, earrings and something else small. A chicken-shaped charm.

Her belly flipped. Not morning sickness, but nerves and excitement.

"Open it."

Slowly, she opened the hinged lid. There sat a white-gold ring with a small oval diamond surrounded by tiny diamonds that flowed partway down the band. It was feminine and romantic. The lights from the Christmas tree gleamed off the diamonds.

She lifted her gaze to Justice. "It's gorgeous... Is this...?" Was this really happening?

"I love you, Beth. Will you marry me?" Before she could answer, he took her free hand, his warmth closing around her fingers, and went on, "Say yes. Marry me before the album drops, before the tour and our life changes. Let's make our vows to each other. Swear to love and protect each other first and always. Promise to be there for one another, through it all, no matter what."

It was the most perfect Christmas present and proposal ever. "Yes."

He slid the ring onto her finger and kissed her.

"I love it." She touched the center oval diamond. "Can we afford this? Rings are expensive." More than his leather coat would cost brand new.

He pushed back a lock of her hair. "One day I'll buy you your own ring—anything you want."

She frowned, trying to follow him. "It's not mine?

What, did you borrow it?" That didn't make sense.

"It's yours. But I took the diamonds from my grandmother's wedding ring and had them reset into a white-gold band for you. She'd like you, Beth. I think she'd approve."

"Oh." She couldn't stay anything else for a moment. She studied her ring, one that had a shared past with Justice's grandmother.

"Beth? It's only temporary. With the tour and my dad's treatment, it was the best I can do right now. But one day, I'll be able to afford any rock you want."

She pulled her hand to her chest, cradling it over her heart. "No. I don't want another ring. This is..." She swallowed the lump of emotion. "You love me enough to give me a ring with your grandmother's diamonds. But you didn't just give me her ring—you had them reset for me. They're mine, but they carry the history of who you are. This ring is special and means everything to me. Everything." She didn't care if she sounded like an idiot.

His eyes cleared to a shimmering blue. "You really love it?"

"So much. And I love you." Going up on her knees, she threw herself at him.

He caught her and lay back on the carpet with her on top of him. "We can't afford a big wedding, and there's no time. Are you okay with getting married at city hall? Then later, after the baby, maybe for our first anniversary, we'll do something big if you want."

Did it really matter? It wasn't like she had a dad to give her away, her aunt wouldn't come, nor would she let her cousins Kristen and Rafe be in the wedding. "I don't have any family who would, or could in my mom's case, come anyway."

"We're a family, Beth. You, me and our baby."

Chapter 11

JUSTICE LEANED BACK ON THE couch in Christine's office in the heart of Los Angeles. Gold and platinum albums and pictures of famous musicians lined the walls. A huge sliding glass door led to a pristine deck that contrasted the dirty gray smog marring the view of the L.A. horizon. But Justice's attention was on the big screen mounted on the wall to his right. They were less than two weeks away from releasing their album and the single "Expired Hero."

"The afterparty at Club Nosh for your release day concert is all set," Bianca, their publicist, said. "Reps from all the major streaming services like iTunes, Spotify, Amazon, Pandora, etc. will be there. We also have reps from several radio stations." She switched screens on her PowerPoint. "Presales for the album are climbing. In closing, we feel your positioning in the market is strong for an indie label."

"Positioning for what, exactly?" Justice asked. "To have a chart topping album?"

Christine stood up. "Not right out of the gate. We're in a brutal business climate. Streaming services have killed sales and—"

"Cut to the chase," Simon snapped from his perch on the arm of the couch. "We're well aware of the current market."

Justice didn't let himself feel the stab of regret. Their loss on *Court of Rock* meant they didn't get the big record label backing them, paying for their production and tours...so yeah...they were behind at the starting gate. But they were still going to fight their way to the top.

"All right." Christine sat on the edge of her desk. "You need to crack the top one-hundred mark in overall sales on the single release. Once you do that, then the song shows up on things like 'also buys,' and it will create its own force. We can use that in our marketing and publicity, and you can do what you do—sing and play—and we'll be able to drive that song into the top fifty, and that's where you start seeing a chance for real attention. And an opportunity to get tapped by World Rock Stage as the indie breakout band."

"Holy fuck," Lynx said. "We'd get a chance to play with the rock gods."

"Dude," River jumped in. "We'd *be* a rock god."

"Hell yeah," Lynx responded.

That dream dangled in front of Justice, right there within his reach. Everything in him wanted to get into that club of rock stars and be someone. He'd prove to all who'd ever doubted him that he was a success. Too famous to ever be abandoned in a jail cell again.

"Quiet," he snapped. "Let's find out how we get to that goal."

Christine gestured to the PowerPoint on the screen. "Those presales are pointing in the right direction. Bianca and her team are getting you some good exposure across all media. Right now, it looks like your competition in the indie category is Jagged Sin."

Justice fisted his hands. "Gene Hayes is backing them. He's up to something." That uneasiness trailed him like a black, swollen thundercloud.

"Doesn't matter that Hayes is listed as a producer, the album is releasing under Jagged Sin's own indie label, not a big-name label like Tangent."

"Our sales are ahead of theirs," Lynx pointed out.

"Just barely," Christine said. "They're appealing to the underbelly of rock and to anyone in the world who ever thought the system has done them wrong. Even their title track reflects that, 'Jagged Revenge'."

Damn, who hadn't felt that way at times? It made sense, and now Justice's worry increased. "We're better than they are. We'll prove it."

"You need an edge." She lifted a hand. "And I have it. I was able to book you into your real shot. We had to shuffle around your tour dates—"

"Wait." Justice looked at Simon. "Did you know about this?" Simon was a little better at reading emails in a timely fashion than the rest of them.

"No." Worry lines dug into Simon's forehead. "This will affect our road crew, the tour bus schedule—"

"It's worth the headache, trust me." Christine's voice vibrated with excitement. "Two weeks into the tour, you're going to take the red eye to New York to appear on *Chatterbox* TV show."

"No shit?" River said. "Fury Run was just on there last month, and their sales shot through the roof."

Justice met Lynx's eyes, and for a second, they were cast back in time to the two teenage boys in juvie who dreamed of a rock band and stardom. And now here they were, so damned close they could taste it.

But they'd been this close before and had it ripped out of their reach at the last second.

"You're right," Simon put in. "*Chatterbox* is worth all the hassle."

"Indeed," Christine said. "Bianca will send you the revised schedule, and you can work it out with your road crew and bus driver. She'll book your flight tickets and add it to your charges."

They all started talking as Bianca packed up her laptop. "I'll go back to my office to send you the revised schedule and see about booking your tickets."

Once the publicist left and closed the door, Justice looked around at the guys. They were so close to their goal now. He didn't want to rock the boat, but he'd withheld information once before, and that ended in a disaster. Rising from the couch, he strode to the door, overlooking the cityscape.

"I have something to tell you." He turned to face the room. "Beth and I are getting married this Friday at city hall."

The high burst like a balloon. Lynx spoke first. "Why so fast? You didn't say a word."

Justice didn't flinch beneath the stares. "She's pregnant."

"Fuck." Simon's face flooded with color as he sprang off the couch. "You swore you weren't going to be distracted this time. That you'd put the band first." He turned, pacing a few steps, and added, "We put everything into this—into the company. We took loans. We trusted you to be there for us, not go out and knock up your girlfriend. If this album and tour fails, we'll be ruined."

That was dead true, they were risking everything. "This doesn't affect my commitment to the band. I'm still in a hundred percent."

River said, "So what now?"

"Nothing changes. We're getting married Friday, and Monday I'll be back in L.A. for rehearsals. The next weekend our record drops, and we'll do our release night at Club Nosh, then we go on tour. Beth will be there for opening night, then fly to Vegas for our show there and then go home. Nothing changes as far as my commitment to our success. She knows that." He'd made it as clear as he could to her, and now he was doing the same with his band. He could do this—be a husband and father, and a rock star. "Look, I know you're shocked, but this is between me and Beth. We're handling it, but I'm committed to the band. No matter what."

The quiet was worse than yelling.

"I'd like to speak to Justice," Christine said. "Alone. We're done here for the day."

Simon turned on his heel and stalked to the door. Once there, he looked back, his eyes frigid. "Don't screw up our shot, Justice. Not this time." He stormed out.

Lynx walked up to Justice. "This what you want?"

What he wanted was everyone to get off his back. He'd make this work. He wasn't going to mess anything up for the band or fail Beth. "Yes."

Lynx nodded. "Let me know if you need a best man." He headed out, followed by River and Gray.

That left him and Christine. Disapproval coated the air like smog.

She swung her gaze to his. "Have you lost your mind? Your girlfriend gets pregnant right before your album comes out, and you agree to marry her? That's lunacy, and worse, downright foolish."

"She didn't get pregnant on purpose." There were two of them in this relationship.

"No?"

He stared at her, refusing to be baited. Beth had told him when she forgot the shot, but that wasn't something he'd discuss with Christine.

"Fine. It was an accident. Now listen up. This is the advice you're paying me for: Don't marry her. It's your kid. You're on the hook for child support. But you marry her, and half of everything you earn from that day forward is hers. It's even more complicated when we get into intellectual rights. If you even discuss a song idea with her, then get divorced, and you write and produce the song? She can make a claim for half the profits. There's a reason big-time athletes and celebrities don't marry their baby mamas."

He cringed at that stupid-ass phrase. "This isn't your business, Christine."

She pinched the bridge of her nose. "You have a blind spot when it comes to Liza, and that's part of why you lost *Court of Rock*. Maybe your band doesn't have the balls to tell you the truth, but I do." She dropped her hand and walked up to him. "So here it is straight up: That girl will destroy you, the band and your career if you don't pull your head out of your ass."

Fury thundered in his brain. Liza trusted him, believed in him, loved him, even when he lost or screwed up. Her simple touch, her sensual peach scent, and the sound of her laugh fired his passion and something more...a love so fierce it hurt.

"Be very careful how you talk about my *wife*." And the mother of his kid.

She dropped her hand to the edge of the desk. "This would be stupid enough with any other girl, but Liza comes with a ticking time bomb."

"Gene Hayes." Anxiety rippled in him. That bastard was always there, a shadow stretching over his life with Beth. "But he hasn't done anything in months."

"No, you haven't *seen* him doing anything, but he won't go away. Hayes has some powerful connections and financial investments in the music industry, both in and out of the U.S."

"How do you know that?"

"Everyone knows it. How do you think he not only got out of the country, but moved so many assets out? He's a quiet partner in multiple ventures." Christine went on, "Hayes is an arrogant son of a bitch who holds a grudge. In his mind, Liza and other girls like her are his due as a rock star. But this girl took him down, and one way or another he'll get revenge."

Deep protectiveness burned until he couldn't stay still. He paced the room. "He can't touch her. If he comes back to the U.S., he'll be arrested."

"Hayes convinced a stupid kid to try and kill Liza. Think about that for a minute—he's so manipulative, he convinced Hans through the internet to stab her. No, he's not giving up, he's plotting something."

Justice whipped around. "What?"

"I don't know. What I do know is we want to stay out of his path. Don't marry Liza. And if you're smart, you'll get her out of your life. Pay the child support, and move on. You're headed for real stardom, and you can screw all the girls you want. Get rid of this one."

Get rid of her? Like she was trash? That was what her aunt and uncle did. And her grandmother. Hell, his own mom had done that to him. But Liza was everything to him.

He crossed his arms. "No." He and the band were locked into a contract with Christine, and that he could live with. But he drew a line when it came to Beth.

Tension filled the office as they glared at one another.

Christine sighed. "Then get a prenuptial agreement.

We'll at least protect you as best we can." She grabbed her phone. "You'll have to delay the marriage until we can get it executed."

Delay and deflect. He knew this tactic, and he didn't need a prenuptial with Liza. "Again, no. And we're done." He headed to the door.

She slammed her phone down. "Do you care about your band at all? Those four guys sacrificing everything, believing that you have their backs and will take them to the top?"

Fury spun him around. He stalked back to her. "Don't ever question my loyalty."

"Then protect them."

"I'm marrying her." She was pregnant. From the beginning of their relationship, he'd told her he was all in and demanded the same from her. He didn't get to cut and run now, nor did he want to. He loved her, needed her.

And he loved his band, needed them.

He could be loyal and committed to both.

"Do the prenup."

"No." All in.

Her face darkened. "What is it about that girl?" Sighing, she got up and went to the window, staring at the city.

Silence filled the office, and Justice stood there, refusing to fill it.

Christine relented first. "I think you're making a mistake, one that will come back and bite you in the ass. But if you're doing it, then let's minimize the damage. We have three problems to manage: One, your fans are females who think you're their wet dream. They don't want you to be married and taken. Two, another part of your fan base hates Liza specifically—she's the girl that ruined a rock star. And three, Gene Hayes—we don't want him focusing on Savaged Illusions, and if you're married to Liza, he'll use that somehow. So ultimately the goal is to keep all media spotlight off Liza and on you and Savaged Illusions."

She had his attention now. Christine was damned good as a business manager. She'd gotten them great gigs for their tour and booked them on *Chatterbox*. What she said made sense. "What's the strategy?"

She turned. "We keep this marriage and pregnancy quiet until after the tour. Don't let her become the story. If we can break you out of the pack with this tour and position you for your next album to do even better, then you'll have enough star power to make any buzz Liza creates work for you, not against you."

Hide Liza. That twisted like a knife in his guts. Could he really ask her to do that? "She'll be at some of our shows."

"No one has to know she's anything more than she's your girlfriend. You don't have to make any big public displays." She fixed a hard stare on him. "You owe this much to your band."

What choice did he have? He had to protect both his band as well as Liza and his child.

Justice took the steps two at a time with Lynx at his side. Traffic had been a bitch getting from Los Angeles to San Diego, and he was running late for his wedding.

"Jagged Sin is still moving up the damned chart," Lynx muttered, staring at his phone.

Justice's neck tensed. "Assholes." The other band's album had dropped last night and was doing better than Justice had expected. He stormed into the building, following the signs to the office they needed. Beth wouldn't get pissed because he was late and leave, would she? She knew he was coming. This wasn't like when he missed the flight home to go with her to the sentencing hearing, he was only a few minutes late.

"There you are." Emily skidded up to them, her face flushed. "Come on, Liza's in there fighting to keep your spot." She turned and jogged, which was impressive in her high heels.

Justice loped up to her side. "We're the last appointment of the day. What's the problem?"

"It's four thirty. You were supposed to be here at four fifteen. The officiant says if you're a second past the fifteen-minute window, you have to reschedule. They close promptly at five."

Fuck. Justice followed as Em pivoted and headed into an office. There was a low counter with partitions stretching across the right. Beth stood between two chairs. "I'm so sorry, but this is the only day we can do it. Please, if you can just wait a couple more minutes, he'll be here."

"I'm sorry, it's four thirty. You'll have to—"

"I'm here," Justice called out, striding into the room.

Beth turned.

He stopped a few feet from her, his breath locking. She wore an ivory satin dress that stopped above her knees. A pearl-beaded strap ran over one shoulder at an angle. Her hair was up in a sleek twist thing, with several strands falling over her shoulders. In her hands she held the bouquet of creamy peach and white roses with delicate ribbons trailing down that he'd had sent to her this morning after he left. His bride was stunning. This was another side to her, sleek and sophisticated.

Drawn to her, he took her one of her hands. "You're gorgeous."

"Thank you, and for the flowers. They're lovely. You look good too." Her gaze slid to the gray-haired woman behind the desk frowning at them. "But I don't know if we can get married today."

This was his fault for not getting his ass here on time. He shifted to the officiant. "I'm sorry for the inconvenience, it's entirely my fault. Can you please make an exception and marry us?" He turned to Beth. "I really want this woman to be my wife."

The woman sighed. "Okay, we'll do this, but we'll have to hurry. We really do close at five." She pushed the opened folder toward him. "Miss Glasner has filled out the documents. Check them over. Sign them, and we'll get this done."

"By all means, let's rush through Liza's wedding," Em muttered. "Wouldn't want this day to be special."

"Hush," Beth said. "I was warned when I asked for the last appointment of the day not to be late. This isn't her fault."

No, it was his. Justice took the pen and quickly signed. Once the paperwork was done, they went to the podium at the end of the room, where they stood together with Emily and Lynx behind them.

The officiant slid on her glasses and read from a form Beth had filled out. "We meet here today for the joyful purpose of joining in marriage Justice Cade and Liza Glasner. This is a moment of joy and excitement as you face a future together. But marriage is more than a legal contract, it is a solemn vow that requires thoughtful consideration of the deep obligations and responsibilities you will pledge this day." She looked up and asked, "Justice and Liza, are you ready today to take this vow?"

"Yes," Justice answered.

"I am," Beth said.

She nodded. "Let us proceed. Turn and face each other to exchange your vows."

Beth handed her flowers to Emily and turned to him.

"I'll go first." Justice faced Beth with both her hands in his and looked into her eyes. "Liza, my Beth, as your husband, I vow to be your friend, lover and partner for as long as we both live. I will put you first before all else. I want to be the one to laugh with you, to hold you when you're sad or scared, to support your dreams, celebrate your triumphs and guard your sleep." After taking the ring from Lynx, he slid it on her finger. "Our hearts are in these rings, and together we are a circle that cannot be broken. I love you, Beth, now and always."

All her fears and frustrations calmed as the cool white-gold band settled into place. Even the hurt that Justice hadn't arrived on time. When Liza had stood there, trying to get the officiant to wait a few more minutes, the pity in the woman's eyes had made her squirm in shame.

Like the times her dad was supposed to come see Liza as a little girl and never showed up.

But now Justice's words sank into her heart, and she couldn't look away from his intensely striking blue eyes. *Guard her sleep.* Of all the things he could have said, that was the one that told her he knew her, understood her deepest fears.

"Liza, do you have your vows?" the officiant asked.

"Yes." She took a second to clear the thickness from

her throat and focused on the man she loved. "Justice, as your wife I vow to be your friend, lover and partner. I will love you with all that makes me who I am today and all that I will be tomorrow and every day after that. I vow to you that no matter how high you soar or hard you fall, I'll be there to fly with you or catch you." Pausing, she took the ring from Emily, a silver band with the infinity symbol etched in black. As she slid it on his finger, she said, "Our hearts are in these rings, and together we are a circle that cannot be broken. I love you, Justice, now and always."

"By virtue of the authority vested in me as Deputy Commissioner of Civil Marriages, for the County of San Diego, I take pleasure in announcing that from this minute on you are husband and wife. You may kiss the bride."

Justice leaned down and settled his mouth over hers. His lips were warm and sweet until he wrapped an arm around her waist and lifted her off her feet. He plunged into her mouth. She gripped his shoulders and kissed him back.

Her husband.

Heat warmed her skin, and ripples of desire danced.

Justice broke the kiss, grinned and puffed out his chest like a pleased rooster. "It's official, you're my wife. There's no escape now."

She beamed at his smug happiness. "When I met you, I never imagined this... I married a rock star."

His eyes crinkled at the edges. "Hell yeah, you did. You're mine. And FYI, husband trumps rock star."

Emily grabbed the camera. "We need a couple pictures."

"Here let me." The officiant took the camera. "We have five minutes before closing."

While they posed, Liza looked up at Justice. "I reserved the romance suite at the Opulence hotel tonight—and it comes with a candlelight dinner for two. And I packed your bag." She couldn't book the honeymoon suite for fear of word getting out that they were married.

His eyes lit up. "Mrs. Cade, are you trying to seduce me?"

"I love the sound of that."

"Seducing me?"

She rolled her eyes, then remembered the camera and flashed another smile. "I meant Mrs. Cade. I wish I could change my name to that now." She wanted Justice's last name so they'd feel like a real family. It was such a little thing, really. But Liza had a different last name than her aunt, uncle and cousins when she lived with them. Just another way she was always on the outside. The whole keeping-their-marriage-secret thing made sense logically, but emotionally...

It stung. Like she was once again being kept on the outside.

"Beth, I'm going to announce to the whole world you're my wife the second this tour is over. I swear it. But right now, with Jagged Sin breathing down our necks—" His jaw tensed as he scowled. "They're doing better than expected, and tonight they're—"

"Hello?" Emily said. "This is your wedding. Think you can focus on that, and not your career?"

Justice flicked his gaze to Em, then back to Liza. "She's annoying, but right. You're my bride, Mrs. Cade, and tonight is about us. And after the tour, we can do another, bigger ceremony."

She lifted an eyebrow. "In April I'll be nearly six months pregnant."

"And still my sexy wife."

"We really have to close now," the older woman said, handing the camera to Emily.

"Thank you for accommodating us." Liza started to walk out.

"Hold on, Mrs. Cade." Justice caught her hand.

Confused, Liza stopped. "What?"

"This." He swept her up into his arms.

She grabbed on to his neck, slightly dizzy. "What are you doing?"

"You're my bride. I might have been late to our wedding, but I'm all in. I'm carrying you all the way to our suite, where I'm claiming you now and forever." He walked out the door, turning down the hallway. The few stragglers left in the building smiled at them.

Emily trotted along, taking pictures. "Perfect!"

Liza laughed. Yeah, he'd been late, and they'd just had the fastest wedding and photos in history.

But the rushed ceremony didn't make it any less real. Even if he was hiding their marriage and baby for the sake of his career.

Chapter 12

LIZA SAT IN THE DRESSING room of Club Nosh, savoring the quiet as she tried to settle her nerves and her stomach. Justice and the band were out doing a meet-and-greet, but she'd gotten overheated and queasy.

Watching the girls in too-tight tank tops touching him, giggling, flirting hadn't helped. Damn, when did she get this possessive?

The door opened. "Hey, Liza, you okay?"

As she rose, it took a second to place the man. "Keith." From Indie Rock Broadcast. She hadn't seen him since Justice and the band had been on *Court of Rock*. The interview with Keith was the one that exposed her to Gene Hayes. But that wasn't Keith's fault, and he was here to cover the release concert and party, not Liza. She was staying under the radar as much as possible. "Good to see you. Justice said they were giving you backstage access."

"I saw you sort of turn pale and rush off. You sick?"

She forced a smile. "Nerves, that's all." Which was probably true. She didn't usually have morning sickness past noon.

He glanced around. "Nice, right?"

The dressing room at Club Nosh had gray walls, red sofas and black coffee tables on a black-and-white rug. Beth picked up two bottles of water from the ice bucket, handed him one and settled on the couch. "It's a great night. Their new album is killer. You can put that on the record." The venue was nearly sold out.

Keith dragged up a chair and opened his bottle. "Hey, listen. That day when we did that interview on the *Court of Rock* stage, I didn't know who you were. I didn't purposely expose you to Hayes." He leaned back in his chair. "It's really bothered me, and you never returned my calls. I wanted you to know I'm sorry that happened."

Liza lowered her water bottle, surprised. "I didn't think you knew, Keith. It was just...I don't talk about it." Except with Justice, and lately she'd told Emily more too. "But I need to thank you."

He widened his eyes. "For?"

"Hayes said on his video that he contacted you, offered you an exclusive."

The man's face twisted in disgust. "I told him if he came back to the states and wanted to fight the charges like a man, then I'd interview him. Or if he wanted to own up to his crimes." Dropping his elbows on his thighs, he said, "Look, I'm not a rock crime fighter, you know? I've interviewed some repulsive characters and promoted music of bands whose members I wouldn't allow near my dog. That's my job. What I don't do is give a voice to scumbags who prey on teenage girls."

Liza liked a man who laid the truth out there. "Fair enough, and I'm still grateful. The *Late Night with Alicia* show is known for underhanded stunts. But you're regarded as legitimate in the rock world. More people would believe Hayes if you'd presented that video."

He grinned. "Yeah, I'm the all-powerful Oz. I need to get a T-shirt made up."

"And modest." She glanced at the clock. The guys had to wrap up the signing and get ready to go onstage. She pressed her hand to her belly. "Feels like an angry beehive in my stomach. I believe they can make it to the big time." And yep, that scared her more than a little. "Do you think this album will get them there?"

"It's kick ass debut." He leaned forward. "Better than Jagged Sin's release last week. Unfortunately, they're getting some good publicity."

Because all Hayes's fans were flocking to Jagged Sin. The fact that Hayes was the producer gave them credibility and legitimacy. "Savaged Illusions will blow them out of the spotlight." They had to.

Keith nodded. "What about you? Are you ready for being back in the spotlight?"

He was smooth. That easy transition almost made her think he was a friend, not media. "Is this an interview?"

"No." He raised a pierced eyebrow. "Otherwise, I'd ask about those wedding rings. We have a Rock Wives segment on our TV show."

Her stomach pitched, sloshing the water she'd drank. Damn, she hadn't thought about her rings. Quickly, she tucked her fingers beneath her thigh. "I've seen the show. You're doing really well, Keith."

He smiled. "Relax, this is off the record. But if you ever want to get your story out there, whether it's about wedding rings or your past, I'd be happy to interview you on IRB. Just putting it out there, I'm not pushing."

For a second, she thought of the potential. If she went on Rock Wives, she'd be able to talk about her special project, SLAM Heroes. It was a temptation, but—

"No," a sharp female voice said. "Absolutely not."

Liza's neck and shoulders tensed as she stood up. "Christine." The band's manager wore caged heels, slicked-on white pants, a draped silk shirt and a fierce expression.

The woman strode into the greenroom and flicked a look at Keith. "Shouldn't you be with the band?"

"My videographer is getting footage of the signing." Keith rose and added, "Liza and I are friends. Nothing she says to me in here is on the record." He turned to her. "You ever need anything, you have my contact info. Later." He headed out.

Christine shut the door and whipped around. "What are you doing? He's the media." She stalked across the floor. "Don't give any interviews, Liza. You're not the story. And don't you dare let it slip that you're married."

Back when she'd first met Christine, she'd been intimated. The woman was sophisticated, powerful, older and much more experienced than Liza.

Yeah, she was over that shit. She worked for a man who took scary to a new level.

"If I wanted to be the story, I'd have made it happen. I'm good enough to do that, Christine, and you might want to remember it. Get your facts straight before you barrel in here and irritate me. I'm nervous enough for Justice and the band without you buzzing around." And a little pissed that Christine had told Justice to hide their marriage and baby. *But Justice agreed, so who are you really mad at?*

Surprise flitted across her face. "Someone's been growing a backbone."

Liza went to the dressing table and perched her ass on the edge. No way would she sit down and allow herself to be smaller than Christine. "Is there something you need?"

"I don't suppose I can talk you into skipping the afterparty and the Vegas shows tomorrow and Sunday? Just watch the show tonight then go home and stay out of the limelight?"

"You supposed correctly." She hoped her morning sickness cooperated. Typically the first couple hours of the day sucked, then she was fine.

"I'm usually right. What I can't decide is if you're real or you got knocked up on purpose to get Justice to marry you before the album dropped." Sitting on the edge of the couch, Christine went on, "He refused to have you sign a prenup."

Huh. She hadn't known he'd considered it. "He never mentioned one."

The other woman checked her phone, tapping out a message. "Would you have signed it?"

Keeping her face blank, Liza said, "Guess we'll never know now." She'd have signed a reasonable prenup, but that was between her and Justice. It made her uneasy how much Christine knew that Liza didn't. What else had Justice and his business manager talked about in relation to her?

"True." Looking up from the phone, Christine let the prenup go. "Now, about tonight and this weekend. First you need to take off those rings."

Instantly she formed a fist with her left hand. "My wedding rings?"

"Yes. We've kept the fact that you're pregnant and Justice married you quiet. He'll announce it after the tour. Until then, don't let it leak." She glanced at Liza's hand. "The rings are a dead giveaway."

That was clearly true since Keith had noticed them, but she didn't like Christine telling her what to do. "What about Justice's ring?"

Annoyance flashed across her features. "He moved

171

it to his right hand. But yours are obvious wedding rings."

Liza moved her rings to her right hand. "Have I ever shown you my mother's wedding rings?"

Christine's mouth tightened. "That will bring up the subject of your mother, which leads right to Gene Hayes." Sighing, she said, "Look, I get it. You're in love, you want the world to know. But you didn't marry an average Joe, you married a rock star. I warned you months ago not to fall in love with him."

That had been the night the band lost *Court of Rock*. Yeah, Christine had warned her, and more. She'd also told her she knew Hayes preyed on young girls but hadn't done a thing to stop him.

"Justice's career is going to come first. And if you want that big payday, and the fame and power that comes with being the wife of a mega rock star, you'll do it. Now lose the rings, and don't go near the pressroom. You stay in your seat or the VIP Lounge. Do what you're told, then you and I will get along great."

"Wrong." It was time to establish her own boundaries. "Let's get something clear, you and me. You're Justice's business manager, but I'm his wife. I sleep with him, I have his children, and, lady, I have his heart. You don't come barreling in here, telling me who I can and can't talk to, whether or not I can wear my rings, or anything else. I won't be treated like a disposable groupie."

Christine lowered her chin, a dangerous glint in her eyes.

Liza didn't budge. Not her stance, her will or her gaze.

The business manager blinked first. "Fine. Would you consider removing your engagement ring and just wearing the band on your right hand when in public with Justice?"

Despite the frigid tone, Liza had won her point. "All right, that's a decent compromise." She switched the band to her right hand and tucked her engagement ring into her purse, then smiled.

After regarding her for a solemn moment, Christine said, "I want him to succeed, Liza."

She opened her mouth, but the door opened, and all the guys spilled in along with Keith and the video crew.

Justice rushed up to her. "You waited."

"I had to wish you luck before I go to my seat." She had seats in the VIP section, where Nikki, Emily and Ben waited with Sloane, Drake and a slew of other friends.

He leaned down, brushing his mouth over hers. "Damn, I'm hyped. And you are fucking hot in that dress. I can't go onstage with a boner." His eyes took on a wicked glint. "Let's find a dark corner. A closet. Any space I can get those panties off you."

She flicked her gaze over his shoulder, but everyone was talking...except Lynx, who'd put his headphones on, had his sticks in his hands and was trapping out some beat on the tabletop. No one could hear her and Justice. Shifting back to him, she whispered, "Who said I was wearing panties?"

A low, sensual groan slid from him. He brushed his hand over her hip. "Beth, fuck. You're killing me."

"Motivating you. Get out on that stage and do your job right, rock star, and you'll get the prize."

He arched a brow. "Money and fame?"

"Amateur stuff. I'm the real prize."

His face softened. "Damn right."

God she loved him. He made her feel this special when this was his moment. He was going on a stage where legends had performed. "Now go out there and rock the house, Rooster. You've got this. You were born to sing."

And she was born to love him. She just hoped that his love for her matched his ambition for stardom.

Justice paced backstage, hands shaking and heart pounding. Christ, it'd suck if he had a stroke right now. The adrenaline rush was as powerful as any drug he'd ever done.

Simon stood against a wall, ripped arms bulging out of the muscle shirt he wore, his jaw set.

Gray gazed at a torn and bent three-by-two-inch photo he always had with him when he performed.

Lynx held his sticks in one hand and fisted the medallion hanging around his neck in the other.

Justice honed in on River. "You taking your phone on stage?"

He glanced up from the device. "No. I'll hand it off in a second."

"Texting now?" Simon snapped.

"It's Cassie."

Justice drew back in surprise. "The girl who came to our last *Court of Rock* show?" He knew Beth stayed in contact with her.

"Yeah. She's wishing us luck." He tapped out a message, then handed his phone off to one of their skeleton road crew.

"You still talk to her?" Simon asked.

"Now and again. She's funny." He shrugged as if it wasn't a big deal.

Justice didn't buy that casual thing. "River—"

He held up a hand. "Don't. I know."

Lynx jerked his head up. "You know what?"

"Cassie. She comes from a regular-type home with people who care about her. The girl is way out of my league. We're just friends, and she's a kid. Barely eighteen. Not going near her, 'kay?"

Justice frowned. "That's not—"

The stage manager announced, "Five minutes. Time to get onstage."

For a second, Justice froze. This was it. The moment.

"We're going out there and hitting it like savages. Yeah?" Lynx said.

"Hell yeah." They all fist bumped. Justice took his guitar and, using the running lights as a guide, found his spot. Simon was on his right, River a step back in the center. Gray took his place at the piano, and Lynx settled in at his drum kit.

Seconds later the introduction began, including a recorded package playing over the big screens placed around the venue that would switch to views of the stage once the curtain went up.

"And now, here they are! Savaged Illusions!"

Applause and some screams broke out as the curtains rose. The colored lights flashed on. Justice raised his arms in greeting to the two thousand people out there clapping and waving their hands. "Hello, Los Angeles! We're stoked to be here tonight!"

"Damn right!" Lynx called out.

"Who's ready to rock?" Justice asked, prowling the lip of the stage, making eye contact with as many people as he could. Energy crackled and popped as the audience roared their excitement. The connection, that living force between him and the spectators, went live.

Justice spun and pointed. "Simon, let's give the

people what they want!" The spotlights dimmed everywhere except on the lead guitarist.

The man launched into the opening riff of "Expired Hero." The others joined in, each spotlight snapping back on. At his cue, Justice hit the first notes of the song. No holds barred, he went all out.

The concert had been freaking amazing. The entire venue had vibrated with the wild energy and the pounding beat of Savaged Illusions. By the final song, Liza's heart had damn near burst out of her chest in pride and joy. The applause had been thunderous. They'd rocked!

Now Liza, along with Em, Ben, Nikki, and some work friends, and a hundred other people, were ensconced in the exclusive Nosh VIP Lounge. The room was bathed in purple and white lights. A bar sat on the left, white leather couches ringed the space, and the center had high bar tables with leather stools. Savaged Illusions music pulsed over the speakers, and the atmosphere teemed with anticipation. The noise level rivaled any bar on a Friday night, and champagne flowed, along with trays of appetizers and desserts.

There were a few whispers too. *That's Elizabeth Ranger. Why's Justice with her?* People gawked at her and made comments, but she did her best to ignore it and sipped her cranberry-flavored sparkling soda.

"You need another one?"

She glanced up at Sloane. "No thanks."

Once Sloane walked away, Tess said, "Finally, now the boss is gone, we can party."

Liza laughed. "The boss brought you all in his limo just so you could party." He'd included Liza's friends,

Emily, Ben and Nikki too. None of them had to worry about driving home.

"Yeah, but he'll take a picture of me snoring and use it to blackmail me into picking up his dry cleaning or something."

"I'd pick up his dry cleaning," Nikki said in her dreamy-plotting voice.

"No!" Liza, Tess and Drake all said at the same time.

Nikki's eyes widened. "What? He's hot, rich and perfect."

Tess put her hand on Nikki's arm. "Trust me on this. He's a great boss and friend, but you don't want to get involved with him. He doesn't date, he makes deals."

"Really?" Her speculative gaze followed Sloane.

Emily rolled her eyes. "Are you that desperate?"

Nikki turned, her hair swinging and eyes frustrated. "My last date had his dog in the car when he picked me up."

"So?" Ben said. "That doesn't sound so bad."

"The dog had died when he was a teenager, but he'd had him stuffed. You know, taxidermy?"

Drake choked on his beer and laughed so hard he coughed.

Tess patted him on the back.

"Yep, I'm that desperate." Nikki finished off the few drops of champagne in her glass and popped up. "I'll go see if hunky Sloane needs help carrying the drinks."

She sashayed off, her sexy red dress swaying.

Liza sighed. "Crap, this could be bad."

"Nah, he'll set her straight," Drake said. "Sloane never gets involved with his employees, their family or friends."

That was true, and Sloane wouldn't be cruel to

Nikki. Relieved, she smiled at the older man across the table from her. It meant so much to Justice that Drake was here tonight. He couldn't ever replace Noah, but he'd provided a strong male influence as a mentor, and Justice wanted to make him proud.

And thinking of Justice—Liza checked her phone, wondering how much longer until he and the band got here. No message. But they'd had to change out of their sweaty stage clothes and do a couple interviews, so it could be a while yet. There was also media here in the VIP room, but so far they'd left her alone. Probably because Sloane and Drake scared them off. Liza suspected Justice had asked them to keep an eye on her.

Em nudged her shoulder. "Where's your ring?"

Setting her phone down, she took in her friend's too-bright eyes beneath heavy lids. "How much champagne did you have?" Okay, it was an attempt to distract her.

"Not enough to make me forget the question."

She glanced around to assure herself they wouldn't be overheard then answered, "Christine." She quickly summed up the encounter in the dressing room.

Em grinned and held up her glass. "Way to summon your inner bitch."

Liza laughed. "She used to scare me a little."

"So what changed?"

She considered that, but the truth was pretty simple. "I did." She'd stopped being so afraid, and a lot of that was due to Justice.

A mic came on. "Ladies and gentlemen, here they are, Savaged Illusions!"

A cheer went up as the guys all jogged in, slapping hands, hugging, and talking. The din of voices rose, and people clumped toward the band. Excitement pitched up, and Liza couldn't wait any longer. She pushed her way through, with Emily, Ben and Nikki on her heels.

"Justice! Over here!" a groupie called out.

"Lynx, I love you!" another one said.

People shouted and vied for the band's attention. Flashes went off as the guys accepted drinks and answered questions.

Christine was in the mix too, and when she saw Liza approaching, she shook her head in warning.

"Did she seriously just try to tell you no? Like you need her *permission*?" Emily shouted.

At that same second, Justice looked over. Seeing her, he broke away, rushed over to scoop her up and swung her around, forcing many people to stumble back to avoid being hit. Camera flashes went off. "So? Did I get the job done?"

As she looked down into his face to see a sheen of sweat mixed with high color and happiness, a rush of heat flashed through her. "You were amazing! The whole band was on fire! I think every woman in that audience had an orgasm watching you sing."

He held her in his arms with her feet still dangling. "Only one woman I want to make come." He dragged his hand over her hip. "You lied, you do have panties on."

She leaned close to his ear as folks around them snapped pictures. "People can hear us."

"I don't care. We did an interview with E! News. We're doing this, Beth. We're making our dreams come true."

She grinned and resisted the urge to kiss him. Not here. She opened her mouth, when a spray of something cold misted her face. "Hey!"

Lynx laughed. "Champagne!" He held up the spewing bottle. "Who wants champagne? 'Expired

Hero' just broke the top five hundred in iTunes on overall sales."

The whole place erupted in excitement. Music burst over the speakers, and they all danced and partied. Justice got pulled away to talk to people, pose for pictures and dance with groupies. Several girls climbed all over the guys under the guise of snapping a selfie with them.

Jealousy simmered, but Liza danced with her friends and told herself that she was the one going back to the hotel with Justice. She was the one he loved. And she wasn't going to be her mom, getting drunk, ridiculous and making a scene.

"I've struck out everywhere tonight." Nikki joined them with a fresh glass of champagne. "Sloane shot me down in two minutes, then I tried to chat up the cute guy with the tat sleeves."

Liza followed her hand gesture to the group by the bar. Justice stood there with several men who had full-arm tats, but she finally narrowed it down. "Keith?"

"He's hot, but he brushed me off. Said he's in a relationship." She sighed. "Let's dance and forget the boys."

"Beth!" Justice called as he broke away, weaving toward her. Catching her hand, he tugged her with him back toward the bar.

Startled, she laughed. "What's up?"

"It's midnight. The new numbers are out."

"Didn't they get the new numbers earlier?" Nikki asked.

Liza's pulse jacked as she quickly said, "They update continuously. Right now we're looking for momentum." She rushed over to her husband. "Well?"

Simon held his phone up. "Jagged Sin is down ten, and we're up another fifty!"

"Fucking A!" Lynx shouted. "The rock feud is on."

"Eat that, Jagged Assholes." River lifted a shot glass high in the air.

The party kicked into overdrive, and ten minutes later, after Liza had lost Justice to more pictures, she planted her butt on one of the couches. This was only the beginning, and the more famous Justice got, the more he'd be pulled away from her. If she was honest with herself, she worried that he'd get blinded by ambition and success, and Liza would become too much of an obstacle.

Especially since he won't claim you as his wife in public.

Internally wincing, Liza shook it off. She'd known what she was getting into when she married Justice, and this was his dream. He deserved it, and she was thrilled for him.

She looked around and spotted Lynx at a corner table making out with some chick—the third one she'd seen him with tonight. An idea hit her.

"Uh-oh." Emily walked over to her. "I know that smile."

"What are you up to?" Nikki demanded.

"Whatever it is, I'm getting a picture," Tess said.

It was totally perfect. She caught the eye of one of the hard-working waitstaff. "Can I get a bottle of champagne?"

The woman brought it and expertly opened it.

"Thanks. I'll take it from here." Rising, Liza marched over to Lynx, who had his hand up the chick's skirt.

Ewww.

Putting her thumb over the lip of the champagne bottle, she shook it and let the spray fly. She tried to aim for Lynx and spare the girl.

"What? Fuck!" Lynx shot up and spun, flinging drops of champagne off his arms.

Flashes went off, but Liza was so busy laughing, she barely noticed. "Payback's a bitch, drummer boy."

Lynx snatched the bottle from her, covered the lip with his thumb and started shaking it.

"Oh crap." Liza, Nikki and Emily all whipped around and ran, dodging people and laughing like lunatics. Her two friends were faster, and Liza thought for sure she was going to get drenched, when a pair of hard and familiar arms wrapped around her.

"Justice!"

His eyes gleamed. "Are you causing trouble?"

"As much as I can. And you?"

He laughed. "I just caught trouble, and now she's all mine." He swung her around in a crazy dance.

Liza clung to him, the whole room spinning and she hadn't touched a drop of alcohol.

Nope, she was high on happiness, and that exhilaration banished her tiny flickers of doubt.

Three hours later, Liza carried her shoes as they headed down the long hallway to their hotel room. "What a great night! Well," she amended, "except when that girl offered to suck your dick."

"She was drunk."

The groupies hanging on Justice had poked at her ugly insecurities and growing possessiveness. "Not that drunk, she was poaching my husband."

He laughed, pushing her up against their door. "I wasn't interested in her."

Liza looked up. His gaze was slightly unfocused. Justice had thrown back two shots and a few beers, but he'd never encouraged the groupies. "I don't care how famous you get, I don't share."

He leaned close to her. "Damn right you don't.

Forget the groupies, it's my wife I want. Let's go inside." He slid the keycard into the slot.

Once Justice opened the door, she walked into the big open room and froze. Rage raced up her back and slammed into her head. "What the hell?"

Right there on their bed was a woman. Naked.

Chapter 13

"OH FUCK." A NAKED GIRL on the bed in his hotel room was nuclear-level bad. He turned to his wife. "Beth, I'll handle this. Why don't you go—?"

She spun to face him, her face flushing, eyes glinting. "You'll handle this?"

"What he means is get out." The girl rose off the bed and strolled to them. "Why would he want a chunky thing like you when he can have all this?" She struck a seductive pose.

Justice couldn't fucking believe this. He knew from experience not to put his hands on the girl. It wouldn't be the first time someone tried to set him or any performer up. But his anger surged at that comment.

"Wrong," he barked, fury growing by the second. This was one of the best fucking nights of his life, and he wasn't letting some groupie tramp or gold digger ruin it. "I want you out of here." Taking Beth's arm, he tugged her with him past the girl to the phone. "Call security, Beth."

"You call them." She shrugged off his hold, picked up the girl's dress and threw it at her. "Get dressed."

The girl deftly caught the garment and dragged it on over her head. "Why did you give me the key if you were going to bring her here?"

Shit. "I didn't give you a keycard." Glancing at his wife, he said, "Don't touch her." He yanked up the phone, called hotel security and reported the incident.

After smoothing the red dress over her hips, the girl smiled at Beth. "I follow the band. Justice always gives me the key to his room. Now he's protecting me from you by telling you not to touch me."

His wife growled. Fucking growled.

"Goddammit." He lunged for Beth and missed. She strode straight up to the girl.

Stopping two feet from her, Beth slapped her hands on her hips and did the up-and-down-body-scan thing girls do. "You're not very good at this, are you?"

The girl's smile fell. "Whattaya mean?"

"I grew up with groupies. The good ones, they know their shit. They love music, I mean love it. They make connections and get invites to parties and hotel rooms. They don't have to bribe hotel clerks or whatever the hell you did to get in here."

"I had the key."

"Yeah? Where is it?"

The cornered expression on the girl's face would be a perfect GIF for *Oh shit I'm in trouble.* "I left it somewhere." She took a step as if looking for it.

Beth moved in front of her. "Name five songs on Savaged Illusions' album."

"What?"

His wife held up her hand, spreading her thumb and fingers. "Five songs from their new album. If you can't count, I'll do it for you." Curling all her fingers in except the index digit, she said, "Song number one?"

"Uh…" the girl stammered.

"Too hard? How about this then. What's his middle name?"

The girl's eyes darted around the room. "Whose?"

"Justice. You know, the man you claim gives you the keycard to his room all the time." Sarcasm dripped from every single word.

"I... Why would I know that?"

"It's on the Savaged Illusions website, dumbass. But you know what? I'll give it to you for free. His name is Justice Noah Cade." She leaned in close until they were almost nose to nose. "And he's mine. You try this shit again, and you're going to deal with me when I'm not in a good mood. You don't want to see me pissed, little girl. You. Do. Not."

The girl turned and hustled her ass out of the room, plowing right into two big security guys.

The first one steadied her, and the second said, "This the intruder?"

Justice strode to the door. "Yes. We found her in the room when we came in. No idea how long she's been here or how she got in."

"Would you like the police called?"

"No." None of them needed the headache. He had to get on a plane tomorrow to Vegas.

"We'll handle it, Mr. Cade. On behalf of the hotel, we apologize. Is there anything else we can get you?"

"No, thanks." After shutting the door, he engaged the swing lock and headed into the bedroom, where he stopped in surprise.

What was Beth doing? Justice watched as she ripped the comforter off the bed and stomped past him. She undid the lock, pulled open the door and threw it out in the hallway. After shutting and relocking the door, she stood there, panting.

For one second, he drank in the sight of her. She

had on the same dress she'd married him in. Ivory, with a single jeweled strap that started at the top of her left breast, snaked over her shoulder at an angle and ended in the middle of her back. The dress molded to her curves—curves he loved. Tonight, her hair was down, and she'd done something to tame her slightly kinky waves into big soft curls. She looked hot.

But watching her handle that girl in his room? "That growl in your voice made me hard as hell." He advanced on her, all caution forgotten. Oh she wasn't leaving him. Nope, she'd fought for him. He knew her—if her plan had been to leave, she'd be gone.

"What growl?"

"The possessive one." They were in the small hallway that opened into a dressing area and bathroom. But he couldn't look away from his fiery beauty or forget the way she'd claimed ownership of him. "You threw the bedspread out."

She tilted her head up, challenge riding her gaze. "That chick's ass was on that bed."

Feral need yanked him to her. He sank his hand in her hair, staring down into her furious eyes. "Say it again."

"What?"

"I'm yours. Say it."

"You're mine. I don't share. Not this." She grabbed his shirt, dragging it up.

He released her hair to tug the shirt off, then regained his hold.

"You want to get onstage and be everyone woman's wet dream, that's fine. But this..." She tore open his belt, undid the snap on his pants and shoved them down his hips.

Justice hissed as her hand wrapped around his hard

length. He was so hyped up, he surged into her hold. "My cock?"

"Yes. And your heart. They're mine."

He shuddered, the words more powerful than even her touch. He slammed his mouth over hers. Some part of his brain tried to remind him she was pregnant, but his more primitive side ruled. Clutching a handful of her dress, he wrenched it up while thrusting his tongue against hers, feeling the wet slide, as her fingers worked his dick.

Heat seared his balls.

But it wasn't enough. Seizing the edge of her panties, he tore them off her. She was his. She'd claimed him, now he had to have her. Bending his knees, he lifted her and pressed her back against the door.

"What I want is you. No one else, Beth." With his hands beneath her thighs, he spread her legs wide. "*Now.* I'm going to fuck you wearing the dress you married me in."

She guided his erection to her opening.

Wet, luscious skin bathed the head of his dick. A groan tore from his throat, but he didn't look away. It took everything he had not to ram inside her, claiming her. "The dress you vowed to love me in."

"Justice."

"You did this." He pushed in, her sweet heat clamping around his cockhead. "My super-smart, organized, romantic wife turned into a fiery hellcat when an invader tried to claim me." He thrust in, all the way, seating his cock in her. He stared into her eyes, her glasses magnifying a hot desperation that he alone could satisfy. It made him feel like a god. "There's no one else. Only you." He needed her to know that, to believe it.

She moaned, her thighs squeezing his waist. "Harder."

Oh hell yeah. She needed this, begged for it, propelled them to a savage mating as he gripped her thighs tighter, pulled out and plunged back in a primal urge to give her everything. Thrusting, pounding, driving himself in to sounds of the wet, fierce mating, which merged with their pants and groans.

Heat and pleasure chased down his back, his balls tightening at the feel of Beth, her slick, snug pussy milking him. "Give it to me, baby. Now." He tilted her hips, hitting the deepest, most sensitive part of her.

Beth slapped her head back against the door. "Yes. God." Her fingers clawed his shoulders.

Every scratch burned into his nerve endings, scrambling his sensors. She was marking him. That thought exploded, sending waves of wild heat through him.

"Justice!" She bowed, fingers digging in, thighs clamping him as she rode his cock and detonated, coming hard.

He thrust in one more time, and his world imploded. Burying his face in her soft neck, he lost himself in the fires of his orgasm.

Two weeks later, Liza approved the promo for an upcoming pay-per-view event for one of SLAM's biggest fighters. She'd checked and double-checked, and every change Sloane had asked for was done.

"Thanks, guys," she told the marketing team, and headed out of the office.

After taking out her phone, she marked that off her list. She'd pushed hard this morning, coming in early and working nonstop. Her heart tripped when she glanced at the time.

Twenty minutes until noon.

Justice and the guys were in New York, appearing on *Chatterbox*. This was huge. "Expired Hero" had slowly inched up the charts, but it hadn't broken the top one hundred. This could do it, no it *would* do it. When Fury Run appeared on the extremely popular talk show six weeks ago, their numbers had surged on music charts.

Liza stepped into the elevator, glanced at her reflection in the shiny panels and pressed a hand to her belly. At three-months pregnant, she wasn't showing yet, and her black-and-white dress still fit. How long before she couldn't hide it anymore? At work, only Sloane and Tess knew.

The elevator stopped, and Liza dropped her hand and headed into the reception area of the executive floor. She'd been Sloane's full-time administrative assistant for about six weeks and loved the challenge. Especially since her morning sickness had faded away, and she was a bit more energetic.

Tess looked up from her computer. "Sloane's plane landed a half hour ago. He's coming into the office. He has a meeting with his lawyers at two and wants all your real estate market research ready, and you'll accompany him."

Liza crossed to the kitchenette and eyed the freshly made coffee. Bummer, but she'd cut back. Instead, she grabbed a bottle of water and her lunch of sun-dried tomato and pasta salad. "I finished it this morning and have it all ready." Sloane moved fast when he made a decision, and Liza'd had a hunch he'd like the property for the new gym he wanted to open in Chicago.

"I'm going to eat lunch in the conference room, if he

gets in and needs me." There were TVs in there so she could watch Justice.

"I'll tell him, and I'll be there in a few minutes. I'm excited."

"Me too." Liza headed to the huge conference room. An oval table stretched down the middle, surrounded by cream-colored leather chairs. One wall had several big screens on it. Liza snatched up the remote, turned it on and muted it.

Her phone vibrated with a text from Em. *Are you watching?*

Just turned it on. You?

Em: *Of course, I've told everyone at the TV station here that I know Justice Cade.* Emily wrote copy and worked in production on the local San Diego news channel. *I'm almost a celebrity today. We have it on.*

Nerves buzzed in Liza's belly as she texted back, *I'm going to call him, talk later."* She switched to FaceTime and made the call.

"Hey." His image filled her screen.

The sight of him tugged hard in her heart. She missed him so damned much. "I wanted to wish you good luck. You guys are going to be awesome."

"We better be. This is huge, Beth. They get something like four-mil viewers. We go on in..." he glanced away, then said, "...eight minutes."

She smiled, feeling his energy crackling through the phone. "You've got this, Rooster. Just go out there and sing."

Before he could answer, another voice broke in with, "Justice, we need to walk to the stage entrance."

Obviously Justice wasn't alone. Liza repressed her annoyance with Christine's intrusion. Truthfully, the pushy-as-hell business manager was doing her job. Getting Savaged Illusions this gig on *Chatterbox* was a tremendous coup. "Go show the world your amazing talent. Love you."

"Love you too, Beth. Miss you." He disconnected.

Even after two weeks without him, it didn't get any easier. But she'd see him in Florida the weekend after next, if all went well. Then a couple weeks after that he'd fly home for her ultrasound.

They'd hopefully find out the sex of their baby.

But right now, *Chatterbox* was starting. Liza put her phone down, unmuted the TV, then opened her Tupperware container and took a bite of the pasta salad.

The hosts walked on, and the audience cheered and clapped. Liza settled back in the leather chair.

The door opened, spilling in Tess with her lunch, followed by Sloane.

"Wow, you made good time from the airport," she said to her boss. "I sent the real estate market research to your email. Are you preparing an offer today?"

He sat at the end of the table and thumbed through his phone. "Very likely." While reading, he asked, "Justice on soon?"

She assumed he was looking over the information she'd compiled. "Yes." Her nerves ratcheted up. *Chatterbox* did everything live. They went on at 3:00 p.m. in New York, which made it noon here in California. If the performance had any problems, even technical glitches, they were screwed. The audience tended to love it though. Some technical glitches went viral and ended up selling more units. *Please let it go well.*

In the back of her mind, playing on a loop, was the *Late Night with Alicia* memory when the talk show host had blindsided the band with a video of Gene Hayes. But that wasn't going to happen this time.

"Today our first guest is Savaged Illusions!"

Liza shifted her focus to the sixty-inch screen. This was it, the pivotal moment that would take Savaged Illusions into the top hundred sales. The guys ran out onto the stage, and all five of them headed straight to the audience, fist bumping the few guys, shaking hands with the girls.

The camera zoomed in on River as he eased an older woman to her feet and kissed her cheek.

She squealed in delight as he held her arm to retake her seat.

Liza sighed, falling half in love with River. Damn, that was a camera-perfect moment brimming with authenticity. It was so like River to do something just like that.

The guys returned to the stage and found their spots to perform.

"Well, after that exciting entrance," the host said, "here now to perform their single 'Expired Hero' from the new album is Savaged Illusions!"

The camera closed in as they launched into the song.

Liza turned up the sound, filling the conference room with Justice's powerful voice wringing out the anger of how the world only wants you when you're a hero, not a mortal man. She could feel the agony and rage. Goose bumps popped out on her arms as they hit the chorus.

A close-up of Justice's hand around the mic showed his bare ring finger. That gave her a pang, but she told herself it didn't mean anything—they'd agreed to keep their marriage quiet.

"They're amazing," Tess said.

Liza glanced over her shoulder and smiled, pride filling her chest.

Once the song ended and they cut for commercial, Liza breathed a sigh of relief at the band's flawless performance. When the show returned, they were all seated around a table. One of the two hosts, Wayne, started off with, "You guys have been steadily climbing the charts with 'Expired Hero.'"

"Thanks, we have awesome fans," Justice responded.

The audience cheered again. Then Wayne said, "You also have some enemies. Jagged Sin's labeling you guys liars and traitors to rock. All the headlines are describing the battle between your two bands as a rock feud."

"They can call us names all they want," Simon responded. "They've demonstrated they're sore losers. I have the scar to prove it." He touched the white line slashing across his cheek.

Good, Liza thought. Remind the audience that Ace and two other members of Jagged Sin were arrested after jumping Simon in a parking garage.

"It's pathetic," River added. "Jagged Sin can't win on their own, so they have to resort to underhanded tactics."

"It's been quite a year for you all," Wayne commented. "But especially you, Justice."

"That's an understatement," the other host, Toby, added. "Your girlfriend was stabbed and your father, a homeless veteran, arrested for the crime. It's like a soap opera. People can't make this stuff up."

Liza hissed in a breath, tension gripping her neck and shoulders.

Justice nodded. "It was pretty surreal. But all that's behind us now."

"You're the one who caught the real attacker." Wayne turned to the screen behind them, the one

194

showing Justice with a bleeding Hans up against a wall in Screech's Nightclub.

Liza fisted her hands, her food forming a lump in her stomach.

Toby added, "How is Liza now?"

Justice ignored the picture on the screen. "She's fine, my father's name was cleared, the real attacker is in prison, and life is good again. Now we, my band and myself, are able to do what we love most, get onstage and perform for our fans. Isn't that right, Lynx?"

She mentally high-fived Justice for skillfully turning the topic back to their music and including another band member.

"Exactly," Lynx answered. "Our concerts on this tour have been close to sold out, and we're having more fun than ever onstage." He glanced over at River. "And offstage, am I right?"

River fist bumped him. "Our fans like to party, and you know..." he turned his dark eyes to the camera, "...we like to party. Even Serious Simon here loosens up around our fans."

Simon smirked. "Serious? Well, compared to you clowns, I guess I am." He shook his head. "When I signed on for lead guitarist, I didn't know I'd also be the clown master, but someone has to keep you guys in line."

The audience laughed.

Gray leaned forward. "Simon has a weird clown phobia."

"And Gray is our biggest prankster," River said. "Do you have that video?"

"What video?" Simon demanded.

Gray flashed a smile so beautiful, Liza felt like she was right there in the room with them.

"The one I gave the hosts," Gray answered. "To

show how we break up the monotony of the long rides on the tour bus."

Wayne snickered, and Toby said, "Let's roll the video."

On the screen appeared a large bus with the words *Savaged Illusions* and their logo across the side. The camera swung around to a close-up of Gray at the steps.

He waved then put a finger to his lips in a signal to be quiet.

The camera view shifted to the inside of the bus, showing a camel-colored couch and small table across from a tiny kitchenette, and settled on a walkway lined with paneling. A door opened, and a man walked out wearing a pair of pajama bottoms.

Liza slapped her hand over her mouth, recognizing the video. Justice had sent it to her a few days ago. It was Simon wearing black bottoms, his back tanned and thick with muscles. He turned his head slightly, and the overhead lights caught the white scar running along his right cheek.

A second later, Simon reached a set of bunks set into the side of the bus. Both the top and lower bunks were closed off by individual dark-brown curtains.

Simon bent slightly—getting a nice shot of his tight butt in those soft cotton pants—reached for the first curtain on the lower bunk and wrenched it back. "Umph!" His back snapped straight, muscles bunched, and he jumped back. "What the hell?"

The camera panned in on the neatly made bunk with a garish, man-sized clown lying there.

Justice, Lynx and River burst into the frame, laughing their butts off. The video stopped, and they went back to the live studio.

Wayne grinned. "You want to rethink that clown-master title?"

Simon raised an eyebrow. "Oh, I got even. We have the best road crew, and they helped me set it up. During sound check, Gray walked to his piano, and the second he passed by, the clown sprang up out of it like a jack-in-the-box."

River said, "The clown is traveling with us on the tour bus now. We've named him Savaged Clown and are finding interesting locations to take pictures with him and post them."

Wayne jumped in. "You guys are having a lot of fun on the road, and it shows. But there are challenges."

Toby nodded. "Going back to your ordeal with Liza's attack. Liza seems to polarize the rock community with her past, and let's be frank, she was attacked by someone who hated her for her involvement with Gene Hayes."

Justice's face tightened, a slight tic forming in his jaw.

"Are you concerned she could be hurting or hindering your career?"

Liza gripped her fork in her fingers. These questions lurked in every interview, a time bomb waiting to explode.

"No," Justice said, his tone measured, then his eyebrows drew together, and he leaned in, looking into the camera. "But truth be told, I am a little worried about that clown. He's getting a lot of hits on social media. He might be trying to knock me off and steal my job as lead singer of Savaged Illusions."

The audience roared with laughter, breaking the tension, and the interview ended on a high note.

"Those boys are doing so well," Tess said, wrapping up the crumbs of her sandwich. "You must be really proud, Liza."

"I am." She closed up her pasta salad container and

breathed out a huge breath, releasing tension she hadn't even realized she'd been holding. Savaged Illusions performance and interview had been flawless.

And there'd been no sign of her deepest fear—Gene Hayes. Maybe he really was going to leave her alone. He wasn't going to be able to ruin Justice's success, Liza's life or their marriage.

Chapter 14

JUSTICE'S EYES BURNED WITH GRIT, but his adrenaline kept him wired. They'd boarded a plane after Wednesday's performance, hit New York, did the TV show, hopped another flight, and now they were in a Houston hotel for the night. After their concert tomorrow, it was back on the bus to make their way through Texas.

Right now, he was stretched out on the bed, talking to his wife on the cell phone with his tablet on his lap.

"You need to sleep," Beth said.

"Says the pregnant woman. It's close to midnight there."

"Can't. I'm too excited. I can't even write, I just hit refresh over and over on my laptop."

He groaned, thinking of Beth sitting in their bed with piles of pillows behind her, laptop balanced on her thighs and glasses sliding down her nose. "Me too." He hit refresh on his tablet. "Oh shit. Eighty-six. We're at fucking eighty-six." "Expired Hero" was climbing up the charts.

"I see it! Look at you guys go."

His head ached with fatigue, but he didn't care. "I

can't believe this is really happening. I wonder if my dad knows."

"I'll text him tomorrow, but I bet he watched the show today."

He smiled at that. Beth had sent his dad videos of Justice's performances. Noah rarely answered her, but the counselor at the transitional center suggested they keep that line of communication open.

"We know Jagged Sin watched," she added. "They've been putting out all kinds of trash talk on their social media."

"Losers." He didn't want to talk about them or have Beth remember their connection to Gene Hayes, especially right before she went to sleep. She still had nightmares about that bastard. He changed the subject to one that made them both happy. "I've been thinking about your book. Your heroine sleeps with the lead singer, then he ignores her, and she almost sleeps with the bassist."

"Right. To make the hero jealous."

"Beth, she likes that bassist. A lot."

"I know, but..." She hesitated for a heartbeat. "She can't sleep with both."

He pushed her. "Why not? The lead singer is sleeping with other girls."

Her silence spread.

"Talk to me," he prompted. Discussing her book was their thing. It was important to him as a way to support her dreams after all she was doing to support his. He didn't want to be the husband and lover who could only talk about his career.

"I want her to get pregnant. If she sleeps with the bassist...she won't know who the father is."

A zing went down his back, the hot recognition of something so special—like when he nailed the words to a song he was writing. He also knew exactly what was holding her back. Beth wrote tidy little romances where bad things were headed off at the last minute *before* they happened. The heroines hovered on the brink of disaster but made the good choice.

The respectable choice.

The safe choice.

But this book screamed for more. For the truth of doing the wrong thing. Excited, he blurted out, "She's in love with both men. It's there, Beth, right fucking there in the pages. When the bassist touches her, she's terrified of how much she wants him when she's in love with the other singer."

"But when she gets pregnant..."

Justice couldn't hold back and jumped into her pause. "It'll rip the band apart. Let her do it. Take the reins off your heroine. Let her be a groupie who falls for both men. Let them really fight for her."

"And one lose?"

"Or both win. What if you wrote something totally forbidden? Sharing happens all the time, but showing two stars committed to one girl? Now that's some power."

"I don't know."

He wanted to reach through the phone and touch his wife, pull her in his arms and soothe her fears while at the same time pushing her to grow as a writer. "Stop censoring. Remember how you told me you found your voice after you went to college? That's why you chose to get your degree in communications?"

"Yeah?"

"Your voice is maturing. Let it happen. Just write, don't worry about where it goes, and send me the pages. It's only you and me who will see it. You can delete it if you hate it."

"It feels risky."

Her voice vibrated with excitement and uncertainty. "Scared?"

"Yes. It feels wicked, and God, I want to do it."

He laughed, the sound rippling up from his belly. "That's my girl. Write it."

"Could you do it? Share a woman?" She let it hang there for a second then said, "The truth."

"A woman? Yeah. I've done it. And I've been with two women. But you?" Fiery possession lanced his gut. "No. Never. I'd kill the man who touched you." Once he started talking, words spilled out. "I can't even stand the thought of Dillion in the same room with you. I know he's touched you, had you, and I want to kill him for that." Yeah, that was honest and a bit homicidal.

"I've noticed."

"Told you, I'm not subtle. When it comes to you, I'm anything but." He touched the headset he used to talk to her while in bed, wishing he could touch her. "I love you, Beth."

"I love you too. And you know what else?"

"You better not tell me you have a fantasy of two men." He'd give her anything else but that.

"Nope. Well, I mean it'd be hot—"

"Beth." That came out a growl, low and feral. She was his. Only his.

Her laughter trilled through the line. "—to write that scene."

He grinned. That he could live with.

"Justice! Hit refresh! You're now eighty-five. 'Expired Hero' is still climbing!"

He closed his eyes, absorbing the joy. "We're getting closer. All our dreams are going to happen."

His dream of superstardom.

Her dream to write.

Their marriage and child. They were going to have it all.

Liza was going to hate herself later for not getting much sleep, but she was too wired now to care. She'd woken at five, checked the numbers for "Expired Hero." Seventy-eight! She couldn't sleep after that and didn't want to wake Justice by calling him.

Instead, she grabbed her laptop and couldn't type fast enough. She loved this story about a twenty-year-old groupie that no one wanted...until two men wanted her.

When she looked up, it was almost seven. She'd have to hustle to get to work by eight. She dressed, dotted on a little concealer and mascara, and tamed her hair into a twist. After leaving the bathroom, she picked up her phone off the nightstand and calculated the time difference. It was seven thirty here and Texas was two hours ahead, so about nine thirty. Would Justice be up? He had a concert tonight, and she didn't want to cut short his sleep.

Deciding it'd be better to call him later from work, she headed out of the room, when her phone buzzed in her hand.

She smiled and answered, "You're awake, did you see it? 'Expired Hero' is at seventy-eight!" It hadn't budged since then, but—

"Beth, turn on the news. Christine called... This isn't good."

Crap, something must have happened. "What's going on?"

"Gene Hayes."

That name sliced her with a blade of cold dread,

and her heel caught on the old shag carpet. Liza slapped her hand down on the back on the couch. "What's he done?"

"She just got word that Gene Hayes is releasing a video. Turn on the news."

Don't panic. After rushing around the couch, she grabbed the remote. Once the flat screen came on, she flipped to a network morning show.

A serious-faced anchor said, "Here now is the just-released video feed from Gene Hayes and one of his lawyers."

Lawyers? He had lawyers? Buzzing pitched up in her head. Her fingers went numb as that hated face appeared on the screen. *Gene Hayes.* He had his dark hair pulled back in a ponytail, with one piece falling over his forehead. Hayes had Johnny Depp eyes that she'd once thought sexy, but now they turned her stomach. Liza couldn't think, her mind cluttered with images. *Hayes wearing only pants, handing her that drink. His voice telling her they were alone. Feeling sick and so scared, wanting her mom...*

Then nothing.

Pain bloomed in her wrist. Glancing down, she saw a spot of blood well at the edge of her oversized watchband. She'd shoved the edge in, cutting her skin. She dragged in a breath. *Stop it, you're safe. He's not in the room with you.*

"Beth, you there?" Justice said.

"Yes. I have it on." Hayes sat at a cloth-covered table with a microphone in front of him, as if it were an official news conference. Beside him sat a youngish woman in a prim dark-gray blazer over a white blouse, very lawyerlike. Liza turned up the sound.

"Today, my lawyers filed the papers to overturn the bogus and radically unfair verdicts against me in the

United States. We've amassed an incredible amount of evidence that Elizabeth Ranger, who is now going by Liza Glasner, is a liar and schemer."

What evidence? That one picture of her he'd shown before? Or that she was dating a rock star? It was old news.

"Liza has tried to convince the world she was a victim, and just a college girl working hard to rebuild her life. It's a lie, a carefully crafted image that's a complete and utter falsehood designed to hoodwink us. But my lawyers and I have spent months compiling the truth of who Liza really is. Let's start with this little video of Liza in Las Vegas."

Liza gaped as a short clip came up of her singing the karaoke song, "Oops!...I Did It Again." She was in front, flanked by Nikki and Em, and belting out the chorus, shaking her hips, leaning forward, her face flushed, eyes bright. Her birthday. She clutched the phone tighter. "Oh God. Where'd the come from? How'd he get it?"

"I don't know. But if that's all he has—" Justice cut himself off as Hayes reappeared on the screen.

"Or here at the same party when she attacked Ace Hollis from the band Jagged Sin."

A still shot of Liza filled the screen. Her face was contorted in rage, and she had her hands on Ace's chest, clearly shoving him back. Ace had both hands out, trying to get his balance as he fell into the pool.

"That's not what happened." The words came out a painful whisper. Yeah, she'd pushed him, but the viewers weren't seeing the way he'd pushed Nikki first and provoked Liza.

"Easy, Beth. I'm right here."

His voice was, but in reality Justice was almost fifteen hundred miles away in Houston, Texas.

"Or this of her partying at Club Nosh's VIP room."

More pictures of her dancing at Club Nosh flashed by, finished off with one of Liza holding a bottle of champagne, spraying Lynx.

Hayes reappeared on the screen. "In case you're still not convinced, did you know that Liza got herself knocked up? And then managed to convince Justice Cade it's his kid and get him to marry her? They're keeping it a secret and lying to the fans of Savaged Illusions."

An ultrasound picture appeared with her name and the date in the left-hand corner. Before Liza could fully comprehend that, a document appeared on the screen.

"That's our marriage license." How was Hayes getting this stuff? She didn't understand.

"That's public record, but the ultrasound isn't," Justice said.

Hayes reappeared. "See the dates? The ultrasound is roughly one month before their wedding. Liza sealed the deal with Justice Cade one week before Justice and his band Savaged Illusions released their new album and single. Which means Liza now gets half of all Justice's earnings as a rock star. And it looks like her gamble is paying off. The band is on tour, and they're making a splash. Reviewers are talking about them as the possible breakout band of the year.

"She's got her claws in Justice, and the dumb kid doesn't even know it. Now she's living in his house, waiting for him to make it big, and then she'll ruin him, their band and everyone connected. Let me ask you this, music lovers: Do you want to support this blackmailing, life-destroying woman? Because every time you go to a Savaged Illusions concert, buy one of their songs, even listen to them on a streaming station, you're supporting her."

Hayes paused, his dark eyes radiating false concern. "To Savaged Illusions, and most especially Justice Cade, I'm telling you now, man. Wise up and leave this woman. Find a way to get your kid away from her...if it *is* your kid."

Hot rage flashed over her skin and boiled her insides. *If it's his kid?* "How dare he? That man's a rapist and a felon, and he dares to question my character?" Her voice shuddered with the blinding force of her anger. This was her child that bastard was talking about.

"As for me," Hayes went on. "I'm fighting these charges with everything I have. Every. Thing. I'm going to win, and then I'm going after Elizabeth Ranger or whatever she calls herself now, with any legal means I have. She must be stopped. I don't want other lives crushed and devastated the way she and her parents did mine.

"And to my fans and supporters, thank you. I wouldn't have made it this far, wouldn't have endured the absolute loneliness of being unfairly branded as a rapist, without your amazing and heartfelt support. You are part of the reason I'm fighting back so hard. I want vindication for you as well as myself." He stared into the camera. "Together we will triumph."

The screen switched back to the newsroom. "This is a bombshell. For more than six months, we've heard little from Gene Hayes."

"That's right," a female anchor chimed in. "But now he's burst back on the scene, and he's got serious credibility with the powerhouse law firm Reyes and Salt."

Liza tried to get air in her lungs, tried to think, but all her anger and frustration made it difficult to focus. "He can't do this."

"He did. And he's going to fuck us up."

"Us?" Dread kicked her hard. "You and me?" Was he doubting her now? Wondering if the baby was his, or—?

"No. Don't be absurd. I'm talking about my band. Our single is climbing the charts, and Hayes just told the whole damned world we're liars, that you're a scammer, that I'm a goddamned moron and...fuck."

Tension balled in her stomach. "Oh." Of course he was upset. They'd worked their asses off, and Hayes was threatening their success. Because of her.

"Beth." Some of the anger in his voice softened. "I don't mean to snap at you. Are you okay?"

Realizing her legs were shaking, she sat on the couch. On the TV screen, lawyers were popping up, discussing what it meant that Hayes had filed appeals and writs and how he was convicted in absentia and whether or not that would hold up if he got an appeal. Her biggest nightmare was being put into clinical legalese that meant nothing to her.

She tried to answer her husband's question. "I don't know. Is the media going to descend on me again?" Hayes was in hiding outside the country. Most believed he was in a small principality that bordered France and Spain. So she wasn't afraid he'd physically show up, but what about the media? Or another lunatic like Hans who was swayed into trying to harm her by Hayes's rhetoric? "What should I do?"

"Is anyone outside the house?"

She hadn't looked. Getting up, she crossed to the window and peeked out the blinds. "Not that I can see."

"Go to work. At least you'll be safer there. Text me when you're inside SLAM."

That made the most sense, but part of her wanted

to stay here and hide. "What about tonight? What if reporters are here?" For the last two weeks she'd been alone, but it wasn't bad. If she couldn't sleep, she talked to Justice, if he was still up, or wrote. But now? "I don't have anywhere else to go." She couldn't go home to Santa Barbara. She hadn't talked to her family in well over six months. They didn't even know she was pregnant. *Well they know now, don't they?* That thought tightened her throat.

"Beth," Justice's voice cut in. "Easy, sweetheart. I wish I was there with you, but I'm trapped in Dallas so we'll do this together by phone. The first thing is to get you out of the house until we understand the fallout of the video. Do you feel safe enough to get to your car and drive to work, or should I call Drake and he'll come get you? Then tonight you can stay with Em or Nikki."

He was offering to send Drake because Justice knew she felt comfortable and secure with him. His thoughtfulness helped, yet part of her wanted to beg him to come home. She even opened her mouth to confess she needed him.

Then she shut it. He couldn't leave without breaking his tour contract, and the band would have to pay to reimburse the tickets plus fines if they missed any concerts.

"Beth, talk to me, please," Justice said. "I need to know you're okay. Drake will be there in fifteen or twenty minutes if I call him."

"No, don't do that." Twice now, Justice had come to her rescue. The first time Hayes released his horrible video, Justice had walked offstage and come right to her. He'd had her stay at his house where she was safe. Then after she was stabbed, he'd taken care of her, moved her things into his house...and now he needed her to handle this.

Determination steeled her spine. "I'll call Drake if I need him, but I think I can handle things here, and you do what you have to there." Plans began to form in her head. It was Friday, so she'd be off for the weekend. Hurrying to the bedroom, she pulled an overnight bag from the closet. "This might blow over. But since word is out now that we're married, I can fly out this weekend, and we'll make a statement together. We'll explain that you didn't want to put your child at risk. After all, I was attacked last June by a man influenced by Hayes's vicious rants. Get the fans on your side. And with me there with you, it'll show them we're not hiding, we're putting our baby's safety first." Liza threw in a few essentials, pajamas and a change of clothes.

"I'll run that by Christine and her publicity department. Text me when you get inside the office, don't forget."

"I won't." Liza gazed at the bed, the one she shared with Justice. Even when he wasn't there, she talked to him while in that bed. Last night and early this morning, they'd been so thrilled, while watching together as his song climbed the charts, and talking about her book. When it was just them, they were close and happy, and now Gene Hayes was threatening that. Apprehension wormed in. "Justice, I love you. We're going to get through this."

"I love you too. Be careful. And, Beth?"

"What?"

"No cutting. Swear it. Don't let that fucker make you cut. Especially now when you're pregnant with our kid."

She lifted her left wrist, the faint smear of blood on her pale skin an accusation. But she hadn't done that on purpose. She hadn't intentionally cut in years now. "I won't."

She meant it. Hayes had taken enough from her and her family. He wasn't getting any more of her blood. Beth wasn't that naïve girl she'd been seven years ago, or even as fragile as she'd been last year.

She could handle this.

Simon muted the TV. "I can't fucking believe this. It's happening again."

Justice poured out more coffee from the two carafes in Simon's room. "You knew Liza was pregnant and that we're married."

"He's right," River said. "This isn't quite the same as last time Hayes released a video, but it's still a problem. He's targeting our fans, and right after our appearance on *Chatterbox*."

"But will they listen?" Gray said. "He's a felon that fled the country."

Simon's laptop chimed.

"That's Christine." Simon accepted the call and positioned the computer on the dresser by the TV.

Christine stared out at them, her eyes grim. "I warned you, Justice. Hayes is a devious bastard, and we know he invested in Jagged Sin. He wants them to succeed and you to fail. You're not only in the way of his band's success, but he wants to destroy Liza."

Anxiety burned like a motherfucker in his gut, but he wasn't throwing his wife to the wolves. He folded his arms over his chest. "I'm not rehashing this, Christine. We're married. Liza offered to fly out and make a joint statement. We can say that we kept our marriage quiet to protect our child, as Liza was attacked in the past. And that attacker had a connection to Hayes."

She shook her head. "Having Liza involved in a statement will draw attention to her, and that's the last thing we want. Tell her to lay low and say nothing. We'll draft a press release that yes, you're married and you're expecting your child this summer, but right now, you're focused on your music, the band and your fans."

Worry for Liza nudged at him. His need to protect her pushed him to either get home or bring her here with him so he could keep her safe. But it'd been after a show that she'd been stabbed last June, so maybe it was better to keep her away for this weekend. One glance at the stone faces of Gray, Lynx, River and Simon added to that last thought. "All right. I'll tell her."

"You'd better find this leak, Justice. How did Hayes get all that information? He has to have a source."

"Jagged Sin," River said. "Ace and Mick were at that pool bar in Vegas. Any one of them could've gotten a hold of someone else's picture of Liza pushing him in the pool."

Justice agreed. "Ace baited her that night, calling out for the DJ to play one of Gene Hayes's songs. I didn't think too much of it then. That's the kind of asshole Ace is. But maybe he did it on purpose. It's possible one of Jagged Sin's band members was hovering around and took that shot."

"True. As for marriage licenses, they're public record," Simon added.

All that made sense, but what bugged Justice was, "How'd he get that ultrasound picture? It looked like the still shot we were given when we left the doctor's office. How the hell would anyone know about that?" He couldn't figure it out.

"Find out," Christine said. "We need this stopped.

Tell Liza to be more careful. She needs to make sure things don't get into the wrong hands."

Justice dropped his hands on the dresser, leaning in. "Liza's lived her life careful since she was fourteen years old."

Christine didn't flinch. "Not that careful. I had to tell her to take her rings off at opening night. She didn't post that ultrasound picture online somewhere, did she?"

"No." That was absurd. "Liza keeps the picture in her wallet, which is in her purse." A thought struck him. "Oh shit. She had it in her purse when she was with me on opening night. She switched to one of those little purses and left her bigger bag in the room."

Christine frowned. "Are you thinking the hotel staff got it or something?"

"There was a naked girl on our bed when we got back to our room that night. Liza was furious, I called security." Frustration bounced and gnawed at him. "That girl could have been snooping. Maybe she was put up to it by Jagged Sin." His eye twitched with his frustration.

"Did security take a report?"

"No. They just escorted her out. I can ask the hotel if they kept information on her."

"Without a police report, I don't think they'll release anything to you," Christine said. "You should have called me. That's what I do, advise you on these things for reasons like this."

"You didn't tell us this either," Simon snapped.

He'd been too hyped and, frankly, hot. Beth's possessiveness had been a huge turn-on, but he also hadn't wanted her embarrassed and worrying about the guys teasing her. She was giving him a hell of a lot of trust. "Because I thought it was handled."

"What else was in the room?" Christine asked.

Justice tried to remember. "Liza's laptop, but she locked that in the hotel safe."

"Are you sure?"

Was he? "As much as I can be."

"Okay," Christine went on. My people are at the courthouse looking to see what Hayes's lawyers filed. I assume it's a motion to overturn the verdict, and that's going to take a long time. But you need to think about protecting the band."

"What the hell do you think I'm doing?" He was here instead of on a goddamned plane going to his wife. *What should I do?* Her shock and fear had trembled in that question. But he had to believe she could handle this. She wasn't the same girl as the last time Hayes blindsided her with a video.

"I'm thinking of your record company. Hayes can't sue Liza in U.S. courts while the verdict stands. But if he gets it overturned, he can bring a huge suit against her. You're married, and you didn't get a prenup."

Shit, shit, shit. He rubbed his hand over his head. "They can't touch our company, can they?"

"I'll check into it," Christine said. "But you need to get her to sign a postnuptial that S.I. Records is not part of the marital assets. She must agree to relinquish any and all claim on the company."

Justice could feel the stares on him from the other guys. "Anything else?"

Christine looked away then back. "Your numbers are holding this morning on the music charts. That's something. Let's go forward. We'll do the press release, you keep on your schedule, and if Liza's name comes up, change the subject. We're going to do a publicity blitz about breaking onto the top one hundred of the charts. Go. We have a busy day."

Justice grabbed his cup of coffee and headed back to his room to shower. He pulled his phone out, but there was no text from Liza, so she wasn't in her office yet. He shot off a quick message of, *Call when you can.*

Chapter 15

LIZA HAD A HEADACHE AND hadn't eaten before leaving the house. Anger and fear had teamed up with that last smidge of morning sickness to torture her stomach.

Once inside the lobby at SLAM, four different people popped up from the sitting area. They had to be reporters. Phones rang incessantly. Glancing at the desk, she saw Sophie had a second person helping her. Both women looked frazzled. Sophie said into her phone headset, "I can give you her email to make a request. No she's not in yet." Sophie's gaze hit hers, anger sharpening the colors in her hazel eyes.

Liza's stomach turned over at the confused betrayal there. When she'd been an intern, she'd helped out at this desk with Sophie a few times and had occasional lunches with her. They were casual friends. Now Sophie must feel blindsided and hurt to find out that Liza was married and pregnant. She barely had a second to process that before other voices called out from the waiting area.

"Liza! What's your reaction to the Gene Hayes video?"

"Miss Glasner! Is it true you trapped Justice Cade?"

"Mrs. Cade, will you recant?"

"Liza—"

Determined to keep her composure, she focused on the reporters. "I have no comment on my personal life. If you'd like to talk about SLAM, please go through the proper channels."

A door opened, and a man strode out wearing a black polo shirt with SLAM SECURITY on the back. He stepped in front of Liza, facing the reporters. "Unless you have an appointment, you'll need to leave." He easily got control of the reporters and herded them out of the building.

She breathed out a sigh of relief then faced Sophie. "I'm sorry this has blown up. We were planning to announce our marriage and the pregnancy in a few weeks."

Sophie looked away. "Sure." She answered the next call.

Liza hauled her tired body and baggage of guilt into the elevator. She'd never thought about how her friends at work might feel when the news of her marriage and pregnancy came out. But then, she hadn't thought it would come out like this.

The elevator doors slid open, and she walked out. "Morning, Tess." She looked pretty in a teal shirt today, and her face was sympathetic.

"You okay? I can't believe all the stations ran that video."

She really didn't know what she was at this point. "I'm shocked, I guess. Mad, upset, scared. Sophie downstairs in reception is angry, and I never thought about..." Liza trailed off. "Does she think I trapped Justice?"

"She's surprised, Liza. She had no warning or inkling, but think about it. She's protected you a few times by screening reporters and handling a few of Justice's super fangirls trying to get to you for whatever reason their hormonal brains dreamed up."

Guilt dug in deeper. When Liza first started here, there'd been a lot of curiosity and some suspicion about her. Over the weeks and months, people had gotten used to her and began to see Liza, not her past and Justice's fame. They trusted her.

And now this.

"I'll apologize again. I didn't know this was going to happen. I'd never let them be blindsided." This was how Justice's band had felt when that first video came out.

"They'll get past it. Right now everyone just feels a little..."

"Betrayed."

Tess sighed. "It'll blow over. But for now, you have a ton of messages from reporters calling to get your comments."

Her phone had been buzzing nonstop. Oh! She needed to text Justice that she'd arrived at work safely. After pulling her cell from her purse, she winced at the sheer amount of calls and texts. Then she saw Justice's message and called him.

"Hey," he answered. "I only have a minute before we have to run to another interview."

"Did you talk to the guys and Christine? Want me to book a flight?"

He paused. "Let's keep our plan for you to meet me in Florida next weekend."

Liza went into the small hallway that led to a kitchenette, trying to tamp down her irritation. "You don't want to handle this together?" Why did this feel like she was being cut out, shoved aside and hidden?

"I don't want you attacked by a crazed fan stirred

up by Hayes and in some kind of crowd frenzy. That's what I'm most worried about. I want you and our baby safe."

His words rolled over her, calming the part that deep down worried his chase for fame would come before her and their child. And it made sense. "Next weekend then."

"Christine brought up a good point about where Hayes is getting his information."

Liza made some tea while listening as Justice explained what he, the band and Christine had discussed. "I had the picture of the ultrasound in a plastic photo sleeve in my wallet. So you think it was that groupie room crasher?" Who else would have seen it? She'd only shown it to Justice and a couple friends.

"Maybe. Either Hayes or Ace could have put her up to it. And clearly he timed this video release to coincide with our *Chatterbox* appearance to put a wrench in our climb up the charts."

And using her to do it. "I haven't looked since I got up this morning. Where are your numbers on the single?"

"Holding at seventy-eight."

She blew out a breath. "That's good, right? There's no loss of momentum. Hayes isn't having an effect."

"Too soon to really tell. I have to get to the local radio station. You'll be okay? I don't want you scared. If you can't handle things there, I'll figure something out."

She stared into her tea. *Be strong, you can do this.* "No. I'm fine. Go, and good luck. Keep the momentum going."

"Love you, later." He hung up.

She grabbed a health bar from the drawer of samples they always had from distributors, opened it and took a bite. *Ugh.* It tasted like dried bran cereal. She made herself take another couple bites while she accessed her work email on her phone. She repressed a groan at the sight of her mailbox.

Tess came in and poured some coffee in her cup covered in bright yellow daffodils. "More problems?"

"There's twenty-five media requests in just the last hour." She tossed the remainder of the health bar in the trash can. "I need to talk to Sloane, then deal with this." It was going to be a long day.

Tess touched her shoulder. "Let me know if you need help or a place to stay."

She appreciated that. "Thank you. But you have kids, and I'm not putting them at risk." She rubbed at the scar behind her neck, then realized what she was doing and stopped. "I'll be fine." After quickly dropping off her purse and tea in her office, she hustled to Sloane's office. She knocked then stuck her head in. "Now a good time?"

He shut his laptop. "Come in."

She tried to read her boss's face, but better people than her had attempted that feat and failed. He was dressed in his usual dark suit, with his hair combed and jaw set. Going to the chair in front of his massive desk, she stood there awkwardly. "I had no idea that Hayes would release that video."

He held up a hand. "Don't waste time with the obvious." His dark eyes flickered with something raw and ruthless. "Hayes is a predator trying to discredit his victim. He's not the first or the last scumbag rapist to try this blame-the-victim shit."

The anger vibrating there wasn't only about her. It was his past, and yeah, she'd Googled him, but it wasn't her place to bring it up. This had clearly touched a nerve for Sloane personally as well as professionally. However, her boss wasn't the type of man to swap stories on their pasts, so she focused on business. "Thanks. How do you want to handle this?"

"Draft a statement that makes it clear you keep your personal and professional life separate. You will, as always, be available to handle any media questions or inquiries directly related to SLAM Inc. We'll post that on our website and send it in release. Otherwise, do your job." He leaned forward. "Am I correct that you can handle this job even when it's personally challenging?"

In other words, suck it up. It wasn't that Sloane didn't care, it was that he didn't fold. He fought back. Much like Justice did. Her husband was going out to give radio interviews and fight for his spot on the music charts.

Liza wouldn't fold either. "Absolutely," she answered, already feeling better with a plan. "I'll get to work on the statement. Once we have that finished, I'll use that in response to the emails, etc." She pulled up Sloane's schedule on her phone, although she already knew this one. "You have a lunch meeting with the writer pitching the reality TV show at 1:00 p.m. at Opulence Dining. Portia from SLAM Entertainment has it on her calendar as well." She lifted her gaze. "Will I be going with you?"

"Yes." He opened his laptop, clearly finished.

Liza walked out. Okay then, time to tackle her job, because she wasn't letting Hayes destroy her life.

"The adult-diaper business must be picking up." Liza looked around the pretty condo Nikki had just moved into.

Nikki snorted. "Nope, my dad helped me out, and I'm renting. I had to suck up to the stepwitch, but it's worth it."

Liza walked through the living room, and damn, she loved that red chair paired with the gray couch and a red-and-gray rug. To the left was a small formal dining room, and ahead a kitchen done in gray quartz countertops, white cupboards and stainless-steel appliances. "This all happened so fast, I guess I haven't caught up. So what made you decide to reach out to your dad and stepmom?"

"Yeah, I'm curious too." Em handed over a bottle of wine she'd brought with her and sat next to Liza at the bar.

Nikki pulled out a corkscrew and got to work on the bottle. "I got a notice that my landlord was raising the rent. I had enough, you know? So I ate my pride and made the call." She popped the cork.

"None for me." Liza got up and grabbed a bottle of water from Nikki's fridge.

"Must have been an awkward conversation," Em said.

Liza had to agree, given all the shit Nikki said about her stepmom.

Nikki shrugged. "I don't want to talk about it. We do what we have to, and move on."

Seeing that Nikki was uncomfortable, Liza felt for her. After all, Liza rarely talked about her mom in prison, and she never talked about her dad.

Retaking her seat at the bar, she changed the subject. "I love this island." She smoothed her hand over the cool gray surface. "You know the wall between the kitchen and dining room of my house? We could take that out and do an island like this. Then put in wood floors and paint." But she'd keep all the chickens.

She wanted to update while retaining some of the character and connection to Justice's grandmother.

Nikki leaned on the counter across from them. "Justice is doing great. You can probably buy a new condo or house soon. Maybe even in someplace swanky like Malibu."

Her heart tugged at the thought of leaving their home. "I don't want to move. I love that house." And they needed to be there for Noah.

Nikki's phone trilled, and she picked it up, listened and answered with, "Okay, buzzing you through." Hanging up, she explained, "Pizza guy at the gate. He'll be here in a minute."

"I'm starved," Em said. "Pizza's on me." She pulled out her card and handed it to Nikki.

"No, I can't let you do that." Liza reached for her purse. Her friends had given up their Friday night to commiserate with her over the Hayes video, and both had offered to have her stay with them. "I'm paying for the pizza."

After relinquishing her card, Em tugged Liza's hand away from her purse. "Probably the last one I'll be able to buy for a while, so enjoy it."

Confused, she eyed her best friend while Nikki answered the door. "Why? Is something wrong? Did you have an unexpected bill or some big expense coming up?"

Em made a face. "I've been ordered to use my connection with you to get the TV station an exclusive interview for the *San Diego Morning Show*. I refused."

"What?" Nikki returned and set the box on the counter. "They expect you to betray a friend for a story?"

Liza blurted out, "You've been getting pressured? You never told me that." That hadn't occurred to her, but it should have. "Why didn't you say anything the two times I talked to you today?"

Anger sparked in Em's eyes. "Because I told them no. And this afternoon, I quit."

"Oh my God. No! If you need a story, we'll figure something out." She'd do anything for Emily.

She dropped a piece of pizza on a paper plate. "My boss accused me of knowing you were married and pregnant. She said I had a golden opportunity to use that to break into reporting. When I refused, she said I'm not cut out for this job." Em picked up her glass of wine. "She's right. I'm not using you for a story."

All through college, Em had been hell-bent on becoming an investigative reporter. But after witnessing Liza's attack, she'd begun having second thoughts. Seeing a crime up close had shifted her perspective and caused her to doubt her ability to deal with that kind of brutality as a reporter. Liza didn't want to be the catalyst that pushed Emily into a choice on her career before she was ready. "Did you tell Ben?"

"Of course. He's okay with it." She took a sip and added, "He knows I hated it."

"It's going to be okay. We'll figure this out together. In the meantime, I know I can help you find a job." Ben was doing his residency, so he wasn't rolling in money either. They had a nice condo, but it was a tiny one-bedroom.

"You're right. I'll get a job somewhere and then worry about my next step."

Liza stood and hugged Em. "I never thought about what it cost you to keep my secrets." Releasing her, Liza sat down and took a bite of her pizza while mentally reviewing her business contacts. "What do you want to do for work?"

"Something that pays my bills. I don't want to mooch off Ben."

She totally understood that. "We'll get you something."

"Thanks, I feel better just talking." Emily scooped up another slice of pizza.

"Hello? What about what I want?" Nikki asked, her voice aggrieved in a teasing way. "I've been keeping Liza's secret. I'm an awesome friend too."

Liza had to agree. She was damn lucky to have such good friends. And Nikki was clearly trying to lighten the mood. Getting into the game, she said, "What do you want?"

"A rich rock-star boyfriend or husband and a cool little dog I can dress up and take with me everywhere." She took a bite of her pizza.

Liza pretended to consider that. "Do you have a rock star in mind?"

"Nah, as long as he's not old, I'm good."

Em rolled her eyes. "Girl, we need to work on your standards."

"I know, right? But I'm tired of being the fifth wheel." She dropped her pizza crust and leaned on the counter, cradling a glass of wine. "You have Ben, and Liza has Justice. I'm just the perky girl with no date."

"And really bad first dates," Em added.

"Last guy?" She shook her head. "He just wanted me to be the designated driver for him and his drunktard buddies. I found out when I ordered a beer and he flipped out. He assumed I was underage."

Emily burst out laughing. "Only you."

"True story." Nikki sighed. "Which is why I don't sign up for dating services. Can you imagine? I'd end up as the getaway driver for a robbery and be totally clueless." She dumped her remaining pizza in the trash. "How about a movie? We need a comedy."

An hour into the movie, Liza's phone buzzed. She glanced at it and frowned in surprise. "It's the San Diego Police Department."

Nikki muted the movie.

"Answer it," Em said.

Was someone hurt? Or had her house been broken into? She'd set the alarm, so wouldn't the company have notified her? Putting her phone to her ear, she answered, "Hello?"

"This is Officer Claremont of the San Diego Police Department. Is this Liza Glasner?"

"Yes. What's wrong?"

"Your father-in-law is Noah Cade, correct?"

Her heart slammed into her throat. "Yes, is he okay? Did something happen?" He was at the PTSD transitional center. Wouldn't they call her if he was sick or hurt?

"There's been an altercation at your house. If you're close by, we can attempt to sort this out now. Or I'll arrest both men and transport them to the station."

Confusion trapped her brain. Altercation? Like a fight? Wait, both men? "Who is the other man?"

"Dillion Gibbs."

Her ex-boyfriend? Surging up from the couch, Liza shoved her feet into her shoes. "I'll be right there. Give me ten minutes."

What the hell was going on? Why would Dillion be at her house? And why had Noah left the transitional center?

But most importantly, was Noah okay?

Liza stared in absolute disbelief as the cop drove off, leaving her with the two men. One drunk and stupid, although he was rapidly sobering up. The other wary and uncommunicative.

What exactly was she supposed to do now?

"Dillion." She turned to him first. "Why are you here?"

Dillion shifted the bag of frozen peas he had pressed to his left cheek. Grass and dirt stained his dress shirt, his tie hung destroyed around his neck, and his eyes were bloodshot. "You didn't return any of my calls or texts. I came over to talk to you."

Noah crossed his arms, stood back by the driveway, and muttered, "That's not an answer."

Oh look, now her father-in-law could speak in complete and coherent sentences. When the cop was talking to him, he'd mostly grunted. Although he had told the officer his name, that Liza was his daughter-in-law, and even gave the man her phone number. So that was something. "I'll handle this, Noah."

The older man leaned back against Justice's Jeep sitting in the driveway, a stubborn expression on his bearded face that was almost exactly like his son's. Noah was pissed. Well join the freaking club.

Liza swung her gaze back to Dillion. "I didn't answer your texts or calls because I didn't want to talk to you. Do the math."

"Do the math? How about you show some gratitude. I could have had that lunatic arrested." He pointed the bag of peas at Noah.

Lunatic? Her fury notched up. "That's my father-in-law. He has every damn right to be here any time he wants. This is his house!" God she was just so mad. This morning, she'd been sleep-deprived but happy, typing so fast on her book, the letters had raced across the screen trying to keep up with her. And Justice's song was in the top one hundred on the charts. She missed him, but they were both working toward their goals and managing to stay close while physically separated.

Then Hayes dropped his video and her day was screwed from there.

She stepped in closer to the man annoying her. "You ever call him a lunatic again, the cops will be arresting me."

Noah made a noise low in this throat, a snorty-growl thing that Liza pointedly ignored.

Dillion, however, jerked his gaze to Noah, the flash of fear evident in his eyes. Clearly her ex was way more afraid of Noah than her. Dillion slapped the bag of peas against his face. "Fine. Whatever."

"Well? You've obviously been drinking, then you drove—" She looked around. "Where's your car?"

"I don't drive when I've been drinking." Some of his petulant arrogance drained. "Stacy Jo and I had a fight. We were out to dinner, and I kept checking my phone, and she got all bitchy and stormed out. I had a couple more martinis while waiting for an Uber."

Liza closed her eyes, fighting for any scrap of patience. "So you came here?" He and his fiancée had a fight, so of course the best way to fix that was to go see his ex. Totally rational.

"You don't understand. I was worried about you, Liza. Stacy Jo is jealous of you and got her panties in a bunch."

"Wait, what? Jealous of me?" She narrowed her gaze. "You dumped me, doesn't she know that?"

He dropped his gaze to the grass beneath his feet. "I broke up with her to see you first."

"You...what?" That last word came out like an owl screech.

"We were sort of engaged when I first met you."

"Sort of engaged?" She sucked in a lungful of cool

night air. "You know what? I don't care. You dumped me in a hot second as soon as you found out who I am. And then you thought I'd still sleep with you." She whipped her head around to see Noah's blue eyes harden on Dillion.

Perfect. She was handling this like a real champ. Now her father-in-law knew that disgusting little morsel from her past.

"You need to protect yourself. Gene Hayes has a powerful legal team. I don't know what their plan is, but you need legal representation." Dillion fished his wallet from his pocket and slid out a business card. "This is the law firm I work for. If you aren't sure where to go for representation, this firm is good."

"Oh." The underlying purpose of his actions was clarified. "You're here to drum up business for your firm."

"I'm here as your friend. Get a lawyer, Liza. A good one. If you don't want this firm, I'll put together a list of reputable candidates." He waved the card at her. "No one there knows we used to date or that I even know you. I'm trying to help."

And she'd believe him why?

"Look, I'm sorry I handled this badly." He flashed another sullen look at Noah. "I'm not trying to start trouble, I just..." He twisted his mouth and looked away.

"You what?"

"I was an ass when I broke up with you, but I was hurt. You hadn't told me who you were. I was angry that I'd broken up with my girlfriend—"

"—who'd been your fiancée." A plot twist Liza hadn't known about. Until tonight, she'd have sworn Dillion hadn't liked her that much. But he'd broken up with his fiancée to date her. "You never mentioned to me you'd been engaged."

He thinned his mouth. "Right. And you didn't tell me that your mom was in prison. Or that you'd been raped. I mean...Jesus, Liza, we slept together."

"Shut. Up." She glanced at Noah. The man pushed off the car, his entire body damn near twanging with the need to attack Dillion.

Could this get any more unreal?

"Sorry." Dillion blew out a breath. "Let me get this off my chest. After you were attacked last June, I finally got what you were living with and that you didn't tell me because you didn't trust me."

Was he for real? She opened her mouth to set him straight.

He held up a hand. "I know you're going to say I broke up with you when I found out, but I was hurt. Really hurt. I had to hear it from my dad? He was livid and made me feel so stupid. I felt betrayed. I thought we had something only to find out you had a whole secret identity."

She'd have more sympathy for him if he'd told her that then instead of treating her like trash and wanting to keep her his dirty little secret on the side. Before she could form a response, he went on.

"I never told anyone who you are, Liza, not a soul. Including Stacy Jo. She found that out on the news like everyone else. She went ballistic, realizing..." He dropped his hand, his shoulders bowing. "I'm still in love with you. I can't do this, I can't marry her. It's you I love."

He what? Her feet grew roots, anchoring her to the grass, while her mind screamed denials. This wasn't happening. Dillion was a child, wanting what he couldn't have. The moment daddy told him no, Liza became the forbidden fruit.

"I'm pregnant," she blurted out, wondering if

Dillion was drunk enough to forget that fact. He hadn't wanted her when he found out about her past, so why would he want her when Hayes loomed threateningly, her reputation was smeared more than ever, *and* she carried another man's child? And Noah, oh my God, what was her father-in-law thinking after hearing all this? His opinion meant so much more than Dillion's ever would. "Justice is—"

A car screeched up and swerved into the driveway, the front wheels plowing into the grass.

Liza swung around and squinted in the beam of the headlights. What fresh hell was this?

A woman jumped out and stomped up to them.

"Stacy Jo," Dillion exclaimed, his brows knitting in confusion. "What are you doing here?"

The lights illuminated Dillion's fiancée's shoulder-length brown hair around a beet-red face. She jammed her hands on slender hips, the massive diamond glinting on her left ring finger. "I knew you'd run here to the gold-digging slut!"

She jerked back, outraged at the audacity of the woman. "What is wrong with you people? I haven't done a damn thing. You're the ones making a scene on my front yard."

"You're the one who lured him here!"

Dillion blanched and tried to grab Stacy Jo's arm. "Calm down."

She slapped his hand away and stabbed her finger at his chest. "You swore it was over! You already left me once for her, and now you're doing it again. You've been screwing her the whole time, haven't you? You're a liar and cheater." She whirled around, rage twisting her face. "And you're a gold-digging, scheming whore. You're married and still fucking my fiancé."

Too many years of having people scream insults at

her and not being allowed to fight back stretched Liza's temper. "Get out of my face. And while you're at it, take your fiancé and get your damned car off my lawn. I was done with Dillion a long time ago. You can have him." Liza spun around and stalked toward the house. She got three steps when something hard and cold struck her in the back.

"Stacy Jo, no!" Dillion yelled.

That woman had just attacked her? Oh hell no. Liza's gaze caught on the hose lying in the grass. She scooped it up and pivoted. At her feet lay the broken bag of frozen peas.

Stacy Jo stalked toward her. "Don't you walk away from me. You're trash, just like your mother. You'll probably end up in prison like her. Oh I know all about it. I found the private investigator's report Dillion's father gave him when he told Dillion to dump your fat ass."

Liza heart beat too fast, her temper stretched too thin. "Shut up."

"Do you even know whose kid you got knocked up with?"

Her temper snapped. Liza twisted the nozzle of the hose. Water streamed out right into Stacy Jo's face.

"Argh! You bitch!" She lunged, grabbing Liza's arm, forcing it up.

Cold water blasted her face, knocking her glasses to the side. It burned up her nose, making her cough as she fought for control of the hose.

"Enough!" Noah roared.

Dillion grabbed Stacy Jo, lifting her off her feet.

Dropping the hose, Liza trembled from cold and adrenaline as water dripped off her face and glasses. Through the film, she saw Dillion dragging a quieter Stacy Jo to the car. Huh, getting doused with cold water iced both their tempers.

Had she really just done that? Gotten in a fight on her own front yard? This whole day was so ridiculous and twisted, she didn't know if she should laugh or cry.

Where was the hose anyway? She spun around and spied Noah by the front door, coiling the hose on the ground with his good arm. Another issue to deal with. Why was Noah here instead of at the transitional center?

As she wrung water out of her hair, she caught sight of Em coming out of the house with a towel that she tossed to Liza, then moved to stand by a stunned looking Nikki. Hell, she'd forgotten all about Emily and Nikki. They'd shown up a minute after Liza had arrived. Em had gone in the house to get the frozen peas for Dillion's face, and then taken Liza's purse inside. Nikki must have remained outside to watch the show.

After wiping her face and wrapping her hair in the terrycloth, she walked by her friends, opened the screen door and said, "Everyone in the house." She appreciated Em and Nikki's support, but they'd given the neighbors gathering outside enough of a show.

Nikki and Emily filed past her. When Liza turned, Noah finished with the hose and limped the few steps toward her. She guessed his hip was hurting, which happened when you jumped a twenty-something man, pinned him to the ground and punched him.

In his defense, Dillion had been pounding on the door and screaming her name. Neighbors had called the cops. Then Noah pounced on him, apparently believing Dillion was there to harm Liza.

Un-freaking-believable.

Dillion had been pretty toasted, but the fight sobered him up some. Well, that and the threat of getting arrested. Not a good thing for a man getting ready to take the bar exam. What a dumbshit. Seriously. But she didn't care about Dillion, she cared about Noah. "Why aren't you at the transitional center? Is something wrong?" He could have texted her if he needed something.

"I saw the video. I was watching the house."

She stared into his blue eyes, feeling that weird zing at the similarity to Justice's gaze. Something really thick moved in her chest, and her anger drained. She wasn't mad at Noah, it was her idiot ex and his psychotic fiancée who infuriated her. But Noah... "You were protecting me. Again." No tears. She wasn't going to cry.

He shrugged. "Justice isn't here, and I'm not letting anyone hurt you again." He pivoted slowly.

She called out, "Noah, where're you going?"

He shrugged and took another lumbering step, clearly favoring his left hip.

She rushed out. "Wait, please."

Pausing, he kept his head down.

Liza hated the shroud of loneliness around him. It hurt her heart. "Thank you."

He gave her a barely perceptible nod.

"You don't believe the things Stacy Jo said, do you?"

He lifted his head, and for a moment, a tiny glitter of humor danced in his eyes. "I hate peas."

"Uh..." What exactly could she say to that? "Justice hates them too."

"Can't trust the judgment of a woman who chooses peas as her weapon."

He didn't believe Stacy Jo. And he was making a joke. How could she not grin at him? "If I promise not to let the peas back in the house, will you come in? Your hip is hurting, and I still have some of the pain pills from your broken arm." She touched his arm, keeping her movement slow and gentle. "This is your home. You have your key, right? And the code to the security alarm. You can leave anytime you want to." She was the one always preaching to Justice about building trust with his dad.

"I'll stay the night." He glanced in the opened door to the house, frowning. "But I'll stay out here. Keep watch."

Over her. Had he been doing this? Leaving the center to check on her? Liza had no idea. She looked over to the door and saw her two friends standing there. Were they the reason he wanted to stay outside? "They're my friends, Emily and Nikki. They aren't staying the night." She wasn't sure how much to push him, but it was February and cold at night. "If you stay out here, I'll worry and won't be able to sleep."

His mouth twitched on one side. "Emotional blackmail?"

She grinned. "Impressive, right? I'm practicing for when I'm a mom. Also it works with Justice most of the time. And when that doesn't work, I threaten his chickens. You know, all the chicken decorations in the kitchen?"

His eyes crinkled. "I guess I'll come in."

Liza led him in, locked the door and rearmed the security. She could hear Nikki and Liza talking in the kitchen. The smell of popcorn told her they were making themselves at home. Turning to Noah, she said, "You hungry?"

"No." He headed toward the hall.

"One second." She rushed into her kitchen.

Nikki was dumping freshly popped corn into a bowl and asked, "That's Justice's dad?"

"Yeah, he's staying the night. Let me get him settled."

Nikki frowned. "With you? Alone? I mean..." She glanced at the doorway to the dining room and back. "Is that safe? I can stay the night if you like."

She grabbed the bottle of pain pills, dumped out two, then got a water from the fridge. Shutting the door, she faced Nikki. "That man saved my life. The only person I'm safer with is Justice." She stalked out, trying to calm that spike of anger.

Noah waited for her by the hallway. "Your friend worries about your safety. Don't be mad." He took the pills and water, shuffled to his room and quietly shut the door.

Liza stared after him, her heart swelling. How could she not love her father-in-law? Even with his issues, he was a million times a better man than her dad had ever been.

For the first time since she was fourteen, she had a family. Justice and Noah, as well as a job and friends who, as Noah had pointed out, worried about her safety.

And her baby. As she settled her hand over her belly, more love and hot determination spread and cemented. She had too much to lose now.

This time she wasn't letting Gene Hayes destroy her family or life.

Chapter 16

Justice PACED BETWEEN THE KITCHEN and table on the bus, automatically adjusting his stride as the vehicle rolled out from the Houston venue towards Dallas. He pulled up Beth's name on his phone and hit call. She'd left a couple voicemails, and he was anxious to find out what was going on. They'd finished the show over an hour ago, followed by an autograph signing. Then Lynx and River made plans to go get shitfaced with some girls...and Justice had to put a kibosh on that idea. They had another interview tomorrow, then a concert, which meant they'd need to be on the bus and rolling out tonight. Simon had backed him up, and so did Gray. But River...

He shot a glare at the back of the bus where the guys were partying with a bottle of tequila.

River's snarling comment blared in his head. *You wouldn't be such a tight-ass bitch if you got laid.*

Fucking asshole. Justice wasn't cheating on his wife. But the point was, he hadn't even seen his wife's messages until he'd boarded the bus, and now he had to find out what was happening with his dad. *Come on, pick up the phone.*

"Justice, hi," Beth answered.

"What the hell is going on there? My dad's been arrested?"

"No, he's fine." Beth sounded tired. "He's here in the house."

"There? He quit treatment? Or was he released?" Justice had seen Noah once at the transitional center, and his dad still hadn't looked at him. Instead, his dad had focused on Beth and gave one-word replies to her questions.

"I didn't ask him that, but I don't think he quit. He's not an inmate, he can come and go. The center is voluntary."

Which meant his dad could be sleeping on the street every fucking night. For all they knew, he was using his room there for a shower and occasional meal. "Is he any better? Will he go back?"

"I didn't exactly have time to do a full evaluation while dealing with the cops and a yard full of crazy. But I'll try to get him to go back tomorrow. In the meantime, he said he'd stay here tonight. He's protecting me, so I believe him."

Yeah, when it came to Beth, his dad would stay. It was Justice who drove him away. A bark of laughter punched out from the back of the bus, reminding him that they weren't alone. He grabbed a beer from the fridge and tried to get his boiling energy to calm the hell down. He was still wired from the performance, the argument with River, and Beth's multiple messages. He could actually hear the buzz in his ears.

If Beth were here, he'd get her in his bunk, kiss her to keep her quiet and slide his aching cock into her. Whisper into her ear to bite his shoulder and arm to keep from crying out as she came for him. Or maybe

Beth didn't want to be silenced, maybe she wanted the whole damned bus to know...

"Justice? You still there?"

"Yeah." Both him and his throbbing cock. *Focus. Get your head back into the conversation.* "So if my dad wasn't arrested, what did happen?"

"I guess he saw the Hayes video and wanted to check on me. But when he got here, a man was pounding on the door and calling my name, so Noah tackled him. That's when the cops showed up. Thankfully, the officer called me."

"What the hell?" He tried to keep up. "Who was the man? A reporter?" Beth had texted him earlier that she was staying at Nikki's new place for just that reason— so the media wouldn't hassle her.

She was taking too long to answer. Suspicion joined the party in his gut. "Beth? What man?"

"Dillion."

Justice froze mid-pace in the tight walkway of the bus. "Are you fucking kidding me? That bastard came to our house looking for you? What is it with him? Has he been there before?"

"No. I haven't heard from Dillion since we saw him at Wylie's months ago. He said he was trying to help me."

Justice listened as she spewed the story about him advising her to get legal representation. "Bullshit. Goddammit, Beth, he wants you. He's always wanted you." He slapped his hand against the paneled wall. The thunk echoed through the vehicle. Leaning on his arm, he dropped his head, staring at the ugly floor. He wanted to punch Dillion's face in.

"It gets worse. You're going to be mad."

He jerked his head up. "Tell me."

"Uh, well—it's so outlandish, I still can't believe it."

"Stop stalling and spill it." The day had been long and frustrating enough.

"Dillion says he still loves me."

The words gonged in his head. "I'm going to kill him. Slowly. I've warned him. But he's afraid of me, so he waited until he thought you were alone and vulnerable. Goddammit." Jealousy and frustration boiled.

"Knock it off."

"What?"

"You heard me. I've had enough tonight. I not only dealt with my ex, but his fiancée showed up and screamed at me, then threw frozen peas at me. I lost my temper and sprayed her with a hose. So you know what, Rooster? I hit my limit of lovesick morons and jealous jerks. I love you, only you, and I'm not a cheater. Don't make me fly out there and kick your ass. 'Cause right now? I just might."

Hearing her rant at him made him think of Beth that night the naked girl had been in their hotel room. She'd been furious and beautiful and *his*. More and more, Beth was becoming fierce, and it was hot. "Wait, you got in a girl fight? On our front lawn?"

"It's not funny."

"Oh it is. And sexy too. Couple chicks in a water fight and I missed it? What were you wearing?"

"Damn it, Rooster, this isn't the time to be a pervert."

"Is everything okay there now?"

"Yes, and honestly I feel better having your dad here tonight."

He knew she did, and if he was being honest, Justice felt better too. His dad had proven exactly how far he'd go to protect Beth. But he didn't want to think about his father right now, he wanted to think about his wife. "Then it's the perfect time to be a pervert." Loneliness closed in on him. "I miss you so damned much, Beth."

She blew out a breath. "I miss you too."

He glanced toward the back of the bus, where voices rose and fell, and up front to Joe, their driver. "I wish we had privacy for some real perversion. But I'm trapped on this bus."

"Em and Nikki are here too. But I'll see you next week in Florida. I mean...if that's still okay? How was your concert tonight? Did the Hayes video affect your sales or anything?"

"I need you, hell yes, it's okay. The concert was fine. There were only a few protesters out front, maybe four or five. No one paid much attention. Our single is still in the eighties. It's all going to blow over." But his band and Christine had been riding him to get the postnuptial agreement to protect S.I. Records. "Listen, is there any way you can take Monday off and stay an extra night in Florida with me? We'll be at the Bayside Manor instead of a hotel. It'll be a chance for us to spend a little time together." It'd be easier to talk to her about the postnup then, and explain he was doing it to protect their future, not just the band.

"I'd like that. Let me check with Sloane, but I think I can do it."

Relief unknotted his neck and shoulder muscles. He'd tell Christine he'd talk to Liza next weekend, and they'd all back off. "I wish you were here now."

"I offered to come out this weekend."

The slight hurt in her voice cut. Things had been going so well until Gene Hayes fucked it up. "I'm just worried about you and wanted to give it a week or so for the media and people to lose interest in the shit Hayes stirred up. I want you safe."

She sighed. "Is your band upset?"

Hell, she would ask that. He phrased his answer carefully. "They're better after seeing there wasn't much protest at tonight's concert. Let's not talk about them, Gene Hayes or the escalating feud with Jagged Sin."

"Then what?"

"You." If he couldn't have her here, then he'd have to settle for second best. "Did you work on more pages?"

"The sex scene." Her voice dropped to a throaty whisper. "The one with the bassist."

"Send it. If I can't go to sleep with you, let me at least have your pages."

"Now? But Emily and Nikki are here. And your dad's in his bedroom."

"So?" He wasn't letting her stall or talk herself out of taking a risk with this book. "It'll take you a minute to get on your laptop and send the file."

"You want them that badly?"

He laid his head back, hearing the sounds of Beth walking through the house. Homesickness lodged in his chest. He missed the little things, like going into the kitchen and finding her making some tea and grumbling that it wasn't coffee since she'd cut back on caffeine for the baby. Or watching her work in the backyard. Or spotting her glasses on the nightstand, or the way candles, pillows and plants kept appearing. And her peach scent...he missed that so much. "I want you. I don't even know if you're showing yet."

"You'll find out next weekend."

Just the thought of stripping her down, touching her everywhere, dragged a thick groan from him.

"Okay, I'm in our room," Beth said. "I'm sending the file with the new pages now from my laptop. Hey!"

Justice sat up. "What? Is it Dillion?" That weasel better not have returned to the house.

"Get away, you snoops." Her voice was far away then returned. "No, not Dillion. My two former friends were standing behind me reading over my shoulder."

He could hear the girls firing questions in the background.

"Hush!" Liza snapped at them.

Justice laughed. "Busted." He didn't think she'd told her friends that she was writing books.

"It was a sex scene. This is your fault. If your dad finds out..." Her voice faded away again as she threatened her friends. "You'll both regret it. Nikki, I'll post every bad-date story about you online. Emily, I'll tell your brothers your job made you cry like a baby. That's what I thought, walk away."

Amusement and lust put on gloves and duked it out inside him. He loved it when Beth got fired up—she was fucking hot.

And she was his.

Excitement danced in her stomach as Liza deplaned and followed the signs in the Tampa Bay airport. She'd finally made it to Florida and couldn't wait to see Justice. She checked her phone.

Rock Rooster: *Outside in the pickup area. Look for a black SUV.*

She'd brought a carry-on bag, so she lugged it through the airport, bypassing baggage claim. No one paid any attention to her, which was exactly how she wanted it. She liked moving anonymously. A little part of her mentally flipped off Gene Hayes. He'd tried to ruin her life, but he failed.

Once she found the sign for the passenger pickup area, she headed outside into the bright eighty-degree sunshine.

"Beth!"

Justice stood by the passenger door of an SUV. Her heart jumped at the sound of his voice, and she ran toward him, dropping her bag and throwing herself into his arms.

He swept her up, burying his face in the side of her neck. "You're here. I've missed you too damned much."

The warm scent of vanilla, wood oil and Justice filled her lungs. Pulling back, he dropped a kiss on her mouth. "No more until I get you alone." He swung her into the seat, then scooped up her bag and tossed it in the back. "That's all you have?"

"I packed light."

He slid into the driver's seat, and they took off.

"Did you rent this car?" She'd expected an Uber or something.

"No. It's from the Manor."

"Bayside Manor? The place you're staying?"

"Yep. They have a fleet of cars we can use. Plus space to park our bus with the hookups. It's really cool. The main house is a mansion right on the bay. There's an outdoor kitchen, a pool, and a dock with a boat and jet skis."

His excitement rippled in the car and touched the spot of unease over all these experiences he was having without her. Liza shrugged it off. She was here now. "Cool. So how was Screech's Tampa club?" She wished she could have gotten here to see the performance, but work kept her tethered to San Diego.

"It was nuclear. That place is over-the-top crazy with a full light show, and the piano under its own spotlight. We performed Screech's song, 'Reaper's

Child,' and the audience loved it. And our stuff too. We signed a slew of autographs, then Lynx and River invited a bunch of people to the mansion, and that party went on well past when I went to bed at 3:00 a.m."

Ugly bile washed up her throat. "Any girls in your bed?" The hard question shot out of her mouth before she could engage her filter. Liza put her hand on her belly, as if she could shield her child from the answer. She remembered those parties from her childhood. Wild drug-and-sex fests. Women with smooth skin, tiny hips and big boobs. Sex was like a handshake for these people. She'd seen more blow jobs and—

"No."

The sharp word pelted through her memories, leaving a weird buzzing between them.

Justice gripped the steering wheel tighter. "I thought you'd want to hear about my night. Obviously I was wrong."

"What are you so pissed about?"

"Because, goddammit, I'm the only one not getting laid. I was excited about you coming here, but you want to start in on me with accusations that I've been fucking around? I don't need this, Beth. I'm working my ass off. I can have a couple drinks without you..." He clamped his mouth shut.

What was happening here? They never fought like this. She turned, looking out the window, seeing the city glide by in the midafternoon. She'd caught a 6:00 a.m. flight, had to run like hell to catch her connection in Dallas, and she lost three more hours in the time change. Tears threatened, but she wasn't doing that. She was tired, but he was the one who'd been living on the road for over a month now.

"I'm sorry. I can't wait to see the manor." She

couldn't look at him, afraid of what she'd see on his face.

Like regret. Justice was the only one saddled with a wife and a kid on the way.

He wrapped his fingers around her suddenly cold hand. "I went to bed alone. Do you know what I did then?"

She wanted to grab his hand in both of hers and clutch it like a desperate chick. Instead she left her fingers limp on her leg. "What?"

"Read your pages. And missed you so damned much. I'm sorry for snapping. I'm not going to fuck this up, okay? Not my career or our relationship. Please, just trust me."

Yet awkwardness bubbled between them. "I'm trying." Not good enough. "I do trust you. But it's hard, Justice. I'm there at the house, dealing with a broken water heater, your dad, my job, reporters on my lawn, or harassing me in routine work press conferences. One even cornered me in the bathroom at a business lunch in an upscale restaurant. She more or less blocked me from leaving while trying to get me to answer questions."

"What did you do?"

She glanced over at him. "Squirted hand lotion on her. I had her send her dry-cleaning bill to SLAM."

His mouth twitched, and he tugged her hand to the armrest and laced their fingers. "Good." His gaze sobered. "How bad is it at the house? Are you safe?"

"Yes. It's just one or two reporters a day trying to catch me coming or going. I ignore them. And we have the alarm system."

"You got the water heater replaced, right?"

"Yes." She kept her gaze focused on the gas stations and convenience stores. "Stuff in one of my boxes we

246

stored in there was ruined, but all your boxes were fine."

"What? Beth, you didn't tell me that. Which box?"

Her throat tightened. "Just some old pictures."

"Oh fuck, the ones of you and your mom before she went to prison?" He paused, then said, "I'm sorry."

Wow, they were getting off to a great start, weren't they? "Forget it. I saved a few on top. It's fine." Everything was fine. She turned and smiled. "I'm looking forward to a couple nights here." She'd taken Monday off and changed her flight out. They'd have all Sunday together.

"I'm taking you out tomorrow. I made a reservation at a steak and seafood place on the bay. Or we can stay in if you'd rather. The manor is fully staffed." He glanced over again. "You can get some rest and be taken care of for a change. You've been handling everything at home." His grin turned wicked. "And it's my turn to handle you."

"Hey, I'm not your groupie, rock star. I'm not a sure thing."

He turned the car toward a gate and pressed a button on the visor. The gate swung open, revealing a long road lined with swaying palm trees. "Wow." She couldn't help but be impressed. They passed smaller roads. "Where do those go?"

"Casitas, a recording studio, some maintenance buildings. I haven't seen everything yet. We can take an ATV or golf cart to check it all out later or tomorrow."

Justice followed a circular driveway to the front of a sprawling sand-colored house. But she had little chance to explore as Justice got out, slung her bag over his shoulder, and tugged her up the steps to a glass-paneled door. Inside was bright and spacious, with white marble floors and white and turquoise furniture in a massive living area. Beyond that, big sliding doors opened to a deck, a big pool and the bay. It was stunning.

"Where is everyone?"

"Might be out on the boat. Come on, I don't want to share you yet." He dragged her to the right and hit a button for an elevator. "We're on the top floor."

A minute later, he opened the door to a big room with a massive king-sized bed covered in a white comforter topped by an emerald-green cloud of pillows and a throw blanket. Just looking at the bed made her hot and needy.

Justice tossed her bag down and pulled her through a dressing area. She had a quick glimpse of the doorway to a bathroom before they ended up in a sitting room flooded with sunlight from a sliding glass door. A couch and two chairs were grouped on a pretty rug. A small dining table with a vase of brightly colored tropical flowers stood by the sliding door. But it was the picturesque scene of the bay that captivated her.

Going to the glass, she scanned the panoramic view. Boats and jet skis created wakes in the water. The edges of the bay were dotted with homes and businesses. "It's gorgeous."

"I want to give you something like this one day."

His voice rumbled so close behind her it sparked shivers that trailed down her neck. Craning her head, she met his steely-hot gaze. All the shades of blue and gray blended together in his irises to make that color uniquely his. "We have a home. But I'd love to vacation here anytime."

Wrapping his hand around her jaw, he drew his thumb along her throat. "We're not living there forever. We'll fix it up for my dad to keep once he's better. But for us, for you and our kid, I want more. I want it all."

When Justice's intensity focused solely on her, she could barely remember her name.

"I want you to strip for me. Right here, in this light. I want to see you, everything I've missed." His hand slid over the slope of her breast to cup the mound contained in her bra. "You're bigger, fuller." Moving lower, he covered her belly. "I want to see you, Beth."

"Some of my pants are getting too tight." Self-consciousness niggled at her.

He kissed down the side of her neck, his mouth warm and wet. Pulling her shirt aside, he brushed his lips over the curve of her shoulder. "You're sexier than ever. I'm going to prove just how much I missed you."

Liza melted into him. Justice made her feel beautiful exactly the way she was.

Chapter 17

JUSTICE GUIDED THE SUV PAST the gates, following Simon and River in the Yukon ahead of him. The thumping on the back of his seat jerked his gaze to the mirror. "Quit kicking my seat."

Lynx sighed. "Drive faster. Jesus, what are you, ninety?"

Justice tried pointing out the obvious. "I'm following Simon."

Lynx crossed his arms. "He's ninety-seven."

He glanced over at Liza. "I don't suppose you could give him a cookie to make him behave?"

"I wish I'd brought some cookies," Beth said wistfully. "Who knew you could make them out of Nutella? That's some delicious brilliance. I can't believe you didn't try at least one."

She'd had three and then begged him to take them away. They'd been sitting on the deck, hanging with the guys, River filling her in on the party, with the video to prove they'd been jumping in the bay naked.

Justice shook his head. He wasn't on that video because he hadn't been a drunk idiot. Manor security put an end to their shenanigans. But Justice hadn't

SAVAGED VOWS

tried to stop River's show-and-tell. It was better that Beth saw for herself that Justice hadn't been involved.

"Hey, Liza," Lynx said. "So you got names picked out for the ankle biter? If it's a boy, Panther would be sick. Panther Cade."

Justice rolled his eyes as he stopped for a red light behind the other SUV.

Liza twisted around in her seat. "What if it's a girl?"

"Sparrow Cade."

"Sparrow?" She seemed to test it out. "Kind of pretty, don't you think, Justice? Oh and Panther, that's all sleek and masculine."

"You can't be serious. We're not naming our kid after a bird or cat. Besides, it's—" He cut off at the smirk on her face.

He'd been had. That was what he got for leaving her out on the deck with his bandmates while he went to the bathroom earlier. They plotted ways to torment him.

"Funny." He flicked his gaze in the mirror to see Lynx's smug face. "Jerk."

"Butt face."

"Children," Gray said from behind Liza's seat. "Stop bickering. Liza, do you know if you're having a boy or girl?"

"No. We might find out at the next ultrasound, if we want to know. I'm not sure. But knowing is better, right? I've been debating, because I want to fix up the nursery, although it probably won't matter to the baby what color their bedroom is."

Her excited chatter amused him. "We'll have to use the front bedroom for the baby. Do you want to paint it?"

She focused on him. "I was thinking soft peach or creamy yellow. Should we find out the sex?"

He was forced to stop at another red light. Simon had made it through and sped off ahead of him. No biggie. They'd all been at the venue earlier, before he'd picked Beth up at the airport, to check the setup and get their bearings. He knew the way. To answer Beth's question, he said, "Sure, why not?"

"We could be surprised."

The pregnancy alone had been enough of a surprise for him. But he'd sound like an asshole if he said that. "It'll be more fun to know."

She rewarded him with a smile, her eyes glittering. Shifting beneath her seat belt, she smoothed her hand over her short dress. He heartily approved of the black lace thing that layered over the pale-pink material of her dress. She'd paired it with sexy black boots. She had a feminine rocker-chick thing going that was uniquely Beth. Especially with curly mahogany hair that seemed to have more red in it than usual. He couldn't wait to show her off tonight. And maybe show off a little for her.

And for his fans. Their single had begun slipping on the music charts, but they hoped the concerts this weekend—especially tonight at the big venue in the heart of Tampa—would give them another push. Justice searched the area, then said, "There it is." He pointed to the big, domed theater rising up in the night sky.

Getting this booking was a feat. They hadn't sold out, but it was a solid sell-through, something like ninety-two percent. Really good. They had to get there for some preshow events, and traffic was moving at a torturous crawl.

"Damn, we're more than two hours early. How can it be this bad?" He couldn't see far enough ahead to figure out what was the holdup.

"That's good, right? It means your show is popular."

Now that they were this close to the venue, his preshow anxiety began climbing. "Yeah." Every show had to be the best one yet, and they needed to push their single up into the top fifty of the chart. They couldn't afford any more fuckups. Well, the Hayes video wasn't a fuckup they could control.

Beth laid her hand on his arm. She didn't say a word, just touched him in a way that soothed some of the boiling energy that surfaced before a show. Looking over, he met her gaze and smiled.

Her eyes sparkled, and she squeezed his arm. "It's going to be a kick-ass night. I want to get pictures to send Noah. Especially when you sing 'Expired Hero.'"

This girl filled him, accessing the place that all the crazed fans in the world couldn't reach—that boy left in a jail cell when his mom walked out. Beth made the boy want to grow up and be a man worthy of her.

"River's calling," Lynx said.

"Put him on speaker," Justice suggested. "He might be far enough ahead to see the problem slowing us."

"What's going on up there? Can you guys see?" Lynx asked.

"Protesters," River's normally smooth voice snapped. "A fuckton of them with signs and shit."

Justice craned his head, trying to peer around the line of cars in front of him. Warnings went off in his brain. Unable to see anything, he looked in the mirror.

Lynx's troubled gaze stared back. Raising his phone, he asked River, "Protesting what?"

"Liza. All the signs have the hashtag *Bring Gene Hayes Home* on them, with things like *Recant! Bring Hayes Home! Cheating Whore! Lyin' Liza! Hayes is Innocent!*"

Beth gasped, her hand covering her mouth. "No. Not again." Her skin flushed to an unhealthy tomato color.

"Now?" Gray said. "We only had a handful last weekend, and no protesters midweek or last night."

"This sounds too organized. What's happening?" Beth said.

"I don't know. Let's—"

A tap on the window had him jerk around to see a cop's face. Once he rolled it down, the cop said, "You're Justice Cade? I need to see I.D."

Justice pulled out his license and handed it over. Once the cop looked at it and handed it back, he moved the flashlight over the faces of all four of them in the car. Obviously satisfied, he said, "Okay, follow me. We're pulling you and the other vehicle out and escorting you to the private entrance. Your car will be moved for you once you're inside."

Damn. He glanced over at his wife. A moment ago, she'd been happy and reassuring him. Now she was stressed. When he shifted his gaze down to her barely noticeable belly, a harsh protectiveness clamped his chest. This was too dangerous. "I don't think you should be here."

"We don't have time to take her back to the manor," Gray pointed out. "It's worse being out here. Go."

Gray was right, so Justice followed the direction as one cop waved him out of the train of cars, while a line of officers kept the others in place.

Horns blared as people realized they were getting special treatment. Would they know Liza was in the car? He followed the cops down the road while Lynx talked to River. "How'd the police know we're here?"

"Simon called our road crew," River answered through the phone. "They alerted the police."

They moved at a crawl, getting around traffic and passing the front of the Tampa Dome.

"Holy crap," Liza said.

The street and sidewalk were covered in a sea of people with massive signs. News cameras bobbed among them, and reporters shoved microphones into people's faces. Screams ramped up, and someone shouted, "There she is! Elizabeth Ranger! Lyin' Liza!"

A crowd surged forward while chanting, "Lying Liza! Recant! Bring Gene Hayes Home!" One woman broke free of the pack, charged the car and swung her sign.

Crack!

The sign slammed into Beth's window.

Beth screamed and threw her arms over her head.

"Fuck." Justice gunned the car to hurl past the knot of lunatics. He didn't care if he ran the bastards over. In the mirror, he had a quick glimpse of several cops tackling the woman to the ground, and more police blocked the protestors. "Beth? You okay?" Her window was caved in with a webbing of fissures, but it hadn't broken. No glass hit her.

She sat up, glasses askew, face chalky, and her eyes bright with tears. "How did this happen? I don't understand."

"Get us in the building," Gray cut in. "Keep going."

Justice's head throbbed by the time they made it past the barricades and around to a back entrance. Security burst out of the building. His door was yanked open. "Let's go. Now."

He shoved out, threw off the arm tugging him and ran around the vehicle just as another security guy helped Beth out. Justice took her arm. "I have her." The man was doing his job, but Beth was his. Memories of the attack last year after the final *Court of*

Rock show tormented him. They all rushed inside, and the door clanged shut.

Surrounded by industrial white brick walls, white floors and exposed piping, they caught their breath for a minute. Then they were ushered along a few twists and turns, and finally into a room with two couches, TVs and a spread of snacks and drinks.

Simon and River were already there, talking to a couple of the security guys.

Simon spun around, his eyes narrowed on them. "Did you know about this?" Anger radiated off him.

"We have no idea what's going on," Justice answered.

Simon picked up a remote and turned up the TV. A harried female reporter with people carrying signs behind her said, "I'm here in front of the Tampa Dome where there's an organized effort to block ticket holders from getting in to see the rock band Savaged Illusions. There's a lot of anger out here. With me is Jillian Shoemaker." She turned and asked, "What brought you here tonight?"

The woman said, "I saw that newest video on the Bring Gene Hayes Home website."

"Website?" Justice hadn't heard of it before now.

The woman went on, "The site announced that Lyin' Liza was going to be here. I liked Savaged Illusions on *Court of Rock* until Justice Cade hooked up with that lying skank Liza. She ruined Gene Hayes's life. We have to stand up for what's right. Boycott Savaged Illusions and force Liza to tell the truth. Bring Gene Hayes home!"

Behind the reporter, the protestors chanted, "Tell the truth. Bring Hayes home!"

"We didn't announce she'd be here." Justice tried to figure out how they knew Liza was going to be at this particular concert.

On the TV, a grim-faced anchor appeared. "Thank you, Regina, for that live report. As most of our viewers know, Gene Hayes was convicted of drugging and raping Elizabeth Ranger, who is now known as Liza Glasner, when she was fourteen. Hayes fled the country, but he has recently surfaced, claiming he was set up. Gene Hayes's lawyers filed an official appeal of the verdict just over a week ago. And now this website, Bring Gene Hayes Home, has been launched with this video that professes to be a Lyin' Liza Truth Bomb.

The screen switched, and Gene Hayes appeared.

"For years I stayed silent after having my life destroyed by Elizabeth Ranger and her conniving, screwed-up parents." He lowered his chin. "As I've said before, I tried to cut Liza some slack—she was a kid. I thought, okay, maybe her parents coerced her into the scheme to seduce and blackmail me, and she was as much a victim as I am. And she suffered enough, right? Her mom is in prison for killing her father that night in my house when the whole plot went bad. Surely Elizabeth Ranger would have learned that you can't lie, cheat and scheme."

Hayes leaned back, crossing his arms. "That's what I thought until I realized this woman has turned into exactly what her parents were—a scheming, blackmailing liar. What we know already is that even though Liza claims to be a traumatized victim of a rock star, she's wormed her way into another rock star's, Justice Cade's, life and moved into his house. Months later, she got knocked up, and then she convinced Justice it's his kid and persuaded him to marry her right before his new album came out. And that's some very convenient timing since Liza now has the right to half the earnings Justice Cade makes off that album. I revealed all that to the world when I announced that we've filed to overturn the unfair verdict against me." Hayes tilted in toward the camera. "But we have so much more. If you're not yet convinced Lyin' Liza's not a victim but a schemer, let me show you what she's been doing while Justice Cade is out on the road working."

Justice could feel all the eyes of his band on him, while Beth stood stiff and frozen.

"We have a video that will show you exactly who she is," Hayes went on. "The man you'll see in there is Lyin' Liza's ex-boyfriend Dillion Gibbs, and the other woman who shows up at the end is his fiancée, Stacy Jo Miller. Now watch this cozy little scene."

"No," Beth whispered. "How could he have gotten this?"

Justice burned with silent rage as the screen shifted to night, but there was enough illumination from the streetlights to make out Dillion holding his hand out to Beth in the front yard of his house. The angle didn't show Beth's face but came from somewhere over her left shoulder.

He watched the whole damned thing beginning with Dillion professing his love for Liza exactly as Beth had described. Then Stacy Jo screeching up in her car, getting out and screaming insults at Liza.

"You're married and still fucking my fiancé."

"Do you even know whose kid you got knocked up with?"

Stacy Jo threw the bag of peas, Liza whirled around, squirting her with the hose, and the two women screamed and battled.

The image died away, and Hayes came back on the screen. "Does this woman look like a victim to you? Did you hear what Stacy Jo said? 'I found the private investigators report Dillion's father gave him when he told Dillion to dump your fat ass.'"

Smug satisfaction radiated from Hayes. "That's right, Liza had dated Dillion, whose father is State Senator Marvin Gibbs. Are you seeing the pattern? She went after the son of a state senator, hoping to hook him. But State Senator Gibbs is apparently no one's fool, and he had Liza investigated. Once he discovered who and what Liza really was, the man put an end to his son's relationship with her. But did Liza go away quietly? Did she show any shame or remorse? Not according to this video in Stacy Jo's own words. Lyin' Liza kept Dillion on her hook while she was dating and married to Justice Cade."

Hayes leaned forward, dark eyes intent on the camera. "It's time for Lyin' Liza to tell the truth. My sources have informed me that she's going to the Savaged Illusions concert at the Tampa Dome tonight. I'm asking all of you who know I'm innocent to show up there and demand that Lyin' Liza be held accountable for all her lies and schemes."

The screen faded to a picture of Hayes with BringGeneHayesHome.com stamped over it.

Simon muted the TV.

Fury spewed from Justice like an out-of-control geyser. Gene Fucking Hayes did this. He was manipulating from his little hideout, making the world see Beth as some lying, cheating whore. He'd failed to get her killed, so instead he was going to ruin her this way until she either recanted or the judge assigned to the case overturned the verdict.

Justice faced his band. "It's lies and accusations. It's a goddamned smear campaign."

"It doesn't matter if it's true." Simon's gold eyes blazed with fury. "You saw the protestors, *they* believe it."

He focused on Beth's too-white face, and his rage

exploded. He pulled away from her, spun around and jogged for the door.

Beth caught his arm. "What are you doing?"

"The fuckers out front are going to get a truth bomb from me. You're my wife. Mine. No one talks about you like that." He yanked free, wrenched the door open and raced down the hall.

"Justice! Goddammit," Simon snarled. "Stop!"

Hell no. He made it through the first turn in the cavernous hallway when a man-sized boulder slammed into his back. He hit the floor, a heavy weight pinning him.

"Jesus, get off me." Coiling his muscles, he flipped Simon aside, leapt up and rolled to the balls of his feet.

Simon jackknifed up, squaring off and blocking Justice from getting to the door. "You're not going out there. You'll make this worse."

More feet pounded around the corner behind him, but he was too pissed to care. "Fuck you, Simon. You don't decide. Beth's my wife. One of those protesters saw her in the car and bashed in her window with a sign, trying to hurt her. I'm not letting this happen." He had to do something.

"What about the band? You gonna go storming out there in a rage and hit someone, is that it, Justice? Beat them up on camera? Make those protestors hate us more than your *wife* already has?" Fury glinted in Simon's eyes. "This is it, man. We're finally breaking out and hitting lists. You can't go off half-cocked, attacking protestors."

"He's right, it won't help." Beth rushed up, taking Justice's hand and unclenching his fist.

His rage dialed down at her touch, replaced with protectiveness. Some color had returned to her cheeks. "You okay?" All this wasn't good for her or the kid. He couldn't let her get hurt like she had when Hans stabbed her.

"I will be." She threaded her fingers in his. "Unless you lose your temper and I have to bail you out of jail tonight."

She amazed him. How this girl could pull herself together when he was losing his shit showed exactly how strong she was. But she wasn't okay, her hand in his was clammy and trembling. Wrapping his arm around her, he walked her back to the greenroom, opened a water and handed it to her.

Beth drank it, then said, "How's he getting this stuff? I don't even know who took that video."

Shit, who had taken it? One of the neighbors? Or was Hayes having her watched? He didn't say that to her. She was already worried and upset. "I don't know. But right now, you need to sit down and—"

"How we doing in here?"

Justice craned his head around as a woman walked in carrying a tablet and a professional smile. He'd met her when they'd been here earlier today—Marla, the manager of the venue.

"Quite a display out front, isn't it? No worries, our security team here at Tampa Dome is the best, and we're coordinating with the police department. Everything is under control." She glanced at her tablet. "You have a meet-and-greet scheduled with some of your street team. They're in our reception room. Are you ready?"

It had completely slipped his mind. The street team was made up of fans who earned special perks by completing certain promotional tasks. He loved meeting fans, but now he hesitated.

"It might be best," Simon said evenly, "if Liza stayed here with security."

Justice bristled. "I'm not leaving her alone."

Simon strode over to him. "This is our job. We promised those fans."

"Just go," Beth said, tiredness thick in her voice.

He glanced around at all the band watching him. Damn it. Justice led Beth to the couch. "I'll be back before we go onstage."

She pulled out her phone and sat down. "Looks like I have a bunch of texts and calls anyway. Emily, Nikki, Tess, Sophie, oh, even Cassie." She looked up. "Did you know she started college this year? She's getting around really well on her prosthetic leg."

Of course he knew because Beth had told him a half-dozen times. That tiny spark of joy in her gaze nearly knocked the breath from his lungs. Beth had been thrown right back in the pool of misery, and yet a text from a girl like Cassie, a girl Beth had helped, gave her joy.

"Go meet your fans, rock star. I'm busy here."

He kissed her. "Stay with security until I get back." He got up and started out with his band. In the doorway, he looked back.

Beth was pressed into the corner of the couch, hunched over her phone, her beautiful face tight with strain. She looked so small and alone, it made his chest ache with the need to rush back, wrap her in his arms and shield her.

Forcing himself to close the door, he turned, coming face-to-face with Simon. "What? Christ, can you just get out of my face?"

"This is on you, Justice. That girl in there? She's already been stabbed once because you dragged her into the limelight. You say you love her, but even after she was attacked, you wouldn't make a choice."

"What the fuck are you talking about?"

"You could have walked away from music and chose her. Or you could have broken up with her and let her go home to make peace with her family. Instead, you're trying to have it all."

Tiny claws of panic tried to sink into him. Music was all he'd had until Beth, it was all he knew how to do. He was only good at one thing—being a rock star.

But Beth owned his heart. He had to be good enough for her.

"You don't understand, she couldn't go back to her family." Liar, they would have taken her back if he'd gotten out of her life. But how could he give her up? Beth was his anchor in the craziness of his world. She was his home and his heart.

"I doubt that, but if you really love her, then get Liza off the radar. She's in serious danger, and you damn well know it. Keep her away from the tour and off any media."

"Hide her?" Like his dirty little secret who he screwed and made babies with on the side? Dillion had tried that shit with Beth, and she'd told him to go fuck himself. Her family had tried to hide and silence Beth too.

Simon's eyes shadowed, going dark and cold. "Yes. Unless you want to end up like me."

"An unfeeling bastard?"

"A broken bastard." Simon walked off.

Justice watched, stunned. He'd told Beth once that nothing would break him. Nothing. His dad had broken. His mom had bailed. Justice swore he'd never be either of them.

But as he watched one of the proudest, most stubborn and determined men he knew walk away, he knew the brutal truth.

Losing Beth would break him too.

He had to find a way to protect her. And Simon was right, after seeing that protester spot Beth in the car and swing the sign at her, she wasn't safe.

He had to keep her safe at any cost. He wouldn't lose her, nor would he let anyone hurt her. He'd find and kill Hayes first.

That thought sank in and began to grow roots.

Liza woke up before she screamed. Oh God, her stomach pitched violently, and sweat slicked her skin. What time was it? She glanced over at the clock. Just after 4:00 a.m.

She didn't dare close her eyes for fear of seeing her nightmare again. Gene Hayes had stood in front of her, wearing sweatpants and holding out that drink, while behind her people closed in with those awful signs raised like baseball bats.

She'd been trapped with no way out and nowhere to run, voices blaring in her head, *Slut! Whore! You wanted it! You begged for it!*

Just the memory of the dream made her queasy. They'd gotten to bed around two, but she couldn't sleep now. In the glow of the clock, she could see Justice. He lay on his side, facing away from her, the big lion inked on his back poised to strike.

Loneliness and fear closed in tighter, the voices rising to an excruciating buzzing that cut into her brain. Her skin ached with the need for pain. Anything to override the horrible drilling whine that made her want to scream.

Carefully she eased back the covers. The chill of the air conditioner bit into her flesh, and she shivered. After getting her glasses, she went in the bathroom.

Almost without thought, her gaze slid to the big shower and her bright purple plastic razor sitting on the shelf next to the bottles of shampoo, conditioner and soap.

Her fingers spasmed with the need to seize that handle. She knew how to crack open the casing and get to the blade.

Forcing her gaze to the mirror, she stared at the woman there. Pale, tired, scared.

Crazy.

Don't cut. No cutting.

Grabbing her makeup case, she dug to the bottom and snatched out a rubber band. Sliding it over her wrist, she snapped it.

The sharp sting shot out from her skin, running through her like spreading cracks draining the intensity of the buzzing in her head.

More.

She did it again and again, raising welts on her wrist to fight the high-pitched static in her head. The screams of haters. The fear.

More. More.

Tears ran down her face, but she couldn't stop. This pain was better than the voices, fear and awful pressure. She didn't want to feel that, didn't want to be so terrified. She was afraid to sleep again.

"Goddammit."

She jerked her head up, her eyes colliding with a furious, steely gaze. Justice's hair stuck out everywhere, his face rough with thick, dark stubble, the blades of his cheekbones sharp enough to cut. He clamped his arms around hers, forcing her fingers to release the band.

Her mouth dried, and shame charred her from head to toe.

He slid the band off and threw it. Then he pulled her wrist up in front of them, the overhead lighting showing ugly red welts.

"I didn't cut." This was her crazy, her worst self.

His arm banded her rib cage, locking her in place. His other hand gripped her jaw to keep her from turning away from his mirror stare. "Talk to me." The growled words vibrated from his chest.

"You're mad."

"You wouldn't talk when we got home. You told me you were okay and you just wanted to sleep. That was a lie. Then you must have had a nightmare, and you didn't wake me up. Fuck yeah, I'm pissed. You don't hide in here and suffer alone. Now talk, right fucking now. I don't care how hard it is, talk."

His jaw bulged, and the veins on his neck stood out. Like seeing her hurting herself had snapped something in him. The shame at her weakness deepened, but she couldn't unhook her gaze from his to look away. As if his stare alone could tame the high-pitched drone of voices in her brain, the rushing thoughts that wouldn't calm. Justice was her lifeline, her safety net. He didn't hide his fury, and he didn't pretend it was okay or ignore her craziness. He confronted it head-on.

It took all her effort to squeeze out, "I had to make it stop."

"Keep going."

The command pulled more from her. "Nightmare, then I woke in terror, trying to scream but no sound came out. No one ever hears me."

"I hear you."

She shuddered and struggled to explain. "It's a dark sense of doom coming for me and everyone I love. Fear that I'll make the wrong choice and end up destroying my family again. You and our baby are my family."

When her fingers dug into her belly, she realized she'd laid her hand over her stomach. How screwed up was she that she wanted to cut when she was pregnant? "I don't deserve this. You, our baby. I don't. I wasn't even allowed to go to my dad's funeral. His family hated me, they said I was a groupie slut like my mom and we were poison. Even strangers hate me too. Like those people carrying the signs at the concert, and that woman who tried to hit me. Now they'll hate you too for loving me." All the words tumbled out, just like the blood had poured from her the day she'd slashed her wrist with that glass. *Shut up. Please.* "I need the pain to make it stop." It came out a tortured whisper.

His nostrils flared like some kind of bull's. "You're better than all of them. Every damned one." His jaw flexed, and his shoulders bunched. "You know Screech's song, 'Reaper's Child'?"

The sudden shift confused her. Now they were talking about a song? "Yeah?"

He turned on the water and shoved her welted skin beneath the stream. The cold water sent icy zings through her. Seconds later it soothed the burn.

"It's about a man fighting the reaper for his son, but he ultimately loses the battle and the reaper takes the kid away." He shut off the water and carefully dried her arm. Ferociousness blazed in mirror-Justice's eyes as he dropped the towel. Gripping her hair in his hand, he tugged her head back, forcing her to meet his eyes without the buffer of a mirror. "Your urge to cut is my reaper. Cutting can take you away from me. One mistake and you could die. I'm not letting that happen. You're mine. I'm not your weak, cowardly family that threw you out. You're mine, and I'll fight any force to keep you with me." He turned her around so they were face-to-face. "This battle you're struggling with? I'm right here fighting with you. Don't shut me out, Beth, like you did when we went to bed. Don't."

She'd done that. He'd tried to get her to talk, but by then, she was too upset. She'd been scared into silence that she didn't know how to break. "I wasn't cutting. The rubber band is how I cope."

He stroked a calloused finger over the welts. "You get the urge to cut when you hold in your feelings or you're afraid to tell me. When you think you have to be quiet and that people are judging you."

He knew her so well, but that didn't stop her rush of anger. "They are. What did I do to those protestors? I didn't do anything, yet they hate me. They think I'm a slut who trapped you into marriage with a kid that might not even be yours. They believe I seduced Hayes for a blackmail scheme, not that he drugged and raped me. My own family hates me." Her worst fear rumbled up and out. "What if you end up hating me too? If one day you believe his lies like everyone else?"

He spun around, slapping his hand against the wall.

With one arm up, his back contoured sharply, all his muscles so defined she could almost see the fibers. His lion tat watched her with predator eyes, the paw lifted, ready to pounce.

Icy sweat seared her skin, and her heart pounded. She couldn't bear it if he doubted her. "You don't believe him, do you? I told you what happened with Dillion that night." Her throat locked up.

Don't talk about it, Liza. You're making it worse. People are judging you. Her aunt's voice joined the others.

He spun around. "I believe you. I'll always believe you. It's him."

"Who? Dillion?"

"No, much as I hate him, you can handle that

douchebag Dillion. I'm talking about Gene Hayes. I want to kill him. Not rough him up. Not ruin him. I want to hunt him down like the animal he is and kill him with my bare hands for what he's done to you. For the rape. For the torment. For inciting others to stalk, harass and stab you." Snatching her wrist, he held it up so the jagged scars and fading welts shown in the light. "For this. But instead, I can't do jack shit because he's out of my reach. I can't touch him."

"I... You can't kill him." The only one who'd killed for her was her mother, and Amber paid for that with every breath she took in prison. Was Liza ruining Justice? "Please, don't go after him. I don't want to turn you into a killer. They'll take you away, lock you up." Like her mom.

"I can't, he's hiding like the rat he is. Yet he gets to do this, hurt my wife and my band."

She shuddered, so overwhelmed she didn't know how to handle this. Justice's love was terrifying and gratifying. Powerful. He hadn't doubted her, he'd been angry. "I feel the same way. Gene Hayes is my reaper, but I don't know how to fight him. I'm so scared he's going to win by tearing us apart. I don't know what he'll do to our child."

He wrapped his arms around her, tugging her against him. His heart thumped next to her face. "He won't. No one can tear us apart."

She lifted her face to his. "Swear it."

"It's our vow, remember? No one comes between us."

Liza desperately wanted to believe him.

Chapter 18

"CHICKEN." JUSTICE LEANED AGAINST A pile of pillows, his wife tucked between his legs with her computer on her lap. Right now, it was just the two them in Beth's book—the place where she brought him into her secret world.

They both needed the escape, a way to channel their raw passion and feelings.

Beth tilted her head back, looking up at him. "I'm thinking."

He grinned. "Do you always cluck when you think?"

She shot her hand out and pulled the hair on his leg.

He caught her fingers. "The scene is damned good, Beth. The hero walking in on her when she and the bassist are doing it the second time. Don't delete it. Go further. Up the stakes. Make the singer realize he loves her, and he has to be enraged at the bassist. He feels betrayed by both of them."

"But they're best friends," she protested. "And they've always shared groupies."

The risk was scaring her, but this was one worth taking. "Don't delete it. Use it. Make them all fall apart."

Resting her head against him, she brushed her fingers over his thigh. "I've never written a story like this. My characters are out of control. I create these worlds so I can make everything come out right."

Tingles raced up his leg to his engorged dick pressed between their bodies. But he focused on her. "Think of it another way."

"Such as?"

"This is your safe place to take risks. Any risk you want. Who's going to see it except you and me? Embrace the risk and the challenge. She's going to be pregnant. The father is one of the two former friends who hate each other because of her." He dropped a kiss on her head, loving the brush of her hair against his face. "Keep the scene and amp it up."

"You believe in me that much?"

This was what he loved—that look of awe and love shimmering in her eyes. He felt like her hero, but she did the same for him. She believed in his dreams as much as he believed in hers.

"Believe?" He shook his head. "I *know* you can do it. Reach for the stars, baby. You've got this." He stroked a lock of her hair and added, "I'd grow fucking wings and fly you into the sky if I could. But the truth is, you don't need a ride to your dream. You just need to quit worrying and write."

She reached up, laying her hand along his jaw. "I need you. You're my courage, Justice."

He looked down at her. "Another lie. You were brave long before you met me. You were surrounded by cowards trying to hold you back. Now quit stalling and write."

She hit save, then closed her computer and set it aside. Her lower back rubbed against his engorged dick. "You want me to write sex scenes."

Ah, now she was ready. His cock had been hard since he'd pulled her between his legs a half hour ago, but he'd savored it instead of rushing, letting Beth come down from her battle with her demons, and the two of them to relax. They didn't have enough time together, and he was greedy for more of her than a quick fuck. "Hell yeah. And fight scenes too, but mostly sex scenes. This one was really hot, especially when the bassist pushed her over the bed, yanked up her dress, and ripped her panties off." Justice slid his hand under her little tank, cupping her breast. She'd gotten bigger and more sensitive with the pregnancy. "It makes you hot to write the scenes. When I'm reading those in my bunk on the bus, I think about you writing and squirming as your pussy gets wet and swollen." He dragged his hand down her stomach and into her panties.

Beth spread her thighs for him.

"Wet." He rumbled the word out, hot hunger pounding. He needed her. "Admit it, writing that scene made you horny."

She pulled his hand out and twisted around until she straddled him. "Yes," she answered, and plucked off her shirt.

Justice lost his train of thought as her tits bounced free, swaying right in front of his face.

"And you know what I was thinking when I wrote it?"

Beth was changing the game on him, but he wasn't fighting it. His mouth dried. Clamping his hands around her hips, he tugged her forward.

"What?" He got the word out an instant before he latched on to her rigid nipple.

Beth arched, a moan breaking from her. Then she bent her head close to his ear. "That I can get you, my biggest fan, so excited you'll rip my panties off. I can make you do that."

A jolt of wicked-hot lust shot straight to his cock. He loved it when she told him what she wanted. Fulfilling his wife's fantasies was a huge turn-on. "You want it, get on your hands and knees." His voice lowered into a thick growl. His excitement wiped out any shred of caution. Beth knew her limits, and if she wanted this, he'd give it to her.

She did it, her sweet ass encased in those shell-pink panties. Tempting as fuck. Grabbing the material, he yanked, ripping the fragile cotton and tearing them off.

Bared. Beth was naked and her ass his. He drew a finger down her crack. "You like teasing your biggest fan? Writing dirty scenes to make me burn for you?"

Her fingers clutched the sheets. "I love it. Sometimes I touch myself, thinking about how you'll react. How big your cock will get."

Jesus. Hot chills lanced his spine. He reared up, gripping her hips. "You're going to find out how big I am." He pressed his dick to her.

The creamy, satin feel of her gloved him. Drove him insane. Unable to stop, he jerked her back as he surged in. He'd never taken Beth this way. His eyes rolled back. He bared his teeth as her pussy clamped around him. Sweat beaded.

Careful, a tiny voice of sanity whispered. *She's pregnant. And this could be a trigger for her too.*

"That all you got, groupie?" Her words tumbled out in pants. "I can write it harder. Wilder."

"Beth," he snarled in warning. All damned night he'd been in control. But this, his woman on her hands and knees, taking his cock and taunting him, frayed the last remnants of his control and sanity.

"Maybe I'll write you out of the scene."

That did it. He smacked her ass. "The hell you will. You're mine, every goddamned scene, every word is mine." He seized hold of her, snapping his hips, and going balls-deep while pulling her back at the same time, making her take every inch of his cock, his everything.

She threw back her head, a cry breaking from her as she came.

Justice lost his mind beneath the power of the blazing-hot pleasure ripping him apart. Minutes or days passed before he could catch his breath and unlock his muscles.

Beth had managed to stay up on her arms and knees, her back bowed and head dropped. He gathered her hair, turning her head to see her face. Her skin was flushed, eyes unnaturally bright. No glasses.

He glanced at the bed a few inches from her, and there they were. "I fucked your glasses right off your face." He smiled at her bemused expression. He knew she'd come hard. Easing from her, he put her glasses on the table. After using her torn panties to clean Beth and him up, he tucked her back to his chest. She was limp and sated.

"Looks like I fucked the wicked-writer attitude out of you too." Male pride damn near choked him. Okay maybe that was love. Because this girl? She was exactly what he needed. Only with her could he lose himself like that. But it was more—her trust. She'd been rendered powerless and hurt by a man before, yet she'd trusted Justice to take her from behind.

"Ha. I made you. I'm the writer."

He barely had the energy to laugh. "You threatened to write me out of the scene. That's a low blow." The thought dug in, burrowing into his fears. "You can't delete me like you wanted to delete that scene tonight."

She turned her head, looking at him in the sweep of light coming in from the partially opened bathroom door. "Never. I mean, I might delete the scene, but never you. You're my life."

Liza rode the elevator down, her stomach fluttering with nerves. She and Justice had had a late breakfast together on the little balcony of their room after checking to see that "Expired Hero" was holding on the charts. Hayes and the protesters hadn't done too much damage.

Once they were done eating, Justice had gone down to talk with his band while she showered and attempted to tame her hair.

And her anxiety. Everyone had been tense on the trip home last night. This morning the media was all over Liza, rehashing and speculating. Trying to get comments from Dillion and Stacy Jo. Those two idiots got a taste of her world, and she'd bet Dillion wasn't so in love with Liza now. Dillion's father probably had a few things to say to his son about that video too.

The elevator stopped, bouncing her from her spinning thoughts. Stepping out, she didn't see anyone in the cavernous living room to her left or massive kitchen straight ahead. It was around 1:00 p.m., so surely others were up by now. She and Justice were planning to explore the grounds and maybe go out on the boat before dinner tonight. Pulling out her phone, she was ready to text Justice when she heard Lynx's voice.

"You have to talk to her, man."

She jerked her head up. *Her?* Far as she knew, she was the only female aside from staff at the manor.

Everyone had been too preoccupied when they came home last night to be in the mood for partying with groupies. Returning her phone to her pocket, she headed to the open sliding doors. The patio had a big outdoor kitchen that led to a sparkling blue pool and beyond that, a dock stretched out over the bay. The afternoon sun, even in February, was warm and brilliant. Her attention honed in on her husband pacing, while the other four band members stared.

"What am I supposed to say to her?" Justice turned around, his face tight. "She's my wife, not one of your groupie chicks you bang and forget."

Lynx was bare-chested, his tats colorful against his skin. "It's all kinds of fucked up, but the four of us agreed. It's nothing against Liza personally."

"Fuck," Justice snarled. "The tour isn't even half over yet."

She held her breath, staying utterly still. They were only a dozen feet from her, but all of them were so focused on their conversation, they weren't aware of her standing there.

"The media only wants to talk about Liza." Simon unfolded from a chair, a coffee cup in his hand. "She, and your marriage, are becoming the story, not our music. And our numbers didn't climb with the concert last night, but Jagged Sin's did. They've passed us up. We should have gotten a bump after the concert, but people are taking sides, calling her Lyin' Liza, and it's getting ugly."

"Like *Court of Rock* all over again," River added.

Gray nodded. "Do you want her hurt? Not only that, Christine got a call from one of our venues saying that if we bring Liza, we have to pop for additional security."

Justice folded his arms, straining the seams of his

blue T-shirt that highlighted the curves and dips of his muscles. Frustrated anger lined every inch of his rigid stance. "You're giving me an ultimatum to ban my wife from the tour. You're supposed to have my back."

Simon stared him down. "And you're supposed to have ours. Have you talked to her about the postnuptial agreement protecting our record company? You said you would this weekend."

Justice turned away, the angle of his jaw unforgiving. "I'll get to it."

Liza pressed her hand on her belly. *Postnuptial agreement. Protect the company? Ban her from their concerts?* They wanted Justice to keep her hidden and neutralized. This felt all too familiar and so damned lonely.

"Not good enough. You have to handle this," Simon said. "Hayes has threatened to destroy her, and if he can find a way to get to our company through your wife—"

"I get it," Justice snapped.

"So what's it going to be?" Simon stared back at him. "Are you going to honor your commitment? Or turn Liza into a Yoko."

Liza slapped her hand over her mouth to stifle a gasp. In the eight months since that fight in the greenroom, she hadn't heard Simon or any of them call her that.

Now it was starting all over again.

Justice turned at a sound and froze for one endless second before he broke free. Striding past Simon, he took her hand. "Beth, you heard that?"

With all five of them staring at her, she refused to get emotional. Pulling herself together just like she did when she handled explosive situations at work, she lifted her chin. "Enough to get the gist. I'm banned from the tour and need to sign a postnuptial. Did I miss anything?" Her words were low and sharp enough to cut glass. "Do you all require a DNA test to prove the baby is Justice's once he or she is born?" She honed in on Justice. "Or is that covered in this mysterious postnuptial that your band knows about but I don't?"

"Hell." Simon rubbed the back of his neck. "We're not saying that Justice isn't the father. It's not personal, this is just business."

Yeah? Because it felt real damn personal. She pulled her fingers from Justice's hand and eyed him. "Well?"

He shot a death glare at the others, then recaptured her hand, his fingers firm. "Let's go for a walk." He tugged her out.

She followed to get answers and to escape the four men who clearly saw her as an obstacle that had be removed.

Justice ignored the pool and bay, turning right to head down some steps and out onto a trail. On one side the bay stretched out, and on the other were palm trees and pretty tropical plants. A cool breeze ruffled the hem of her tunic over cropped jeans. It was a serene, beautiful place.

Unlike her mind, which was filled with slime-coated trails of hurt and betrayal.

Minutes passed before she finally said, "Are you going to talk? Or are you looking for a place to dump my body to get rid of me permanently?"

"Not funny," he snapped.

She yanked her hand from his grip and crossed her arms. "What is the postnuptial for?"

He shoved his hands in the pockets of his shorts. "To specify that S.I. Records is not a part of our marital assets. But, of course, any income I make paid out by

S.I. Records is. That way if Hayes gets that verdict overturned and sues you, he won't be able to touch the company's assets."

"I see."

"It's not just my company, Beth. I have to protect my business partners."

What could she say? "Christine said she tried to talk you into having me sign a prenup. Why didn't you do it then?"

He jammed his fingers through his hair. "Because I didn't want to." Settling his palms on her biceps, he added, "I'm not protecting S.I. Records from you, I'm protecting it from Hayes."

The warmth of his touch and his reassurance flowed into her muscles, calming her enough to think. "I'll sign the postnup."

Shock widened his eyes. "You will?"

"Yes." She tried to sort out the threads of her upset.

He rubbed her arms. "So you're not mad?"

"Not about that." She turned out of his hold and walked along the path. Palm trees swayed gently in the breeze, creating a tranquility that contrasted sharply with her churning feelings.

Justice fell into step next to her.

"Last Friday on the phone, when you told me you missed me so much and wanted an extra day—it was to convince me to sign the postnup, wasn't it?"

Justice caught her arm, swinging her around to see the fire burning in his eyes. "No. I missed the fuck out of you and wanted you here so we could be together. You're pregnant with our child, and I'm not taking care of you. I feel that every damn day. Instead you're working, paying most of our bills, taking care of the house and my dad. So I wanted you here, and I wanted just once to give you a break, a chance to relax and be a little spoiled. But fucking Gene Hayes ruins every goddamned thing, and what I am is furious."

The hairs on her arms jacked up with the enraged energy pouring off him. Yet his fingers wrapped around her biceps were gentle. She swallowed, trying to control that sudden surge of relief in her throat. Justice did care. "Then why didn't you just tell me you needed the postnup instead of waiting? Because hearing it like that sucked. So did hearing your band has the power to ban me from your tour."

He winced and took her hand, resuming their walk. "Hayes is a serious trigger for you, Beth. Look what happened last night. You were close to cutting. But at least I was here with you. When you're home and I'm out on the road, I'm fucking helpless. You're out of my reach, and that scares me."

"You were scared I'd take the postnuptial as rejection?" Yeah, it hurt a little bit, but she understood the necessity.

His fingers tightened around hers. "I just didn't want to add to your stress. Plus you were dealing with Douchebag Dillion and my dad showing up. I don't know. It made sense at the time. But then I saw your face and realized I fucked up."

Beth stayed quiet, listening to the boats on the bay and a dog barking in the distance. Up ahead, a pretty white gazebo sat on a rise. She headed that way, climbing the steps to find a porch swing. She took a seat.

Justice settled next to her, put his arm around her and tugged her to his side. "Are we okay?"

"Don't keep secrets from me. It feels like I'm being manipulated and controlled." Leaning her head back, she looked up at the ceiling of the structure. Everything was so clean. Did the staff wash it down weekly? "Obviously my dad and Hayes concocted the plan to get me to his house that night, and I didn't know anything about it. I believed my dad, but he had this secret agenda, you know?"

"Fuck. You can't think this is the same thing."

Twisting her head to see him, she said, "No, but I still felt blindsided and hurt. It's bad enough your band doesn't want me around. But you—"

He laid a hand on her face. "I want you with me every single day. I'd fight the band on this, Beth, except for one thing."

"What?"

"It's not safe. You could have been hurt last night. I can't go through that again." He leaned his forehead against hers. "I'd have given anything to trade places with you when you were crumpled on the ground, bleeding, in pain and terrified after you were stabbed. That's why I'm not fighting. I'll come home and see you. But I need you safe, Beth. And I need you to trust me."

His words were sweet, but it was the way he pressed his head to hers, his arm around her, his eyes piercing in their intensity that convinced her heart he really was trying to protect her. He'd taken care of her after she'd been hurt, stood by her and loved her. The risk to her was real. "You're right. I don't want our baby hurt either."

"I'm trying to protect both of you. You know that, right?"

Liza wanted to believe that, but a tiny doubt flickered. Justice had told her when they discovered she was pregnant not to make him choose between her and the baby, and his dream of being a rock star.

He hadn't chosen her over his band today. Sure, Liza understood his reasons intellectually. But a part of her feared pushing him into a real choice.

Because he might not choose her.

Chapter 19

LIZA HUGGED HER TWO FRIENDS then sat at the square table with the snowy linen tablecloth in the gorgeous restaurant. The huge window gave them a perfect view of the sun setting over the Pacific Ocean. She'd been tense ever since she'd returned from Tampa less than a month ago, and a night out with the girls was exactly what she needed.

Taking her seat, she raised her eyebrows at Emily. "Someone's showing off. I can't afford to eat here when it's not on SLAM's dime."

Emily grinned. "I love this job. And I couldn't wait to use my discount, so order whatever you want. It's my thank you for helping me get this job, Liza." She shifted to Nikki. "And both of you for helping me with my resume."

Nikki picked up her menu. "You just started this week and already get perks. I'm so jealous. Event Coordinator for the Opulence Hotel. Now that's glamorous."

Liza assured Nikki, "We'll find something awesome for you too."

"I know. But I have a job, Emily's need was more

urgent." A wicked smile curved Nikki's mouth. "Although I was tempted to apply for the job, because...look around this place. This is the life."

The waiter stopped by their table. Once they ordered, Liza asked, "So what's the most exciting thing about your job so far?"

"Let me think." Emily bit into a slice of warm, crusty bread. After swallowing, she went on, "I'm getting up to date on a few weddings and conferences we're doing this spring and summer. One stands out though—that wedding has a baseball theme."

"Baseball?" Liza looked up from buttering her bread.

"Like...the game?" Nikki asked.

"Like they want a batting cage at the reception." Emily took her wine from the waiter and sipped it.

Liza tried to picture that. "How will you pull that off?" She didn't have a clue how to set up a batting cage. Or why anyone would want a baseball-themed wedding.

Em laughed, clearly happy. "Anything is possible with money. They met at a baseball game, and this is what they want."

"Wow," Liza said. "If I were planning a wedding, it wouldn't be with a baseball theme." Her own marriage at city hall seemed more romantic than that.

"My dream would be a destination wedding in Italy, or maybe Hawaii." Nikki's eyes gleamed. "Or Greece."

"Not me. I just want my brothers not to embarrass the shit out of me at my wedding," Em groused.

Liza grinned at her. "Not only will they torment you, Ben will probably help them. You should elope if you ever marry."

"The way you did it might be smarter. Simple and no fuss. Way less expensive too."

"You mean the knocked-up quickie?" She scrunched her nose. "Or as some social media site called it, Lying Liza's trap." She really needed to stay off that website, *Bring Gene Hayes Home*. The headlines and stories, like *Lying Liza Banned from Savaged Illusions Tour*, stung.

"Assholes," Em muttered. "Where are they getting this stuff?"

"Maybe someone on the band's road crew is leaking it," Nikki suggested. "They must overhear the band talking about things."

"I don't know. But it was like this when I was fourteen. No matter what my aunt and the prosecutor's office did, things got out to the media. Reporters and creeps dug through our trash. They even hounded my two younger cousins. The media finds out stuff, or they make it up. The truth doesn't matter. People love the sensationalism."

"It matters to me," Em said.

"And me," Nikki added. "This whole thing is surreal." After chewing a bite of her steak, she went on. "I can't believe Jagged Sin pulled their shit together enough to release an album."

Liza nodded. "And now it's this huge indie rock feud between them and Savaged Illusions. The last week, it's almost all Justice talked about."

"He's excited about coming home though, right?" Em said. "You guys will find out the baby's sex at your ultrasound."

She barely tasted her shrimp. "He says he is. He's flying in tomorrow afternoon, and the appointment is Thursday morning."

"Liza." Em leaned forward. "Is something wrong? You guys aren't fighting, are you?"

"No. Nothing like that. I just miss him, and you

know..." It'd been three weeks since she saw him in Tampa. "I had to reschedule the ultrasound once because something came up." They talked, and she sent him her pages, same as usual, except he'd been more distracted the last few days. Now she was being the downer. "But he's coming home, and that will help. Oh, and I have news."

"What?" Emily dug into her fish.

"I got an offer to appear on IRB's TV show in the Rock Wives segment."

Nikki set her fork down. "Oh my God, Liza! You have to do it!"

"Sh." She didn't want anyone to overhear. Her nerves tangled. "I'm thinking about it. I've told Keith no in the past, but—"

Em slapped her hand on the table. "Why the hell not?" Her eyes blazed fire. "It's time you fought back against the media."

She was torn, knowing how easy it was for anything she said or did to be twisted. "The last time I was in an interview with IRB, that's how Gene Hayes found me. Plus, the band wants me to stay quiet." Just like her aunt and grandmother had.

"That's bullshit," Emily snapped. "I'm getting really damned tired of hearing you defend this crap."

"I negotiated a little and got Keith to agree that if I do the Rock Wives segment, it'll be about the project I'm passionate about. We'll still touch on being married to Justice, life as a rock star's wife, but I can really put this program out there."

"SLAM Heroes?" Nikki asked.

That was what drew her to the idea. She could show people how much most of their fighters cared about helping victims feel safe. It was her chance to really showcase her beloved project that she'd developed with Drake's invaluable help. She refused to talk about Gene Hayes, except in the context of how Liza understood how scary it was to testify and face your attacker in court, and how that led her to establish the SLAM Heroes program. "Sloane and publicity are okay with it. I just have to talk to Justice."

"You are not asking his permission." Em glared.

Liza hated the way that sounded. "No, I wanted to—"

Her phone played "Expired Hero," her ringtone for Justice. He didn't usually call this early in the evening. He was playing in a club tonight...somewhere. "Uh, that's Justice." Tugging out her phone, she answered, "Hi."

"Beth, World Rock Stage posted the short list for Indie Breakout Band. We're on it! We made the short list."

She flushed with excitement. "Congratulations! How many bands?"

"Five." He listed them. "According to Christine, the only one who's real competition is Jagged Sin."

He sneered that name though the cell. Liza smiled. "You'll win, rock star. This is your time. We'll celebrate after you get home tomorrow."

"About that—"

Her heart dropped into her stomach.

"—I can't make it home, Beth. I'm sorry."

She closed her eyes as disappointment crashed over her. "I rescheduled the ultrasound for you. Don't you want to know our baby is healthy? If we're having a boy or girl? Justice—"

"We're in the chase now, sweetheart. We're flying to New York tomorrow for a round of cocktail parties, interviews and a photo shoot. There's nothing I can do."

"You could come home." Her eyes pricked, and that pissed her off.

"Beth, please, I know you're disappointed, but this is important. If we get the Indie Breakout Band nod, we go to the World Rock Concert in France. That will make our careers."

"More important than our child?" Or her? She could hear the pleading tone in her voice and hated herself. She was in the middle of a restaurant with two friends. *Snap out of it.* She wasn't doing this now.

"Of course not. Can you reschedule the ultrasound? Maybe in a couple weeks?"

"No."

She heard voices and a female giggle in the background of the call.

"I'm on the phone," Justice snapped. "I'll be there in a minute."

Liza took a slow breath, trying to drown the ugly jealousy swimming around her brain. "Who was that?"

"River and two chicks he's practically wearing as skin. I called to share the good news. I'm sorry I can't be there Thursday, but you can send me a video."

She wondered if those skintight chicks would be going with them to New York while Liza sat at home. "Will I be sending you a video of your child's birth too?" Did that sound bitchy? Because it felt pretty damned good.

"Fuck. Are you really doing this? I'm busting my ass traveling the entire country, singing four to seven nights a week in different venues, trying to make it. For you and the kid."

"That's a lie. It's for you, for your dream, the one that drives every decision you make." *Like banning me from the tour.* "I've been supportive, I've sacrificed. All I asked you to do is come home one time to see your child's ultrasound." She cut off before her voice broke and weeks of pain, fear and loneliness spilled out.

"You're overreacting and stomping my balls because I can't make one doctor appointment. This is my job, Beth."

And she was only his wife. The one he'd knocked up and felt obligated to marry. She stared down at her pretty rings he'd had made from his grandmother's diamonds. She loved them so much.

She loved him.

But each day it felt like they were being torn apart. It was a physical pain, as if something were being ripped from her body.

"Beth? I'm sorry. Christ, I'm just...I can't do it."

For a horrible second, the pretty restaurant in San Diego faded away, and Liza was a kid again maybe about eight, sleeping in some crappy trailer and woken by screaming.

Her mom and her latest boyfriend—another stringy-haired, drugged-up musician—had been out screwing around. Liza had snuck out to see her mom screaming and throwing whatever she could, her face a twisted mask of hatred. The place had stunk of old beer, cigarettes and broken, bloody dreams.

Was that who she and Justice would become? Ravaging each other?

Had her aunt been right all along?

Pressing her fingers against her stomach in a desperate attempt to protect her child from the pain she'd suffered, she got control of herself. "You're right. It's one appointment. We'll talk later. I'm happy for you guys making the short list."

"Shit, they're calling me to get back onstage for our last set. I'll call you tonight, okay? Love you."

The line went dead, and heaviness settled on her chest.

"You okay?" Nikki laid a hand on her arm.

She tried to shake off the ghost of her past. She was here in a lovely restaurant with two friends who'd obviously heard enough of the conversation to get the gist. This was her life, and she'd deal with it. "Fantastic. I'm a rock star's wife." She shoved her half-eaten dinner away. "Where's the dessert menu?"

"Making that short list is legit." Lynx slugged down half his beer.

Justice finished off his brew in the stuffy tour bus as he and Lynx waited for the rest of the band to get their asses on board. They had an early morning flight to New York, and he had to wind down and try to get some sleep. "Best night in a long time." Or it had been until he talked to Beth.

Fuck.

He leaned his head back on the couch, legs stretched out and feet touching the opposite wall. She'd been so damned upset. *Because you let her down, and you damn well know it.*

He had to call her back now that the night's concert was over. But what would he say? *Sorry, but I'm not giving up this shot?* Or how about, *I'd already cancelled the flight before I called you?* Yeah, that'd be even better.

"What's eating you, J?"

This was his oldest friend. He didn't have to lie. "Beth. What am I supposed to do here?"

Lynx set his bottle on the floor and picked up his sticks, tapping out a beat on the seat. "This life fucks up a marriage. You've seen the shit that goes on. Some women can do it, but they're rare." He cut his gaze over. "Regrets? I mean you could be chasing pussy.

Hell, you wouldn't have to chase, they're all over you."

They were all over Lynx too. He'd had a girl in the bus tonight while they were on break between sets, and Justice had been standing in the dirty alleyway talking on the phone to Beth. He closed his eyes. He was a guy, so sure, he looked, and yeah, temptation happened. But he wasn't a cheater. "If I'm going to fuck around, I'd tell Beth we're done. I'd own that."

"Straight up way to be. I hate liars. But your deal with Liza? That's harder. She heard us talking about banning her from the tour. She's dealing with the smears in the media. Everything is leaking out, even that you two have a postnuptial. Then you bail on the ultrasound, and, well, you know chicks and babies."

But this wasn't just a chick and a baby, they were his. "This is what Simon warned me about." Going after superstardom didn't mix with love. You couldn't have two all-consuming passions. Something had to give.

"Yeah, and you bail on us now, I'll kick your ass. All of us will. We didn't work this hard to get sabotaged by our lead singer."

Exactly. Caught between a rock and a hard place.

"Finally, Christ, I've been texting you for forty minutes." Simon's voice came from outside the bus. "We need to roll."

"Fuck off." The bus shifted as River climbed aboard and turned down the aisle.

Justice caught a whiff of him. "You smell like a perfume factory. Open a window."

River swung his gaze to him. "It's called getting laid with girls, not my hand. Try it sometime." He grabbed a beer out of the fridge. "So the short list for Indie Breakout Band." He lifted the beer in a toast. "To us, best damned rock band. And no one to give a shit beyond a hard fuck." He downed several swallows of the brew.

Justice could almost feel the loneliness rolling off River, even though he'd clearly just been with a girl or two. Both Lynx and River didn't have family. Well, Lynx had had his mom until she'd overdosed.

But River? Nada. He didn't even remember a lot of his childhood or how he came to be wandering the streets one night as a kid. The peacemaker and charmer in their band was fraying at the edges. "Not true. Drake, Sloane, all the guys give a fuck," Justice said. That was what Fighters to Mentors gave them—a connection to people who cared what became of you.

He opened his mouth to ask if River had texted Cassie, the sweet, funny girl who always cheered him up, but Gray and Simon boarded, followed by their driver. In five minutes, they were rolling out.

"Only competition on that short list is Jagged Sin." Simon passed more beers around where they'd settled at the table.

"Yeah," River agreed. "Who'd have thought we'd ever consider them real competition."

Justice lifted his head, his mind spinning. "They've upped their game, I'll give them that. But we're better." And he still hated the bastards, especially now that they were in business with Hayes.

"We don't take our foot off the gas now, it's pedal to the metal," Simon said. "We have to stay focused and work harder."

He started to answer when his phone rang. He glanced at the screen.

Beth.

For an instant, he considered sending it to voicemail. He just wasn't up for another dip in the guilt pool. But he wasn't a pussy either, and Beth deserved better. Getting up, he answered, "Hi, baby. I'm sorry about—"

She cut him off. "I'm calling about your dad. The transitional center called earlier. He's sick with a cough and running a fever, and he was trying to leave."

"Leave? Where?" He stopped at his upper bunk, pressing his forehead to the wood frame.

"Apparently he comes and goes from the center, often spending nights on the street instead of his room. They called me because he's running a one hundred and two fever and coughing. He won't go to the hospital, so I picked him up and brought him home. Ben came by and diagnosed bronchitis. Nikki went to the pharmacy to pick up the prescription Ben called in for him."

The bus turned a corner, and Justice gripped the edge of his bunk to brace himself. He tried to absorb it all. "Is he going to be all right?"

"I think so. I had to beg him to come home with me, and then to let Ben look at him. He's...haunted. I know it's the fever, but I hate seeing it."

He climbed into his bunk and stretched out. God he was tired. "It's not working, is it? He's not getting better with the center's treatment." His dad's head was still in that war zone he'd physically left years ago.

"This is who he is now," she said gently.

He wasn't the father Justice remembered. Part of him understood why his mom had left—sometimes it was just too hard to stay. "He can get better than this, he has to try."

"He's trying, or he wouldn't go back to the center when he leaves."

Her soft kindness overwhelmed him. He pictured her there at home, dealing with his sick and tormented dad. What if Noah woke up screaming? What would Beth do? Damn it. This was Justice's big chance, but it was his dad. His wife. His kid. "What do you want me to do? He won't listen if I talk to him. Even if I came home...he'd leave. There's no point."

Silence rocked between them.

"Beth? Are you okay?"

"No point in you coming home?"

It struck him how that sounded to her. "I meant with my dad. Not you. Of course I want to see you, but I can't right now." He was fucking this up worse.

"What's happening to us?"

Her whispered pain cut into his heart. "It's just stress. We'll get through this. We knew it'd be hard, right?"

"It feels like you're slipping away from me and our family into the life of a rock star."

"What am I supposed to do?" He fought to get the defensive tone out of his voice. "You knew what my life was going to be like when you married me. You knew I was going on tour." But she hadn't known she'd be banned, now had she?

"That's true. We had to work in a quick marriage ceremony around your release and tour." There wasn't any bitterness in those words, just a sad resignation. Was she having real regrets?

Not knowing what else to say, he blurted out, "Do you want me to come home? I can try to get a flight tonight, then fly to New York tomorrow." And what, squeeze her in for a couple hours?

She sighed. "No, go to New York. Your dad's fine here, it's his home."

The distance between them stretched like an endless chasm. He didn't know how to reach across it. "I love you, and I need you to trust me. Can you hang in there with me? It's only a few more weeks, then I'll be home, and things will be the way they used to be between us. You'll see, okay?"

"Okay, but I need the same trust from you."

"Trust how?" One thing popped in his head. "Has that fucker Dillion been around again? If he—"

"No. Other than a one-line apology text from him, I haven't heard a word from him or his fiancée. I was hoping to talk to you about this in person, but I've been asked to go on Rock Wives."

"The IRB show?" They usually wanted the wives of rich stars for that segment. But Beth wasn't just a rock star's wife, she was the girl who ruined another rock star. Everyone wanted to get her story.

"Yes. It's been hard, Justice. I sit here while people say things about me. Every day, there's something on that *Bring Gene Hayes Home* site." Her voice cracked. "They even had a story that my aunt who raised me had cut me off."

Fuck. He hadn't seen that one. He tried to think of something to say to make her feel better, but what?

"I want to do this interview. It's a chance to show I'm more than the lying, scheming slut Hayes is putting out there. Most of the women on the show get to feature a cause, and mine is SLAM Heroes."

She really wanted this, but it was too risky. "If you go on that show, it's going to get all the protesters riled up. Who knows what shit Hayes will pull next? We're in the final few weeks."

He heard a shuddery breath. "I was hoping you'd trust me more than that. Believe in me."

"I do." Damn it. She didn't ask him for much, but this could really backfire. *Think.* There had to be a way... Wait. "Beth, does it have to be right now? Can you do this after the tour? If we get the Indie Breakout

Band nod, we'll be going to Paris in May, so how about after that?"

"Will I be invited to go with you, or staying home while you're in France?"

That punched him smack in his center. "You think I'd go without you? I know how much you've done and sacrificed to help us." He'd damn well take her to Paris. In fact... "We could go a few days early and be tourists." If they got that invitation to World Rock Stage, they were set, and even his band couldn't object to Beth going with them. And if they did, he'd tell them to kiss his ass. He was taking his wife.

"A few days in Paris," she said, her voice going warm with building excitement. "Like the honeymoon we never had. Real time together before the baby comes."

Finally he'd found a way to make her happy and stay on track to superstardom. "We get that invitation for Indie Breakout Band, and we're going to Paris."

"All right, I'll postpone Rock Wives until their fall taping. That'll be after the baby comes. Now go win me a trip to Paris, rock star."

He wouldn't disappoint her again.

"Justice!"

The screaming girls kicked up his pulse, and Justice grinned and waved. Half the time he barely remembered what state he was in, but that thrill never died. Recognition. Adulation.

"Lynx, can I play with your stick?" another voice called.

"Anytime, baby!" Lynx called back.

"Justice, your wife is a skank!"

He froze.

Simon grabbed his arm. "Keep walking." Once inside, they passed through the security check and made their way into the greenroom. Justice slammed his hand flat against a wall. "When will this shit stop? I swear—"

"I can help relax you." A warm hand slid down his arm. Cloying perfume clogged his nose.

A flash went off.

"What the fuck?" Justice whirled away, startled to see a blonde chick with a huge rack purring at him. Behind her in the doorway was another woman with gothic-black hair and a pinched expression, backed up by a guy with a camera.

The dark-haired woman pushed in, forcing the blonde back. "I'm Rachelle from *Thump Beat*. I was told to meet you in here for an interview." She glanced at the blonde. "You can come back later."

River stepped in front of the blonde. "What's your name?"

"Tiffany."

"Nice to meet you, I'm River. As you can see..." he gestured to the reporter and camera, "...we have some business to take care of. But how about after the show, I buy you a drink?"

The girl melted. "Really?"

"Yep." He eyed the badge around her neck. "You have a backstage pass, find me after the show."

"I will." The girl bounced in excitement as River deftly steered her out of the room.

"Is he really going to meet with her, or is that his brush-off line? Rumor is River's a huge playboy," the reporter asked.

Justice had forgotten they had an interview scheduled, and that had been an awkward start. Getting his head into the game, he shook the reporter's hand. "I'm Justice, and yeah, River meant it. I won't lie, River's a total dog, but he genuinely likes women."

River walked back in, and they all settled on the couch and chairs.

Rachelle began with, "This battle is heating up between Savaged Illusions and Jagged Sin. It's down to you and them to get the coveted Indie Breakout Band from World Rock Stage. Do you guys think you can win the title?"

They were running neck and neck thanks to that damned Bring Gene Hayes Home website.

"One hundred percent," Lynx said.

"Absolutely. We're the better band," Simon added.

She turned to Justice. "What about you? Do you think you can win when many rock fans hate your wife? Word is she's been banned from your shows."

Shit. Every fucking interview it came back to Liza. "You guys hear about this ban?"

River frowned. "No. Only thing on my banned list is Brussels sprouts. What about you, Gray?"

"Dude, you should try Brussels sprouts roasted with some garlic. Broaden your horizons."

"Not happening. Brussels sprouts are demon food." River turned to the interviewer. "Do you like Brussels sprouts? Tell Gray here I'm right. Brussels sprouts are creepy."

Rachelle blinked. "Let's stay on topic. Rumors are running rampant that your wife is cheating, and the baby might not be yours. The Bring Gene Hayes Home website posted today that you refused to go to doctor appointments and want nothing to do with the kid. Is it true?"

Justice surged up to his feet. Where the fuck were they getting this stuff? Jesus Christ. Jerking out his phone, he pulled up the site.

Justice Cade out partying in Manhattan while his wife goes to doctor appointment alone. There was a picture of him at one of the cocktail parties in New York, his arm slung around a redhead in a slinky black dress. She had her hand on his chest, her eyes screaming *fuck me.* In the bottom corner was a picture of Liza walking into a medical building by herself.

Yeah, he'd been a bit wasted, but he didn't touch that girl beyond the pictures. He'd gone back to his room and read Beth's pages featuring the threesome and jerked off, thinking of his wife.

Beth had likely seen this. She saw it all. Had he even talked to her today? He glanced at the picture again. Two days after that party, he'd called Beth from the airport, and she'd been sick with the same crap-ass cold his dad had.

And Justice had flown to the Midwest to continue his tour.

He shifted his gaze back to Rachelle. "Not a shred of truth. Liza's my wife, and that baby is our child." Daughter. They were having a girl. "And I'm damned lucky Liza is putting up with all this shit." But how long would she do it? It'd been almost five weeks since he'd seen her.

He kept letting her down.

And then stuff like this? How would he feel if he saw a picture of Liza with some man all over her? Like Dillion. Oh fuck no, he'd kill the bastard.

He really wanted to kill Gene Hayes. More each day. Too agitated to continue, he said, "I have something to take care of. I'll let you guys finish the interview." Justice stalked out of the room. Winding around the hallway, he found an empty room, went inside and called his wife.

"Justice, don't you have to go onstage?"

Her voice had the husky note he loved so much. He leaned against the wall. "I miss you, Beth. I walked out of an interview just to hear your voice. Talk to me. How are you feeling?"

"I'm better now. Cold's gone."

"My dad still showing up at night?"

"Sometimes. When I took him back the other morning, I talked to one of his counselors. He thinks you should come in to try some family therapy with your dad. He's not forming any bonds there, and they're worried. They're hoping bringing you in will trigger a breakthrough."

More pressure squeezed his heart. "This was the other day? Why didn't you tell me?"

She hesitated. "I told them you were on tour and wouldn't be back until the week after next. But I should have texted you right then, I'm sorry. I meant to do it when I got to work, but I walked into... Never mind. Sorry."

What was he doing? "You have nothing to be sorry for. I know you were sick, sweetheart. I was just surprised since my dad didn't even talk to me the one time I was there. I'll give them a call tomorrow and set something up at the transitional center."

"Will you be home sooner than expected?"

Tension crackled down the airwaves. "I don't think I can, unless we cancel a show. If I do that, it costs us a fortune in penalties and ticket refunds."

"I know."

Right, and that was why she hadn't rushed to tell him about his dad. The dad she was obviously taking care of. He had to tell her why he called. "Beth, the picture that came out today, I didn't touch her once the photo was done." He stared at the economy-sized packages of paper towels and toilet paper lined up on shelves. He was in a storage closet. Lovely.

The pause killed him before she said, "Okay."

"You believe me, right?"

"I'm trying. I really am."

Her pain ripped through the cell line and made him feel like shit. "It's only another week and few days. Just hold on and I'll be home. I'm not cheating on you." He needed to get his ass back to San Diego and help her, take care of her. Go to a damned doctor appointment.

"Good luck tonight. Have a great show."

She obviously didn't want to talk about it. "I love you, Beth. I'll text tonight to see if you're still awake after the concert."

"Okay. Love you." She hung up.

He stood in the storage room, cold fear seeping in. When had things gotten so hard and awkward? They'd been a lot of things—honest, raw, pissed, happy, and turned on. But never this distance until after Tampa. It just kept growing.

He couldn't lose her. The old sense of abandonment closed around him. A pit of loneliness engulfed him, making him feel so fucking worthless.

Shoving off the wall, he headed out of the dank room. Time to get out onstage.

The one place he could make them love him.

Chapter 20

LIZA JUGGLED TWO BAGS OF groceries around her five-and-a-half-month-pregnant belly, her purse and her keys. "Sorry, baby, don't mean to squish you. But I have news. Your daddy's coming home tomorrow. The tour is finally over."

A gentle flutter in her belly made her laugh. "Yeah, I'm excited too." And a little scared. He'd been surrounded by beautiful, sexy girls, and nope, not going down this road tonight. Sliding in her key, she unlocked the door, then froze when she heard music blasting.

The hair on the back of her neck stood. *Run!* But wait...she checked the alarm. It flashed the warning that the door had been opened just now, which meant it was on and worked, so no one could have broken in. But her father-in-law had a key and the alarm code. After entering the code to disarm the system, she crouched down, setting the bags and her purse on the floor, and grabbed her phone. "Noah?"

"No, it's me, Beth." Justice strode out from the kitchen, wiping his hands on a towel.

Wait, what? She was picking him up tomorrow. "I

didn't... You're..." She couldn't think what to say. Instead she drank in the sight of her husband. His hair was longer and brushed back, face a little sharper, blue eyes glittering as he slid his gaze over her, locking on her belly.

"You're showing."

Her hand flew to her stomach, unsure if she was boasting or hiding. "Five and a half months. She flutters around in there. It feels like butterfly wings."

"Beth."

"What?"

He tossed the towel over his shoulder and opened his arms. "Come here. I need to hug my girls."

Whatever held her frozen cracked. She kicked off her heels and ran to him. The second his arms closed around her, warmth engulfed her. The feel of his hard chest crushing her breasts, his ridged stomach against her rounded one, filled her with joy. His scent flooded her, and she inhaled, desperate to replace all the loneliness and uncertainty that had been festering for weeks.

His hands caught her butt, lifting her. "Damn, baby, I'm already hard for you. It's been too long."

Liza kissed his neck, her nipples throbbing. "Now."

He pulled back, his lips curving in a wicked grin. "Horny?"

"God yes. You don't know what it's like with all these hormones running amok like sex-starved teenagers."

His laughter rumbled, teasing her nipples.

She didn't want to wait. "Let's go—"

"Not yet."

"Why?" She could feel his erection pressing against her, thick, hard, and straining the fabric of his jeans.

His breath blew across her neck. "I made you dinner. Fried chicken. And I have a surprise."

Surprise? Oh, did he say fried chicken? She twisted her head toward the doorway to the kitchen and inhaled. Sure enough, she caught the mouthwatering aroma of old-fashioned fried chicken. It was his grandmother's recipe from the diner she'd owned and Justice had grown up in.

And something else too, an acerbic, familiar scent. "Do I smell paint?"

"That's my other surprise. Well, one of them." He slid her down to her feet. "I hope you like it. If not, I'll redo it, I just..." He scrunched up his face. "I'm actually nervous. This is worse than my preshow jitters."

She was still trying to get her bearings. "What is? Did you take up painting? Did you paint a chicken? Oh, I know, it's a rooster." Why was she babbling?

Taking her hand, he tugged her toward the hallway. "Nope. I painted this." He led her to the doorway of the first bedroom on the right.

She glanced in and gasped. "You did this?" The double bed, bookshelf, and dresser were gone. The room was empty, with a fresh coat of soft, sweet yellow. It was like walking into the first rays of morning sunshine, warm and embracing. "You did all this? When?"

"I flew in this morning and hauled ass here to paint the room before you got home. I spent a week looking at colors and talking to Ben and begging him to get Em to help. She was so pissed at me."

"Em helped you choose this?"

He turned her to face him, hands on her shoulders, eyes boring into hers. "I want our baby, Beth. Our daughter. You were so hurt when I couldn't get home for the ultrasound. I want to show you I'm here and I'm in. All in. I love you. I'm going to take better care of you now that I'm home."

She couldn't quite breathe. "Remember those hormones I was telling you about?"

"The sex-starved teenagers?"

"They're getting all weepy and messy." She blinked, trying to keep from crying.

He laughed. "Do you like it? The color I picked? You mentioned peach or yellow, but peach is your color."

"Mine?"

"You smell like peaches, and it's a turn-on. I can't have that in my daughter's room. So I chose yellow for her. Is it okay?"

Liza gazed at the room again. "I love it. Thank you."

He kissed her, then groaned. "Don't tempt me. Once I get you in bed, I'm keeping you and your sex-starved hormones there." He glanced down at her dress. "I need five minutes to mash the potatoes and make the gravy."

"Oh, I left the groceries by the front door."

"I'll get them. That dress is pretty on you, but go get comfortable. You're going to be naked very soon anyway."

She rushed to put on her yoga pants and tank, no bra just to torture him. They ate in the dining room and did the dishes together like old times, talking, laughing, and finally Justice pulled her into his arms. "I have one more surprise."

"What?"

"The announcement will come out at midnight EST, but we got the notification."

Her heart rate jumped, and Liza went up on her toes. "You got it?"

"You're looking at the lead singer of the Indie Breakout Band for World Rock Stage. And he's taking his wife on a belated honeymoon to Paris."

Liza squealed, so damned happy and proud of Justice. "I have a honeymoon to plan! How many days will we have in France before the show?"

He laughed as he scooped her up as if she hadn't gained any weight, and walked down the hallway. "Three days all to ourselves before the practice and events start." In their room, he laid her on the bed. "You can plan tomorrow. Tonight is all about making love to my wife."

She was totally on board with that.

"I grabbed you a coffee." Lynx handed over the to-go cup.

Justice accepted it and took a long drink of the strong brew. "Thanks, man." Lynx had known Justice had an appointment today at the transitional center. The family therapy session left him with a killer headache. For forty minutes, his dad refused to look at him and gave muttered, one-word answers.

Then the counselor brought up his mother.

Justice winced again as the memory replayed.

She bailed like the coward she is, Justice had said.

Watch the way you talk about your mother, Noah replied.

Justice couldn't fucking believe his dad said that. They'd had words, then Justice's temper snapped. *She left me. I got arrested, and she left me to rot in jail. Informed me I was a loser and left. So don't fucking tell me to have respect for her.*

Robin did that?

He should have reined it in then. The utter shock on his dad's scarred face had been more than he could take. *You both did. The only one who gave a damn was Grandma.* Justice had walked outside to cool down and get control of himself. When he'd gone back inside, his dad was gone. Everyone assumed he'd gone to his room, but when Justice checked, he wasn't there.

Noah had left the center.

Once again, Justice with his big fucking mouth had driven his dad away. He hadn't even told Beth yet, just got his ass on the road to L.A. to sign the contracts for World Rock Stage.

He popped a couple Advil and chased it with another hit of hot caffeine. What was wrong with him that he kept lashing out at his dad? He'd been shocked and pissed that his dad would defend his mom. Okay, it was a sore spot with him.

"He bailed," Lynx said.

"Yep." What else could he say? His friend knew his dad's pattern of disappearing and not wanting to be found.

"Therapy is a crock of shit. Never did a lick of good for my junkie mom."

"Or us in juvie." He leaned against his Jeep in the parking garage of the building. He wasn't ready to go inside yet.

"Those juvie shrinks were smug, self-righteous, overeducated pricks. They didn't know what it was like. Did they ever eat uncooked macaroni from the box 'cause they were starving? Or rotting food out of a trash can? No."

Jesus. However bad Justice had had it, he'd always had food and a place to live and someone who cared— his grandmother. Lynx had spent much of his childhood in crack houses or worse.

"The counselors in juvie didn't know shit," Justice agreed. "But this guy we were talking to at the transitional center, he's ex-military. He's lived some of the life my dad has. He's not bad, it's just..." What?

"Your dad's fucked up."

It hurt like a son of a bitch every time he saw the ragged shell that once was his dad. "I don't know how Beth does it. She looks at my dad and sees something else. He loves her. Talks to her." But Justice, his own son? Nope. *Grow up, dude, it's time to get over your daddy issues.* Yeah, that.

"How's Liza?"

He welcomed the change of topic. "She's good." He thought of her with the baby swell, her body softening and changing. He wanted her more than ever. "If you'd told me a year ago a pregnant woman would ring my bell, I'd have laughed in your face." He wanted to kiss her, touch her, and fuck her every damned second. Even her scent was stronger. And she wasn't kidding about those sex-starved hormones of hers. "She woke me at 3:00 a.m. Girl's got it bad for me."

Lynx snorted. "Mega TMI."

Probably, but this was his longtime friend, so he didn't care if the man knew how hot Justice was for his pregnant wife. "I'm taking her to Paris a few days early. It's going to cost a shitload, but she deserves it."

"Well, then we better get up to the office and sign those contracts, or you won't have a reason to go to France at all." Lynx studied him. "Ready?"

In other words, had he gotten his head back on? "Let's go sign. Jagged Sin is in meltdown mode. They're ranting all over social media how we sucked dick to get this spot."

"If I was gonna suck dick, it'd be for a Grammy win."

Justice laughed. "Now that's some TMI." They

headed up the elevator, through reception and into Christine's office.

Gray, Simon and River were already there.

"Nice of you to drop by," River commented.

"I thought so." Lynx sprawled on the couch. "Miss me?"

Justice lifted his hand in greeting and took a chair.

Christine turned from talking with her staff and faced the group. "And here we are. The launch and tour was a success."

Simon cleared his throat. "To the extent that we broke into the top fifty and got invited to World Rock Stage, yes. But our income for S.I. is lagging. We spent a hell of a lot of money with extra flights, hotels, adding more shows. Not all sales are in yet, but we're still in the red."

"I'm aware. However, you get a substantial signing bonus from World Rock Stage, and your flights, food, lodging and security are paid for." She shifted to Justice. "Designers are already vying for Liza to wear their clothes—all of which she'll get for free."

He loved the idea of them fawning over her. This was what he wanted, to spoil his wife and give her the world. "Cool."

Christine refocused on the group. "In addition, you can expect more sales, and that invitation has given us some offers for endorsements for apparel and jewelry that you'll wear onstage. In other words, you sign this contract..." she held up legal-sized sheets of paper, "...and you guys will be golden. All the work, the sacrifice, it's all paying off."

The last of Justice's headache vanished in the rush of joy and vindication. World Rock Stage was seen in multiple countries. The opportunities from that would pay off for years. They had finally captured the brass ring.

And he was going to take his wife to Paris and show her a good time. "Where do we sign?"

She waved a hand at her assistant, who snapped into action, passing out copies.

"We've already made a couple changes. The version you have is ready. Look it over, and let me know if you have any questions. We'll sign it, I'll send for countersignatures, and it's a done deal. Also attached are the endorsement deals, which hinge on signing the contract. I'll give you guys some time to look it over."

She moved back to her desk.

Justice took his copy, first looking at the endorsement deals. And damn, that was some serious money. They'd be able to pay off everything they owed for the tour, invest more in the company and all take a very healthy draw too. Justice would be able to pay off the second on the house and start taking care of his family the right way.

He was anxious to sign, then go home and take Beth to dinner and shopping for baby furniture. At this rate, they could look for a new house in a year or so.

They were going to be rich. Famous. Powerful.

He'd be able to find a treatment that worked for his dad.

Realizing his mind was drifting, he focused, reading through the dense clauses jam-packed with the usual legal speak. Getting to the end, he flipped to the signature page. Lines and typed names filled the page—all five band members, their representation, Christine Castle, and the owners of World Rock Stage. He scanned down the list then froze on one name.

Gene Hayes.

"What the blazing fuck?" He jackknifed up, his

blood defying gravity to surge up and pummel his eardrums. "Gene fucking Hayes is an owner?"

Christine lifted her gaze from her phone, eyes cold and hard. "Yes. Sign, Justice."

"Sign?" His voice dropped. Pain stabbed his temples, probably from his impending stroke. He'd never in his life laid an unwanted hand on a woman. Never. But he was seconds from turning into a monster. "You knew? It wasn't on the website. I never saw his name connected."

"He bought in a few years ago as a silent partner."

"And you knew this?"

Lynx and River both got up, flanking him. Justice could feel the look pass between them. They thought he was going to lose it and attack.

Smart men.

"Back off," he warned them.

"J, sit, we'll figure this out."

He swung to Lynx. "It's already figured out. We aren't doing this. We aren't helping that rapist make money. We aren't getting into bed with him." He threw the contract at Christine, shoved River out of his way and stormed toward the door. He had to get out, leave. Before he hit a woman.

"You'll be ruined, Cade. Bankrupted. Your career dead," Christine said. "You won't be able to get a job singing at a kid's birthday party. You walk out that door, and you're a nobody loser."

His muscles locked down an arm's length from the door. He was pretty sure it was a rich wood color, but all he could see was the red haze of pulsing rage so vivid his body twitched.

He turned, his gaze pinging around the room. Simon stood, hands fisted, cold predator eyes burning.

River and Lynx wore similar masks of anger.

It was Gray who strode to Christine's desk, kicked a chair out of his way, and demanded, "How long have you known this and kept it from us?"

"I heard about the deal when it happened."

"And you didn't tell us? Justice?"

Her stare cut to him. "I warned him that Hayes was powerful and had long tentacles in the music world. I told him Liza was a problem. He made his choice. But no, I didn't tell any of you about Hayes."

River spun, all his muscles going fluid, his dark hair fanning out. "Why the fuck not?"

Lynx shot his hand out, gripping River's forearm.

Justice saw it all: River going into his fighting stance, and the man was freaking dangerous when he got pissed. Lynx leashing him. Christine staring down her nose at them.

Because they were her pawns, her bitches.

"You wanted to win, to get to the top? Grow up, men, this is how it's done. You don't get to pick and choose from the moral high ground. Winning means you get in the trenches with the dirty cocksuckers and deal with it. You'll sign the contract, or you're done. On top of losing everything, I'll sue for breach of contract. Now stop whining. This isn't just your shot, this is it. The big fucking deal. The dream every wannabe rocker in the universe dreams about—and it's right here." She held up the contract. "Gene Hayes isn't going to be there. No one has seen him there since the trial."

All his band members turned to look at him.

So did Christine. "You're the one who has the most to lose if you don't sign. Because Hayes won't stop in his quest for revenge on Liza. So if you really want to protect her, then you'd better get rich and powerful enough to hire a legion of attorneys and fight. So what's it going to be?"

Liza. Holy Christ on the cross, what should he do? If he walked, they'd end up destitute. He'd be fighting lawsuits, because Christine would come after them with all her shark teeth exposed. And Liza, how would he protect her from Hayes and everything else?

How would he take care of their baby?

If he walked out that door, he was a loser. No question.

If he signed that contract, he'd betray Beth. He felt that all the way to his soul.

What could he do?

Justice stalked to his car, ready to kill. He'd never felt like more of a traitor in his life.

"Wait up."

He spun, facing Simon. "I almost killed Christine. I could see myself doing it."

"Right there with you. We're trapped."

"When our contract is up or we're rich enough to buy Christine out, she's fucking fired." He dropped his back to the cool metal of his Jeep. "She manipulated us like a bunch of eager, wet-behind-the-ears pussies."

Simon braced a hand against the hood, staring at the ground. "It never ends. The getting fucked over."

True goddamned story.

Simon lifted his head, the scar on his cheek a slash of white across the dark flush riding his face. "I thought going on TV to tell Julie's story was bad. The worst thing I could do. A betrayal of my wife's memory, of the pain she suffered. But this..."

Justice would never forget that day. Sitting in the studio on the red couch while Simon verbally ripped open a piece of his heart and told the world his wife had committed suicide. All because Jagged Sin tried to use Julie's suicide to win more votes for their band by casting Simon as the one who drove his wife to kill herself. They had tried to get the public to turn on Simon and Savaged Illusions.

Simon sold his soul that day to achieve fame.

Justice sold his today.

"I wouldn't have asked you to do this if we weren't in too deep," Simon said. "There's no way out. We walk away, we're ruined and done."

"I can't walk away. I have a kid coming. Beth's already sacrificed so much. We told her she was banned from our tour. I had her sign a postnup. I asked her to postpone her own moment of glory with a chance to appear on Rock Wives because I didn't want to risk any more negative publicity for our band. Now I have to do this, work for the man who took everything from her once—her innocence, her family, even her trust." He closed his eyes, a wave of pure terror clutching him. "I can't tell her."

"Are you sure? Hayes's name isn't on anything aside from the contracts, and he won't be in France, but still, wouldn't it be better to come clean? Just tell her now?"

"No. Remember the last video in Tampa? She had nightmares, and I found her huddled in the bathroom." The image flooded his mind, the tears streaming down Beth's face as she frantically snapped that rubber band. "She cuts."

"Still?"

"She's struggling with it again. Between Hayes, the shit I put her through and the baby, the urge is there. She's almost six months, and she'll be nearly seven months when we go to France. If she finds out, I don't know what she'll do. I can't tell her, not now." He had to protect her. Give her this one thing—a honeymoon in Paris. He'd do the show, and they'd come home. Then after the baby was born, he'd explain.

"Don't let her see the contract. Otherwise, Hayes's name won't come up. He's a silent investor," Simon said. "I doubt anyone connected with World Rock Stage wants his association known."

Justice hated keeping this from her, but he didn't have a choice. If she found out, Liza would lose control. They'd fight. She'd walk.

Or cut.

He couldn't take the risk.

Chapter 21

Paris, France

LIZA TOOK A PHOTO OF their next gorgeous dish.

"Are you going to take a picture of every bite?" Justice teased her.

Okay, yeah, she'd taken a lot of images for the last three days. But come on, *she was in Paris, France.* This was the experience of a lifetime, one she'd never conceived of as a kid living in rat-infested motel rooms or leaking mobile homes. Even after moving in with her aunt and she'd learned to escape in her stories, she'd never really envisioned this.

Paris, France.

With her rock-star husband.

People had recognized him here too. Of course he was appearing at the AccorHotels Arena for the World Rock Stage Extravaganza. Whenever she saw the posters featuring Justice and the guys as the *Indie Breakout Rock Band, Savaged Illusions,* she wanted to squeal like a groupie.

A part of her considered sending a picture to her aunt and grandmother to gloat a little bit. They'd

315

brutally cut her out of their lives for dating Justice. Told her she was making bad decisions exactly as her mother had that would lead to disaster.

And maybe she'd begun to wonder that too after Tampa.

"Hey, Earth to Beth?"

Justice's amused voice pulled her back. She set her phone down. "Every dish is a work of art. I want to remember this." She picked up her fork, scooping up a bite of duck, cherries, almonds and a juice somehow related to hibiscus. She tasted it. Delicious. So tender and the flavor... A slow moan slid out.

"Good?" Justice leaned close. They were side by side at the bar in L'Atelier De Joël Robuchon, experiencing the tasting menu. Dish after amazing dish was presented with flair.

She dipped her fork in and shared a bite with him.

"Damn." He took a sip of his wine, then held it out to her. "Want to try it? Your doctor said it's fine to indulge in a few sips here and there."

She eyed the glass for a second, the ruby liquid matching the dark and indulgent red-and-black interior of the famous restaurant. Accepting the glass, she took a small sip, allowing the wine to settle on her tongue.

Then she scrunched her nose. "Not a fan."

He laughed a deep chuckle.

The baby kicked. She captured his hand and pressed his palm to the side of her belly. "Do it again. Talk. Laugh."

"On command? Demanding, aren't—?"

The baby kicked again.

The glitter of amusement in his eyes softened to almost boyish wonder. "I felt it this time. That's our girl?"

"You sing to her every night. Even when you were gone, you talked to her or sang over the phone or Skype. She knows her dad's voice. And she likes it when you laugh. I swear she wiggles."

Leaning forward, he kissed Liza, his mouth more sweet than sensual. "She's going to be strong. You're not quite seven months. She's like, what, maybe two pounds?"

A surprised gasp huffed out of her. "You know how big she is."

"The doctor's office is covered in those charts on the baby's size. It was either that or stare at graphic pictures of delivery. I memorized the baby size charts." He stroked her stomach.

The baby shifted again. "She's going to be a daddy's girl." Her heart melted at the thought of seeing Justice holding their daughter. She'd never had a dad who adored her, but this baby would.

"You're both my girls."

He pulled back as their next course was delivered. They sampled every dish, talking about the sights they'd seen over the last three days.

"I think my favorite was the Seine River Cruise and the Eiffel Tower lit up at night. But the stained-glass windows in Sainte-Chapelle were stunning." Liza shook her head. "I don't know if I captured the magnificence in pictures." Her thoughts skipped around. "I can't wait to show my mom. Although I can only take in a few photos at each visit." Being pregnant had made her long for her mom, but she didn't want to dwell on that now.

"We'll visit her after we get home and you rest up."

"I don't want go home. I don't want this to end," Liza said.

Justice held out his fork with a bite of dessert.

"We'll come back. And we can travel to other places."

"We'll have the baby. Right now it's just us." And a piece of her wanted to hold on to this moment forever.

"She'll come with us. I know it'll be different, but still good. We'll make it work."

Pushing away her plate, she said, "This has been a magical honeymoon. It's been nice to get away from the tension and worries." It had been good at home for the last month too, except their worry about Noah. Justice had gone out looking for him a few nights, and Liza hated his anxiety. His guilt about what he'd said to Noah in the session haunted him. The pressures of his growing fame pulled at Justice and the band daily. They'd gone back to writing songs for a new album, but that wasn't going well, fraying their tempers.

Justice's relationship with Christine had soured to the point he'd told Liza not to answer or talk to the business manager if she called Liza's phone. When she tried to find out more, he deflected, usually changing the subject to their Paris trip, the baby or her book. *And you let him*, a voice in her head reminded her. She just didn't want to rock the boat. Liza still hadn't quite gotten over the way things had gone when he was on tour. That distance and growing feeling that she was second to his career, band and fans.

And why was she dwelling on this now?

"Have you thought of more names?" Justice asked.

She lifted her gaze to his, and even in the darkened atmosphere of L'Atelier, she caught the flicker of unease in his gaze and the slight clamping of his jaw. What was it? Maybe he'd be more willing to talk now? "Justice, you can tell me if something's bothering you."

The sounds of the bustling restaurant filled his pause. After a few seconds, he said, "I'm getting a little anxious about the show, that's all. It's going to be televised worldwide. We have the endorsements, and some of the footage will be in a commercial for the shoe company." He smiled, shaking his head. "We'll deal with that tomorrow when the preshow stuff begins. Tonight is you and me." He settled his hand on her stomach. "And our girl. So names. I was thinking, my grandmother's middle name was Rose."

"Rose," she repeated. They had a long list of names, but Liza already had her favorite. "It's pretty, but I still love Savanna. How about Savanna Rose Cade?"

His lips curved, and his eyes warmed. "I like it. Let's move that one to the top of the list."

That smile woke up the pregnancy-enhanced sex drive. She threaded their fingers together. "I'm ready to go back to our room."

His grin widened. "Still haven't had enough, huh?" He leaned close, his mouth brushing her cheek to her ear. "Sex-starved hormones?"

A shiver went through her. Around Justice, she'd always had a big sexual appetite. But since he'd come home, it'd grown to something that bordered on desperate greed. She'd be embarrassed if Justice didn't seem to love it so much. She turned her head, bringing her eye to eye with her husband. All the noise of the chef calling out orders, dishes clinking, food searing and people chatting faded to the background.

"You have one job, rock star." This had been their motto for their trip.

"Keeping my perpetually aroused wife satisfied."

"Bingo."

His gaze slid to her mouth.

That made her squirm on her seat. Going down on him had become an obsession too. She just wanted him.

"Let's go back to our room." He stood, helping her from the stool, and they walked hand in hand.

It was a beautiful night in Paris, and Liza tried to soak it all in, right down to the feel of the man next to her. The long months when he'd been on tour had tested them, but they came out on this side of it stronger and more in love.

This trip was cementing their bond. By the time they went home, they'd be ready to start seriously planning for the arrival of their daughter and life as married lovers and parents.

The tour of the AccorHotels Arena left Justice awed. He'd watched the World Rock Stage show for years and dreamed of the moment he'd step out on that stage. Here he was in their private luxury box that was to be the Savaged Illusions loge on the night of the show. He looked through the massive viewing window down on the stage that had hosted world-famous singers.

It had been reconfigured to World Rock Stage specifications so the audience would surround the performers on three sides. An enormous screen would be behind them, magnifying their images so everyone in the arena would have a view. Their S.I. logo would be beamed on the stage floor and the ceiling.

"Scared?" River asked.

Was he? His nerves hummed. Tomorrow before they went on, he'd be wired to the hilt. At this second, it was an internal pressure building. Like a racehorse pawing the ground at the start gate. Or the revving of a car engine, waiting for the flag. "I want to get out there with every damned seat filled, those cameras on us, showing the whole world we're Savaged Illusions and we've made it." This was what success felt like—and it was damned good.

River gazed out. With his hair up in the man-bun thing that made Lynx scissor-happy, his jaw was bared and tight. "The kid no one knew. You'll fucking know me now."

The dark tone rivaled the low throb of his bass. This wasn't a side River showed often. The deep and silent fury that lived in him came out with his bass in his hands or when he sparred. Otherwise, he showed the world the charming, happy playboy.

But Justice knew. River wasn't even the name he was born with. No one had ever found his identity or where he came from. When River said, "The kid no one knew," he meant it literally.

Justice shoulder bumped him. "You're in the spotlight for a piece of 'Expired Hero.' Everyone will know you."

River didn't respond, and Justice didn't expect it. All of them had their moment of glory because they'd earned it. It meant something different to each of them.

"Hey." Beth came into the suite, her voice bubbling in that single syllable.

He turned, smiling. She spilled in with three other women, all looking radiant. Two wives and a girlfriend of one of World Rock Stage owners had found out they were sharing the same designer as Beth. They'd reached out to her and planned some events together. Today had been lunch and final fitting for the clothes they were wearing to the show tomorrow.

Beth had been wide-eyed with nerves this morning when the car came to pick her up. Justice walked her down to keep her from bolting, teasing her the whole way that she better get used to the life of rock royalty. Hobnobbing with stars and having designers falling all over themselves for the chance to get her to wear their clothes. And look at her now, she was glowing. The life agreed with her.

"We just toured the place. Oh my God, Justice, this arena is dazzling."

He kissed Beth, said hello to the other women and introduced River. Simon, Gray and Lynx picked that moment to spill in, and the chatter ratcheted up.

Justice tugged Beth aside. "How'd it go?"

"We had so much fun! My outfit is so rock-chick cool. I mean..." She glanced down. "Well, I'm pregnant and not..." She waved her hand at the other tall and thin girls.

He tugged her chin up. "Don't gloat, baby. Not everyone can be as beautiful as you."

Her smile burned brighter than the spotlights on the stage. "Yeah, that's what I was going to say. Anyway, it's so surreal. I can't believe they're giving me a dress and shoes and..." She shrugged.

He loved to see her reaping the benefits of his success.

"Tomorrow, I'm going to their room. They have a whole spa thing set up, hair, makeup and nails. And get this, their nail technician can do your logo on my nails. I love that! Oh, and a catered lunch, and champagne that I can't have, but they'll have sparking water or juice for me. And chocolate. I'm going to take a million pictures."

And he'd been worried about what Beth would do while he was working.

Finally pausing to take a breath, she said, "I forgot to ask. How'd practice go?"

Fighting a laugh, he pulled her against him, feeling her growing belly. "Know what I think?"

"What?"

"You're getting spoiled and forgetting who's the star of this family."

"Huh, I was wondering when your ego would show up, Rooster."

Wrapping an arm around her, he led her to the floor-to-ceiling viewing glass. "Look at this. Isn't it incredible?" He gestured to the thousands and thousands of seats curving around the stage.

She leaned her head against his shoulder. "You're going to be amazing, and I'm going to be right here watching you."

He looked down at his wife, and a deep, fierce love gripped his throat. There had been nights on the road when a hot body and his restless dick briefly tempted him. But he'd resisted, and this was why. Sex was easy, but this? The love and sharing with Beth?

Priceless.

It was Beth that anchored and gave him a reason to keep it all in perspective. Her and their kid.

Justice nodded as the reps kept chatting and slugging back the champagne. He knew the importance of schmoozing with VIPs, but damn, all he wanted to do was get out there on the stage and perform. His gaze shifted to the glass overlooking the venue.

The seats were packed shoulder-to-shoulder with people. Energy revved up his system, creating a familiar buzz in his ears. The only downside to the night—their business manager was here. She'd arrived yesterday for the cocktail parties.

Christine's voice droned on and on as she talked and complimented and sucked up so hard, she could have a second career as a vacuum cleaner. Justice refused to allow his manipulative bitch of a manager to ruin his night. They'd all known she'd be there.

"Justice, let's get a picture of you with Myra," Christine said. "Be sure that your cuff shows. We want to post it on your site to show the rock jewelry collection."

He played the part, getting a few shots with the former model turned entrepreneur who'd offered Savaged Illusions a killer endorsement deal. After that he called the other band members over to do a few group shots.

Several boring pics later, River charmed Myra into letting him sweep her up, her long, bare legs draped over his arm. The rest of them gathered around as Myra squealed with laughter.

Now they had a more unique shot as the guys held up her legs and at the same time displayed the silver and leather jewelry.

The fact that the unscripted move annoyed Christine was a bonus.

"Well that looks like fun." Liza walked in, flanked by a security guard.

Justice let go of Myra's legs and crossed to his wife. She'd stopped just inside the door by the champagne bar. She'd spent the late morning and early afternoon getting ready with her new friends, and come over in their limo. His breath caught at his first look at her. Beth's hair sheeted down in a shining mahogany curtain to the curve of her back, with wisps cut around her face. Although he loved her wavy hair, this was a stunning transformation. She had on a gunmetal-gray slouch dress that emphasized her bust and baby bump. Over that, she had a thin leather jacket with the sleeves pushed up. Silver bangles clattered on her wrists. Her legs were bared down to some ankle boots that exposed her painted toes.

"Damn, you look hot."

"Thanks, we had fun. Did you know all the wives have their own security for tonight?" She waved toward the guy hovering behind her. "He was waiting for me when I got here."

"Yep. World Rock Stage hired them. I don't want you going out into the auditorium though. Stay in the suites, okay?" No one had bothered her here in France, but Justice wasn't taking any chances with her safety.

"I won't. Besides I'm—"

"Hello, Liza," Christine cut her off. "We're in the middle of something here. Perhaps you'd like to sit down and rest while we continue?"

Before he could tell Christine to fuck off, Myra interrupted by touching Liza on the shoulder and saying, "I love your shoes! Where did you get them?"

Liza turned her back on Christine. "Thank you! I'm Liza, and you must be Myra." They walked away, Liza's security guard close to her side as she told Myra all about her designer and exclaimed over the other woman's jewelry collection.

"And you were worried," Simon said below his breath.

"Justice," Christine cut in. "This isn't the time for Liza to suddenly play rock-star wife. We—"

The door opened, and their attendant announced, "Time to head to the stage. You guys ready?"

"Hell yeah." Going to Beth, he laid a hand on her back. "Walk with me?"

"Of course." She turned to Myra. "I'll be in touch, and thank you."

"I'll see you after the show, Myra. Enjoy," Justice added. He high-fived the reps from their other two endorsement deals and listened to Christine's reminders, as if he gave a shit what she said. Done, they headed out the door and followed the attendant.

People rushed up and down the halls with carts moving food and drinks for the different loges. Justice's mind was on the show, mentally running through their set and trying to keep his growing nerves controlled. Squeezing Beth's hand, he said, "Did you see the crowds in the arena?"

Her eyes shined behind her glasses. "It's crazy. I've never seen so many rock fans in one place."

They stopped at a doorway leading to the tunnel. The attendant smiled and looked at Liza. "You'll have to say goodbye here," she said in a heavy French accent. "Band only past this point."

Justice nodded. Security was tight, as it should be. The only people in this section of the arena were cleared and badged. "This is it." He bounced on his toes, the energy snapping and crackling. Hot need pushed and prodded with the urge to get out there and perform. They were going to rise from the bottom in a dramatic opening for the concert.

"When you get off that stage tonight, you're going to be world famous," Beth said. "A true rock star."

That got him focused on her. "You told me you don't even like rock stars." She'd said that the first time they met. It'd become one of their ongoing jokes.

"I didn't." She shrugged carelessly. "You're growing on me."

He laughed and laid his hand on her belly. "That's my girl growing inside you." He leaned down, kissing her, his tongue just touching hers. Electric heat sizzled between them, and he broke it off, a groan sliding from his chest. "You're making me hard."

Her eyes flitted to his band, the attendant and the security detail.

"I don't care if they know. Eyes on me, baby."

A flush warmed her face, and her tongue darted out to glide over her lips, as if she wanted to capture his kiss. Her gaze slid to his.

It seared right through him. "On that stage, I belong to the world. But offstage..."

"You're mine."

"Always." With a kiss to her forehead—because he didn't trust himself with her mouth when he was this amped—Justice stepped back. Meeting the gaze of a security guard, he said, "Appreciate it if you make sure she's safe."

The guard nodded. "Madam Cade has been invited to join the other wives. They're in a luxe suite upstairs. I will escort her."

A second of unease gripped him. "Why didn't they tell her themselves when she was with them earlier?"

Liza frowned at him. "They did in the limo on the way over. I was going to mention it earlier when Christine interrupted us. Why are you being weird?"

He relaxed, realizing he was overreacting. "Okay, I just... Nerves, you know?" He held out his hands, showing her his usual tremble, the one that always settled the second he got onstage. Beth was fine. Hayes was a silent and absent partner. No one wanted to bring that kind of controversy to World Rock Stage. He switched the subject. "You'll be watching me, right? I need to know you're with me."

Her expression softened into tenderness. "My rooster."

God he loved her. Did this woman have any idea how much he wanted to protect her? "You're my song, Beth. I told you that once, and I meant it. Singing is something I do, it's what I am—a singer. And loving you isn't something I just feel, it's who I am—yours. You're my song." With that he let her go and walked to the door that would take them to the stage. He looked back for a second.

His beautiful wife with the softly swollen belly carrying their child and clutching his heart with a fiercely tender, all-consuming sweet pain. His Beth truly was his song, and the love of his life.

Chapter 22

LIZA STOOD THERE A MOMENT after the door closed, drowning in Justice's words. She was his song, and he was her reason to breathe and live.

"Madam? You will go up to join the other wives? I was instructed to escort you up immediately so you don't miss any of the show."

Right. She hadn't committed to the other wives yet, but it was a pretty easy choice. Christine was back in the Savaged Illusions suite. Did she want to share this moment with the business manager who irritated her and who Justice had come to despise? Or go up with her new friends?

A flash of pride streaked into her excitement for Justice. Liza was fitting in as his wife, and happiness filled her. She answered the guard, "I'll go upstairs to the luxe suite. Thank you."

The guard strode across to the glass-and-steel elevator and slid in his card. Next to that was a door that she assumed was for the stairs. Normally for one flight, she'd walk.

But considering her four-inch heeled, peep-toed boots, she'd go with the elevator. As they shot up, she thought of Emily, Nikki and Tess. Maybe next time she could bring them along too. Liza could have her very own entourage of girlfriends and be able to share this with them. After all, wasn't that what wives of superstars did?

That thought made her smile as the doors opened to a light-filled area with thick-cushioned couches and chairs. But no one was here. A hallway snaked to the right and left. Straight ahead, the floor-to-ceiling windows displayed the massive arena packed with people. Hidden speakers piped in sound. "Welcome to the World Rock Stage!"

Liza recognized the voice of a legendary rock star opening the show before Savaged Illusions went on. Excitement built in her. This night was something she'd never forget.

Applause came rolling down the hallway. Was that from the right? With the speakers on, sound was getting harder to source. She began to pivot that way. Her nerves danced, and she wished she could indulge in a glass of champagne.

"This way, madam."

Turning, she realized her security guard was going left. Liza hurried after him, not wanting to miss a second of Justice's performance.

The guard knocked and opened the door. "Madam Cade." The guard stepped back and waited for her to go through.

Liza smiled at him. "Thank you." She walked in a few steps and stalled out. Wait. The room was too quiet. Only the barest sounds of the stage and crowds filtered in. Where were the ladies? It was a plush private room with a polished wood bar edged in padded leather at her left. Behind it, top-shelf liquor bottles rested on clear glass shelves. Groups of mahogany leather chairs faced the massive window overlooking the stage. The room must be soundproofed and the speakers turned off.

Agitation tightened her muscles. This wasn't right. She dug her custom-designed fingernails into her palms.

As far as she could tell there was only one other person in the room. She could see the back of their head rising over the chair. Dark-brown hair.

"Hello?"

Wrong. Turn and get the hell out. Her heart pounded until it became a throb in her ears.

That chair began to turn.

Not that fast spin like on *The Voice*. This was slow and torturous, and everything in her knew. "No." Had she said that out loud? The whole room tilted, and Liza grabbed the edge of the bar, her fingers biting into the black leather border. It couldn't be, it made no sense. But the chair rotated a hundred and eighty degrees to reveal a man lounging there.

This wasn't just a man.

It was her nightmare.

Gene Hayes rose from the chair.

Run. Oh God, run. But where? What was happening? Where was her security guard? Liza held on to the edge of the bar, struggling to make sense of this. "You can't be here. You're a felon."

Hayes stopped five feet from her. His dark hair flowed to his shoulders, deep-set eyes piercing her from beneath heavy brows. And his lips, they were too perfect... She shuddered.

Oh God. The baby moved, as if sensing her mother's panic. "How?"

"Didn't your husband tell you? I'm one of the owners of World Rock Stage."

"No." She shook her head, her freshly straightened hair whipping across her face and glasses.

"Yes." He grabbed up a document sitting on the bar. "Read it."

She backed up. "I'm getting security. They'll arrest you!"

His lip curled. "Who do you think arranged for your personal security guard? I'm sure he's already out of the building now. His job is done."

She desperately tried to make sense of this. "It was a setup? The girls—" Her throat tightened. Had her new friends lured her here? Made her think she was part of the group of rock-star wives?

"Those power-hungry whores?" Derision dripped off every word. "No. They're as stupid as you, not knowing I'm a part owner. They're on the other side of the floor, expecting you to show up. You're just like them, a bitch trying to climb the ladder with your mouth open and legs spread."

His hatred of women was tangible and terrifying. More frightening was the power he'd exerted to set this up and get her in here. He'd hired a fake security guard. Got him clearance to work the VIP floors. The scope of his influence caged her in, pinning her in place. But she wasn't a powerless child anymore.

Don't freeze. Run! She spun, sprinted to the door, grabbed the doorknob and twisted to yank it open.

A hand slammed against the wood.

Liza stared at that hand. The long fingers with short, buffed nails. She'd seen it before—holding out the drink that had drugged her. Oh God. Her heart stuttered.

"You ruined my fucking life, you fat cunt. I'm going to ruin yours, hurt you in ways you can't even imagine. And FYI, no one knows I'm here except my closest friends. You can go scream it all you want, no one will believe you, Lyin' Liza. I've been in Paris for days, watching you." He leaned closer.

He smelled of burnt ash and cigars. Her stomach roiled, that scent dragging her back to that room when the darkness stole into her head, tugging her from consciousness. She'd been crying for her mom as the drugs he and her dad had fed her took effect.

Get out. Don't stand here. He can't touch you. All she had to do was open that door and scream for help.

"Jagged Sin was supposed to win Indie Breakout Band. My band with my name attached. I flew them to my house, paid for the production of their album, so I could show the world they couldn't hold me back. You were supposed to destroy Savaged Illusions. But even when the World Rock Stage committee voted for Savaged Illusions, I figured once your husband found out I was involved with World Rock Stage group, then he'd refuse to sign the contract and perform."

Justice knew? "You're lying!"

He slapped the page against the door in front of her face. "Read it."

She was too close with her glasses, but Liza fought to focus. She pulled her head back, and the blurs crystallized into two columns of typed names with signatures. She spotted Justice's, along with Lynx's, Gray's, River's, Simon's, and then Christine's as their representation.

She'd known Justice had signed the contract.

She scanned down, and her heart froze into a painful clump.

Gene Hayes. His name typed beneath *owners,* along with the five others, and his signature.

Unable to stop herself, she looked up.

His dark eyes stared back, malevolent hate burning

on her. "He signed. He's taking the fame and money."

Every last drop of blood drained from her face. Black spots danced in the edge of her vision. "I—"

"He's not the only one who betrayed you. Did you wonder how I got a copy of that ultrasound? All the info on you? How I knew you'd be here in France? I know what hotel you're staying at. I know your room number."

She backed up, not daring to take her eyes off him. *Get away. Run.*

"Nikki. That's right, your good friend? I paid her to spy on you. She took a cell phone picture of that ultrasound, and she shot video of you in your yard. She told me how your own family cut you off. She even told me about that porn you write, but she couldn't get alone time with your computer to steal any pages. She's made a lot of money off betraying you."

Nikki? No. Liza retreated until her back hit a wall. "She wouldn't do that." Nikki's new and pretty condo flashed in Liza's head. Where had she gotten the money for it?

"Oh, she would." He sauntered to the bar and dropped the papers there. "Your friend takes my money. Your husband takes my money. You're nothing but a trashy groupie whore." He stalked toward her.

Fear struck her chest like a slap. Liza turned, running for the door. Her numb fingers slid off the knob. Her eyes burned with tears.

A sob tore up her throat.

Fame. Justice chose fame over her. Nikki sold her out for money. Her world shattered into a thousand shards.

His hand thunked against the door, blocking her in again. "This isn't over, bitch."

Goose bumps erupted on her arms, and panic clawed. He was behind her. Too close.

"I'm getting this verdict overturned. I've bought off your friend, I've got your husband on my payroll, I've got the best lawyers money can buy, and soon I'll get a judge that will tell the whole world you're a lying whore. And once I'm back in the U.S., I'll find a way to kill you and that kid you're carrying. No one will care."

Her kid, her baby. No. A flood of fiercely protective strength released. Liza bent her arm and slammed her elbow into his gut.

Oof! He stumbled back.

She yanked open the door. Pounding music poured in, Justice's powerful voice filling the air.

Betrayal pierced her head, and her knees tried to buckle. *No, block it, just think of the baby. Get to safety.* Liza lurched into the hall, hung a left and opened her mouth to scream for help. *He's a wanted felon! A fugitive!*

Her throat squeezed, locking down the words. Years of conditioning kicked in, and her aunt's voice admonished, *Don't talk about it, Liza. You're making it worse. People are judging you. Us. Just keep your head down, and stay quiet.*

Her voice wouldn't work. But she wasn't giving in. She had to get off this floor, and away from Hayes. She'd keep her baby safe, then figure out what to do. Liza skidded to a stop by the elevator, windmilling her arms to keep from falling. Once balanced, she looked down the hall.

Hayes stood there by the suite she'd just escaped, arms crossed, eyes vicious.

Go!

Forget waiting for the elevator. She lunged for the

door to the stairs, yanked it open and raced through.

Too fast.

The floor was as slick as ice, and her shoes slid right off the first step. Liza hit her left hip, and pain tore through her middle as she tumbled down the stairs.

The wild energy of the packed arena crackled like a live wire as Justice sang "Expired Hero." They were surrounded by fans on three sides and backlit by a towering screen flashing their image. He strutted the stage, making security insane as he leaned down to high-five fans.

Justice didn't care. He fucking loved being onstage and connecting with the audience. The compelling adulation was the magic, the sensation he craved.

He really was a cocky-ass rooster, exactly as Beth described him.

Returning to center stage, he lined up next to Simon with River, Lynx and Gray spread behind them. As they hit the chorus, Justice pivoted, facing Simon as the other man unleashed his powerful vocals.

Damn, Simon was on fire and forced Justice to push hard, drawing deep to feel the song about the man no one wanted when he failed. Thinking of his dad opened the wounds to allow the pain, shame and rejection to pour out.

At the end of the song, the crowd surged to their feet, dancing and screaming.

It took several amazing minutes to calm their fans before they launched into their next song.

By the time they reached the finale, Justice poured sweat and damned near drowned in the glory of a full-bore standing ovation. They'd done it! Justice and

Savaged Illusions had rocked the house and secured their place as international rock stars.

Best night ever.

When they finally left the stage, he jogged out into the wings, looking for Beth. Was she still upstairs in the luxe suite? He had to find her, to share this magnificent, perfect moment with the woman he loved.

"Justice!" Christine ran up.

"Not now." He pushed past her, heading to the Savaged Illusions loge first. People cluttered the hallway, whispering in groups. A strange chill ran down his spine. He and his band had killed it out there, so what was the weirdly subdued vibe from?

He caught the arm of a passing security guy. "Where's my wife? Beth, I mean Liza?"

The man's face paled. "Sir? I—"

"I'll tell him," Christine jumped in.

Justice shifted to her grim face. Something had happened. "What's going on?" Had Beth left?

"Liza fell on some stairs. An ambulance came, and she's on her way to the hospital now."

Chapter 23

JUSTICE HAD A HELL OF a fight trying to get to Beth. He couldn't speak French, couldn't get his point across. He was losing his damned mind. Gray showed up at the hospital a few minutes later and translated. At that point, Justice learned they couldn't get the baby's heartbeat when they got her to the hospital, and Liza was in advanced premature labor. That was all they would tell him, and they refused to let him see her.

What the fuck could he do? He paced, ready to tear this hospital apart until he located her. But he'd tried that once already and found himself face-down on the floor, with security or cops or whatever yelling at him that he'd go to jail.

Gray managed to talk them out of actually arresting him. No one would tell him anything more, except that Liza refused to have him with her.

What the hell?

He slapped his hand against the wall. They were in a waiting room of whatever the French version of a maternity ward was. Lynx, River and Simon all hovered.

All he knew was Beth had been found on the

landing of the stairs between the Premier Luxe and the VIP floors early in Justice and the band's performance.

No one had told him. The entire time he'd been performing, Liza... Shit. Did she think he'd chosen not to rush to her side? Was that why she wouldn't see him? How the fuck had this happened? His head throbbed, and terror snapped and clawed.

Christine and security had sworn Beth was alive but having back and stomach pains.

"Mr. Cade."

He swung around, relieved at the barely accented English. A woman in a skirt, blouse and tailored jacket said, "Come with me."

Finally. Gray put his hand on Justice's shoulder. "I'll come with you until you reach the room. I can translate if you talk to a doctor."

He nodded, grateful for the man's help. The need to get to his wife overrode everything else. They followed the woman through the doors he'd been tackled at an hour ago. A baby cried somewhere, and Justice turned toward it.

"Sir." She led him into a smaller room with a few chairs around a table.

"Where's my wife?"

"I need to talk to you. Sit."

He dropped his ass in the chair. He'd get to Beth faster if he cooperated. Gray stood just inside the room by the door.

The woman introduced herself as some kind of counselor, and said, "Mr. Cade, your wife has miscarried. It was fast and hard, and by the time they got her here, there was no stopping the delivery. Your daughter was born about an hour ago, but she did not survive."

Their baby died? A mental image of Beth formed of

the last moment he'd seen her before going onstage. Beautiful and full of joy, her hand on her belly...their child.

Dead.

Pain squeezed his chest. He couldn't breathe and dropped his arms on the table, letting his head fall forward. He didn't get to meet his daughter, would never hear her cry or see her smile. Terrible pressure crushed his lungs with an unbearable loss.

A hand settled on his shoulder.

Justice looked up into the Gray's sad eyes. "Beth was fine. You saw her. How could the baby—" Hot worry stabbed him. "Beth!" Oh Christ. This would kill her. He surged to his feet.

Gray stepped back, giving him space.

Justice homed in on the woman. "Is she okay? Where is she?" The frantic need to get to her wiped out his shock.

"Sit down, Mr. Cade, or I will call security, and this time you will be arrested."

He slapped his hands on the table. "Tell me if Liza's okay. She's my wife."

"Mrs. Cade came through the delivery. She is okay, but, well, she has been refusing to see you. However, I have convinced her that you should have a chance to..." Her eyes pooled with sympathy. "You have a right to see your child. Your wife relented. You will wait here, and I will collect the child and bring her to you."

He straightened. That made no fucking sense. What was going on? "Take me to my wife."

The woman rose, her face set. "She does not want to see you."

Fuck this. He swung around and bolted for the door. Once in the hallway, he heard an argument between Gray and the woman, but he didn't care.

"Beth! Liza!" He stopped at every room, barreling in and rushing out when he didn't see Beth.

At the third one, he burst in and stopped cold. There on the bed lay Beth with her eyes closed. Her glasses were missing, and quiet tears rolled down her face, dripping onto her shoulder covered in a hospital gown. Her skin was sickly pale, hair stuck to her head, and the shadow of a bruise marred her forehead.

In her arms was a tiny bundle wrapped in a blanket, so small it could fit in his hand.

Their baby.

Behind him he heard Gray speaking rapid French to security, probably trying to keep Justice out of jail. But all that mattered to Justice was in the hospital bed, and he wasn't leaving.

Pain slashed his chest, biting as deep as the first time he saw his father broken and burned in a hospital bed.

Only this was worse. This was his wife and baby. And somehow he'd fucked up so badly she'd refused to see him.

Going to the bed, he stared down at the perfect little face. The baby's eyes were closed, tiny little eyelashes lying against her rounded cheek. Two perfect little eyebrows, a tiny nose and lips. A soft tuft of pale reddish-blonde hair lay against Beth's arm. She was exquisite.

And gone.

His throat swelled. How had this happened? "Beth? Sweetheart, I'm here. They wouldn't let me in. I tried to get to you."

Slowly she lifted her lids. The green he loved had dulled to utter misery. "I trusted you. How could you do this?"

The harsh agony in her voice wrecked him. Sitting on the bed, he reached for her. "What—?"

"Don't touch me." Her eyes filled with more tears. She dropped her head to the baby she cradled and sobbed.

She was breaking his fucking heart. "Beth, please. What happened? How did you fall?"

"I saw him. Gene Hayes. He showed me what you'd done by signing that contract."

Every muscle, tendon and nerve snapped awake and hot. His heart pounded with the violent thump of murder. Gene Hayes had been at the arena? No fucking way. "He can't have been there. He's a wanted man." *So?* a harsh ugly voice said. He was rich, powerful, and famous enough to be able to get away with it.

Justice was going to kill him. All this time, while he'd been out on that stage, Hayes had been there in that building and torturing Beth.

"I can't bear it. I can't," Beth said. "If that wasn't enough, he told me Nikki's been selling pictures, videos and information."

Nikki? That bitch betrayed Beth? He'd never even guessed.

"I ran. Then..." Beth looked down at the tiny child in her arms. "She died before we got to the hospital."

Her anguished voice tamped down his rage over Hayes. She needed him. He couldn't lose control and go after Hayes right now.

"He took everything once before. Everything. Now he's taken her, he killed my daughter. And you let him." With the baby tucked against her, she rolled to her side, her entire body shaking with wrenching sobs.

Beth's suffering shredded him. Circling the bed, he

crouched to her eye level. Tears flooded from her with horrible wrenching sounds. Mascara ran onto the bed.

Don't think about Hayes right now. He'd find him later. Right now, he focused on his woman. "Let me touch you."

She cried harder, her entire body jerking.

A nurse ran in, holding a syringe and giving orders in French. Seeming to remember her patient didn't speak French, she slowed and focused on Justice. "You must leave."

He glanced in the doorway to see Gray with two security guards. He assumed they didn't want to traumatize Beth more by dragging him out. Returning his attention to the nurse, he said, "I won't leave my wife. You bring security or police in here, and you'll upset her further. No one is taking me from her."

The nurse hesitated, then looked toward the door and shook her head.

The guards backed off, and Gray followed them.

Once the doorway was clear, the nurse held up the syringe. "This will calm Madam Cade. We'll take the baby."

Liza rolled to her back, took one look at the needle, and sat up, throwing herself toward Justice, while cradling the baby. "No! Don't let them drug me. Please."

His response was automatic. He closed his arms around her, protecting her from that deep terror. "Sh, it's okay. No one will drug you unless you want it." Her fear of being drugged and forced into the black nothingness where she'd be rendered helpless and vulnerable was all too real from what Hayes had done to her when she was fourteen. Stroking her hair, he asked the nurse over her head, "How badly is she hurt?"

The woman frowned in concern. "Bruises and contusions from the fall. The delivery was uncomplicated, but she's bleeding and must rest. She'll heal, but her grief...she needs a lot of support to help her accept the child is gone."

Justice recognized the sympathy in the woman's expression, understood that she meant to help, yet he wanted to shake her. Could she not see his wife? "She knows." Nothing else could break Beth like this. She curled into his chest, her body heaving while their baby girl lay too fucking still in her arms.

The only consolation was that in her moment of fear, she'd thrown herself at him.

"She knows," he repeated. "Just leave us. She needs time." He didn't care what they thought was healthy or right, this was what Beth needed. He gently lifted her in his arms, settled on the bed and held his sobbing wife and their baby.

Twenty minutes later the storm passed. Justice rubbed her back, keeping his touch light for fear of hurting her. Beth had to be in physical pain. She'd fallen down a half flight of hard stairs and then suffered a miscarriage. Rage flickered, threatening to erupt into a forest fire of raw, lethal fury.

Not yet. Hold it together for Beth. Don't think about going after Hayes until later.

She shuddered. "Her name is Savanna Rose. Will your grandmother recognize her if they have the same middle name, do you think? Take care of her? I don't want her in the dark by herself."

His eyes welled up. He hadn't cried in years, not since the day his mom walked out and left him in jail.

344

But Beth holding their child, begging him to promise his dead grandmother would care for their baby, tore him apart. "I promise. She loves children." He stroked the tiny baby's cheek. "Savanna Rose." His voice trembled on her name.

Their daughter. A beautiful, torturous love ballooned his chest. He'd had no idea, no concept of what he'd feel when he saw his child. A terrible and bright feeling made of all that he was. But right now, he had to give Beth some peace and solace. "Savanna Rose will have her great-grandmother to love and watch over her until we see her again."

"Will we?" Beth looked up at him with so much raw vulnerability and awful grief.

"Yes." They would one day. They had to.

She curled back into him, quiet and limp with sorrow.

The nurse returned, checking on her. "Mrs. Cade? Would you like more time?"

Beth lifted the baby to her lips, kissing her head. "Mommy loves you, Savanna Rose Cade." She tried to hold the baby up, but her arms trembled.

Justice pressed Liza to his chest. "I've got her, Beth. Hold on to me."

He slid his hands beneath his daughter. Beth let her go, wrapping her arms around him.

For a heartbeat, he held his tiny, perfect little girl and wished they could have a lifetime. He'd trade his soul for her life, but he was powerless. He kissed her head. "Daddy loves you too."

"We'll take good care of her," the nurse said.

Beth trembled against him, and Justice gently enfolded her in his arms.

But the wrath in his mind, the fires of hatred, flamed.

He was going to find and kill the man who'd done this.

Gene Hayes.

Liza hated herself. If she could trade places with her baby, she would. Why hadn't she died and the baby lived? How could she let Justice touch her after what he'd done?

She scrambled off him, then yelped as pain bit into her hip. Her shoulder, arm and knee were sore. Her empty belly ached. Blood gushed between her legs, but she deserved it.

They both did. Maybe this was their hell—living with the pain of knowing they'd failed their child in the worst possible way.

"Beth—"

"I have to go to the bathroom."

Before she could rise, he rolled off the bed, then his arm wrapped around her shoulders, easing her up. "I'll help you. Stand slowly, I've got you."

She wanted to argue, but she was weak, tired and fogged. She let him help her up and walk her to the small bathroom. At the door, he tugged her face up. "Can you do it?"

"Yes." His kindness hurt so much more than if he didn't care. Justice loved her, but when faced with a choice—he chose his career, and their baby paid the price.

He hesitated, and said, "No one told me, Beth. I was out there onstage singing, and you were going through this. I'd have left the stage."

Liza couldn't see his eyes clearly without her glasses, but she could feel his desperation for her to believe him. But her ability to do that had died with their daughter. "We'll never know. I can't believe you anymore. The cost is too high." She pulled from him and went inside, shutting the door.

Every step and movement hurt. She'd been told she didn't have any broken bones. It took everything she had just to use the facilities. What should have taken three minutes took fifteen. Weary, she barely got the door open when she heard Justice's voice.

"Find out, Em. Please."

Liza stopped, gripping the door. While his voice was clear to her, his image was fuzzy. "You're talking to Emily?" She took a step and another, aiming for the bed.

"Beth." He put an arm around her, his scent warm and safe.

"I can do it," she snapped.

He ignored her, easily taking her weight. "Do you want to talk to Emily? I was letting her know."

She shook her head. She couldn't, her throat had closed up.

"Em, I'll call you later, okay? Take care of— Yeah. I'll tell her." He slid his phone in his pants. "Em said she and Ben love you. She'll talk to you after you sleep. Anytime. And Gray's going to our hotel room to find your spare glasses and gather some clothes. They'll probably release you tomorrow, but we'll stay in France until you're cleared to fly."

Reaching the bed, she put her hand on it and turned out of his hold. The question burning her soul spilled out. "Why? Why did you do it?" The pain was too much, Liza couldn't think rationally. Nor could she get back in the bed where she'd held her daughter for the first and last time.

She couldn't. Hysteria bubbled and clawed, and yet she was so tired.

Justice's hand closed around her arm. "We'll talk tomorrow. You need to sleep. Rest."

She jerked away. Another shaft of pain made her hiss. "I can't do this. Go away. Go back to the hotel, or go party. You got what you wanted." Her inner bitch snarled and snapped.

He reared back as if she'd hit him. "I'm not leaving you. You're mine, now and always. I never wanted this to happen. Christ, how can you even say that? I didn't want to lose our baby."

"You wanted your dream more. You signed that contract. Hayes showed me."

"Hayes." He barked the name, pacing like a caged animal. Then he stopped. "I didn't know he'd be at the arena. Are you sure it was him?"

"Am I sure?" A bitter noise escaped her, half sob, half laugh. "He was there. He had me summoned by that security guard he apparently hired specifically for that reason. Like the idiot I am, I walked right into the room where Hayes waited. And do you know why? Because I trusted you. It never occurred to me you'd keep something like Hayes being a part of World Rock Stage from me." The moment of seeing Hayes was forever burned on her brain. "Just like I trusted my dad." She wrapped her arms around herself.

Justice lunged to her, his hands curling around her arms. "Beth...he wasn't supposed to be there! You have to believe me. I'd never have signed the fucking contract."

She looked up, and another wave of betrayal rode through her, trampling over everything she'd ever loved and believed. "But you did sign. You knew he was an owner. His name was right there." Her nose clogged, and more tears fell.

"I had no choice. We still owed money from the

tour, and if we didn't sign, we'd be ruined. All of us. I wouldn't be able to protect you, take care of my dad and our baby."

She flinched. Their baby. Savanna Rose. The agony rose and tried to swallow her. She wanted to hate Justice, it'd be easier. Better. Because those moments when he'd held her and their baby earlier, she'd felt his grief, his tears, his comfort. She craved nothing more than his arms. Even now he tempted her. A part of her wanted to run to him, to cry with him, to endure until they could breathe again.

But he'd betrayed her, their child and their love.

"You sold out your wife and child to become an international rock star. That was more important to you than us." She shrugged out of his hold and sat on the bed, grateful she didn't have her glasses. She didn't want to see his face.

He dropped to the floor at her feet, taking her hands in his. "I was trying to protect you. I screwed up. Please, Beth, forgive me."

"I can't." She took her hands away, crawling into the bed and closing her eyes. "I can't forgive you or me. I deserve this, but she didn't. She should have lived and I should have died."

"He's where?" Justice said into his phone, unable to believe this as he stood in the hallway outside his wife's hospital room. "In the St. Andre hotel?" It was only a few minutes from the hotel he and Beth were staying at. All the bands were spread among three hotels.

"That's the one," Emily said. "It was booked by World Rock Stage. Do you know it?"

"Yes." They'd had a cocktail party there the previous night in one of the suites. He'd had Beth right there with him. Jesus. Red coated his vision. Hayes had balls. He'd tormented Liza until she fell down the stairs and lost their baby, and he hadn't run to the hole he'd slithered out of? Thought he could just stay in Paris like no one would do anything? "How sure are you Nikki is telling the truth?"

"Very. She broke down entirely when I told her Liza lost the baby. She told me it all started in Vegas on Liza's birthday. Nikki was desperate for money, Ace made her an offer. That whole scene when he pushed Nikki was set up to get Liza to react."

He closed his eyes for a second, recalling another time Liza had defended Nikki at the Sandcastle Contest and Concert a year ago. Ace and Nikki had known it would work. He expected that shit from Ace, but not Nikki.

Emily went on, "Then it just ballooned, until Hayes was demanding more and more. And soon he was threatening to expose Nikki on the Bring Gene Hayes Home website if she didn't keep feeding him information. Hayes's money was paying for that condo Nikki is living in." Emily's voice trembled. "I wanted to choke her."

"Don't, Em. We'll deal with her, but Beth's going to need you." He meant it. Emily was like a sister to Beth. She'd already been betrayed by one friend she trusted. And him.

"I can't stand this," Em said. "How is she?"

"Asleep. She finally agreed to take some pain meds, and they've numbed her enough to rest." Which was why he had to handle this now, before Beth woke. "So how does Nikki know Hayes is still here?"

"She called him right in front of me. He's so sure of

her, he bragged about getting Liza to come into that room and showing her the contract. I could hear him. He's an animal. Call the French authorities, get him arrested. He belongs in a cage."

"Fuck that. I'm going to see him myself."

"Justice! Wait—"

"Thanks, Em." He hung up and went back into the room, looking down at his wife. In sleep her face was ravaged, dark craters beneath her eyes, her breath ragged from crying. Gene Hayes had hurt her.

And caused her to lose their child.

The rage exploded, roiling up until his skin burned with it. "He's going to pay, Beth. Now." He walked out. In the waiting room, Gray shot to his feet.

"Justice. How's Liza?"

"Asleep. Can you stay with her? I need to do something."

The man's eyes narrowed. "What?"

"Don't leave her alone. I owe you." He broke into a jog, going out into the dark.

Fifteen minutes later, a car dropped him off at the hotel. Justice strode in, bypassed the elevators to take the stairs to the third floor and found the room. Music thumped, and laughter rolled out.

He knocked.

A girl answered.

Justice lunged inside, forcing her to jump back. He scanned the room, looking past the half-naked, too-damn-young girls mixing among the men. There were at least fifteen people in the room, some snorting blow, others making out, drinking. Two girls were dancing and pulling clothes off each other.

Ten feet away, Gene Hayes sat in a chair, glass in one hand, eyes fixed on the two girls making out.

The last hold on Justice's sanity snapped. His wife

lay in a hospital bed, their daughter dead, and this pervert was getting off watching two girls. A roar of agonized rage tore from him. He rushed across the room, grabbed Hayes by the shirt and jerked him to his feet. His drink tumbled out of his hand and hit the carpet.

Screams erupted. Music screeched to a stop.

Justice slammed Hayes against the wall and plowed his fist into his nose, trying to drive bone straight back into his brain.

Blood sprayed Justice's face, feeding his fury. People grabbed at him, but Justice threw them off. He had one goal—to destroy Hayes.

Hayes shoved him, broke free and ran two steps.

Justice leapt, tackling him to the floor and driving his fist into the man's kidney.

Hayes screamed, "Get him off me!"

Bending down to his ear, Justice said, "I'm going to kill you for hurting Liza and murdering our child." He got in one more shot before he was tackled by security or bodyguards.

Justice took several punches as Hayes got up, blood dripping from his busted nose. "Kill him."

Oh shit, he hadn't thought about Hayes having security. Two cold-eyed brutes stared down at him as girls around them sobbed.

A boot caught him in the ribs. *Crack*. Pain exploded out his side. Fuck. If he died...no. Beth. He was all she had. He tried to raise his arms.

Shouts froze everyone.

Justice was hauled to his feet. He recognized the uniforms of French police. Someone had called the cops. He focused on the cop closest to him. "Arrest him." He pointed at Hayes. Agony lanced his ribs, but he didn't care. "He's Gene Hayes, an escaped felon from the U.S." Blood poured into his eye. One of the punches must have split his eyebrow.

Another man jumped in, gesturing angrily as he explained something in French.

A minute later, Justice was dragged out and put into a car. Desperately, he looked around. "What about Hayes?"

The officer spoke rapid French from the driver's seat.

Justice grasped enough to realize that he was going to jail while Hayes would remain free.

In both English and French he was screwed.

Chapter 24

FOR TWO DAMNED DAYS, JUSTICE had tried to make the authorities in France comprehend that Gene Hayes was a wanted man. Unfortunately it didn't matter. Hayes was gone by the time the authorities sorted it out and went to apprehend him.

When they finally released Justice, it was with the understanding that he leave Paris on the first flight out.

Justice sat in the back of the rented car, rage, grief and worry eating his guts. On top of it, his cracked rib hurt like a bitch, and he had a couple stitches in his eyebrow. But his aches were nothing compared to his concern about Beth.

"You're damn lucky," Simon snapped. "The French authorities had good reason to charge you."

"But they didn't. Because Gene Hayes was right there under their noses and they did nothing." When would he wake from this endless nightmare?

"How the hell would they have known? You went to the hotel, shoved into the room and attacked him. He was using an assumed name with identification. It took them a while to sort it out." Simon glared at him. "If you'd done this right, Hayes would be arrested. Instead, he's gone."

He closed his eyes. Did he ever not fuck up? "Just get me to the hotel. I need to see Liza." His Beth. He had to beg her forgiveness. For everything. He hadn't even been there when she was released from the hospital.

The only good news was Emily had flown in on Sloane's plane to be there with her. Emily would take care of her. And Sloane had sent some lawyer to get Justice out of this mess.

It was several minutes before he realized Simon hadn't said another world. "What are you not telling me?"

"You have to stay calm."

The car had stopped directly in front of the hotel. Calm? One look at the regret and sympathy in Simon's eyes tripped his adrenaline. Justice shoved out of the car, nearly tripping as pain lanced his side and stole his breath. Sick sweat burned his skin, but he didn't care. Forcing his body past the hurt, he raced into the hotel, ignoring the elevators to take the stairs two at a time. *Faster, get to her. Don't let this happen.*

On the fourth floor, heaving from exhausted terror and near-blinding agony, he limped to his room and shoved in the key. Pushing inside, he stopped.

The echo of emptiness pierced into his soul. The bed stood perfectly made with the gold-striped blue comforter. Two blue chairs framed the window with the partial view of the Eiffel Tower. But no sign of Beth. A bare thread of hope propelled him to check the bathroom.

Empty.

Gone.

His legs shook as he crossed to the closet and slowly

opened the doors. Only his clothes, suitcase and somehow his guitar were stored there. Had he even had it in his hand when he left the stage after their set ended? He didn't remember. All he could see was Beth's ravaged face as she held their baby.

He turned in a helpless circle, when his gaze caught on a thick cream-colored envelope propped against the lamp on the bedside table.

Justice was scrolled across the front in blue pen, the letters rigid and thick, as if she'd held the pen too tight in her hand. Drawn to that envelope, he felt like he was walking toward a death sentence.

Toward the end.

How long did he stand there, staring down at it?

He wasn't going to be able to bear what was in there.

Yet he reached out and snatched it up. After ripping open the sealed flap, he withdrew a folded sheet of paper.

Clink.

That tiny sound wrenched his heart. Setting the unread sheet aside, he held up his hand and poured out the contents.

Beth's rings. Her engagement ring he'd had made from his grandmother's diamonds, and the plain wedding band.

All the air rushed from his lungs. She'd left him. While he'd been in jail, Beth had left. His eyes burned, and pressure clamped his chest. Fisting the rings, he picked up the paper.

Dear Justice,
When I got pregnant and you told me, 'Don't make me choose between the baby and my dream...' *I didn't* want *to understand. I loved you with everything I*

had. I truly was all in every second. I believed you when you told me you loved me, that I was your song. I would have sacrificed anything for you—anything but our baby.

But the blame doesn't just lie with you. I knew who I was—the girl who ruined a rock star and destroyed my family. People who didn't even know me hated me. My own family disowned me because I was making reckless, selfish decisions. I thought they were all wrong.

But they were right.

I understand now, but it's too little, too late.

Let me go, Justice. Go be a rock star.

The paper blurred, and Justice squeezed the rings so tight he could feel them cutting into his skin.

"Justice."

He lifted his gaze. Some part of him wondered why Drake stood there, his mentor from long ago. "How did you get here?"

"I flew over with Sloane and Emily. Sloane went home with Liza to make sure she's safe. The media is going wild. They know she had a miscarriage and you were arrested, but not anything else. Sloane and Emily arranged to get Liza checked out at the hospital once they land."

"She left me."

"I know."

"While I was in jail. She left me there to rot and—"

"No. She begged Sloane to help you, on the phone and once we arrived here. She made me swear to stay with you. Sloane's sending the plane back for us. The baby will be brought home too. Those arrangements have been made." Drake poured out two shots of tequila and handed him one.

Justice nodded. "She wants me to let her go."

"And?" Drake asked.

Justice got up, walking to the window. Darkness had fallen, and the slice of the Eiffel Tower he could see through the window was lit up against the Paris sky. "No."

"No what?"

"I'm not letting her go. I'm all in. Now and always."

Beth was his. He'd betrayed her, and he'd own that. But he wouldn't let his wife go. Opening his palm, he looked at the rings in his hand. Tiny specks of his blood spattered the diamonds, yet they still sparkled in the lights from the tower. Their love was like that.

They'd lost and bled a little.

But their love was still there, still real enough to catch fire.

"I'll fight to win her back."

Until his very last breath.

Coming Fall 2017
The exciting, powerful conclusion to
Justice and Liza's story!

Savaged

Devotion

SAVAGED ILLUSIONS TRILOGY • BOOK THREE

JENNIFER LYON

Other Books by Jennifer Lyon

THE SAVAGED ILLUSIONS SERIES

Savaged Surrender, a novella

SAVAGED ILLUSIONS TRILOGY

Savaged Dreams (Book #1)

Savaged Vows (Book #2)

Savaged Devotion (Book #3) – Release September 2017

THE PLUS ONE CHRONICLES TRILOGY

The Proposition (Book #1)

Possession (Book #2)

Obsession (Book #3)

The Plus One Chronicles Boxed Set

THE WING SLAYER HUNTER SERIES

Blood Magic (Book #1)

Soul Magic (Book #2)

Night Magic (Book #3)

Sinful Magic (Book #4)

Forbidden Magic (Book #4.5 a novella)

Caged Magic (Book #5)

Jennifer Lyon writing as Jennifer Apodaca

The Sex on the Beach Book Club
Good, Bad & Sexy, a novella

Writing as Jennifer Apodaca

ONCE A MARINE SERIES

The Baby Bargain (Book #1)
Her Temporary Hero (Book #2)
Exposing The Heiress (Book #3)

About the Author

Jennifer Lyon is the pseudonym for USA Today Bestselling Author Jennifer Apodaca. Jen lives in Southern California where she continually plots ways to convince her husband that they should get a dog. After all, they met at the dog pound, fell in love, married and had three wonderful sons. So far, however, she has failed in her doggy endeavor. She consoles herself by pouring her passion into writing books. To date, Jen has published more than twenty books and novellas, won numerous awards and had her books translated into multiple languages, but she still hasn't come up with a way to persuade her husband that they need a dog.

Jen loves connecting with fans. Visit her website at www.jenniferlyonbooks.com or follow her at https://www.facebook.com/jenniferlyonbooks.

www.ingramcontent.com/pod-product-compliance
Lightning Source LLC
Chambersburg PA
CBHW021524250626
47154CB00006BA/1967